VERTIGO

A catalogue record for this
book is available from the
National Library of Australia

ISBN 9781760992248 (paperback)
ISBN 9781760992255 (ebook)

Fremantle Press is supported by the State Government through the
Department of Local Government, Sport and Cultural Industries.

Fremantle Press respectfully acknowledges the Wadjak people of the
Noongar nation as the Traditional Owners and Custodians of the land
where we work in Walyalap.

VERTIGO

KAREN HERBERT

 FREMANTLE PRESS

ABOUT THE AUTHOR

Karen Herbert is the author of *The River Mouth* and *The Cast Aways of Harewood Hall*. She spent her childhood in Geraldton on the midwest coast of Australia, attending local schools before moving to Perth to study at The University of Western Australia where she attained a Bachelor of Commerce and Master of Science in Applied Psychology. Karen has worked in aged care, disability services, higher education, Indigenous land management, social housing and the public sector, and is a graduate member of the Australian Institute of Company Directors. She is immediate past president of the Fellowship of Australian Writers (WA) and a board member of Advocare. Karen lives in Perth, Western Australia with her husband, Ross, and the occasional fledgling.

For Ross, my husband.

CHAPTER ONE

'No-one ever made a movie about the murder of a bureaucrat.' Eric dumped his laptop bag and backpack onto his desk. Sweat dampened the blond hair at his temples. 'Why is it so hot out there? Spring's only just started.'

Belinda, James and I turned away from our screens to look at him. Eric was short and movie-star handsome and, if you knew to listen for it, spoke with a small clip that I once assumed came from European parents. He opened the backpack and pulled out a wad of manila folders. They were stamped with the state government crest and fat blue serial numbers ran along their spines.

'Why don't you use a wheelie case for those?' said James. 'You'd make it a lot easier for yourself. Less sweaty.' James shaves his head and has the muscled forearms and broad hands of a farmer, which is what he is, really. His family runs a market garden north of the city. I suspect that he's only an accountant to get some respite from the dust. James wouldn't be seen dead with a wheelie case.

'Wheelie cases are for sissies,' said Eric, shunting the folders to the corner of his desk. He reconnected his laptop and reached for the power cable that was threaded through the round hole in the desktop. It slid away from him and vanished under the surface. I watched as he got down on his hands and knees to feed it back up. As well as being handsome, Eric also rode his bike to work every day. Even Belinda risked a quick glance.

The end of the cable poked above the desk and James grabbed for it as Eric climbed back out. 'You can use a bulldog clip to hold those in place, you know.'

'Yeah, yeah,' said Eric. 'Full of good advice today, aren't you?'

'*Silkwood*,' James replied. 'Movie about the murder of a bureau-crat. Meryl Streep.'

'She was a nuclear whistleblower; that's different.'

'Why?'

'Because she threatened the entire nuclear industry by calling out non-compliance with safety regulations.' Eric's laptop made its start-up noise. Satisfied, he dropped into his chair and swung around to mirror James. They both put their feet up on the table that occupied the space in the middle of our pod.

'*You* call out non-compliance,' James pointed out, tilting his beer at him. In Eric's absence, James had announced beer o'clock fifteen minutes ago and returned from the staff kitchen with three Coronas. Mine was halfway down and Belinda's sat sweating on her desk, still full.

'Non-compliance with Health Department policy about patient discharge planning. It's not exactly big-picture stuff. It's not in my job description to lobby for changes to government regulations.'

'I don't think it was in Karen Silkwood's job description to testify to the Atomic Energy Commission, but she did it anyway.' James pointed at his beer and Eric shook his head and indicated a carton of iced coffee on his desk. James shrugged. 'Tell us again why you're complaining about not being murdered.'

'Well, I mean, it's not like we do anything earth-shattering, is it? No-one cares if we find out that twenty per cent of public health patients don't get follow-up appointments after they leave hospital.'

'The patients probably care when they end up in emergency again. And why are you working on that inquiry anyway? Health's not your portfolio.'

'CorpEx has brought the tabling date forward and the team needs help tying up some loose ends.'

James and I lifted our beers in unison and drank silently. Eric's own inquiry, after being touted as a potential toppler of governments, had been scaled back and he'd been shifted sideways.

He shrugged. 'It's okay, turns out there was nothing to see on the police inquiry. Not that there's anything in the health inquiry either. It'll be on page five of *The West*, the Leader of the Opposition will ask questions in parliament, the minister will wring his hands and complain about the Commonwealth–State funding agreement, and everyone will forget about it by the game on the weekend.'

'Yeah, sorry about that, mate,' said James. 'I know you had high hopes for the police inquiry. And we're all here to keep the bastards honest. I just don't think I want to upset anyone enough to incite them to murder. I'd rather be the main character in a movie where the bureaucrat exposes the corruption and lives happily ever after.'

'That's a fairytale, James. Only little kids believe in fairytales.'

'Doesn't mean it can't happen though. How about *public investigator exposes billion-dollar hole in public health services, retires, becomes pro-surfer*. That's interesting. You could make a movie about that. Put yourself in the starring role.'

'I can't surf,' Eric pointed out.

'You could learn.'

'Yeah, yeah. And get eaten by a shark before I even stand up. Anyway, the movies I want to make don't involve people.'

The overhead lights flicked off, sending the open-plan office into darkness except for the twilight through the windows. We all looked at our phones.

'Is that the time?' Eric lifted his feet off the table with a grunt and planted them on the floor. 'Where did everyone else go?' he asked, as he walked to the timer switch that would give us another hour of artificial light.

'Scarpered. There's some concert on in Kings Park.' James nodded at the trees across the road, a dark shadow in the middle of the city. I could see the glow of the floodlights around the stage beginning to emerge from its centre.

'Nice evening for it. They got lucky at this time of the year. What are you doing tonight?'

'Nothing, going home. Surfing tomorrow though. D'you want to come?' James grinned. 'I've got an extra board.'

'Nah, mate. We're having a barbeque for Granny's birthday. She's ninety.'

'Can I come?' We all turned to Belinda, whose workstation faced the corner window. It sounds like the best position, which technically Eric should have occupied as our team leader, but it was the worst. You had your back to whoever walked toward us, which meant everyone could see what was on your screen, and the afternoon sun in summer made you sweat. Belinda wore sunscreen on the backs of her hands while she was at her desk. The Hello Kitty plush toys that she'd lined up on the windowsill were faded and shedding brittle fur.

'To Granny's barbeque?'

'No, surfing.' She clicked her mouse and swung her chair around to face the rest of us. Her feet hung above the carpet, and she picked up her beer.

'I didn't know you could surf.' James leaned back in his chair.

'I can't, but you said Eric could learn. You can teach me.' She leaned back in her own chair and rocked her feet backwards and forwards.

James regarded her. I could see his tongue moving against the side of his cheek. 'Yeah, okay. Why not? We're going early though, and don't forget it's an hour to my place from where you live.'

'Cool.' Belinda swung back to her screen, her little finger tapping on the bottle.

'Do you have a wetsuit?' James said to her back. 'The water's still cold at this time of the year.'

'Yep.' She didn't turn around, but I could hear the smile in her voice. James dipped his head in salute.

Eric winked at me. 'What about you, Frances? Keen to tangle with some Noahs tomorrow morning?'

'I'll give it a miss.'

'Wise choice.' He turned back to his workstation and I took it as a cue to turn back to mine.

Eric was right, what we do doesn't change the world, but James was right too, we might change the world for one person. I hang onto that while I'm picking through purchase orders for office consumables, tallying up the invoices, and comparing the totals to supply contract variations and the delegated authorities for approving them. Eric wanted the big one, the inquiry that would expose corruption on a scale big enough to bring down a government. He had a deep suspicion of big business, big banks, and global media even before conspiracy theories became mainstream. I couldn't see it myself. The big, audacious rip-offs might be out there, but I doubt there are as many of them as Eric thought there were. It's the routine, casual rorting that I chase. The procurement manager who slips his children's annual schoolbook purchases into a million-dollar stationery contract. The chief of staff who hires backpackers to vacuum the floors of ministerial offices for cash at twenty per cent under the minimum wage. There's something deeply satisfying about pinging a self-important bureaucrat for ripping off the state while he's enforcing the rules for everyone else.

Don't get me wrong, I'm committed to public service. I think most of our public servants are saints. You'd have to be to work in a job where your boss changes every four years, and then overturns everything you've been doing because the *previous administration* made a mess of things. A new government comes in, goalposts shift, departments restructure, stationery is rebranded, and just when they start to get going again, there's another election. I wonder sometimes whether democracy is the right basis for running a country after all.

I'm lucky because my boss reports directly to the parliament, so technically he's independent. Neil does what he does year in and year out and only the law can change that. Government still controls his purse strings though. After a particularly damning inquiry by our office, the premier will mutter dark words about the high cost of watchdogs, taxpayer value for money and the possibility of budgetary constraints. We watch him on telly, laugh and tell him *good luck with that*. Still, it's a shame the police inquiry was shutdown. It was the most exciting one any of us had worked on.

A laptop lid slapped shut behind me and I turned my head to see Eric raise his arms and stretch. 'That's it for me. Go home everyone and have a good weekend.'

The rest of us sighed and clicked save. We didn't have to stay until Eric left – he wouldn't care if I left at lunchtime as long as I met my deadlines – but somehow, it had become a thing.

'Give Granny my best birthday wishes.' James closed his own computer and reached under the desk for his bag.

'Will do. And you look after our Belinda in the water. I need her here next week for work that she won't be able to do from inside a great white.' Eric shouldered his backpack and walked back down the corridor.

That was the last time any of us saw him.

CHAPTER TWO – *ONE YEAR LATER*

The front corner of the room begins to slide upwards. It is tentative, testing. I look hard at the point of the brown-and-gold carpet where it meets the ridged skirting board. I don't turn my head, just my eyes, because it is easier that way and for a moment I get a mental image of myself giving the corner a mean side-eye. I figure I must look either crazy or bored. The speaker is engrossed in her PowerPoint and the participants are scribbling notes. No-one is watching me to notice. I breathe in and out. The corner recedes, reluctantly, it seems. Has anyone else in the world anthropomorphised the corner of a seminar room? I have to keep an eye on it because I know where it wants to go. I reach up and tuck my hair behind my right ear. That's the bad one, the one that makes me dizzy. I let my fingers linger there, rubbing the base of my skull.

The speaker is explaining the government's plans to solve the homelessness problem. They want to decentralise, open up subsidised rental to the private sector. She's working hard to sell the idea even though the seminar was billed as a *consultation* forum. The room is packed with charities and social welfare advocates. The Tenants Advisory Group has already asked some pointed questions about accountability. The speaker reassures us that landlords will need to register with the government, meet a set of criteria, and let themselves be audited once a year. But the room is sceptical, the programme will give the private sector a guaranteed supply of tenants – the thirty thousand people on the public housing waiting list – and access to a government subsidy if they keep them in a home for more than twelve months. The TAG isn't buying it.

'What margin does the private sector need to make this worth its while?' A woman the shape of a pencil and dressed in black has been scribbling and pursing her lips on the other side of the room. 'Five percent? Ten percent? Twenty percent? Social housing providers run on a margin of three. Where's the incentive?'

The speaker smiles with her teeth and folds her hands over the remote control. 'We have received enormous interest from the private property sector locally, nationally and internationally,' she tells the TAG woman. 'The sector is very keen to expand its social responsibility platform. They are acutely aware of the tsunami of older people retiring and still in the rental market, a market they won't be able to afford when they are only receiving an aged pension. Most of those people are single women.'

She clicks the remote, the crowd murmurs and I risk a look at the screen. It shows the front page of yesterday's paper. *Froze To Death*. The headline is superimposed on a bush setting. A white shelter, the type you buy in camping stores, has been erected between prickly melaleuca bushes and a once-red station wagon. All of the car's doors, including the tailgate, are open and I can see the end of a mattress hanging out the back. It will, I know, smell of damp, mould and sweat. The grey sand in the foreground is littered with bottles and cans. Another mattress on the ground beside the car's rear wheel arch is partly screened by the bushes and covered with a sheet that outlines the shape of a body.

'Stacey Miles died while sleeping rough at a bush camp south of the city last weekend,' says the speaker. 'She had been homeless since leaving an abusive relationship two years ago. She was on the public housing waiting list and the Department of Housing understands she had been couch surfing with various relatives across the metropolitan area. We don't know why she returned to the bush camp at this time of year. Overnight temperatures on the weekend dropped to less than two degrees. We need more low-cost housing to prevent this from happening.'

She presses the remote again to bring up an image of a

construction site. Front and centre are Simon Tallent, the Minister for Housing, and the developer: suited, smiling and clutching takeaway coffees from a popular inner-city café. The site signage board is still shiny and, above pictures of safety equipment and a stern prohibition against onsite alcohol, announces *Lignum Partners* as the developer. I recognise the name. Lignum is a tiny settlement – thirty households at a stretch – on Yamatji country inland from my hometown. I squint at the screen to see if the developer is anyone I know, but at that moment Belinda raises her hand. It is her left hand, next to my right ear, and I feel a rush of motion and jerk my head away. I eyeball the corner. It has seized the day and is bolting to the ceiling. The carpet follows, rising up like it's being pulled on a string. I grip the table and close my eyes. It doesn't help and I feel sweat, both hot and cold, on my forehead. Belinda is asking about the registration criteria for landlords. People will be looking at her. I compose my face in what I hope looks like profound, closed-eyed contemplation of my colleague's query. I squeeze my fingertips into the underside of the composite wooden surface, breathe and wait for morning tea to be announced.

I'm here because our office is investigating the government's previous homelessness programme, which opened up public housing to not-for-profit landlords. It was a half-step to privatisation. *Social housing*, not *public housing*, the Minister for Housing had called it last year, as if there was a difference between having a charity or the government as your landlord when your only other option was the back seat of a car. I suspect the tenants themselves don't care as long as they have a roof over their heads. The social housing programme has made a considerable dent in the waiting list, which is a great success story for the government, but accounts are coming through about building faults – walls cracking, high power bills, that sort of thing. My boss wants to know whether it is stopping the government from putting people into homes. My guess is that the rush to get the new homes built has stretched the already overheated housing market, and the department is turning a blind eye to shoddy work in order to meet ministerial demands.

Across the room, the Assistant Director for Homelessness Strategies meets my eye and winds his way through the crowd. I say 'winds' but, in reality, Dr Duncan Wolf walks directly toward me, cup in one hand, a plate in the other, and elbows out. Seniority, determination, and bulk clear his path. He reaches me, exhales, and sips his tea. He has dirty fingernails, and despite his size, his black suit hangs in folds like he's recently lost weight.

'Good to see you and your colleagues here, Frances.'

'Duncan,' I nod. 'Thank you for inviting us.'

'It's in everyone's best interests to keep the commissioner's office abreast of what we are doing. I like to have everyone on board and on the same page. Pulling together.'

'Keeping your enemies close?' I add. Oops. I'll get pulled up for that later. I wonder whether Duncan will text, email or call Neil about my snarky behaviour and whether he'll do it before or after morning tea ends. He's impassive, which means he's considering which option will do the most damage.

'How is the inquiry going?' he asks.

'On time and on budget.'

'Of course it is. With you at the helm, Frances, it wouldn't be any other way. And what about your findings? Anything useful you can tell me? No surprises and all that.'

That's a dig at our office values. *No surprises.* We tell the departments under inquiry as soon as anything comes to light. Procedural fairness, one of the tenets of administrative law. It gives the department the best opportunity to either convince us that we've got it wrong or prepare their damage control for the media.

'Nothing yet,' I reply.

'Early days, hmm?' He balances the plate on top of his cup and uses his free hand to lift a sandwich to his mouth. It looks good. I've always preferred savoury instead of sweet at morning tea. I wonder if there will be any left to take back to the seminar room when we reconvene.

Alarmingly, Duncan steps forward. He is too close now and he blocks my view of the far wall, which I was relying on to keep steady. Without an anchor, the ceiling makes a slow dive to the right. My throat tightens and my right hand reaches for the sideboard behind me.

'It would be very helpful, Frances, if you could wind up the fieldwork by the end of the week. My staff are stretched enough as it is trying to reduce the waiting list, and with your inquiry we are at risk of missing our own minister's KPIs.'

I lower my head to get a view of the floor, hoping I'm looking thoughtful and not submissive. The brown and gold swirls on the carpet don't help. I press my tongue to the roof of my mouth, count to three and breathe out.

'Your team has been very accommodating, thank you, Duncan, but I'm expecting we will still need to go into next week.'

His face is way too close, and I see him taking in the sweat on my forehead. 'Is that because you're unwell?' he asks. There's canniness there, and no concern.

'No, it's because we need to review the files for the north metropolitan district.'

'Perhaps I should speak to the commissioner.'

'Perhaps you should.'

The bell rings and Duncan glides away. It occurs to me that he must take long, smooth steps to move like that, or lots of tiny ones, like a ballet dancer doing *bourrées*. I look at his feet. He strides. Of course he does.

I cross the room to the morning tea table. All of the scones and biscuits are gone, but the crowd has left behind a nice selection of sandwiches. I find a fat triangle of chicken breast, avocado and lettuce on soft white bread and an exciting wedge of rye embracing beef, mustard and pickles. I put them on a plate and walk as fast as

I dare through the doors just before they are closed by a smirking usher who looks like he should be preparing for his final exams instead of opening and closing doors. I pause to adjust to the lower light before rejoining my table. At the back of the room, Duncan has pushed his chair away from his own table and is leaning backwards, right ankle hooked over left knee. He is tapping on his phone like his life depends on it.

CHAPTER THREE

The day after the housing seminar, I stop by the supermarket to buy Tim Tams and bananas. The biscuits are for the team, and the bananas are for potassium. I shouldn't be going to work today – I'll suffer for it for the rest of the week – but it's not optional. This Sunday will be twelve months since Eric disappeared. Today we will work quietly, have chocolate biscuits for morning tea, someone will make a joke about the legendary Tim Tam eating competition (I won) and we will all go home at five.

According to the police and the building management company, twelve months ago, Eric took the lift from our floor to the basement carpark and cycled up the car ramp. He turned left onto Kings Park Road and circled the roundabout into the park itself. Our gardener, Jason, was clearing the footpath ahead of some government function the next morning and said Eric had waved to him from his bike. Jason remembered, he said, because Eric and another cyclist were almost cleaned up by a Mercedes in the right-hand lane, and Eric had looked back and given Jason the thumbs-up to show he was okay. The last Jason saw of him was his red-and-silver reflective handlebar tape as he cycled down the darkening avenue under the line of pale, lemon-scented gums.

I've completed two inquiries since then. I've moved up from a level five analyst to a level seven project manager, taking over the housing and justice portfolios that Eric used to manage, and skipping a whole level in the public service hierarchy. I write project plans, prepare budgets, submit inquiry proposals to CorpEx, and report on our findings. I pore over maintenance logs, rental payments, and court security contracts, and inform the Western Australian public about the missteps and, occasionally, misappropriations made by public servants in their expenditure of taxpayers' money. I love it.

Eric was a level seven project manager when he vanished. It felt odd, the day I got my promotion, to be the same level as he was. To a level five, level sevens are big time; important people who wield control over project budgets and deadlines. They keep their teams in line with whips, and their torches blaze into the night as they check timesheets for any unauthorised hours and minutes that you might have booked to their project. Level seven project managers who bring their projects in on time and on budget are office heroes. If they also get front page coverage of their inquiry reports, they are legends. And if Dean Alston, the statewide daily newspaper's political cartoonist, is inspired to make a wry comment on your findings, your work will be memorialised on the office walls of the Commissioner for Public Inquiries.

*

I'm fine until I turn into the baking aisle. The shelves are too high and too close, and my dodgy ear makes the floor shift under my feet. I step my left foot across my right to escape the looming packets of flour and then have to step my right foot wide to compensate. My right arm follows it, palm upward to ward off the sugar on the other side. I stand, mid-aisle, feet apart and arm out, willing the floor to stop moving. I breathe in and out again and open my eyes. A woman not much older than me is standing two metres away, clutching the handrail of her shopping trolley. I could do with a trolley to clutch right now. I wonder if she'll let me hang onto it too. She has a small boy behind her knee and a horrified look on her face, so I guess not. I realise my mouth is hanging open, so I draw in limbs and jaw, and offer her an apologetic smile. The alarm on her face only deepens in response and she angles her trolley to move around me, one arm reaching behind her to shield her child. *You're too young to be so judgy*, I tell her in my head. At least she'll have something to talk about at playgroup today. The drunk woman in a suit at Coles *at eight thirty in the morning on a weekday, can you believe it?*

I wait until she turns the corner (she shoots me another suspicious look as she angles the trolley around) and hold out both arms to keep an even distance between my malfunctioning vestibular system and the baking items. I aeroplane to the end. I don't even know why I came down here. I navigate two aisles over, choose four different packets of Tim Tams and head to the fresh produce section for my chewable, yellow potassium pills.

It's close to nine when I get to the bus stop, so I get to sit down on the bus without excuses. I gave up using the special needs seats a couple of years ago. The drama of dealing with the outraged stares just got to be too much. If the bus is full, I just stand and deal with it. Today, most commuters are already in the city, marching to their offices or opening their shop doors. I sit at the front, where there is less movement, and lean my head against the back of the seat. Today, I need to review the defects reports that James sent me yesterday. It's the end of the month, so I also need to approve timesheets and finish my progress report for next week's CorpEx meeting. The bus crosses the intersection at Thomas Street and enters Kings Park Road. The plane trees on the left are pruned in a high arc over the traffic and are coming into leaf. I feel the light and shade across my face like fingertips. The bus stops, discharges commuters, then stops again, and again. I close my throat against the gentle rocking of the brakes and breathe. One more stop and I can get down.

After lunch, we feel rather than hear the usual office murmur fade. It's like the welcome drop in temperature before the sea breeze comes in, or the sense of foreboding you feel when you hear the roar of a million bees swarming down the street toward you.

'Today's CorpEx is finished then,' says James.

Belinda grunts without turning around.

I lift my head to look down the corridor toward reception and see a cluster of dark suits shaking hands. Among them is a white-jacketed, skirted anomaly.

'Who's the outsider?' I ask.

'Neil's equivalent in Victoria,' says James. 'She's here for a gathering of the clan.'

I watch as my boss moves to pat the Victorian commissioner on the back and then thinks better of it. He stands awkwardly, hand in mid-air, as she walks toward the lifts and out of my view, then realises he can avoid physical contact by waving instead. I can almost see the motor neurons firing down his arm to his hand. They hesitate, reconsider the image of himself waving to a senior public servant three metres away inside a liftwell, and wisely blink out. His hand flops back down to his side. He looks over his shoulder down the corridor, meets my eye and remembers. I hunch forward into my desk hoping he'll get sidetracked.

He doesn't.

'Frances, James, Belinda' – *Eric*, I add in my head – 'how are we today?'

'Great, thanks boss,' James replies on behalf of us all.

'Good, good.' He puts his hands deep in his pockets. I wonder how much mental energy he puts into working out what to do with them. 'Housing inquiry going well?'

'On time and on budget, boss.' James again. The commissioner looks at me.

'Really well, thanks, Neil,' I say, because I'm the project manager and the one who should be replying, not James. 'The department has been really helpful.' Really, really.

'Good to hear, Frances.' He looks out over the trees, removes his hands from his pockets, and swings them like he is about to launch through the window and into the park. 'Can I have a word?'

'Sure.' I follow him back up the corridor. It's a long walk. I can feel my team watching my back and Belinda leaning forward to explain to

James. She'd seen the exchange with Duncan at morning tea yesterday.

'Thank goodness,' she'd said when I'd returned to our table with my sandwiches. 'I thought Duncan was going to suck out your soul.' A man at the next table shushed her and Belinda waited until I sat down before whispering. 'What'd the great dementor want?'

'An end to his pain,' I hissed back.

'I hope you told him that wasn't going to happen.'

'Not until I'm ready.'

'Good woman.' She lifted up the top slice of rye and stole the pickle. 'Where does he get off? He thinks he's God's gift just because he managed some construction project.'

'Some several construction projects,' I remind her. 'Projects of State Importance. He didn't get an Australia Day Honours for nothing.'

'Whatever,' Belinda threw a look at the shushing man, 'it doesn't mean he's not a jerk.'

'I might have a been a jerk too,' I admitted, grimacing at her.

'Oh excellent, what did you say?'

'Something about keeping your enemies close.'

'Nice.' She twisted in her seat to look at the back corner of the room. 'Is that why he's texting? Reporting you to Neil?'

'That or updating his online dating profile.' It was common knowledge in the public sector that Duncan used dating apps – which wasn't in itself a bad thing, most of my single friends hook up that way – but Duncan's devotion to his phone was good fodder for jokes about his romantic life. Not that anyone could prove that he was chatting up potential dates during budget meetings. He was diligent about keeping the screen angled away from his colleagues and it always went straight back into his jacket pocket.

'Will you please show some respect?' The shushing man upped the ante, and we were getting frowns from other tables. Belinda made a show of peering at his name badge and writing it down on her notepad. We both pressed our lips together and turned to face the front of the room.

*

As Neil and I approach his office, Neil nods at his executive assistant, who gives me a sympathetic look, and ushers me inside. Neil has the opposite corner to Belinda, but five times the space and enclosing walls. He also has a couch, several framed Alston prints, and a minibar. He gestures for me to sit on the couch, changes his mind, and offers me the chair in front of his desk. He sits in his own chair, looks out the window, adjusts a stack of papers and pats his phone. I smile and he looks back down at his desktop.

'I had a call from the Assistant Director for Homelessness Strategies yesterday,' he says, before stopping, clearing his throat, and grasping the glass of water at the top of his blotter. 'Duncan is very impressed with your progress on the inquiry; says you've covered a large amount of ground already.'

'His team has been more than forthcoming,' I answer, 'so he can take some of the credit for that.'

'He's very impressed with your project management skills.' Neil leans back in his chair, and I do the same. He notices me mirroring and nods to himself. I remember what James said about Neil taking empathy coaching. I put my hands in my lap and he does that too, wriggling slightly to adjust his seat. 'He was wondering if – given the progress you've made and the substantial number of files you've already reviewed – you have sufficient information to make a finding.'

'Not really, no,' I say, using my best reasonable voice. What I really want to say is *for fuck's sake, Neil, grow a pair*, but of course I don't. 'We haven't started on the north metropolitan district and, as you know, that's where many of the complaints originated.'

'Ah, yes.' He lifts his elbows to the arms of his chair and presses his fingertips together. I copy him but he doesn't notice this time. 'You see, the department is under terrible pressure to roll out this new housing strategy ...'

'The private sector one.'

'… yes. If what the minister is saying is right, it will go a long way to reducing the waiting list, which of course is what we all want.' He pauses so I can acknowledge this universal goal.

'Mmm.'

'And Duncan was wondering, given your excellent progress, if we could perhaps close out the fieldwork this week.'

I have to hand it to Duncan, he's taken my *keeping your enemies close* comment to heart.

'I don't think we can, Neil,' I say, tipping my head to one side. 'How would we explain that we'd cut the scope of the inquiry when it was the north metropolitan district where the building complaints originated? And some of those complaints came through the sitting opposition member's office, didn't they? What's her name? Jaelyn Worner?'

Neil flinches. Jaelyn Worner is a Yamatji woman with spiky hair, red lipstick that looks like it was applied in a moving vehicle while she was fording a river, and a pre-parliamentary career as a defence counsel. She remembers everything you say and can brandish facts and figures that you won't need to check because she is right every single time. In the last election, Jaelyn swung her seat from a four per cent margin in favour of the government to a three percent margin in favour of the opposition. Shortsheeting Jaelyn's electorate in a public inquiry would not be a good move. I watch Neil's neurons make new pathways.

'Yes, of course,' he says. He looks out the window and purses his lips. It makes his chin wrinkle. 'How many files do you need to review in the north metro district?'

'The project plan says fifty.' I watch the joints of his fingers whiten as he presses the tips together.

'And how many did you review in the other districts?'

'The same percentage. So, sixty files in the south, forty-five in the east.'

'And what's coming out of them?'

'About one in five defects reports haven't been acquitted.'

He raises his eyebrows. 'Twenty per cent?'

'Yep.' I try to keep the schadenfreude out of my voice but there's no mistaking it. Defects reports are the main quality control at the end of a construction project. They have to be acquitted before the project manager can sign off. Neil gives me a look. He understands.

'And that's consistent across districts?'

I nod.

'And what about the occupancy data? What percentage of the new builds are still empty?'

'Not sure yet, we're still waiting on access to the files.'

'Hmm.' Neil gazes at the trees and I wait. He's working out who he's most afraid of and balancing it against the opportunity to add another Alston to his wall. Duncan's boss, the current Minister for Housing, is also a lawyer, but unlike Jaelyn his background is in public prosecutions, and he campaigned on a law-and-order platform. The Hon. Simon Tallent is popular and tipped to become deputy premier if his party stays in power at the next election and the current premier stands down. He's also been vocal about interference from unelected officials with, he says, the power to stand in the way of election mandates. Neil has been in his sights before.

'Review twenty files and let me know the result. If it's coming up consistent with the other districts, I'll call it in.'

I open my mouth and shut it again while he stands and walks over to the window, hands safely back in his pockets. I'm dismissed.

CHAPTER FOUR

The vertigo episode at the seminar wasn't my first. They don't often happen in public though. They don't happen very much at all these days if I take my meds. They started when I was twenty-one, on a beach in India. The sea tipped to the right and slid under my feet. The sand rose up after it, turning over my head. I thought it was drugs. I'd smoked hash for the first time on that trip and hadn't expected it to be so strong. Apparently, I'd fallen asleep pretty much straight after the first toke and spent the whole day snoring on my beach towel. It took two people to carry me back to the hotel. I'd woken up at lunchtime the day after, foggy, sunburnt and hungry. Three days later, I was standing very still on the same beach, watching the world turn, fascinated by the psychoactive properties of marijuana until I remembered I hadn't ingested anything more exotic than a mango lassi since my last adventure. Then I panicked.

'Madam, did you come here for narcotics purposes?' A barefoot man in an olive suit stood in front of me. He was stationary against the revolving background. His sentence dipped in unexpected places.

'Um.' How do you explain that the world is turning but, no, you are not stoned, when you are clearly a middle-class white girl playing at being a hippie on a beach in Goa? You don't. You get saved by your friends.

'Leave her alone, creep.' Maggie gripped my arm and dragged me back to our nest of towels and striped cotton bags. She passed me a bottle of water. 'Sunstroke?'

'Yes. No. Everything is spinning and my ears feel like they're full of fluid. It's weird. I need to sit down.'

'Maybe you're just dehydrated. Drink more water.' She settled back onto her elbows, sat up and adjusted her bikini line and leaned back again. I picked up her hat from the sand and dropped it onto her head. 'Thanks, buddy.'

We stayed on the sand for the rest of the afternoon while Maggie coaxed more melanin to the surface of her skin, and I hid my own flesh under layers of paisley cotton. Maggie tanned better than I did. A Portuguese heritage does that for you. My Scottish–German DNA is not so happy in subcontinental sunlight. I rolled over onto my stomach and Maggie flicked my tasselled skirt down to cover my legs to my ankles. I looked back at the olive-suited man. He was standing in the shade of the lassi van, talking to the owner and sucking on ice chips. I hoped they'd give him diarrhoea, then remembered that diarrhoea can be a death sentence in this part of the world and took it back.

'Do you think ice really is unsafe?' I asked Maggie.

She snorted. 'I'm not going to try it.'

I looked down at my book. It was set in India and written by a convicted bank robber who escaped from an Australian prison and went to live in Bombay. I was up to the part where he returns after smuggling guns in Afghanistan, but the words were doing the revolving thing too. I tried following them around the page, tilting my head to keep track, but it didn't work. I turned the book over, hugged my arms across my chest and closed my eyes.

*

'Well?' James swings his chair around as I return from Neil's office.

'I've been told to give you your First Formal Warning.'

'Was it the beer in the staff fridge or the bribe I took from those prison officers?'

'The beer. Neil says no self-respecting staff member of his drinks Coronas without a slice of lemon.'

'How does he know I didn't put lemon in?'

'He went through the bin under your desk.'

'Damn.'

'He is a public sector investigator after all,' says Belinda, standing at the printer. 'You can't put anything past him.' She waves pages at me. 'Can we go through these before you go home?'

'Sure.' I watch her flick the back of James' head before she sits down. He reaches over to swat her without taking his eyes off his screen. She shimmies out of the way, and he misses. I can see his reflection grinning in the monitor.

My own workstation is buried in paper, and I can't recall what I was working on before Neil invited me to the other end of the floor. I shuffle the piles into rectangular shapes and collect up three tide-marked mugs. Eric would have laughed.

'Who wants a coffee?'

James looks at his watch. 'Nah, not for me.'

Belinda passes her mug behind her without taking her eyes off the spreadsheet on her screen.

'We'll go through those papers in a minute, hey?' I say to her.

She nods, absorbed.

'Oh yeah,' James looks up, 'Bigfoot was looking for you.'

I look over my shoulder down the corridor expecting to see our director materialise. She has a way of appearing, silently, when you are not expecting it. 'What'd she want?'

'Didn't say.'

'Oh crap,' says Belinda to her screen. 'I have to renew my password for this stinking tenancy database.'

'So just do it,' says James.

'This will be, like, the third time and I'm running out of ideas. They don't let you repeat old passwords.'

'What's your formula?'

'What do you mean, what's my formula?'

'You know, you work through your friends' names and substitute the letters for numbers, that sort of thing. Like J A M 3 5.'

I watch Belinda copy the letters and numbers onto her notepad. James looks at me and grins.

'Oh. I get it, it spells James,' she turns to him. 'Does this mean we're friends?'

'Only if you use his name as your password,' I tell her. 'But it won't be long enough. You'll need to add his birth year at the end. If you know it.'

I take the mugs to the staff kitchen, four square metres of space tucked in behind the liftwell. It's the dead hour before five, so I don't have to squeeze around anyone else to reach the coffee machine, fridge or sugar. I wash and dry the mugs in front of a laminated A4 poster that tells me my mother doesn't work here and I need to do my own dishes. My mother bought a dishwasher two weeks after she moved out of her childhood home. *Life's too short*, and all that.

'There you are, Frances.' Catherine Matthews – Bigfoot – Director of Public Inquiries and my immediate line manager, is standing in the doorway, two lines creased between her pale eyebrows. That's not fashionable, these days. If your eyebrows are not heavy enough to need soldering to your face, they might as well not be there. My own brows are – measurably – two shades darker than my hair, thanks to a box of dye under my bathroom sink. There's not much that is fashionable about Bigfoot, though. She dresses for work like she's wearing a uniform. Black pants suit, white button-down, incongruously large lace-up shoes, pale hair in a ponytail, pale face clear of make-up. Her wardrobe must look very ordered. Zen. I wonder if that is the secret to her silent appearances. She blends in. 'Can you come to my office? Be quick, we'll need a while and I have a physio appointment after work.'

*

The office lights have timed out by the time I return to the pod. So much for leaving at five today. James' and Belinda's workstations are empty, the screens blank, the desks clear. In the absence of lockable offices, we have a clean desk policy. All project records, especially any that might contain sensitive information, have to be locked in the filing cabinets or in the mobile pedestals under our desks. James and Belinda are diligent about it – me, not so much. On Eric's workstation, there is nothing but dust. Even the monitor is gone, re-allocated to another staff member.

I'm surprised his desk is still vacant. Space is always tight in the public sector. We have a policy of fifteen square metres per person, including meeting rooms, liftwells, reception, and wet areas. So far, Neil has managed to find other desks for new staff, but that's about to come to an end. We are moving next week. The whole office is relocating to the CBD to clear out our building for government ministers. It's better for security, apparently, to put them all together in one location. I'm not sure of the logic of that myself. It seems to me someone could take out the whole state Cabinet in one fell swoop, but what would I know. Personally, I think they are doing it so ministers don't have to cross paths with grubby public servants. They'll be able to drive their government cars straight into the basement and take dedicated lifts up to their floors without coming into contact with one of us and having to work out if we are a level two payroll assistant or a member of the Senior Executive Service. I'm not sure which would be better or worse.

I shut down my computer and lock up my papers. I peer into James' bin and find one empty, lemon-less, Corona bottle. It has a faint smudge of lipstick around the top. I smile and head for the liftwell.

CHAPTER FIVE

It's late so I get a seat on the bus. That's twice in one day. Above the tree canopy the sky is fading and cockatoos screech as they come back to the park to roost. The flocks look bigger this year. Dad said it's the same up home, that a run of good seasons has bumped up the population. Apparently, they are stripping the Norfolk Island pines in the town and making a mess in the carparks. I can see one of the park's signature lemon-scented gums covered in white wings, and branches falling to the ground. Parrot beaks are strong.

In the disappearing light, the understorey has deepened. Pools of green and brown pass by. They can't be penetrated by the streetlights. A hiking path disappears into a tunnel that starts out olive and rapidly becomes black. It will be cool in there already. Twigs will snap and leaves rustle as ground-based animals large and small find their own hidey-holes for the night. Or emerge from them. The park has foxes, and rabbits, and kangaroos. I've been in there when it's dark, with other drunken students, armed with torches. I've seen animal eyes looking back at me. They don't move, frozen but unaware that the reflective layer behind their irises is giving away their position.

It's not the wild fauna in Kings Park that you need to worry about. Foxes and rabbits and kangaroos (depending on how big they are) are scared of you. They remain motionless until they don't; then they disappear. It's disconcerting. You wonder if they are going to reappear in front of your face. The carnivorous kangaroo of your nightmares, bloody fangs bared and clawed hind legs poised to rip through your intestines. That's ridiculous though. As much as we like to wind up tourists with stories of man-eating marsupials, there's nothing in the bush that wants to kill you except other humans. Bodies have been found in the park before. Some have been homeless people who have died from exposure or lack of medical treatment (ironically, the state's largest tertiary hospital is across the road), but others have been victims of actual crimes. I wonder how many bodies are still buried there. I wonder how many have been carried out of the park by their assailants. I wonder if Eric's was one of them.

The bus crosses Thomas Street and I am back in the suburbs. We trundle past weatherboard cottages and a glowing outline of a snapper. *Western Pescado.* Children in school uniforms follow their fathers into bottle shops and come out again clutching bags of chips and bottles of soft drink. Dad has a wine for Mum and a sixpack for himself. It is Friday, after all. My bus dives under the railway line and up the other side. More school children scurry along the footpath to a floodlit playing field. They wear yellow shin guards and flash alarming yellow and red striped grins at each other. Their mothers trudge behind them carrying camp chairs and pulling wheeled cooler bags.

The bus turns down an avenue of Norfolk Island pines and I ring the bell. I alight under the canopy (not yet savaged by white cockatoos), thank the driver, and look up at my building. Lights glow from every apartment on my floor except mine, the one on the end. It is the best one, at the top and with a wraparound balcony that lets me sit in the winter sun without having to endure the southerly. I take my cue from the dads and visit the bottle shop before I get in the lift.

The corridors in my apartment block are wide, carpeted, and punctuated with framed Indigenous prints and pots of native flowers. My apartment is at the end farthest from the liftwell. The real estate agent told me I'd never be bothered by people walking past, but with the heavy fire door and soft flooring, I don't know how he thought I'd ever know.

One advantage of being the end apartment – one that the real estate agent didn't point out – is the huge Norfolk Island pine outside my balcony. I can see it through the window at the end of the corridor as I walk to my door if I get home in the daylight. It is home and breakfast bar for red-tailed black cockatoos and, at the right time of year, I can see them sitting on the branches. They are big birds, bigger than the white cockatoos, with red feathers in their tails, and beaks that look like they are smiling. Tonight, all I can see through the window is me reflected back in the corridor. I put my bottle on the carpet while I rummage for my keys and let myself in.

With so much balcony and glass, my apartment heats up during the day if I don't draw the blinds in the morning, even in winter. I forgot today, so I open the balcony doors and let in the sea breeze. It blows the mail off my kitchen bench. I swear and plonk the bottle on top of the recovered stack. The top envelope immediately begins to soak up the condensation from the glass. It's a power bill so I leave it, pull last night's takeaway laksa from the fridge, and put it in the microwave. I make myself a nest of pinot gris and paperwork, and settle into the couch.

The papers are from Bigfoot and, as she had warned me that afternoon, they are a mess. A forgotten file from an old community health inquiry had been uncovered as part of the office clean-up ahead of the move. She'd go through them herself, she said, but she's been allocated a PID and has to make that her priority. Investigating PIDs – public interest disclosures (not pelvic inflammatory diseases as Belinda claims, even though they create a similar level of discomfort), more commonly known as whistleblowers – is part of Neil's mandate as commissioner, and he's supposed to act on them as soon as they come in. I want to ask if the whistleblower is a public servant or a member of the public, but Bigfoot has said enough already. PID investigations are supposed to be top secret.

'I know health isn't your portfolio,' she had said, nodding at a folder optimistically held together with what looked like dressmaker's binding ribbon, 'but we're all under the pump right now and the follow-up review is due.'

That didn't sound right to me, but I figured she must be getting ahead of the game. Making sure she meets her KPIs. 'Is this a serviette?' I asked, pulling out a square of soft pink paper.

'Possibly, yes.'

'Who worked on the project?' I peeked under the top corner of the folder, wondering if the food that accompanied the serviette was still there, squashed between the pages.

'Here's the annotated inquiry report.' Bigfoot passed me a familiar, neater folder, barcoded, and stamped with the name of our office. It would, I knew, contain a marked-up copy of the official report and copies of the evidence for each of the findings. 'I need you to identify anything in this folder that's relevant to the key findings and add them to the annotations.'

'And shred the rest.'

'No, put the rest in here' – she had passed me a folder with *Miscellaneous* helpfully written on the front cover – 'and give it back to me. Can you do it by Monday? I need the papers put in order for the follow-up review. I'll give you approval to sign the files out of the office.'

I slurp a mouthful of noodles, chase them with wine, and open the annotated report. It was a year-old inquiry into community health services, the one Eric was seconded to when his police inquiry was pulled. It hadn't set the world on fire. The findings were all about the lack of communication between tertiary hospitals and health clinics in the suburbs. The Department of Health, we'd said, needed to close the gap between the different parts of the system. Better communication would lead to better outpatient follow-up which could potentially reduce the number of avoidable emergency department presentations. That's public-inquiry speak for admitting we hadn't been able to actually prove that anyone had died because they'd missed a follow-up appointment.

Predictably, the media took the populist angle when the report was tabled in parliament. The nanny state shouldn't be holding the hands of individuals who can't take responsibility for themselves, said one page-three reporter. It wasn't a coincidence, he sneered, that seventy-five percent of the patient files that we audited were people who live in public housing. I looked him up. His last article included a photo of himself, holding a notepad and scowling in front of a house with no curtains and a lawn strewn with car bodies and a stained mattress.

I set the bundle of papers free, eat some more noodles, drink some more wine. The top page is a photocopy of the Department of Health brochure *What happens when you leave hospital?* Someone has underlined a sentence about *a call from your community health service provider* in green pen. I check the annotated report, find the reference to the brochure and the brochure itself in its correct numbered position in the file. I put the photocopy into Bigfoot's *Miscellaneous* folder and move on. Second in the bundle is a partial database printout, sorted alphabetically by outpatient name. The list ends at Townsend. I flick through the bundle to find the rest of the alphabet. Toward the bottom, I pass over a page of newsprint. I pull it out and turn it over but can't see how it relates to the report. I'm about to put it in the *Miscellaneous* folder when I recognise the date. Two weeks after Eric disappeared. In the bottom right-hand corner, I find a single column article. It isn't even four centimetres long. *No sign of missing public servant,* it says. I fold it into my pocket and go to bed.

CHAPTER SIX

I have my own theories about what happened the day Eric disappeared and why. Of course I do, there's a reason I'm a public investigator. Eric's last project was the big one, his *magnum opus*, his lead story on the nightly news. If he was going to expose high-stakes corruption, the police inquiry was it. He'd pushed for it himself, pitching it to the commissioner as the best opportunity yet to make a difference. Forensic evidence, Eric had told Neil, was collected from the scene of a crime, swabbed, bagged, and tagged, and held in the evidence room at the local police station where access was restricted and logged. Right?

Wrong. Local coppers, especially those of a certain vintage, don't trust the administration. They hang onto their evidence, keeping it close. They're smart enough, in these days of DNA analysis, to put their treasure in sealed evidence bags, but from that point, it stays in pockets, car boots, home garages and desk drawers. The retired detective in crime thrillers with cold case evidence in a shoebox under his bed? There's a reason that's a trope, Eric told Neil.

Neil was doubtful. He'd been doing his daily rounds of the office floor and Eric had cornered him in our pod. Neil wanted to know how Eric would prove that police officers held onto evidence outside the system. They weren't going to simply volunteer the information. It would land them in front of a judge themselves. And our legislation doesn't allow Neil to give witnesses protection from prosecution.

'I know,' Eric replied, 'but that's not the angle. What if police officers are right to be cautious? What if evidence does actually go missing in the system? It doesn't have to be because there's someone deliberately removing it. What if evidence bags get numbered incorrectly, or go missing when they are moved from the evidence room to the forensic testing labs, or even the pathology labs in the health department, and back again? Some jurisdictions have radio frequency devices attached to their evidence bags so they can record any breaks in the chain of custody. We don't have that here.'

I saw Belinda and James glance at each other. Neil was nothing if not a technology freak. Anything that smelled of a shiny new electronic system had his instant attention. We watched him watch Eric, his hands at rest in his pockets, absorbing the intricacies of using radio frequency systems to track and log the movement of forensic evidence. He was smitten. You'd think Eric was showing him how he could fly to the moon.

'Which jurisdictions have implemented these systems?' Neil asked.

'Queensland and California.'

'Well, we're not budgeted for international travel, but it wouldn't hurt to go over east and have a look at what they've done there.' He gazed out the window, rocking backwards and forwards on his heels.

'Always good to learn from the people who've gone before, sir,' said Eric.

James pulled a face at Belinda, and she swung back to her screen with her hand to her mouth.

'But, just thinking this through,' Neil contemplated the treetops, 'this has the potential to bring the integrity of thousands of items of evidence into question. It could throw the justice system into chaos.'

'I know,' Eric replied, beaming, 'think of it. But also think about the hundreds of people who might have been wrongfully convicted.'

And then he used his master stroke. The human element also works with Neil. He loves personal stories he can recount to the media.

'Remember that guy who spent ten years in prison for murdering his mate?' Eric asked him. 'The one who was found in the desert up north?'

Neil frowned.

'The one who was pardoned after an inmate at Greenough Prison confessed to the murder?' Eric prompted. 'He was a cook on a mining camp.'

'That was the guy where the only evidence they had on him was his DNA on the knife found at the scene. Scottish guy.'

'That's the one. Apparently, when Internal Affairs reviewed the case, they found a discrepancy between the date the knife was logged out of the evidence room and into the forensics lab across town. No-one knows where it was for three days.'

'Is that right? How do you know that?'

'My brother-in-law works for Internal Affairs.'

Neil raised his eyebrows at this potential conflict of interest but let it go. 'Could have been a data entry error.'

'Yeah, it could,' Eric acknowledged, 'but the point is, the DNA had to travel from the police evidence room to the state forensics lab, to the state pathology lab without being contaminated. It's hard to prove no contamination if they can't account for the knife's whereabouts for three days.'

'So did the guy's DNA get on the knife at the scene or after it was bagged?'

'No-one knows, that's the problem. But the evidence wasn't secure and shouldn't have been used to obtain a conviction.'

Neil wasn't won over immediately, but then a gap came up in our programme the next year, and Eric was given a project budget and a reporting date.

My theory is that someone got wind of Eric's project. Someone who knew about a conviction that was unsound. Maybe some underling had taken the rap for their criminal boss. Maybe a crooked cop had tampered with evidence. Whatever it was, someone didn't want a mid-level public servant raking over their case and was prepared to go to any lengths to stop him.

I think that person killed Eric.

Trouble is, I have no idea who that would be or what evidence they wanted to protect. Tens of thousands of pieces of forensic evidence travel through the court system each year.

James disagreed. 'That's ridiculous,' he said when I shared my theory on a Friday in the pod after everyone else had gone home.

'No, it's not. I think Fran has a point,' said Belinda, swinging her legs. 'There are potentially hundreds of people who would want Eric dead.'

'Maybe, yeah, before the report was tabled. Not much point offing him afterwards though, is there?'

'Revenge.'

'Revenge for what? The inquiry was pulled. Watered down. The report didn't say anything in the end.'

James was right. Eric's great exposé had faltered in the home straight. There wasn't enough, Neil had said, to warrant a finding that forensic evidence was compromised on any significant scale. The best we could do was comment on inefficiencies in the justice system caused by a processing backlog. Eric had been gutted. But no-one gets murdered for pointing out government inefficiency.

CHAPTER SEVEN

I wake up to optimistic sunlight and do a stocktake. It's Saturday, I have a week's worth of laundry in my basket and an empty fridge. The game on the oval behind my apartment will start at one and the game at the stadium will start at six. I said I would have coffee with Steph at eleven. Eric is still missing. I slide my feet onto the floor and experiment with being vertical. It's fine. I decide to start with putting a load of laundry in the machine.

I remember to rescue the newspaper clipping from my pocket before I put my pants in the darks pile. I smooth it out and tuck it inside a hardback book of African landscape photography to flatten the creases. The book has become my go-to storage for random but interesting pieces of paper. I never look at them. Their torn edges poke out from underneath a jacket cover showing orange sand dunes rising over a silvery river. Long shadows track down the faces of the dunes. I wonder why the publisher didn't put a picture with animals on the cover. They should be at the water's edge, drinking in the late afternoon light. Perhaps that was considered too obvious, too safari-kitsch. I leave the clipping there to flatten, swallow my meds, eat a banana, take the lift downstairs, and walk to the supermarket.

My apartment block backs onto a football oval that is the home ground for the local league team. Downstairs, yellow and navy balloons are flying outside the bottle shop, and the supermarket patrons wear striped scarves around their necks. It's a home game. The Tigers are at the top of the ladder and today they play the Sharks. It will be a good north-of-the-river, south-of-the-river stoush. By lunchtime, my street will be flooded with blue-and-white pouring off the Fremantle train, and the public swimming pool across the road will have erected a *Pool Patrons Only* sign at the entrance to their carpark. If I get home from Steph's in time, I'll be on my balcony for the bouncedown.

I have a list and a pen, and cruise the aisles from the freezers to the fresh produce, marking off items as I go. Ice-cream, frozen peas, toilet bleach, deodorant. Tinned tomatoes, rice, peanuts, muesli. I stand in front of the bread shelves. I prefer sourdough, but I've worked out that when I'm dizzy, I also get reflux. I wonder if that's a Meniere's Disease thing or a gluten thing. The internet says that six percent of people are gluten intolerant. I pick up a packet of gluten-free sliced bread. I hate it. I can feel my lower lip drop. I put it in my trolley anyway.

At the end of the aisle, a tall, erect man is considering the flavoured milks. He is decked out in tiger stripes, jeans that look like they've been ironed and bright white runners. His spider sense sees me staring and he turns his head, flashes me a smile. It's not one of those dentist-brilliant, surface smiles. It is warm, with crinkly eyes, and an underlying expectation that you will be nice. It's typical of politicians, I've found, at least the ones I've met in person. They genuinely like people and will happily spend their days chatting to constituents about street trees and the neighbour's dog and whether something can be done to help the old lady down the road with her shopping. In my opinion, they are unsuited to politics. You have to be thick-skinned and rat-cunning to run a government. You can't be worried about pleasing people. I've never been able to work out how calculating Cabinet ministers develop out of the skins of ordinary, voter-chatting local representatives.

The smiling man is our local member of parliament and a Cabinet minister. The Minister for Housing, actually. The same ex-public prosecutor, law-and-order campaigner that Neil was weighing up yesterday. He is also my best friend's cousin's husband, but he doesn't know that. Steph and I figure he doesn't need to be aware that she has the inside running on official inquiries into his portfolio. He knows me though, and where I work. I've briefed him twice on inquiry findings in his wood-panelled office in Parliament House. They don't forget names and faces, these guys. It's an admirable superpower. He raises his hand in greeting, picks up a litre of chocolate milk and walks toward me.

'Frances, lovely to see you. Are you well?'

'I am, thank you, Minister. And you?'

'Simon, please.' He looks genuinely embarrassed and diverts attention to his purchase. 'Supplies for the game today,' he says, shaking the carton. 'Teenage boys drink litres of this stuff. I don't know where they put it.'

'I hope there'll be a sausage roll as well.'

'Multiple sausage rolls. We're taking two of my son's friends.'

'Make sure you stop by an ATM on the way there, although I guess it's all tap and go now.'

'Yes, no more getting caught short at the footy! Are you going?'

'I've got a bit to do this morning, but I'm hoping to watch it, yeah.' Technically, I'm not actually going to the ground, just watching from above, but Simon Tallent doesn't need to know where I live.

'Neil cracking the whip, hey?' he answers with a knowing, if incorrectly motivated, smile. 'We're going to be without Venter, apparently. He's been called up to the AFL.'

'The team will miss him.'

'So, will the ladies in the crowd.' The knowing smile again.

'But it'll give that new kid a chance.'

'The boy from Mullewa?' He frowns and I catch a glimpse of the Cabinet minister. 'Yes, I suppose it will, although I doubt that he'll keep clean long enough to make use of the opportunity. Anyway, got to go feed the hordes. Lovely to see you.'

'You too. Go Tigers.'

'The mighty yellow and blue.' He grins, brandishes the chocolate milk cartoon and jogs – actually jogs – down the aisle toward the cash registers.

By the time I've made my own way to the checkout, I'm too laden to get above a slow walk. I added to the list during my journey from the frozen food section and my trolley is piled higher than I planned. Carting it all back to my apartment, even with the groceries inside the granny cart that I've parked at the front doors, is going to be a trek. I make a token effort to lighten the burden by ditching the gluten free bread.

*

Two hours later, I've unpacked the groceries, hung out two loads of washing, cleaned the toilet and am sitting at Steph's kitchen bench cradling a cup of tea.

'Guess who I saw at the shops today.'

She narrows her eyes. We've been playing this game since we moved to the city. She always, always gets it right. It's her own superpower.

'The Honourable Simon Tallent.'

'Geez Louise, how do you do that?'

'No idea.' She turns her mouth down and her eyes twinkle. 'How was the lovely minister?'

I think about Tallent's *keep clean* dig at Venter's replacement on the football team, but let it go. We've been around that block before. 'He's still tall. I forget how tall he is every time I see him.'

'Yeah, that side of the family are all giants. Did he invite you to his church on Sunday, tell you that God wants you to prosper?'

'I don't think he was thinking further than thrashing East Fremantle this afternoon.'

'So, he should. Bloody socialists.'

'Are they though?'

'Well, the ward probably leans right, but the electorate is left. Green left. Remember the wetlands campaign?'

'Of course.'

'I know a story about Simon.'

'Do I want to know?' Steph knows political gossip makes me squirm.

'No, you probably don't, Franny.' She pats my arm. 'I'll give you the latest on Jana instead.'

We spend the next half hour laughing at the adventures of Steph's sister. Jana (rhymes with banana) moved to a south-west hippie town after finishing a PhD in microbiology. She grew a set of blonde dreadlocks, married an evangelist and gave birth – at home in the bath – to two children in the next two years. The evangelist is also a successful winemaker and now that the kids are in school, Jana spends her days campaigning against logging in old-growth forests as part of her stewardship of God's creation. In the last local government elections, she got herself a seat on the shire council.

'So apparently she turned up for the first meeting with no shoes,' Steph laughs, a short, sharp bark.

'Barefoot? How did she even think that was okay?' I remember the etiquette sheet I was given when I visited parliament for the first time. Enclosed footwear was mandatory. No toes on show. Apparently, previous etiquette sheets also specified no trousers for women. I can't imagine local government would be any different.

'You know Jana, she plays by her own rules.'

'But dress codes aside, isn't it cold down there?'

'Maybe she figured the chambers were heated. Anyway, the security guard said she couldn't come in with bare feet. He said it was because they'd just installed new carpet.'

'New carpet?'

'Apparently. So, Jana said *when we're barefoot, we're closer to God.* And then she offered to go back to the ute and get her wellies but told him she'd need somewhere to wash them first because she'd been pulling arum lilies out of the creek that morning and they were still caked in mud.'

'I'm guessing he declined her suggestion.'

'Yeah.'

'And she went to the meeting barefoot.'

'She sure did.'

An hour later, Steph collects our mugs and puts them in the sink. 'I've got to kick you out I'm afraid. Clare's game finished ten minutes ago, and I have to pick her up.' On the verge, we look at the sky to the west. 'Nice day for the footy. Will you watch it this afternoon?'

'Might as well, it's right there.'

She gives me a sad face. 'One year tomorrow, right?'

'Yeah.'

'I'm sorry, Franny.' She pulls me into her, and I hang my chin over her shoulder.

CHAPTER EIGHT

I miss the bounce-down, but I also miss the pre-game traffic, so there's that. When I open the doors to the balcony off my bedroom, the roar of the crowd smacks me in the face. It makes me smile. It's not a big capacity ground, six thousand at the most, but the crowd is happy to be here, and a solid contingent has caught the train up from Fremantle. I can see the blue-and-white block behind the southern goalposts. The scoreboard tells me the visitors have kicked one behind and the home team have yet to score. I go back inside to the kitchen and return with gluten-packed bread, cheese, sausage, and wine.

I've watched two full seasons of local football (the oval ball, not the round one) since I moved here. I used to follow only the AFL, going to the games at the stadium, but it's easy to park up on my own balcony with my own food and wine and look out over the ground, so now I follow my local club as well. I know the players and their positions, and where the team is on the ladder. I know who's injured and who's on suspension. I have yellow and navy streamers to hang off the railing for finals games.

I search the forward line for Venter, but Simon Tallent was right, he's not there. I'm disappointed and feel bad about it. It's good for his career to get a game in the national competition. I wonder if James or Belinda will come with me if I go to the game at the stadium tonight. I cut a piece of cheese and text them.

Dad used to come to home games with me, but he doesn't make it to the city so much anymore, which is a shame because he enjoys live footy. He kept coming after Mum died, driving down every two weeks in the Nissan during the season, but then he started to find excuses. He wasn't feeling well. He had to help a mate with some fencing. There was no-one to look after the dog.

'Bring her with you,' I told him.

'Nah, she'll fret while we're out.'

'I'll have someone come sit with her.'

'Nah, too much trouble.'

'Get her registered as my disability assistance dog and she can come to the game.'

'Now you're being ridiculous.'

He keeps his membership though, which means that I now have a spare seat on offer for every home game. You'd think it would make me popular with all the boys, and it did for a while. Not anymore though.

My phone pings. It's Belinda. *The seat is mine.*

Cool. C U @ the gate @ 6.

The crowd roars and I look up. Venter's replacement is inside our fifty-metre line, ball on the ground and pulling up his socks. I missed the mark while I was texting. He lines up. The Sharks centre half-back is waving his arms like a clock gone wrong and their full-back bumps shoulders with our forwards under the goalposts. The new boy kicks, one long, skinny leg angled high above his shoulder and the other pointing straight at the ground. A perfect picture for the back page. The ball sails through, dead centre and high over the heads of the defenders. He punches the air. The Tigers are on the board.

I watch until quarter time then return inside for a top-up and Bigfoot's papers. The Tigers have pulled ahead by nine points, but the Sharks kicked the last two goals. One of them was the second for the boy from Mullewa. The phone rings. It's Dad.

'Are you watching the game?'

'Tigers are up.'

'Good. Going tonight?'

'Yep. Belinda's using your ticket.'

'Make sure she wears the right scarf this time. Tell her she can take mine.'

'I will. What's the weather like up there?'

He pauses and I picture him looking out the window at the sea. 'Windy.'

'Did you get any of that rain?'

'Nah.'

'Is the sale of the business going okay?'

'Yeah, good.'

'No problems with settlement?'

'Nah.'

'And how's Jess?'

'She's good.'

'Good.'

'Good.'

Even when it's Dad calling me and not the other way around, it's hard to get a conversation out of him.

'What's news then, Dad? Have you been into town lately?'

'Yeah, I went into town. Did the shopping. Went to Bunnings. Had a check-up.'

Now he tells me. 'What did the doctor say?'

'It's all good. I had a blood test.'

'What for? Cholesterol?'

'Yeah, something like that.'

Dad has heart disease, has had it for years. Mum used to make sure he took his medication and saw his GP once a quarter but now he has to do it himself. He's not exactly what you'd call an engaged patient. Dr Vahala is the same generation, not much of a talker either. I can't begin to imagine how they communicate in his rooms.

How're you doing Joe?

Good thanks, Doc.

That's good. Been feeling alright?

Yeah, good.

Good.

Good, yeah.

'When do you get the results?' I ask him.

'Sometime next week, I guess.'

'Are you calling them or are they calling you?'

'Dunno.'

'How about I call them?'

'Yeah, that'd be good.'

'Good.'

It's usually at this point that Dad will say, *I'll get your mother,* or, *have you seen your brother lately,* but of course he doesn't do that anymore. We sit in silence.

'Well, I'll let you go then,' he says instead. 'The next quarter will be starting.'

'Okay, Dad, have a good weekend.'

'Yeah, I will.'

'I love you.'

'I love you too.'

'Bye.'

'Bye.'

I wait until he hangs up.

Outside, the Tigers have come out fighting and kicked two quick goals, taking them twenty-one points up. I open Bigfoot's folder and continue sorting the dross from the papers that are relevant to the inquiry findings. I find another pink napkin, and (strictly in compliance with my boss's instructions) put it in the *Miscellaneous* folder. Next is a sheet of paper with what looks like a Venn diagram, hand-drawn in green ink. It joins the pink napkin.

After that is a screenshot that I recognise from my own project. It's the Department of Housing's tenancy database and the screenshot is of one tenant's inspection records. I don't know how it's got mixed up in a health inquiry archive box, but Eric wasn't known for his filing prowess. The tenant is question was a model citizen, it seems. The printout shows neat six-monthly inspection records. *Oven cleaned and cockroach baits laid. Renew tenancy.* I put it in the *Miscellaneous* folder and put my plate on top to stop it from blowing away.

Next is a draft chapter of the inquiry report and two crumpled pages of a spreadsheet that look as though they have been prised from the teeth of a jammed photocopier. *Miscellaneous.* Underneath the gnawed pages is an A5 page with the left edge savaged, this one from being ripped from a spiral binder. It has a list of ten serial numbers – six numbers followed by three letters written in the same green ink as the incomplete Venn diagram. I pick at the dangling shreds of the torn holes as I contemplate the familiar handwriting and sip my wine.

CHAPTER NINE

It's Monday morning and I ride the bus past Kings Park on the way to the office. I've outlived another weekend. A runner shoots out of the hiking path tunnel and turns down the road toward the city. He keeps pace with us, pulls ahead when we stop, falls back when we speed up again. He's fast. He will reach my stop before I do. He's already run the road that Eric cycled, into the park under the avenue of lemon-scented gums, and all the way to the park restaurant overlooking the river and the city. He will have looked out at the water, silver at this time of day and heard the roar of the traffic commuting up from the south. From the restaurant, he will have turned right, along the road lined with memorial plaques for fallen service men, some dating from the First World War.

No-one knows which way Eric turned when he reached the restaurant that day. That seems incredible to me. On a night when the park was swarming with people, no-one saw a movie-star handsome man cycling home from work. That's exactly why no-one saw him, said the detective in charge of the investigation. There were hundreds of people there, all looking for places to park their cars, carrying picnic bags, wondering what they had forgotten, trying to find their tickets, trying to find their friends. They would have paid him no notice. He was just another person in the park trying to get to the same place they were going. A competitor for a good spot on the lawn.

Eric vanished into that crowd and never came out. He would have slowed as he approached the concert venue, a bowl of startlingly green grass surrounded by the browns and olives of the native bush. I've been to concerts there, both before and since we lost him.

People leave their cars all over the park, anywhere they can get a spot for free, and walk to the venue along the hiking trails and the roads. Cars slow to a walking pace to avoid flattening pedestrians, and cyclists have to dismount when they lose the momentum that keeps them upright. Eric would have dismounted and walked his bike through to the other side. If he made it to the other side.

Weeks later, even after the date of the newspaper clipping, it was reported that two sisters found a bike lamp on the ridge above the river. The lamp was below a limestone outcrop overlooking the water. The girls were at a family picnic and had been sitting on the rocks in the sun, when they saw it in the grass and climbed down. They didn't tell their parents about the find. They'd been told not to leave the path, that the slope below the ridge was dangerous and they'd fall all the way to the highway at the bottom if they weren't careful. Only the week before, a jogger had slipped on what he thought was a track down to the road and lay there with a broken ankle until someone spotted him.

The girls' mother cleaned out their bags at the end of the school term and found the lamp among discarded school notices and dried up mandarin peel. The police said it must have been dislodged from the bike or thrown *with some force* to have fallen from the road to below the outcrop. As to the question of whether its location proved that Eric had ridden that way or, indeed was his lamp at all, they said, the answer was inconclusive.

*

Belinda and I are based at the Department of Housing's north metropolitan office all week, so I check out a car and we drive through the heat haze to the outer suburbs. The office is a three-storey, red-brick rectangle fronted by a two-hundred bay carpark. I put the car in a visitor's bay under a bare-limbed jacaranda tree.

'Where's the parking card?' asks Belinda, searching the glove box.

'Use mine.' I pass her the laminated square that I keep behind my ID card on my lanyard and she puts it on the dashboard. It identifies us as being from the commissioner's office and is meant to ensure that we don't get a ticket for using the visitors bay all day. It doesn't always work.

In reception, we take our place in line behind tired women with prams and skinny men with blank faces. The man in front of me clutches a sheaf of papers. I can see a bank statement, a birth certificate, an electricity bill and a passport. He is wearing steel cap boots and his jeans are shiny with grease.

'Next please.'

He steps up to the reception and hands over his papers. The receptionist looks at the documents in turn, shaking her head as she puts each one aside. 'We can't use this one I'm afraid' – she holds up the passport – 'because it's expired. And this is only a birth extract. You need the full certificate.' She swivels the other documents around and arranges them in front of him. Her voice is warm. Patient. 'For your secondary documents, this account is not in your name, so we can't use that either. But this one' – she points to the bank statement and smiles up at him like he's won a prize – 'is great, and I'll take a copy now, so you don't need to bring it in again. Do you have your Medicare card with you?'

He reaches into his back pocket and pulls out a thin wallet. She beams.

'That's marvellous, I'll copy this one too.' She puts both documents into the scanner and hands them back to him. 'Now you just need to go to Births, Deaths and Marriages for the birth certificate' – she makes a circle on a map and passes it to him – 'right here. It will cost you fifty dollars. I'll put your application in the queue anyway, but we will need the full certificate before you accept a tenancy.'

The man mutters something at her and shuffles away, his eyes down. His arm dangling the sheaf of papers by his side is so loose I worry that they are going to spill across the floor.

'Next please.'

I turn back to the receptionist. Her eyes light up as though she's been waiting her entire life for me to turn up at her desk. I can't help but smile back.

'Frances Geller and Belinda Lim to see Jennifer Lawson please.'

'From the commissioner's office, of course. Lovely to see you again. Come through.' She pushes a button under her counter and a glass door to the left makes a distinct click. 'Jennifer will be down in a moment. Next please.' We wheel our trolley bags through, and the door clicks decisively behind us.

We settle into the cushioned armchairs in the waiting room off the liftwell. The wall opposite displays a collage of botanical drawings. They were Duncan's choice, apparently, and are rumoured to be depictions of the flora and fauna found on his property. I once heard him explaining the behaviour of the red wattlebird to a visiting member of parliament who at the time was heading a fiscal austerity review. The wattlebird, Duncan told him, is one of the largest nectivorous birds in the world. The honourable member made noises about symbiosis and native animals adapting to the local food sources. Duncan responded by telling him that the wattlebird is also highly aggressive and territorial and will band together with other wattlebirds to mob larger birds like magpies. The honourable member said *indeed* and found someone else to talk to.

Today, the coffee table in front of the armchairs is strewn with disembowelled newspapers. The headlines lament the crack epidemic that is suffocating the health system. Emergency rooms and mental health clinics say ninety percent of their clients have experienced some form of methamphetamine-related crisis in the past month. I look back through the glass security doors where it is standing room or plastic seats only and wonder how many of the people waiting there will go home to a length of plastic tubing and a needle to escape from their day. I wonder how many of my fellow accountants do the same.

'How did you pull up on Sunday morning?' Belinda asks.

'Yeah, not so great.' Our trip to the stadium to watch Venter play in the big league had involved a few trips to the overpriced bar.

'Me neither.' She slumps into her chair. 'I've still got a headache. Good game though.'

'Wasn't it? I didn't think we'd get over the line.'

'How was that mark?' It was taken right in front of our seats, just inside the fifty-metre line, from a leap over the back of the pack that was appropriately tiger-like in focus.'

'Venter? Freaking awesome.'

'How tall is he? Six-two, six-three?'

'Does it even matter when you're over six foot?'

I look at her. Her feet just touch the floor on this couch. 'When the other team's backline is still taller than you, yeah, I think it probably does. At least he has no tatts.'

'Not that we know about anyway.' She sniggers.

'Christ, we're shallow.'

'Yeah.' She looks away and I change the subject.

'Sorry I didn't get to go through those papers with you on Friday.'

'No drama,' she shrugs, 'I figured Bigfoot got to you first.'

'She did.'

'I bet she gave you more work.'

'Afraid so.'

Belinda waits for me to tell her what I've been assigned, but my mind has drifted back to Eric's handwriting and the list of green serial numbers. We stare at the flora and fauna on the wall until I snap out of it and ask her what papers she wanted me to look at. She pulls them out of her wheelie case.

'They're defects reports from the Dryandra housing estate,' she says. 'More of what we've already seen. Same trades.'

I flick through them. 'Have you checked the project managers' acquittals?'

'Doing it this week.'

A shadow falls across the coffee table and into our laps. I look up and the ceiling immediately dips to the right. Duncan's head, which takes up most of my field of vision, remains still, front and centre.

'Ladies, good to see you, although you're looking a bit peaky, Frances,' he says. 'Still unwell?'

'I'm fine. I thought we were meeting with Jennifer.'

'Jen's busy. And I'm working here today, so I thought I'd greet you myself.'

'That's very kind of you, Duncan,' Belinda says, standing up. The top of her head reaches almost as high as his armpit. 'I like your white gum pictures.'

'The locals call it wandoo,' he replies. 'Although I don't suppose you'd know that. You came here on a student visa, didn't you?'

Belinda just blanks him. She grabs her wheelie case and walks to the lifts. He turns to me instead.

'I see you've read the papers.'

I shuffle the eviscerated newspaper into a pile while he stands over me. At the same time, I curse myself for being easy to intimidate.

'Terrible thing, that meth,' Duncan says over the top of my head. 'People need more incentives to stay away from it.'

'I think that's simplifying the issue a bit, don't you?'

'Yes, well, I guess you'd know all about it.' He studies my face and I work hard not to blink. 'Anyway, enough of that. I believe you won't be here as long as you had originally planned.'

'No longer than absolutely necessary.'

'The commissioner assured me at the game that the fieldwork would be finished by the end of this week.'

I doubt that's true, but who knows? Men in team colours say a whole lot of things to each other that they might not mean at the time, especially when there's a corporate box and free beer involved. I wonder what sort of sandwiches they had. I follow him, counting the number of giant steps he takes to get to the lift.

On level three, the lift doors glide apart to reveal the rows of workstations that form the north metropolitan public housing office. The interior architect has positioned a line of shelves between the lift doors and the first workstations to demarcate the circulation space. Pots of mother-in-law's tongue sit on top, managing to be both spiky and fleshy. It is not the most spiritually enriching work environment but my own soul lifts when a familiar, broad, female accent exclaims, and Duncan shrinks by my side.

'Duncan, we had a ten o'clock, I've been waiting.' The pencil-shaped woman from the Tenants Advisory Group is standing in front of the lifts with a jumble of folders. Up close, I can see she has a nose piercing, a lip piercing, a line of studs from her ear lobe to her helix and a sparkle in her eyes that is at odds with her tone. I finger my own, solitary helix piercing and look at Duncan for his reaction.

'Meredith, so sorry.' His tone is anything but. 'Shall we go to my office?' He gestures away from the lift (and me and Belinda) and all but shoves her in the back to move her along.

Meredith plants her feet and takes us in. I've seen her on the television as well as at the housing seminar. She's both smaller and more intimidating up close.

'You're from the commissioner's office. I saw you at that consultation thing.' Her tone has an accusing edge to it, and she leans on *consultation* like it's a dirty word. I feel my tongue collapse to the floor of my mouth.

'Yes, we are.' My tiny colleague steps forward and holds out her hand. 'I'm Belinda Lim.'

Meredith eyeballs her then shifts her gaze back to me. 'And you are?'

'Frances Geller.'

'Geller. I thought so.' Two lines appear between her eyes. 'I know you from Weymouth, don't I? You were two years ahead of me at high school. Sorry about your brother.'

'Thanks.' I frown back at her, wrongfooted. 'I don't think I remember you.'

'Older kids never know the names of the younger ones. And I was quieter then.' She shrugs it off. 'Meredith Johnson. I'm with the Tenants Advisory Group.' She eyeballs Duncan. 'We keep these bastards honest. Like you.'

'Meredith is a fierce advocate for public housing tenants.' Duncan's hands flap at his sides.

'Too right I am. What are you girls looking at?'

'The social housing programme,' Belinda answers.

'Spoken with any tenants yet?'

'No.'

'Planning to?'

'It isn't in the audit scope,' I offer. I know what's coming.

'Is that right? I thought your commissioner's charter said something about public consultation.'

Belinda looks at her shoes and Duncan blinks. I'm still searching for a justification when Meredith saves me.

'Never mind, Frances. I get it, budgets and all that. That was Duncan's excuse too, but we fixed it, didn't we, Duncan? Tell you what, I'll take you out to a few properties later in the week. Won't take long. We can catch up on the Weymouth gossip while we're at it.'

'Meredith, I'm sure Frances and her team know what they're doing,' Duncan chimes in. 'What sort of useful input are tenants going to give them anyway?'

'I guess we won't know until we ask them, Duncan.' She leans on his name, and I can see Belinda's lips twitch upwards.

'It's really not part of TAG's remit—' Duncan begins, but Meredith cuts him off.

'I'll decide what's part of TAG's remit, thanks.' She turns back to me. 'I'll call you.'

She follows Duncan down the corridor to a glassed-in office in the corner. We hear her hiss under her breath as she walks away.

'Fucking Nazi.'

CHAPTER TEN

On Sunday, I'd taken the mutilated A5 sheet of paper with the green numbers out of my back pocket and put it inside the photography book with the newspaper clipping. They belonged together, one recording Eric's spiked, uniform handwriting, the other his unexplained vanishing. I figured the numbers had to be some sort of serial or identification numbers, something relevant to one of Eric's projects. I made a list of every serial number I could think of and looked them up online. Tax file numbers, employee payroll numbers, student identification numbers at each of the local universities, tenant identification numbers. I'd come up with nothing. None of them had the same six-number, three-letter format. Still, I thought, if I let them sit there long enough, something would float to the surface.

Eric was first reported missing on the Saturday morning by his girlfriend. He was supposed to meet her for a bike ride around the bridges but didn't show. She went to his apartment, found it empty, and called his parents, who were already worried that he hadn't turned up to his granny's birthday party. They called the police, the police called Neil, Neil called Bigfoot, who called me. I called James and Belinda, and by that Saturday afternoon the three of us were sitting on the couch in my apartment waiting for news and trying to work out how to be useful.

'It'll be something boring and predictable,' said James. 'He'll have met someone in Kings Park, gone to the bar to have a drink, taken advantage of a free ticket to the concert. He's probably sleeping off a hangover in Morley.'

'Morley? Who lives in Morley?'

'I don't know, Belinda. Some random person who he knew from uni, or film classes, or something.'

'Where's his bike then?'

'In the back of their Hilux.'

'So, he's hungover on the couch of a Hilux-driving arts graduate from Morley.'

'Best I can do at this point.'

My phone rang. It was Steph.

'I've just seen the news.'

'What? What news?' I reached for the television remote and saw it next to James' elbow. 'James, put the television on. What channel, Steph?'

'Ten. It's him, isn't it? Eric? Your boss. I recognised the photo.'

'What did they say?'

She told me as I watched it myself on the television, a blue ribbon running along the bottom of the screen. *Fears held for missing public servant.* The station's crime reporter stood in front of the park entrance, talking into the camera as a police car circled the roundabout and cruised down the avenue under the gum trees.

'Why are they searching the park?' asked Belinda, taking the remote from James and pressing the volume up button. 'What about the roads from the park to his apartment? He could have fallen off his bike anywhere along there.'

'Remember when he was sideswiped by a white van a few months ago? All he had was scrapes and bruises, but it could've been a lot worse.'

It was too much. I'd held it together up to that point, but that last comment released the floodgates and I felt them crack open in my chest, a physical pain that tightened my throat and made my lips tingle.

'Hey, Fran, hey.' I felt Belinda sink onto the arm of the couch, her arms fold around me, and her chin rest on my head. 'We've got you, we're here.'

I squeezed my eyes, pushing it all back in, but that never works. A tissue appeared under my nose.

'Can we go there?'

'Where, Franny?'

'To the park.'

'Of course we can, babe.'

'You can't, they've put up a cordon.'

I looked up at the television. More police cars were pulled up at the end of the avenue in front of the restaurant. A line of tape was already strung between the grey trunks of the gum trees on either side. 'They've only put it up along the road, not through the bush.'

'Well, no, but now's probably not the right time for bush bashing through a, well, you know.'

'What?'

'She means crime scene.'

The three of us watched as a forensics van pulled up to the police cars and an officer lifted the tape to let it through. It trundled into the empty park.

'I'm going.' I stood up and pressed the tissue into my eyes. 'Who's coming?'

'We will.' Belinda stood up and clicked off the television.

'Not me.' I'd forgotten about Steph on the phone. 'Unless you want three sulking kids with you. Let me know when you hear something.'

'Thanks, buddy.'

'I love you.'

'I love you too.'

The three of us went in James' car and drove into the park at the southern entrance, nearest to the university, the entry we used for our night-time student ramblings, the same one Eric would have used to leave the park on his bike the night before.

'I think we should walk from here.' I pointed James to the carpark opposite the student residences.

'Why? It's three kilometres away.'

'Fraser Avenue is, yeah, but we don't know where he was last seen. He would have ridden this way.'

'And you want to walk all the way there?'

'Why not? There might be something on the road. He might have come off his bike.'

'Oh god, what if he's still here?' Belinda prodded James' shoulder. 'Fran's right, pull over, we should walk.'

So we walked, all the way to Fraser Avenue. No cars came towards us, although a few drove up behind, did a U-turn, and went back the way they'd come. I guess they were hoping to do some rubbernecking, but the sight of James stalking down the middle of the road in a high-vis vest put them off.

'Where did you get that from?' said Belinda when he dug it out of the boot.

'Mum makes me wear it when I'm burning off the verge at the orchard.'

I saw her smirk and remembered they were supposed to have been surfing that morning. There was no sign of sun on Belinda's face but that was to be expected given her dedication to daily thirty-plus. She tugged a bucket hat down low on her head, handed a matching one to me, and allocated our positions. James got the middle of the road by virtue of his PPE, and I got the ridge looking out across the river.

I was sweating by the time the road swung around to face the city. The bridge emerged from behind the trees as we walked, cars streaming north and south soundlessly as though nothing significant had happened in the world that day. The fat stretch of water on the other side was similarly untroubled. Two ferries slid toward each other in the haze, merged, and continued to the opposite sides of the river. At my feet, the roadside pea gravel slid and slipped, and heat rolled up the scarp from the dark bushes on its slopes. The pressure behind my eyes was turning into a headache and I glanced at the horizon. At least that was steady.

'Hey, have some of this.' James passed me a water bottle. It was Belinda's, the same green-and-white stainless-steel column that sat on her workstation, strategically placed out of the sun. *Powered by plants,* it said on the side. I drank and James took it back, swapping it for a collection of road-pickings that he tipped into my hand. A two-dollar coin, a matchbox racer, and a pair of tortoiseshell Raybans, astonishingly unbroken. 'Some kid's gunna be missing that car.'

'Nice glasses, though.' I held them in front of my face and blinked as the world turned blue.

'Expensive. Nice tint.'

I poured the treasure into my pocket and kept walking, my eyes back on the undergrowth below the road. I couldn't see far into it, just the odd bottle and scrap of paper. Under the sun, nothing moved, not even in the shade of the bushes. From time to time, the limestone ridge capping would appear, and I could smell the dust of summer through the drying topsoil even though it was only just the start of spring. I wrinkled my nose, suddenly irritated by the heat and the light.

'Stop.' Belinda was facing the bush on her side of the road, looking down a sand track, her hands cupping her eyes. 'What's that?' The track under the she-oaks and banksias was white sand. It ran in a straight line into the bush then veered off after thirty metres, winter grass growing at its edges. The sun filtered between the trees close to the road, but the shadows deepened until the bend in the track was a wall of dark green.

James left the tarmac to stand behind Belinda and followed her gaze.

'What?'

'On the right, about two thirds of the way down. A brown shape.'

'Rabbit?'

'Too big.'

'You haven't seen the rabbits in my orchard.'

'It's not a rabbit.'

'It looks like a paper bag, probably dumped by someone who couldn't be bothered carting their crap out of the park.'

'Go have a look.'

'What? Why me? You go.'

'I can't, the sand is too soft. You're wearing boots.'

I walked past them both, glad to get out of the sun. The air was cooler under the trees and unlike the open ridge, smelled of damp soil and fleshy grasses. A deeper, riper smell pushed its way through as I walked. Rotting leaves and fallen branches being turned back into soil by white ants. In tens of thousands of years, millions probably, the topsoil up there will be thicker, enclosing precious carbon and the left-behind evidence of bush picnics. I looked back. James and Belinda were only twenty metres away, but were dark shapes, lit from behind with their faces in shadow.

'What is it?' Belinda called.

The brown shape she had seen hadn't moved. It wasn't a rabbit then, or at least not a live one. But not a laughable mistake either. It was a brown corduroy jacket, bundled and left at the side of the path. I prodded it with my toe, then tested it again with more weight. It gave way, much as you'd expect from a discarded piece of clothing. I picked it up and shook it out, then jumped back. I might have yelped.

'What? Are you OK?'

I heard boots in soft sand coming up behind me.

'Oh, that's disgusting.'

Knickers – soiled – and a condom lay side by side in the sand. I flung the jacket back on top of them.

'Concert goers or university students?' James asked. We turned to look back toward the student residences but couldn't see farther than a few metres through the bush.

'I don't know, and I don't care,' Belinda replied.

We retreated to the road and continued on, following the tarmac as it turned away from the ridge until we were surrounded by bush on both sides. The minute I lost sight of the bridge and the river, the temperature and the humidity increased. Mowed lawn appeared on the left, and then a toilet block, followed by the entrance for the lookout carpark. Two police cars were parked across the road. The uniformed officers levered themselves off the bonnets and walked toward us, hands out in front.

'This area is closed off. You'll have to turn around and go back.'

'We're only passing through.' Belinda blinked at him. 'We're not staying.'

'Sorry, ma'am, you'll need to go around the park.'

'Can we take another path? It's a long way to go back.'

'I'm afraid not. We're searching the area and can't have anyone come in until we're done.'

'Is it because of that guy that's missing?'

'Yes, it is, so you won't be able to come in until we open up the park again.'

'Can we help? We're good at that sort of thing. I have my first aid certificate.'

I watched the officer's mouth twitch. Beside me, I felt James shake his head.

'That's very kind of you, ma'am, but the State Emergency Services is here. We have plenty of trained volunteers.' He put the smallest emphasis on the word trained.

I was about to tell him that we are *trained* investigators, but I felt James' hand on my arm.

'That's okay, officer, we understand. I hope you find him soon.' James steered both of us back in in the direction we'd just walked. I let him do it, but I chewed my lip hard enough to make it bleed. Belinda tugged her sleeves down over her wrists and the three of us walked back to the car in silence.

*

Despite refilling Belinda's water bottle, refilled twice at the lookout carpark, I'd got home from our trek dehydrated and off-balance. I made a show of watching the footy on television but fell asleep on the couch with my toes cramping and twitching. When I woke up two hours later, Fremantle had gone down to Sydney by twenty-four points and the world was spinning. I took my meds, ate a banana, went back to the couch and flicked through Facebook. By the time the spins had stopped, the day was gone and the evening news was starting.

Search for missing Perth man continues was the lead story on each of the commercial channels. Helicopter footage showed lines of orange-suited SES volunteers inching through the bush and along roadsides. The story cut to police headquarters at the other end of the CBD. A long-faced officer with epaulettes on his blue shirt looked into the camera and said police were gravely concerned for the man, who hadn't been seen since he left his workplace in West Perth on Friday night.

'We know Mr Steyn rode his bike into Kings Park along Fraser Avenue. At some point, he would have encountered the crowd attending the benefit concert in the park.' The police commissioner's eyes drooped. 'Mr Steyn's family are appealing to any person who attended the concert and who thinks they might have seen Mr Steyn to come forward.'

The camera angle widened to include a woman sitting next to him. I recognised her, of course. Alice Rensburg, Eric's sister. We met her when she hosted Eric's thirtieth birthday at her house in the hill. We mingled on her terrace and gazed across the suburban coastal plain to the city while the national park around us came alive with birds flying in to roost. Her rescued greyhounds wandered mournfully between us, searching the ground for scraps of chicken satay and flaky pastry, and occasionally huffing at hikers trudging past on the Bibbulmun Track.

Alice was short, like Eric, and, also like Eric, impossibly, movie-star beautiful.

'I don't get it,' James had said after the birthday party. 'She's not that special.'

'What do you mean *not that special*?' Belinda scoffed. 'She's spectacular. Like' – she waved her arms in the air as though she might magic up an angel – 'Charlize Theron, or Scarlett Johansson.'

'Nah, Charlize is way taller. And Alice is a stick compared to Scarlett.'

Alice was also smart and owned a string of pharmacies. On the television, her hair was longer and straighter than I remembered, and she wore a blue blouse. Not the same blue as the police commissioner. Hers was a cool ice-blue, with a soft V-neck and no stiff, official collar. I imagined viewers all over the state staring slack-jawed in their loungerooms. She held a photo of Eric with his bike. It was taken on her terrace, with the city view behind him. He had one foot on a pedal and a helmet on his head and was grinning into the camera.

'Our brother is very special to us, like all brothers.' She glanced at the man on her other side. 'We were celebrating our grandmother's ninetieth birthday and she is absolutely distraught. It is completely unlike Eric not to turn up. Please call Crime Stoppers if you think you have seen him.'

CHAPTER ELEVEN

I consider the untidy stack of files that have been dumped onto a spare workstation at the north metropolitan office of the Department of Housing. Belinda and I don't see Duncan again, but Meredith emails to say she's arranged for me to come on her rounds the following Tuesday. I'm to be at her office in East Perth at one.

Government departments are supposed to give us enclosed workspaces when we are onsite. Spaces where we can review confidential files and lock up each night. There's only one enclosed office on this floor though, and that's the one Duncan uses when he's here. It's locked when he's not. The two meeting rooms are fully booked, we're told, and can't be made available. Belinda and I work at a narrow table wedged in among the human resources team. I suppose whoever put us here figures we all have the same understanding of confidentiality.

We don't all have the same understanding of appropriate noise levels though. Apparently. Or of appropriate language. I guess we've been sheltered, my little gang, in our corner pod overlooking the park. There, we are barricaded in by filing cabinets even though the floor is supposed to be open plan, and no-one minds if we get a bit sweary. Here, poring over Department of Housing project files, Belinda cackles.

'Oh, for fuck's sake! Frances, check this out.'

One of the human resources staffers snaps his head around and glares at her. 'Excuse me?' Offence is written across his face.

'Sorry, um, Colin,' she replies, leaning over the table and reading the magnetic name plate on his workstation.

'We have a code of conduct, you know.' He adjusts his shoulders and cracks his neck. 'I expect your office does as well.' He looks at me for confirmation.

'We do, yes,' I acknowledge. 'Belinda, please keep it down. Remember, we are guests here.'

'Yes, boss.' She sinks into her seat, flips the file around to face me, and whispers. 'Get a load of this.'

The file is open to a building defects report. I read the handwritten margin notes and snort. Colin flinches.

'Roof insulation?'

'Roof insulation indeed,' Belinda confirms. 'Shall I put it on the list for a site inspection?'

'Oh yes.'

I've seen the floor plans for our new office. The arrangement is more or less the same as our current floor, with me, Belinda, and James in a corner pod. The filing cabinets have been sacrificed. We are all being encouraged to file our papers electronically to save space and archiving costs. Everything is expected to sit in the cloud, wherever that is. Belinda said she'd like to sit in the cloud too and got a sharp reprimand from Bigfoot that she would be the first to trial hotdesking if she wasn't careful with her tone.

The pod in our new office is a pod of four. *Graduate Analyst* has been written above the fourth workstation on the floor plan. The next intake won't be until March next year, when all the university students come back from their last long summer holiday ever. They'll arrive in our office in new suits and unsuitable shoes. They'll have that special combination of excitement of their first real job tempered with the horrible realisation that if the weather is nice on a weekday, they won't be able to go to the beach. They'll be tanned, thin and profoundly dehydrated every Monday morning. By the end of the second week, they'll be falling asleep at their desks and wondering how anyone has the energy to do this five days a week until they turn sixty-five.

I was like that when I started. The commissioner's office was my first job out of university, a plum placement for a graduate with a double major in accounting and constitutional law. Here, I would be able to complete my professional year and qualify for my CPA registration, as well as get exposure to the inner workings of government. I loved it from the start. I was allocated to Eric's team and put to work reconciling the Department of Housing's payroll. I found multiple instances of under and over payments and a failure to pass on the latest award increases. My work was tabled in parliament and hundreds of public servants had their pays backdated. Best of all, Eric brought Tim Tams to the office the next day and praised me in front of the rest of the team.

My phone buzzes on the desk and I take it to the circulation area outside the lift doors and out of Colin's earshot. I can see tiny midges flitting between the fleshy spikes of the mother-in-law's tongue. One lands on the back of my hand, and I flick it away before it can bite me.

'Hey, boss, how's life in the colonies?' It's James, checking in.

'Noisy.'

'I hope that's not preventing you from getting through those files by the end of the week.'

'No, it won't, and neither will access to documents.' I look back at our tiny table, laden with files that Duncan arranged to be delivered yesterday, *all ready for you.*

'Dr Duncan Wolf PSM, the model of a cooperative public official.'

'Isn't he, though? How's it going at your end?'

'I'm about eighty percent through the defects reports for the Riverside Seniors' Housing project in the South West.'

'And?'

'Pretty much the same as you: twenty percent not fully acquitted.'

'What sorts of things are we talking?'

'Don't know yet. I need to look at the complete project files.'

'Are they online?'

'Sadly, no.' James laughs. 'Hard copy only.'

'I see. What's the swell going to be down south this weekend?'

'Two metres,' says Belinda, walking up behind me. 'But you can tell James he can't go until next week. It's my sister's engagement party this weekend.'

'Tell Belinda she'll have more fun without me.'

'Tell her yourself.' I pass the phone to Belinda and return to our table.

If what James says is right, my housing inquiry is headed for the front page. The social housing programme in the South West is a big deal. The Department of Housing built apartments on land that had since doubled and tripled in value as baby boomers cashed out and retired to wine country. Low-cost housing that once sat next to a light industrial area is now surrounded by homeowners who park their four-wheel drives in double garages and their boats on the front lawn. No-one wants to live across the road from a block of rentals, even if it has a fancy name and is managed by the state's most reputable social housing provider. I consider the outcry if the local residents learn that a good number of the apartments weren't properly inspected or signed off by the project manager. That defects were identified, but never fixed. Or maybe not. Maybe the locals don't care as long as they don't have to live in them.

I slide between the table and the wall to get to my chair and give Colin an apologetic smile. He blanks me and tilts his head into his phone.

'If you want to make a formal complaint, you'll need to complete a grievance form,' I hear him say. 'HRF17. You can find it on the intranet.' He glances back at me, sees me listening, and scowls. 'That's right, it's completely confidential, just email it direct to me. Thanks, Saraj.'

Belinda returns as Colin puts down the phone. They shuffle around each other, and Colin stomps down the corridor to the staff kitchen, cradling his mug. It's one of those personalised mugs that friends buy you for your birthday and has a photo of an indifferent orange cat on the side. The cat's name is Hamish.

'Colin's not having a good day, then?' Belinda asks.

'Apparently not.'

'He's been on the same call since James phoned. It sounded a bit fraught.'

'I heard him mention a grievance form. Some project manager being bullied by his boss.'

Belinda pulls a face. 'You couldn't pay me to work in HR. People suck sometimes.'

CHAPTER TWELVE

Belinda and I stay at the north metropolitan office until Thursday. On Friday I walk out of the lifts and toward the reception desk in our own building. It is our last day here. The view across the park is as beautiful as it has ever been. Behind our receptionist's head, I can see blue sky, that deep, saturated colour that emerges on clear days in spring. On the other side of Christmas, it will be dry and washed-out, scoured by wind and salt from the west, and dulled with dust and bushfire smoke from the east. It will stay like that until Easter when we enter early autumn – Djeran – the best season on our side of the continent. In April and May, the days are warm, the wind drops away and the night-time temperatures fall. The sun stays in the sky for long enough to walk on the beach after work or drink wine on the grass at twilight picnics, unlike spring, when you take your chances with the weather if you want to drink outside in the evening. In spring – Djilba – the blue sky is pretty, but it still holds water, and rain clouds can move in fast from the west.

Underneath the sky I can see water and trees. The river reflects the clear blue, and the trees are still shiny from the last rain. From our fifth floor, this view lets us kid ourselves that the grumbling CBD is not at our heels, that the river and the park are all that exist outside our windows. It is a fantasy that we blithely discard when we take the lifts to the ground floor and walk less than ten minutes to the nearest government offices. Our working environment is not a challenging one; we get the best of both worlds. It won't be the same when we move. Our new office squats among other concrete and glass towers. One of the squattest, it won't give us views or green trees. All we will see is other office workers staring back at us.

I look at the bronze lettering on the face of the reception desk. The *Inq* in *Parliamentary Inquiries Office* has rubbed back to a dull grey over the years as my workmates and I have leaned against it to sign in and out. I wonder if I could steal the letters when we go and how many people are in line before me to do the same thing.

'Belinda already brought in a chisel and a mallet,' says Julie. The number one criterion for a receptionist is the ability to read minds and the contents of handbags.

'I have boltcutters,' I lie.

'You'll need them. James has already chained himself to his workstation.'

I look down the corridor toward our pod. 'James in chains. It has a ring to it.'

'You could start a band.' Julie passes me a roll of sticky labels pre-printed with the name of the removal company and our new address. My heart folds a little and I scold myself for being a sook. It is such a middle-class problem, getting upset that my new office doesn't have a view and my commute will be ten minutes longer. I don't even need to take a different bus.

Julie passes me the new floorplan. She's handwritten numbers on each workstation and highlights mine in fluorescent yellow. 'Write your name and the number of your new workstation on each label and stick them to your boxes. You can leave the boxes on the floor; the removal company will pick them up and deliver them on the weekend.'

'Thanks.' I take the roll and trudge down the corridor. The senior staff in the enclosed offices look up from their screens as I pass. Some of them say hi, some just give me a sad smile as their fingers pause over their keyboards. You'd think we were being relocated to Weymouth. The open-plan workstations are already stacked with archive boxes. Junior staff in jeans and t-shirts stand in front of filing cabinets swearing at the state of suspension files that have discharged their contents to the bottom of the drawers.

'Is that from the community health inquiry?' I stop as a level five analyst forces an elastic band around an overstuffed and crooked file. Pink-and-white corners poke out at angles. I wonder if there are serviettes inside.

'Sorry,' she replies, 'sorry. I didn't know it was still here.'

'That should have been scanned and shredded two years ago.'

'I know. Sorry. Sorry.'

'When you were, what, still at uni? Hardly your fault, is it? Anyway, I think I know who was responsible for those files. Don't sweat it.'

She pauses, then gives me a grateful smile. 'Thanks, Frances. I can do it now if you want?'

I wave her away. 'You've put it together already. Just shred it when you unpack everything at the new office.'

'The new office where the document management system will work, and we won't need paper files?' James walks toward us down the corridor. He is chainless and otherwise attired the same as always. James, as I was told on my first day here, does not wear suits, so he doesn't get to dress down today like the rest of us. He's in his usual jeans, work boots, and checked shirt. The sleeves are rolled up to the elbow and he has pushed them farther up his arms. It couldn't be for comfort because the fabric is cutting into his biceps. Vanity then. Well, good for him. He spends every hour that he's not in the office working in his family's market garden and if that means he has guns to show off, then why shouldn't he?

'That's the one,' I tell him.

'Because if it doesn't work, we'll have nowhere to put our files except to sit on them.'

'Paperless, James, we will be truly paperless,' I intone.

I was chair of the Office Consultative Committee during the planning for the office relocation. That meant towing the line on government policy to move to the cloud and reducing the square metres of government office space given over to paper files. If every government agency reduced their physical storage needs by ten per cent, I was told, government would save forty million dollars a year. That would be enough to employ a trillion more nurses.

Nursing shortages notwithstanding, the paperless office idea wasn't popular with the public service rank and file, at least not on our floor. Electronic document management systems were famously effective at losing documents, as the unwilling participants in our paperless inquiry into government subcontracting were still telling us. The inquiry was late in reporting to parliament because we had to scan in hundreds of hard copy maintenance receipts. (Mum-and-dad plumbing contractors hadn't joined the paperless economy at that point.) The beautiful irony was not lost on my colleagues.

'We'll see.' James relieves me of the roll of sticky labels. 'Thanks, Belinda needs more of these.'

He turns and I walk behind him, label-less, to our pod. Taped archive boxes sit on the floor waiting for the trolleys that will cart them to the truck in the basement and then to their new home. Our sad, fourth workstation, I notice, is still empty. James and Belinda have not put any boxes on its surface.

'What's happening to the workstations when we leave?' I ask.

'The fit-out is being gutted,' replies Belinda. She is standing at her desk, trying to make lever arch files fit into an archive box. I watch as she alternates their spines to turn their triangles into rectangles. The final file doesn't quite fit, and she hammers it with the side of her fist. The side of the box splits and a staple comes loose and digs into her hand. She swears and sucks at the bead of blood. 'Some minister is taking this floor and apparently his staff can't work in open plan.'

'Ministerial privilege?'

'Yeah, but not in the way you mean.'

James laughs and Belinda pats Eric's workstation. We smile at each other. She knows why I asked.

'Come here and squeeze the sides together while I tape this up, will you?' Belinda reaches over the top of the box to find the roll of tape she's been using. I crabwalk between the boxes and files and stacked in-trays. Belinda's even, sloped handwriting is already printed on labels and stuck on the top lefthand corners.

'James, where's all your stuff?' I ask as I brace the box.

'Where it's always been.'

I look at Belinda, who presses her lips together and dimples her cheeks.

'Don't you think …'

'There's plenty of time. I'll do it later; before the party.'

'Bigfoot won't be happy if you're not ready when the removal company comes in.'

'Bigfoot also said deadlines wouldn't be extended because of the relocation.'

'You've got nothing to worry about, though, have you?' I frown as I squeeze the bulging box of files, taking care to avoid the loose staple, while Belinda wraps it in tape. As far as I know, James is tracking ahead of his work schedule.

'She's given me a job on another project and it's due Monday.'

I grit my teeth and avoid looking at Belinda. Our director has a habit of picking off staff for special projects when project managers drop their guard. Now she's done it to me and my most senior team member in one week. I cleaned up her community health file and handed it back to her on Monday like she asked (no thank you for working overtime, just a disappointed grimace when I told her there were no loose ends to tie up), but James is supposed to be allocated to my project fulltime until it's finished, and I can't afford for him to spend time on other work. Bigfoot knows that. I wonder if it is part of her plan to sabotage my chance of promotion. We're all expecting one of the other directors to pick up a senior executive posting at another agency next year and I'm one of three project managers most likely to get his job. I'm fairly sure Bigfoot doesn't fancy me being the same level as her.

'Hey.'

I look up. James has swung around on his chair and put his feet up on a stack of boxes.

'Don't be like that,' he says.

'I didn't say a word.'

'But you thought it. I could see it on your face. You get this frown.' He rubs the spot between his eyes, then picks up his coffee cup and grimaces as he looks inside. 'The job's a follow-up review of the police inquiry. It's not taking any time away from our project. I'll still get those numbers to you by Wednesday.'

'Are you sure? I can go speak to her.'

'You can't, she's not here. Physio appointment.'

'Again? What's with that?

'She was clipped by a car while she was out running eighteen months ago. Tore something or other in her hip. It's why she walks funny. Exercise is bad for you, what can I say?'

'Okay. But no more extra work, right?' There's not much I can do. The review will have a statutory reporting date. We're required to follow up our inquiries within two years and report to parliament on the government's progress in implementing our recommendations.

'What can I say?' He opens his arms wide and grins. 'Bigfoot loves me. She'd be gutted if I turned her down.'

'Not as gutted as you'll be at your next performance appraisal if I miss my deadlines.'

James snorts and swings back to face his screen. He's right not to care. He knows I'm still terrified of conducting performance appraisals and I haven't yet marked anyone as less than perfect. He also knows he'll never let me down. James has more capacity than anyone I know to work overtime to bring in deadlines. We've had more than a few overnighters in our little corner of the office, watching the sun set and the lights come on over the other side of the river. We order in Vietnamese food and work until we're done. I've even slept under my desk while James has kept going, cross-checking findings against the evidence file, making sure everything is tight.

Then we have breakfast in the café downstairs the next day, shower in the basement bathroom and, if we're lucky, convince the concierge to let us sleep for an hour in the backseats of garaged ministerial cars before we troop back upstairs.

Grizzling about Bigfoot reminds me that I never caught up with Belinda after I got sidetracked in the kitchen.

'Hey, Belinda, we never got around to discussing those papers last week, did we?'

'Yeah, we did.'

'We did? When?'

'Monday. They were the defects reports. The ones for the Dryandra Estate.'

'Of course we did. You were going to check the acquittals.'

'That's right.'

'And you've done that already.'

She grins.

'Of course you have. Give me the good news.'

'All signed off by the project manager.'

'Including the non-existent roof insulation?'

'Including the non-existent roof insulation.'

This is what I live for. 'Shall we go have a chat to the project manager's boss?'

'The Assistant Director for Homelessness Strategies? Absolutely we should.'

CHAPTER THIRTEEN

I consider Eric's workstation. I've already unburdened my shelves and mobile pedestal ahead of the big move. The green wheelie bin next to the pod is full and anything that I want to keep, I've put into labelled files. The hole-punch and stapler have been put to good use and I've even deployed coloured file dividers. My workstation looks like an advertisement for Officeworks. All I need to do now is slide the files into an archive box (floor seven, workstation thirty-six) and pack up Eric's old papers.

Eric's mobile pedestal hasn't been opened in six months. I was the last one to close it. The key is still hanging in the lock. It sticks when I turn it and, for a horrible moment, I think it might break off.

'Let me.' Belinda wriggles the key out of the lock and rubs the edges over the tip of a pencil. 'Try it now.'

The key slides in and turns without complaint. Belinda high fives James.

The suspension files in the drawer are labelled with blue plastic clips and hold manila folders. There are no loose pages; everything is hole-punched, stapled and threaded into file binders. This orderliness is not a credit to Eric, but to me. I was the person delegated to give the police access to his working papers after he disappeared, and I wasn't going to hand them over in the condition I knew they lived in. I flick through the pages and even I, Queen of Invoice Reconciliations, have to admit they're boring. Excel spreadsheets with rows and rows of patient names accompanied by a string of dates, ticks and crosses. Handwritten interview notes with health administrators explaining how they follow discharge protocols and why their patient records are incomplete (the hospital's fault if the administrator worked for an outpatient clinic and the clinic's fault if the administrator was based in a hospital). It would have driven Eric crazy. Not exactly the big picture stuff he craved.

One of the rows is underlined in green pen. *Helen Stewart.* The name is familiar and I look for her in the back of the file. Ms Stewart spent three days in hospital for asthma complications. Her discharge plan is hole-punched and threaded into its correct place, along with records of her follow-up appointments. Behind them are tenancy inspection reports, stamped with a familiar blue logo. Helen Stewart, it seems, is one of the public housing tenants that so offended the page-three reporter, although I can't see the relevance of the tenancy reports to the community health inquiry. She's a single mum with one dependent and neat six-monthly inspection records – and I realise she rings a bell because she is the same tenant whose misfiled records I put in Bigfoot's *Miscellaneous* folder. *Oven cleaned and cockroach baits laid. Renew tenancy.* Well done, Ms Stewart.

I put the file in the last space in my own archive box, then stop. I figure I might as well set an example. I take the file to the photocopier, where I unthread the papers, lever out the staples with my fingernails, and scan each document. I reassemble the file and mark it as archived. On my way back to the pod, I cross paths with the level five analyst who'd been trying to file the other community health inquiry papers. I hand her the folder.

'This belongs with those other papers,' I tell her. 'I've scanned it in but it's best if you keep all the hard copies together.'

She beams. 'Thanks, Frances. Bigf— Catherine gave me some papers as well, so we should have them all together now.'

'Brilliant. You can shred it when I've confirmed that the documents are in the cloud where I hope I've just put them.'

Her face is already red from the Bigfoot slip-up, and she blushes deeper at the implied imperfection of our new technology.

'Don't worry,' I tell her, 'I'm sure it will be fine.'

I return to the pod and close the drawer of Eric's now-empty mobile pedestal. Something swishes along the bottom. I frown, annoyed that I've missed something, and pull it open again. I've left a photo lying in the bottom of the drawer. It is small, maybe five by seven, and faded. I hold it to the window. It's well composed: a river, sand dunes, and a picnic setting in the bottom right-hand corner. It could be the river on the cover of my landscapes book, but the colours are so washed out that the dunes could just as easily be the white dunes of my own childhood. I flip it over. *2005.* No location, very enigmatic. I tuck the photo into my handbag and take my empty cup to the tearoom. Then my phone rings and everything goes to shit.

CHAPTER FOURTEEN

The sun has set by the time I reach the outer suburbs of Weymouth and I drive to the hospital along the port road under orange floodlights. The wide intersections are empty except for the road trains carrying ore from the mines. I watch a prime mover with three trailers haul itself out of the traffic lights. A dog looks down at me from the passenger seat. I have a chip bucket in my cup holder, empty except for a crumpled Chiko Roll wrapper, and I wonder if he can smell the fat and the salt through my open window. I make kissing noises at him, but he's impassive. They will unload and turn around again tonight, making the return trip so they can reload in the morning, ready to do it again. The paddocks along the way will be starting to change colour but they won't see much in the dark, just the oncoming beams from other road trains. The traffic light turns red before the last trailer makes it through. I wait for it to pass then take my own turn through the intersection.

The hospital is also floodlit. A couple of families sit on the grass under gumtrees. The white trunks glow under the lights, and shadows stretch along the ground. The adults cluster around butcher's paper from the corner fish and chip shop, and barefoot children drink from cans of Coke. The carpark is all but empty. I pull in to a bay closest to the after-hours entrance, shoulder my bag and walk past the kids. They are gathering she-oak fruits, preparing, no doubt, for a coming war that will end in dark bruises and tears.

The receptionist looks up my dad in her admissions records and sends me to the ward. Behind her and the security glass, emergency department staff are drinking tea and completing paperwork at an island desk surrounded by empty beds. This is where the ambulance would have brought him yesterday. He would have been hooked up to an oxygen monitor and an electrocardiograph, and had his bloods done. I know they gave him IV heparin, nitroglycerine and beta blockers. I know he's been scheduled for an angiogram tomorrow morning. Best case is he will come out with a stent or two.

Dad's bed is closest to the nurses station. I can see his white dressing-gown hanging over a plastic chair, and it occurs to me that he won't have anything else with him. The hospital told me on the phone that he'd called triple zero at seven am, taken aspirin and unlocked the front door as instructed by the call centre operator, then laid himself down in the hallway. They found him there, in his slippers and dressing-gown, blue-lipped and sweating, Jess on the floorboards next to him.

He raises his fingers off the bed when he sees me.

'Hi there, Frances.'

'Hi, Dad.'

'Good trip up?'

'Not too bad.'

'Much traffic?'

'Just the usual.'

'You were okay to drive then?'

'Yeah. I'm fine.'

He raises his eyebrows at this and runs out of questions.

'So, you've had a heart attack?' I ask the obvious.

'Looks that way.'

'How're you feeling?'

'A bit weak. Shaky.' He raises his hand to demonstrate, and it flops back down on the bed.

'What'd the doctor say?'

'I have to have some sort of procedure tomorrow. Ask the nurse.' He waves the same hand in the direction of the nurses station. 'She'll know.'

On cue, a nurse in a blue-and-white tunic and long pants arrives at the end of the bed. He picks up Dad's chart and squints at him.

'I'd have taken an RDO if I knew your daughter was coming in tonight, Joe.'

Dad laughs, which becomes a cough, which becomes a wheeze.

'Jeez mate, it wasn't that funny.' The nurse levers the bed to sit him up further.

'Good thing you didn't go into stand-up, Dave,' I say.

'Oh, but I did. Every Sunday night at the Murchison Tavern.' Dave offers me his hand, which I miss because he's a funny man, and whips it away again.

'Gotcha.' He looks at the monitor and enters the numbers into his notes. 'You're in the city now, aren't you, Fran? Working for government?'

'That's right.'

'Taken the day off?'

'Yep.'

'She's a good daughter, isn't she Joe? Coming all this way just for you.'

'She is, yeah.' Dad beams at me, even though Dave's tone has an edge to it.

'You're not married are you, Fran?' Dave hangs the chart over the foot of the bed. 'Yet.'

'No.'

'Hmm. You here for long?'

'I don't know yet. Depends on when Dad is discharged.'

'He'll be here a few days yet. You should come out with me and Jack tomorrow night. There's a band playing at the Murch.'

'Right.' I look at Dad, expecting a scowl, but he's not paying attention. Dad doesn't approve of Jack. Never did.

'Alright then, Joe,' Dave says, 'you're all good. Can I get you anything? Cup of tea? Beer? Rum and coke? You're allowed fluids until midnight, then nothing until after the procedure.'

'Nah, I'm good,' Dad replies.

'What about you, Fran?'

'I'm fine.'

'Good, good. I'll see you tomorrow night then. Eight o'clock. Be there or be—'

'Not there.'

'You were never any fun, Franny.'

'Fuck off, David.'

He grins and gives me the finger as he walks away.

'What can I get you from home, Dad?' I ask.

'A toothbrush and some proper toothpaste. And some thongs.'

'Why the thongs? Don't you have slippers?'

'Don't want to get them dirty outside.'

'Do you really think you'll be going outside?'

'Just in case then,' he concedes.

'How about some pyjamas?'

'Don't have any.'

'I'll get you some from Target.'

'Nah, don't bother, this is fine.'

'I'll get you some pyjamas.'

He sighs. 'Then get me a lotto ticket while you're there. You know my numbers. And the newspaper. Not that big one that you read, the local one.'

'Will do. Anything else?'

'Nah, you'd better get going, Jess'll be hungry. Her dinner is on the kitchen bench where I left it.'

'Got it.'

'And she'll want to sleep inside tonight.'

I raise my eyebrows at him.

'Since your mum, you know.'

'She wouldn't approve.'

'She won't know.'

'She might.' I bend over to kiss him goodnight.

'Thanks for coming up.'

'Of course I came up.'

'Don't listen to David.'

'I won't.'

'And stay away from Jack.'

Outside the hospital, the families on the lawn have left and the pile of she-oak fruits is still on the footpath. I pick up one and put it in my pocket. Fish and chips is the only real choice for takeaway food in Weymouth at this time of night, so I drive to the corner, order a piece of battered shark, a minimum chips and a pineapple fritter and take them to the wharf. It's a still night and the lights reflect off the flat water. The bay curves away to my right, white sand punctuated by breakwaters all the way to the marina. Seagulls are quick to gather around the car. It's the only one in the carpark so I guess I'm it. They stand on the grass between the bonnet and the beach, expectant. As I eat, the closest gull arches his neck and rushes any others that threaten his position. He doesn't know I always go for the underdog.

I told Dad the truth; I am okay to drive. Sometimes I'm not, but my ears have been clear for the last two days and the spins have stopped. I find it a bit odd that no-one has ever told me I shouldn't have a licence. People with epilepsy aren't allowed to drive and their seizures aren't all that different to my drop attacks. I don't have fits like they do, I just fall over, but you can't drive a car when you're horizontal and the world is turning in odd directions. I guess epileptic fits are spontaneous – they don't get warnings – but mine only happen when I'm symptomatic so I take the bus if my ears are clogged.

The batter on the shark is thin and crisp and they've given me two pieces. I eat the first, think about saving the second for lunch tomorrow, then eat it anyway. The Chiko Roll and chips were five hours ago and I'm hungry. The gulls won't be getting much out of me tonight. I pull the batter off the pineapple ring and eat that next, the mix of sweet and salt and tang from the fruit mingling on my tongue. It's the best I've ever had. Or maybe I'm hungrier than I thought. I chase it with the pineapple and shake the paper on my lap to jostle the chips into a pile. The seagulls edge closer.

At the end of the breakwater, a man is standing on the rocks, throwing pebbles into the sea. He dusts his hands on his jeans, turns and clambers awkwardly toward the beach. The rocks are wet, and they shine. The flat water must be deceptive. As I watch, the swell climbs after the retreating scrambler. He beats it effortlessly, and it falls back without breaking, glutinous and silent. I imagine getting the spins on a pile of rocks in the middle of the water, sucked at by a viscid sea. How long would it take me to crawl back to shore? The thought makes my stomach churn and the fat and salt from the batter rises up my throat. I wash it down with my water bottle. I don't feel like the chips any more. I open the door and pour them into an unhelpful pile next to the car. I narrowly miss a seagull as I clap the door shut against the squawking horde.

I back out slowly to avoid any unnecessary roadkill and by the time I've swung the car toward the exit, the chip pile is no longer. The birds are gone too. The person on the breakwater is back on flat ground and crossing the road toward the houses on the other side of the wharf. They are single-storey weatherboard bungalows with iron roofs and low front fences. Behind them, a new building rises, four storeys and clad in those perforated metal panels you see everywhere now. I recognise the building. Harbour Lights, the Department of Housing called it. I can't see the detail in the dark, but I know the cut-outs in the panels make an image of a flock of seagulls. I follow the breakwater-scrambler as he turns the corner and walks to the ground floor entrance.

I have to give Duncan his due. Up close, the building looks good. The panelling is positioned to let the sea breeze pour into opened windows but stop the afternoon sun from blasting the western wall. And you'd think the seagull motif would be naff for up here, but it works, the lines of the birds softening the building's heavy block shape. Even the gardens look good, which is no mean feat on this coast, where the sun and the wind are not kind to vegetation. They've planted spinifex and banksias and I can see purple pigface flowers peeping out behind soft grey cushion bush. Lavender lines the footpath in a nod to the neighbours' cottage gardens up and down the road.

A light flicks on two storeys up. I guess it's the breakwater guy. I can see the shape of him move across the window and the light come on in the adjacent room behind a gap in the metal panels. I watch him as he opens the window, hear the crack of the lock and the creak of the frame when he pushes and looks out. I immediately slump into my seat and turn my face, now flaming with heat. I've just followed Jack home. I turn my head back as far as I dare, but he's gone, his shadow disappearing into the building. I start the car and pull away from the curb.

CHAPTER FIFTEEN

The thing about high school sweethearts is that you remember how good they smelled, even when you're still cringing about the time that they dumped you. Seeing Jack in the window brought back that sharp, overheated boy smell, something that was still a novelty when I was sixteen. I'd pretend to be cold as an excuse to wear one of his jumpers, then I'd forget to take it off when I went home and wear it to bed, wrapped up in heady teenage musk. Driving to Dad's house, I wind the windows down to get some fresh air into the car.

Jess is snuffling at the front door when I turn the key in the lock. She twists and wags when I push it open then bounds toward the kitchen. I leave my case by the door and follow her. First things first. If ever I was going to have trouble finding the dog food, Jess wasn't. She has her paws on the kitchen bench and nose pointing to the ziplock bag where her minced chicken has defrosted. I mop up the ice-melt and take the bag outside to where Dad keeps her food bowl. She sits without being told, her haunches tense, her butt barely touching the ground.

'Are you a good girl, Jess?'

She barks, once.

'Really truly?'

She barks twice. *Woof, woof.*

'Good girl.'

I squeeze the pale, mushy meat into the bowl and she leaps at it. She's finished by the time I reach the back door. As I close it, I see her circling the lawn looking for the best place to poop.

My bedroom is at the other end of the house, the opposite end to my parents' room. I drag my wheelie case past the loungeroom and Matt's room and lean it against my bed. The curtains are open, and I can see across rooftops to the orange harbour lights and the water. I open the window and the sound of the sea fills the room. Outside the protection of the harbour, it is free to break onto the beach, and I can hear the thud and slap of the waves. I breathe it in and the salt tingles my sinuses and rushes all the way down the back of my throat.

I haven't been able to smell or hear the sea from my bedroom since I left home. The first room I had was in a residential college. It looked out at treetops, which at least swished in the sea breeze. That room was noisy in more insistent ways; thumps and shouts from students on either side, calling over their pocket balconies or running down corridors that were barely narrower than our bedrooms. *No running in the hallways,* said the signs. Yeah, right.

The second room was closer to the sea but not close enough to hear it moving. Sometimes, when the wind was right and I stood on the front veranda, I thought I could smell the salt, the clean air not yet tainted with the oil of eucalyptus leaves or the fertiliser on struggling English gardens. It's not really salt that you can smell when you smell the sea; it's dimethyl sulphide, a gas released by bacteria that feed on decaying seaweed. So, it's bacteria fart in my lungs, not pure, cleansing salt.

There were five of us in that house. Two couples and me, alone in another skinny room on a sloping, enclosed back porch. It was a house with a long and proud history of student rentals. At Eric's thirtieth, I discovered that Alice had lived there seven years before I took over the sleepout. *Did you discover the cellar?* she'd asked. Of course we'd discovered it. When I moved in, the subterranean garden was already twenty centimetres high, and a light shone up through the floorboards day and night. The gardener, a medical student from down south, shouted us Friday night pizza once a month in appreciation of our silence.

I still don't have a sea view in my apartment, but I can hear the sea on most days, especially when a storm has been through, and the swell makes the waves boom on the sand. Here, in my childhood bedroom, I open the windows and curtains before I go to sleep so the sea can wake me in the morning. I burrow under the blankets, listening to the water mutter, and turn my face to the cold air falling through the window. I drift. Behind my closed eyes I see the dark, unbroken swell against the rocks on the breakwater, watch it chase Jack's heels and cover the pale crabs. I breathe out as it recedes, sliding away before it gathers itself again, seeking out the cracks and crevasses, pushing higher. Then together we exhale, and I feel myself drift a little deeper. Eric is telling me about his grandmother's birthday party. She's changed her mind at the last minute and wants to go to the concert in the park. Do I know where they can get tickets? He has his feet on the table in the pod, but the table is Dad's kitchen table, and I can't work out why it fits in the small office space. I am worrying that the table might have been broken at some point when a car starts up next door and I hear voices leaving for the day. *Don't forget your lunch. I love you. I love you too.*

I swing my feet to the floor and look at the ocean.

*

By the time the hospital calls to say that Dad is out of theatre, I've caught up on my emails from yesterday. I fold the laptop shut and push it away across the kitchen table. This is the table from my dream, where we sat in real life, the four of us in a line so we could all eat looking at the water. It sounds unfriendly, but we still talked. Mum especially. She couldn't eat in silence. She'd interrogate Matt and me about school, about football, about netball, about our friends, and then when she'd exhausted our day, she'd grill Dad. *Did those parts arrive today? Why not? Well did you call them? Do you want me to do it tomorrow?* And then when she'd exhausted him, she'd tell us about her own day, about the storeman who kept losing consignment notes and how she'd never get ready for the audit if she had to do everything herself.

I close the curtains against the heat that has started to build despite the cold morning easterly, ruffle the dog's head, collect the newspaper from the doorstep, and drive to the supermarket. I buy bananas, two jam doughnuts, and two takeaway lattes, juggle them back to the car, then juggle them into the hospital. Dad brightens at the treats and reaches for the paper.

'How's Jess?'

'She's fine.'

'Did you feed her?'

'Damn, I forgot.' I take a deep bite of my doughnut and jam spurts out the other side and onto my lap.

'Yeah, right.' He passes me a paper napkin. 'Make sure you take her for a walk today. Did she sleep inside?'

'She sure did.'

'On the big bed?'

'Yep. I could hear her snoring from my room. How do you stand it?'

'I slept next to your mother for thirty years.'

'Mum didn't snore, you did.'

His mouth is full of doughnut, and he just shakes his head and jabs his finger at a colour photo on page three.

'What's that?'

He chases the doughnut with coffee. I peer over his shoulder. The photo is part of an advertisement *For Sale by Public Tender – Guaranteed Rental Income*. It seems Harbour Lights is a front-runner in the government's privatisation agenda.

'All the tall blond people. Look at them. You'd think the Dutch had made it ashore after all.' He tosses the paper onto the bed. 'Don't tell me any of the people in that photo actually live there.'

I start to tell him that the newspaper advertisement would have been made in Perth and the people recruited from a metropolitan modelling agency when a nurse comes in with Dad's meds.

'Hi, I'm Mei, you must be Joe's daughter.'

'Frances.'

'Your dad's told me all about you. Never stops. I've heard all about how it was you who exposed the government's maintenance contracts stuff-up last year.'

'Yeah.'

'Those incompetent bastards. They should sack the lot of them. I saw the pictures of the houses they live in. One of them's even got a yacht moored in the marina up here.'

'Nah, that bit's not true.'

'Well, you've got them on the run. I hope you got a promotion out of that.' She gives Dad his meds and points to the picture in the paper, lying open on the bed where Dad tossed it. 'Oh, that's Harbour Lights. Are you looking into that now? There's plenty of people up here who could tell you some stories about that place. Ask about Weymouth Builders and how they got the job. That'll be another front-page story for you.'

'I'll do that, thanks.' I have no intention of looking up Weymouth Builders. People give me hot tips all the time. If I followed up all of them, I'd single-handedly bring the state government to a stand-still while I rifled through their files.

'Just make sure they put any money you find into employing more nurses. We could do with some extra hands up here.' She takes Dad's pulse and writes up his chart. 'Do you know what they call that place? The White Palace.'

Dad nods. 'Tell her why.'

'Because that's where you get all the good white stuff.' She presses a finger against one nostril, sniffs, and grins.

Dave twitches the curtain. 'No, you've got that all wrong, it's because you have to be a whitey to live there. No blacks or Asians allowed.'

I blink and Dad clears his throat. Mei presses her lips together and they turn pale against the blush on her cheeks.

'I don't think they can do that, Dave,' I tell him.

'Oh, Frances, there's what people are allowed to do according to the rules, and what they actually do out here in the sticks. Or have you forgotten?' He lifts Dad's chart. 'Never mind, we'll get you back on the right path tonight at the Murch. Gin should do the trick. Time for handover, Mei.'

She follows him out of the room. Dad looks at me and shrugs.

CHAPTER SIXTEEN

The next morning I wake up at the White Palace and my first thought is that I forgot to take Jess for a walk last night. Above my head, the ceiling is white, and the light bulb is shaded with a white paper lantern in a bamboo print. There is a lot of light in the room, bouncing freely off the white walls, white bedspread, white chest of drawers, and the mirror on the wall above it. I thought single men were supposed to prefer dark colours for their interior decor. Black leather couches, and all that. I roll onto my side. Through the open door, I can see the arm of a beige couch and a framed poster of the seventies' tennis girl. Someone has blu-tacked an A4 print of Pat Cash in the same pose on the wall next to it. I feel myself smiling and the shooting pain behind my eyes at the same time.

'There's water on the bedside table.' Jack blocks the view of the naked tennis butts. 'Do you want a coffee?'

'Yes please.' I squeeze my eyes and open them again.

'And some Panadol?'

'Please.'

He's showered and dressed when he returns and hands me the painkillers. I can smell toothpaste. I edge myself upwards and look at the skirting board. It's stable.

'All good?'

'Yep.'

'You were a riot last night.'

'At the pub or after?'

He laughs. 'Nah, you're all good. Nothing untoward happened. You were pretty quiet by the time we got here.'

'What were those drinks Dave was buying?'

'Gin Negronis.'

'They went down easily.'

'You seemed to like them.'

'His girlfriend's nice.'

'Michelle? You were lucky to meet her. She's only just finished her swing.'

'An itinerant like you, hey?'

'Itchy feet, what can I say?' He grins, as well he should. Jack left school at fifteen, worked on the cray boats as a deckhand, got his skipper's ticket, and a job taking tourists on whale-watching day trips out of Exmouth. One of them took a shine to him and asked Jack to deliver his superyacht to Queensland. From there, it's been rolling gigs, one after the other, skippering multimillion-dollar boats through South-East Asia and even as far as the Middle East and Africa. Although the work must've dried up if he's living in public housing now.

'Can I get you some toast? There's a spare towel in the bathroom if you want a shower.'

'Do I need one?'

'Yeah, you do.'

I wait for him to move out of sight and then flop my face into the pillow next to me. The unchecked sideways move makes the room lurch to the left but it's worth it. The smell is the same.

The shower, coffee, drugs, and toast scaffold me into human shape and I look down at the street where I'd parked two nights before. Jack says we got a lift home last night and we'll need to collect both of our cars this morning. I nod. I don't remember the ride home or the decision to leave the pub. Or the decision to come back here. Only one side of the bed has been slept in as far as I can tell, and a blue-and-white striped doona is folded on the arm of the beige couch.

The rest of the apartment is similarly neat and doesn't gel with the Jack I remember from school. Shoes are lined up next to the front door, and in the kitchen there are no dishes on the draining board or in the sink. A pile of papers is held together with a bulldog clip in the middle of the (white) dining table, the edges squared away. The top page is a pathology request form. The notes box says *opiates and amphetamine* in typical doctor scrawl.

'What's the deal with that?' I ask. He leans over me to see. His hip is warm through my t-shirt, and I catch myself wondering what it would be like to snuggle against him in bed now I'm sober.

'Oh that. It's from my last job. The owner wanted to know if I was clean before he handed over the keys. The gig got cancelled before I went for the test.' He looks down at me and squeezes my shoulder. 'There's nothing like that going on anymore, you don't need to worry. Most workplaces make you get one when you apply for a job these days and then every six months or so, especially if you work FIFO like Michelle. Occupational safety and health. If you test positive, it's instant dismissal.'

'Are many people sacked for drugs?'

'Sure are. At the pub last night there would have been a good four, maybe five, people who've lost their jobs because they were high at work.'

'Far out.'

'I know right? Drug addicts in this town, who would have thought?' He tips a poached egg onto my toast. 'Shame they weren't able to get that Griffiths guy on trafficking charges though.'

Jack means the famous drug bust a few years back. The local police hauled a forty-four-gallon drum packed with meth out of the sea north of town. It had a battery-powered beacon strapped to the top and a GPS tracker stowed inside. Local Weymouth people were done for it, but the alleged brains behind the business was Graham Griffiths, a Sydney businessman with a flash penthouse on Perth's northern beaches. The police couldn't make the trafficking charge stick and now he's doing time in Perth for a lesser supply conviction. I don't care either way, as long as the drugs are off the street and not ruining the lives of people like my brother. Jack changes the subject.

'You still working for the government then? Don't you want to do more exciting stuff by now?'

'Like what?'

'I dunno, come up here and run your dad's business.'

'Nah, he's selling it anyway. Cashing in.'

'Good for him. You could still get work here though. Do the accounts for the port or one of the schools.'

'Yeah, nah. I'm still good where I am.'

'You like living in the city, hey?'

I do, he's right. I can buy takeaway laksa at ten o'clock at night and go shopping seven days a week. And if and when I do want a different job – which I don't – there are plenty of city-based companies happy to pick up a government-trained accountant with my level of experience.

'How long have you been out of work?' I ask him.

'Four months.'

'And you got into public housing that quick?'

He shrugs. 'A vacancy came up.'

'But still, that's unheard of. Surely there were dozens of people in the queue in front of you.'

'Well,' he looks out the window, where we can see the breakwater and white horses starting to rise outside the harbour. 'I guess it helps if you're the right person.'

The phone rings before I can ask him what the hell that actually means. It's the hospital. I have to go. Dad's had a stroke.

Jack comes with me in the taxi. I want to say no, remembering Dad's scowl two days ago, but I look at the Scandinavian minimalist flat and his navy polo shirt and figure my need outweighs Dad's disapproval. It turns out Dad's not in a position to notice anyway. When we arrive, he's already been prepped for theatre and all I can do is squeeze his hand as they wheel him in. Mei is on shift, and she takes me to the visitors waiting room.

'He'll be fine,' she says, 'it's not uncommon. The surgeon will know what he's doing.'

'Why did it happen?'

'Sometimes patients throw a clot after a procedure.' She sees the blank look on my face and takes me back a few steps to explain. 'The blockages in a coronary artery that cause a heart attack – like with your dad – can come loose during an angioplasty and cause a blood clot, and that can travel to the brain. We use blood thinners to reduce the risk, but it can still happen.'

She tells me that Dad's having a thrombectomy to remove the clot and restore the blood flow. They'll use a catheter the same way they did for the angioplasty, but this time, they'll suck out the clot instead of inserting a stent. We won't know if he'll have any long-term side effects from the stroke until after the surgery.

'But the prognosis is good,' she says, patting my leg. 'He was in the best place for something like this to happen.'

Jack comes back into the room carrying takeaway hot chocolates from the café downstairs. 'I figured you'll be keyed up enough without additional caffeine.'

Mei brightens. 'Hey, Jack.' She turns back to me. 'You didn't say you knew Jack.' She has the tiniest hint of accusation in her voice.

'Neither did you.'

'Jack and I play five-a-side together when he's in town.' She waits for me to justify myself. Jack steps in instead.

'I went to school with Frances' brother.'

Mei looks relieved and I figure she thinks she has the higher claim. *We also lost our virginity to each other,* I say to her in my head. Jack asks Mei when Dad will be out of surgery.

'We don't know how long Mr Geller's procedure will take, but he won't be up for a visit until this afternoon, if that's what you mean.

There's not much point staying. Maybe come back around three?'

'Will you still be on shift? Could you call us maybe?' Jack beams down at her and I swear she grows an inch.

'Of course I can, of course. I have your mobile number.' She glances at me as she says it.

'We won't be far, just back at Jack's place,' I tell her.

CHAPTER SEVENTEEN

There was a breakthrough six days into the investigation into Eric's disappearance. A truck driver reported seeing a blond man who *looked like that bloke from Home and Away* at the Cataby roadhouse. The police drove north to speak to the staff and so did the news crews.

'Aye, that's your man,' confirmed the shift manager, Orla, a nurse from Galway who had been working her way around Australia until she met a farmer from Dandaragan. 'Nice fella, very clean. He said he was an accountant and had a job up north. I remember him because he wanted a fancy iced coffee that we don't stock.' She smiled into the camera as her long-lashed eyes filled with tears.

'She remembered him because he was cute, not because of the brand of coffee he drank,' Belinda said when we saw her on the news.

The police took the roadhouse CCTV and transaction records but neither revealed any sign of Eric. The police also questioned every cash register attendant and short-order cook from Cataby to Derby and came up with nothing. If Eric had been north of Perth since his granny's birthday, there was no evidence of that apart from Orla's word.

For a while, I entertained a fantasy that Orla was right: Eric had been at the roadhouse during her shift and had travelled on to Weymouth, where he was hiding out in one of the small holdings outside the town. In my mind, Eric had used his contacts to engineer his own disappearance. The contacts, of course, included my father, whom Eric had met at my apartment once when Dad was still coming to the football every other weekend. The fantasy built on my forensic evidence theory. Eric was being pursued by the underworld – I wasn't specific about who – and needed to lie low somewhere out of the city. The only person he knew in the country was my dad, who put him in touch with one of the families who run the market gardens outside Weymouth. They arranged to pick him up in a truck they use to transport produce to Perth and brought him back to Weymouth on the return trip. That's when Orla saw him, using cash to buy iced coffee after spending three hours in the back of the otherwise empty truck.

Seduced by my own imagination, I found reasons to travel home at least once a month over the past year. I've spent weekends watching my dad, waiting for him to drop hints, or even suggest a trip out to the hills. In my mind, he would need to make an unscheduled visit to a friend. We'd pull into a dusty driveway flanked by Doric columns and chipped concrete lions, and drive past the main house to the rows of greenhouses at the back, my dad tight-lipped about the friend's name. The workers would turn around, surprised by the unexpected visitors. One of them (I pictured him wearing dark blue work shorts and a surf brand t-shirt and holding a white hose) would frown and then his face would split apart as he realised. He would drop the hose (still running and sending a dark stream of water through the red dirt) and run to the car, where he would gather me into his arms and tell me how much he had missed me. Dad would beam at the two of us. Later I would chastise him about keeping secrets and he and Eric would drink beer and refuse to tell me how they did it. *It's best if you don't know, Fran,* Dad would say.

I was undecided how the happily-ever-after would play out after the initial reunion. In one scenario, I would take an accounting job with the local council (the first one available, way below my paygrade, but I wouldn't mind, as long as I could be with him), sell the apartment, and buy a house on a remote cliff north of town.

In another, we'd conduct a long-distance relationship until we found the perfect hideaway in the South West (also on a sea cliff) figuring that Weymouth would be too obvious. We'd let James in on our secret and he'd quit the public service and join us to establish our own (wildly successful) market garden and teach us both to surf.

*

James went surfing on the weekend, Belinda tells me via Microsoft Teams on Monday morning. I have my laptop open on the kitchen table where I can look at the sea. The reception cuts out every now and again, making James and Belinda freeze with their eyes half closed, but otherwise I could be back in the pod. James asks me to flip the screen so he can check the swell.

'It's a bit small in this part of the bay,' I tell him. 'There's too much reef. You have to go north to the river mouth.'

'Still looks pretty good though. How come we've never cracked an invite to Joe's place?'

'I didn't know you were interested.'

'How could you think we're not interested? Maybe we'll just come up anyway when he's better. Some weekend that the Eagles have a home game, so we'll know you'll be in Perth and the bedroom is free.'

'You guys are not sleeping in my bed.'

'You'll never know.'

'Dad won't let you, and anyway there's Matt's old room.'

'With a view?'

'Yes, with a view.'

'Alright. Hey, Bel, we're going to Weymouth.'

I can see the back of Belinda's head and her hand when she raises it to acknowledge the arrangement.

'How's the new office?' I ask. They moved without me. Today is their first day.

'Not much different to the last one,' he replies. 'We're in the corner again, only now we face north' – I watch him turn his head from side to side – 'east. Ish. It's warm, but we only get the sun in the morning, not the afternoon. Belinda has ditched the sunscreen.'

'And the boxes all arrived?'

'The ones from our floor. We've put yours on your desk, but we have to go back this week and get the last boxes out of the basement archive room. Apparently, a couple got left behind when we moved everything to Iron Mountain. But the server is up and running, and there's a surprisingly adequate amount of filing space.'

'See, I told you.'

'That's because we've used yours as well,' Belinda chips in.

'Yeah, right. Is Neil happy?'

'Neil's happy. He's done his rounds already.'

'And what's the plan for today?'

'I'm going to the north metro housing office with Belinda, seeing as you've skived off.'

'What about the South West trip?'

'We'll get these done first.'

'Cool.' I watch him give me the thumbs-up and then slide sideways. Belinda's head fills the screen.

'Hey, Fran, aren't you supposed to be going out with Meredith tomorrow?'

'Damn, yes.' I'd forgotten. 'I'll have to call her.'

'Do you want one of us to go instead?'

'No, I'm good, I'll reschedule. It's not urgent.'

'Cool beans!' She slides away to make room for James. I call her back, remembering Dave's crack about the White Palace.

'Hey Belinda, do we have that tenant occupancy data yet?'

'We sure do. Duncan's office gave it to us in one flat spreadsheet. I had to filter them by postcode. It was a pain in the arse.'

'Can you send me the file?'

'I'll do it now before we leave. Anything else?'

'No, I'm all good. Go do some work.'

I get another thumbs-up and a wave before she logs off. I decide to take a break from the screen and I'm in the kitchen waiting for the kettle to boil when I hear the ping of the email. I bring my laptop to the kitchen bench to check it.

I love data. I love spreadsheets. Give me an Excel workbook full of numbers and I'll be quiet for hours. By the end of the day, I'll produce a set of charts and be able to give you breakdowns, percentages, trends, and insights into your government programme that you never thought to ask about. That's exactly what I do for the next three hours. I don't even register lunchtime coming and going or the sun drifting through the windows on the western side. I do hear the sea breeze, though, and when the windows rattle, I click save and call the hospital. Reception transfers me to the ward and Dave picks up on the third ring.

'Well, well, well, Ms Geller, how are we feeling today?'

'Fine thanks, Dave, how are you?'

'Splendid. That was quite the show you put on for us on Saturday night. I forgot you could dance.'

'I forgot you thought you could sing.'

'Triple threat, me.'

'You're not, you know.'

'Oh, I am though, you just haven't seen the full me yet.'

'How's my dad?'

'Joe!' I swear he screeches directly into the phone and I pull my mobile away from my ear. 'Joe, you there? Franny wants to know how you are. You OK down there, Joe?'

I wait for the dramatic pause.

'He says he's fine, Fran, but he's very disappointed in you.'

'Right.'

'You know he never liked Jack.'

'And you've given him a reason to not like him again.'

'Not me, Francesca, you.'

'It's just Frances, actually.'

'Yes, I know that Franola-Granola, I did it to get a rise out of you.'

'No kidding. Is he up for a visit?'

'From you, Fran, he will accept any crumbs. See you in ten.' He hangs up on me. I shut down the computer, collect my bag, and head for the hospital.

CHAPTER EIGHTEEN

Mei was right, the prognosis is good, but Dad isn't buying it. He's ready to chuck it all in and become an old person.

'What do you mean, you want me to put the house on the market?' I ask.

'It's too big for me to manage on my own.'

I look at him in the hospital bed. To be fair, he doesn't look like he could boil water, let along vacuum a floor. 'You might feel like rubbish now, Dad, but give it a few days. You'll be back to your old self. Don't make decisions that you'll regret when you're back on your feet.'

He waves me away. 'Just go see Ray, he'll look after it.'

Ray Emanuel is Dad's accountant. He's the person I've always been told to contact if anything ever happened to my parents. Ray lives on ten acres of riverfront south of town, and smells of straw and horse manure and cigarettes. He taught me and Matt how to ride. For a while, when I was still in primary school, our horses were agisted on his property. We used to take them down onto the riverbed in summer when it was dry. His son, Vince, was a stockier version of my brother and he'd come with us, cantering ahead with Matt to put distance between themselves and the embarrassing little sister.

'And where are you going to live?'

'I'll go to The Village. They've got vacancies. You can go up there and reserve one for me. The corner villa, with the view. Do it today, could you?'

'How do you even know if that one is vacant?'

'Sandra Davies' mum, Joan, is there. She told me at the tennis club.'

'Sandra Davies' mum is in her eighties,' I protest. 'You're not even seventy.'

'That's what Joan said. She reckons I should move in sooner rather than later so I can enjoy the facilities while I can. Get involved. Make some friends.'

'You have friends already.'

'Just go up there and reserve it for me. I don't want to end up out the back looking at the railway line.' He pushes down on the mattress to lift himself up.

'Where do you think you're going, Mr Geller?' Dave marches into the room, clicking the pen in his hand. He holds it to my face. *Click, click, click.* I push him away.

'Stop that.'

'Stop what, Franny?' *Click, click, click.*

Dad chuckles. 'Go easy on her, Dave, she's already annoyed.'

'Oh, I see. I told you she wouldn't like it, Joe.'

'You were right.'

'You've told Dave about this already?'

'He thinks it's a good idea.'

'Dave also thinks he can sing.'

'Now, now, don't get personal.' Dave attaches a cuff to Dad's arm, and it swells. 'Joe's an adult, he can talk to whoever he likes.'

'But he's fine, you said it yourself. He's got a stent in and there was no damage from the stroke.'

'Where there's a stroke, there's fire.'

'Jeez, Dave, that's awful. I hope that's not the material you're using at the Murch.'

He writes in Dad's chart and puts his pen back in his pocket. When he turns to me, he has his medical-professional face on. 'A heart attack followed by a stroke is pretty serious stuff, Fran. Joe did a great job in calling the ambulance on Friday, but next time he might not be able to get to his phone. At The Village, he'll have an emergency pendant that will call an ambulance just by pressing a button. He won't even have to speak. They'll have all his details on file, and they'll come straight to him.'

'But what are the chances that there'll be a next time? The artery's clear and the new meds will keep his cholesterol on track.'

'They will, and the chances are low, but what if he does? Wouldn't you rather he was closer to help?'

I look at my dad, watching me and Dave discuss him across his hospital bed. I hate it, but Dave's right. 'Fine. So, you're selling the house and the business.'

'Sold. The business settled on Thursday.' He rubs a hand over the blanket. 'I was going to tell you on Friday.'

'Right. And now you want to sell the house and buy into The Village.'

'Yep.'

I sigh, possibly louder than necessary. Mum always said there's no point fighting with Dad when his mind is made up. 'Do I need to give them a deposit or anything?'

'Don't know.' He waves his hand at me. 'Sort all that out with Ray.'

I feel my face crumple into a scowl but promise Dad I'll call Ray today. 'Is there anything else you need?'

'No, I'm good.'

'What about lunch? Can I get you a pie? A salad roll? Doughnut?'

'Are you saying we don't feed our patients?' Dave plants his feet and puts his hands on his hips. I can see it now, the theatrics of the stand-up.

'No, but I bet you bring your own lunch.'

'That's because the taxpayer doesn't spring for my meals. As you would know.'

'Even so.'

'Even so, it's a good thing Joe has such a devoted daughter. The new café at the town beach does a good line in bratwurst dogs.

You can get me one while you're there. Sauerkraut and mustard. No tomato sauce.'

I look at Dad.

'Same.'

From the car, I call Ray and ask him to put my childhood home on the market and reserve the corner villa at The Village.

CHAPTER NINETEEN

The following morning, I don't go to the hospital to see Dad. I tell him I'll see him in the afternoon. Instead, I go to the White Palace to help Jack with job applications. There's a reason why he hasn't found work yet. He can't write. He never could. He's applied for three jobs in the past month that he should have won. None of them needed more than his skipper's ticket and four years of experience, which he has twice over, but his job applications could have been written in crayon by a six-year-old for all the good they would have done him. I need to talk to him about addressing selection criteria and using whole sentences.

Yesterday at the hospital, Dad didn't appear as fazed about my encounter with Jack as Dave made out.

'What's with the Scandi-chic décor?' I'd asked Dave as we sat beside the bed eating our bratwurst dogs. They were good, I was surprised. You don't expect to get good German sausage at the far northern end of the wheatbelt, but there you go. If I could get sausage and sauerkraut for lunch every day, maybe I'd consider moving up here.

'At Jack's place? Who knows? Maybe with all that time on his hands now, he's been getting into home decorating.'

'Well, his parents are from Denmark,' said Dad, pausing in the middle of his bratwurst dog to chase it down with the milkshake I bought him. 'You've been to their house. Don't you remember all the pine?'

I do now. It was on the ceiling as well as the walls and made the house look like a cabin. There were also brown-and-orange cushions and a shag pile carpet. Jack and Dave lived on the same street, and Dave's parents' house was a standard 1980s cream brick-and-tile with imitation iron lacework, a poured concrete driveway, and a basketball hoop.

'Your parents emigrated from Europe too, didn't they, Dave?'

'Holland. The Netherlands. Statistically, we're taller than the Danes.'

'You could have been in that ad.' Dad grinned at me through a mouthful of sausage and bun. A string of sauerkraut was caught at the side of his mouth and for a moment I got a glimpse of him as an old man, propped up in a hospital bed, needing a nurse to wipe his face after he eats. I realised that when he goes, I'll be on my own.

'No-one in this town is from here,' I said.

'Statistically, ninety-seven percent of the people in this town are not from here,' Dad pointed out.

'You and I are from here,' I replied, 'the three percenters.'

'Not sure that's what your dad meant,' chipped in Dave.

I winced. Dave was shamelessly enjoying the opportunity to score points off me, but he was right, and Dad looked disappointed. In a town where the difference in living circumstances between Yamatji and non-Yamatji residents is in your face every day, Dad had made sure my brother and I understood that we were newcomers. My three percenters quip would have made him feel like he's failed.

'Jack's not ever here,' Dave added. 'He spends more time at sea in his floating palaces than on land. You should go with him sometime, Fran. Just you and Jack and the sea. You could be pirates together.'

I blanched. Boats and I don't mix, for a start, but the last thing Dad would want is me and Jack getting involved again. Dave, Jack, and Ray's son Vince were the bad boys at my school, famous for leaping off bridges into flooded rivers. When they were twelve, the Weymouth Sea Rescue had their only boat in the water for six hours looking for them after they were swept into the bay on their boogie boards. Matt was with them.

'They're nice people, the Pedersens.' Dad pivoted back to Jack's family, stopping me mid chew in surprise. 'They owned the bakery on the main street. Your mum used to like their cinnamon rolls.'

I was quick to riff on the unexpected positivity. 'And you used to buy me their sticky buns, with all the icing on top, when I came to the shop after school.'

He laughed. 'You loved those. You used to sit on the shop counter and eat them. I'd have to wipe the fingermarks off afterwards.'

*

I resist the temptation to stop at the shops on my way to Jack's. He's promised me lunch in exchange for helping him get a job and, going by the state of his flat and the perfect poached egg he gave me on Sunday, there's a good chance of something other than sandwiches.

I'm right about lunch. I can smell it in the corridor when I get out of the lift on Jack's floor. Meat and pastry. I follow my nose and the door opens before I knock.

'When did you turn into a domestic goddess?' I ask him.

'Goddess? That's a bit sexist, isn't it? Men are allowed to cook too.'

'Yeah, fair enough.' I leave my laptop and my handbag on the kitchen table and peer through the glass oven door. 'Did you hang out at the shop after school much when you were a kid?'

'Some, not much. Mum had usually finished up by then, so I just went home with her. If she was still working, Justin was at home anyway.' Justin was David's seven-years-older brother.

'Where's he now?'

'On the rigs. Caning it. He's bought a house in the city.'

'Can't he get you a job? Skippering a supply boat, something like that?'

'Yeah, maybe.'

'Have you asked?'

'Nah.'

I roll my eyes. 'Maybe you should.'

We eat. Jack serves individual pies with buttery crust, mince, potato, carrots and long strings of melted cheese. He places a bowl of salad and a pot of chutney in the centre of the table. As I chew, I search for Justin's company on my laptop. Their website says they're hiring. Jack will need to provide scanned copies of his identification, skipper's ticket, and consent to pre-employment drug screening. He shrugs, *might as well, I guess,* and I start work on his resumé, leaving greasy fingerprints and flakes of pastry on my keyboard. By the time I've finished and written a cover letter, he's washed our plates and wiped down the table.

'Save it,' he says, leaning over my shoulder. He presses the lid flat and takes my hand. 'I need a lie down after all that food.'

*

Later in the afternoon, euphemistic lie down completed, I've retrieved my laptop from the kitchen table and propped it against my thighs. At my back are thick European pillows that Jack pulled out from under the bed. I'm reading through the contract that Ray has sent me for Dad's corner villa at The Village. It is two hundred pages long and I've created my own Excel spreadsheet to keep track of the fees and charges. Jack looks over my shoulder and laughs.

'You can tell you're an accountant. Tea?'

'Yes please.'

I put the laptop aside, curl back into the bed, and wriggle my toes into the sheets. Dad had been right to distrust Jack when we were dating. Jack was my bad-boy crush, my three-years-older, blond, tanned surfer-dude with a car and a woollen jumper that smelled of sex. He taught me to drink, to smoke, to sneak in late and sleep until midday. He showed me an alternative approach to exams – *if you get over fifty percent, you studied too hard* – and a disdain for two-piece-suit corporate city life.

Despite the boogie board incident, Dad didn't discourage the relationship so much as ignore it, figuring I'd outgrow sleeping on the beach and waiting for hours while Jack surfed. He was right. I moved to the city, hung out with university students in three-hundred-dollar jeans, and became an accountant on the Terrace. Jack breezed in and out of town between deliveries, cashed up and ready to party. That's when he reconnected with Matt, and Dad took a more active dislike to him.

'Do you remember that time you all got washed into the bay when the river flooded?' The domestic sounds from the kitchen pause just long enough to indicate that he does and maybe the memory isn't welcome. He appears in the doorway again with my tea, looking contrite.

'I'm not sure we're allowed to forget.'

'Was it that bad?'

'Bad enough for Vince's mum to take him back to Perth and your parents to put Matt in a different school.'

'I thought Vince left to play rugby.' Vince had been an outlier in our Aussie Rules–dominated town, following teams we'd never heard of. I'd always assumed his move to the city was about sport, and I'd forgotten about the link between the boogie board incident and Matt changing schools. But that was only a couple of years before Mum, and all that came afterwards, so maybe I never even made the connection. I struggle to get a mental image of him. The best I can do is a light-blue rugby jersey with an Italia crest. 'Did you ever hear from Vince after that?'

'Not much. He got a job with one of his dad's clients. He went to one or two of Matt's games and I think they planned to go riding sometime. Not sure if it ever happened.' Jack flushes and squeezes the teabag against the side of the cup. 'Probably a good thing; I heard Vince got mixed up with a bad crowd.' When he looks up, his eyes are full of apology.

It feels good to know that Matt wanted to go riding after he moved to the city, even if maybe he never actually did it. Matt stopped riding after Mum died. He started going out most nights after dinner and was too tired to come out to Ray's with me after school. Dad said to let him go, it was Matt's way of coping, that he would exercise Matt's horse himself on the weekends. But Dad had already left for work when it was time for us to go to school each day and he didn't find out Matt hadn't been going to classes until he ran into Matt's teacher in the supermarket. By then, it was too late, and the school psychologist recommended that Matt take a break and come back the following year. Then he got an apprenticeship with the local building company. Then he got sacked for not turning up to work and left town for good.

'So, you're the only one who stayed.'

That comes out all wrong because, of course, staying in Weymouth is not necessarily a virtue and the consequences of leaving were complicated at best. I cover up my clumsiness by pulling him under the sheets. To Jack's credit, he lets me save face and obliges.

Later, the sea breeze finds its way through the metal seagulls and the bedroom window to my bare shoulders. I drag my t-shirt off the floor and over my head. The afternoon light makes patterns on the bedspread, and I can smell the sea. Beside me, Jack rolls over and drapes one arm over my hip. Neither of us have had any long-term partners as far as I know, and I at least have no plans for one. This could be nice, though, I think. I drag my laptop in front of me, log into Seek, and type *Weymouth* into the location tab.

*

'What percentage of public housing tenants would you guess are Anglo?' I ask James and Belinda the next day on Teams. I've sent them the work I did yesterday on the occupancy data. I've created graphs and pie charts on tenant age, gender, cultural background and length of stay.

'What do you mean?' I watch James shift his gaze to his second screen, where he's opened the spreadsheet.

'The pie chart in the second tab. Everyone living in Duncan's pet project up here is white and speaks English.'

'Nooo, that can't be right,' he says, his eyes flicking back and forth across the rows and columns of numbers. 'I know public housing's mostly old white women, but not all of it.'

'Just about. Look at the third sheet.' This one has a time series graph. 'See this? I thought Indigenous people were an identified at-risk group, especially in Weymouth, but the percentage of Indigenous households is falling.'

'Define Indigenous,' Belinda's face appears on my screen as she pulls her chair in and bumps James out of the way.

'Where the principal tenant identifies as Indigenous.'

'Maybe fewer people are identifying as Indigenous,' she suggests.

'You can't be serious.'

'Sure, I can.' I watch her stretch her back, hands braced on her hips. I bet she's been sitting at her desk for the past three hours without a break. That'll be my fault. I told her the tenancy application forms had to be audited by the end of the day. 'I don't identify as Asian.'

'But you are Asian,' I point out.

'No, I'm not, Frances. I'm Australian.'

'Well, yes, your nationality is Australian but ethnically you're Asian.'

'Nope. Mum's Scottish. We celebrate Hogmanay.'

'Yeah but ...'

'... I look Asian?' She leans into the screen and smirks. Up close, I can see the grey cloud in her eye that she hates.

'Most people would say you're Asian.'

'Doesn't mean I have to say I am. You don't identify as having a disability.'

'That's because I don't.'

'But *most people* would say that you do.'

'No, they wouldn't. I don't ...'

'… look disabled?'

'Exactly, and most of the time it doesn't affect me.'

'Except when it does, and then you're a vomiting, spinning mess on the floor.'

'*Most people* just think I'm drunk.'

'Jeez, girls, give it a rest.' In the background, James stands up and collects two mugs. 'I'm going to make tea. Frances, are you sticking around?'

'No, I'm good.' I check the time. It's four o'clock already. 'Going in to see Dad.'

'Tell him to get your brother's old room ready.'

CHAPTER TWENTY

I drive back to the city on Friday. Dad left hospital with a post-discharge care plan, a bag of meds, and an appointment for a home visit from the community health nurse. Jess ran in circles when he walked in the front door, and Dad demonstrated his ability to boil water while I made us sandwiches. There wasn't any need for me to stay on, he told me. If I left after lunch, I could be home before dark, and I'd be able to go to the game on the weekend. I didn't protest. I figured he didn't want me to see him shuffling around the house and that all he really wanted to do was sleep uninterrupted. I could come up again in a few weeks when he was feeling better, maybe help him pack up the house, maybe sleep over at the new villa.

I did as I was told and said goodbye after lunch. He wouldn't let me do the dishes. I called in at Jack's before leaving town. He's watching the football, his bony, tanned feet on the white coffee table, an early beer in hand. I shook my head when he offered me one.

'Nah, sorry, I'm off.'

'Off, off? Like, back to Perth?'

'Yeah. I think Dad wants some alone time.'

'He's settled back in then?'

I nodded, my throat abruptly closing.

'I'll call in tomorrow. Check up on him. Take Jess for a walk.'

'That'd be good.'

'I'll walk you downstairs.'

I'm rubbish at goodbyes and got it over with as quickly as I could without being callous. Jack told me to drive safe and we made promises to keep in touch. We both felt bad, but what can you do? If we wanted to give it another shot, he'd have to move to Perth, or I'd have to move here. Despite my post-coital adventure on Seek, I wasn't giving up my job, and I couldn't see Jack living in an apartment in the city, even if it was only between trips. And it didn't work out last time, so the odds were if one of us moved, we'd be moving back again eventually. He patted the roof of my car as I drove away.

Dave calls me just before I get out of mobile range.

'I heard you've skipped town.'

'You heard right.'

'Did your dad kick you out again?'

'Something like that.'

'Can't say I blame him. It's been good having you up here for a while, though.'

'Yeah. Thanks for looking after Dad.'

'Jack's already crying into his beer.'

'That's because his team is going to lose today.'

I hear him start to reply but then the reception cuts out and the only noise coming from my phone is beeping.

*

On my first day back at work, I ride the bus past the park, past my old office, and down the hill into the CBD. I see Jason the gardener from the bus window, clearing the footpath with his blower vac. He sees me waving and waves back. On the Terrace, the glass and steel towers close over my head, and I hear Jack's words about becoming a corporate wage slave. I defend myself to him in my head. *It's not true, I actually love my job.* The bus empties us onto concrete and bitumen and I walk through a musty arcade of closed shopfronts, cross an empty and leaf-strewn pedestrian mall, and step through the sliding glass doors of my new workplace. The lift here is newer than in our old office and I zoom up to level six. This is a heritage building, refurbished to make public servants rise and fall efficiently through the floors while giving the appearance of stability and calm. When the lift doors open, I am greeted by our corporate colours and Julie at the reception desk. There is no sunlit blue river behind her, only the office name and logo stamped on the wall. It feels smaller.

My team, Julie tells me, is to the right and then left, in the corner. I walk past a bank of meeting rooms with frosted glass walls. Heads are raised and lowered around circular tables as the office clocks my return. In the far corner I can see a single Hello Kitty plush toy mounted above a workstation, and I make my way toward it.

'Um, Frances?' It is the level five analyst with the unarchived community health files. 'Sorry to bother you. Is this okay to shred now?'

I flick through the papers, recognising the misfiled tenancy report and the outpatient spreadsheet. The spreadsheet is not the same version as the one I read. It has a second column added. I put my bag on the floor so I can read it.

'What are these?' I run my finger down the page. Each cell in the added column contains a familiar combination of six numbers followed by three letters. This spreadsheet, I can see now, is a photocopy, with the top of the page, including the column headings, sliced off.

'I don't know, I haven't looked through it.' She blushes. 'I can check in the cloud if you want.'

'No that's fine, leave it to me, I'll talk to the director who oversaw the inquiry.'

'I've shown it to Bigfoot already. She said to bring it to you.'

I press my tongue to the roof of my mouth, annoyed in spite of myself. This wasn't my project; I don't see how I can shed any light on stray paperwork that Bigfoot can't already identify. But it does help me out with my own personal snooping.

'Don't worry,' I tell her, 'I'll deal with it.'

'Thanks, Frances.'

'Not a problem.'

I tuck the file into my bag and find James and Belinda in the corner. My archive box, as they promised, is sitting on my desk, the lid open but otherwise intact.

'You didn't think you might unpack it for me?'

'Wouldn't dream of going through your stuff, boss. There might be something personal in there.'

'Like my teacup, for instance?' I pick up the cup that is sitting on James' desk. Cold tea sloshes inside.

'Couldn't find mine. I noticed you didn't wash it before you packed it away. I had to do it before I used it. A bit inconsiderate, I thought.'

I unfold the lid of the packing box. The newspaper that I'd used to stuff the cup during transport has been tossed back inside.

'So,' Belinda says, crossing her legs and leaning forward, her elbows on her thighs, 'we have news. You know how we had to go back for the archive boxes in the basement? You wouldn't recognise it. Jason has expanded now that the archive room has been cleared out. It's full of hedge trimmers and jars of washers.'

'And it stinks.' James adds. 'There's no ventilation and he keeps weedkiller in there. Major OSH issue.'

'Anyway, we got the boxes and brought them back here. But Jason asked how the missing persons investigation was going into Eric's disappearance, and – get this – he wanted to know whether that drug dealer had been questioned about it yet.'

'What drug dealer?'

'You know, the one from last year. The one who they failed to get convicted on the trafficking charge for bringing drugs in through the beaches up your way. Graham Griffiths, remember? The guy from Sydney. He was done for the meth stashed in his bicycle frame instead.' James nods at an Alston pinned to his workstation.

I recognise it. The long-faced police commissioner is standing on the side of a road, with the ocean in the background. He is questioning a lycra-encased cyclist with veined eyes and plastic bags taped to the seat post, top tube, down tube, fork, handlebars, anything that doesn't spin. *It's just for personal use, officer,* the cyclist is explaining. A street sign behind him says *Speed limit 28g.*

'I don't get it. What does Graham Griffiths have to do with Eric?'

'It was his car. The one that nearly took out Eric on the night he disappeared. Jason saw the driver and recognised him from the photos in the paper.'

CHAPTER TWENTY-ONE

I call Meredith from the carpark. She picks up on the first ring and promises to be *out in just a tick*. I swing the car around to face back down the driveway and wait. The carpark used to be someone's backyard. Now it's paved and the worker's cottage at the front of the block is the headquarters for TAG and the plumbers' union. Half of the parking spaces are occupied by white trades vans. I watch two men with thick forearms emerge from the cab of one and walk with rolling gaits to the back door. They carry clipboards with Southern Cross stickers. One shakes his head in that flat way men do when they can't believe what they've just seen. I picture them on a building site, maybe half an hour ago, making notes about improperly constructed scaffolding and unsecured chemicals and pointing clubbed fingers at the corporate HSEQ officer.

The cottage is a hold-out. The suburb used to be a worker's dormitory, walking distance to the city and adjacent to the rail yards. This street would have been lined with weatherboards, with lemon trees in the backyards and brick outhouses against the back fence. Now the city is bleeding into the suburbs. All three sides of the carpark are bordered with boundary fire walls, grazed by the tilt-up walls of commercial office buildings. I can see strip-lights in the second-floor ceiling panels from where I sit in my car, as well as workstations, pot plants and sticky notes on the windows.

The screen door of the ex-cottage swings open and clatters against the wall. The union men walk in, and Meredith walks out and down the stacked bricks that serve as steps to the old veranda. She cradles a stack of files in one arm and holds out the other to stop the door from rebounding on her.

'Some bastard helped himself to the door closer last weekend,' she says as she bends down to car window level. Her files shift in her arms and drop with a thump against the door. 'Oops. Here, can you hold these? I'll move my car and you can put yours in my bay.' She feeds the files through the window, and I juggle them across to the passenger seat. Unburdened, she searches her handbag, swears, apologises, then jogs back to the cottage. She's wearing the same black cardigan, jeans, and trainers that she'd been wearing at the housing seminar. I watch her fling the door open and leap inside before it catches her.

I straighten up the puddle of files on the passenger seat. They're the same type we use – manila – with coloured stickers to indicate their allocated place in the filing system. These are client files, I realise, some as thick as a plumber's forearm, some with only one or two documents. I pick up a thin one. Aaron Abadi. The file contains his Residential Tenancy Agreement and a personal details form. Aaron is thirty-four, I read, and has lived in his current tenancy for six months. His last job was with a builder based in Myaree. His personal details form says that he's a plumber by trade and his six-year-old son will be living with him for seven nights out of every fourteen.

The back door clatters again and Meredith jogs across the carpark shaking her keys at me. She whips her car backwards out of her parking spot, only just missing the bumper of a station wagon parked on the other side and flings it into the driveway in front of mine. I have a bad feeling about the car ride ahead. An arm appears from the driver's window pointing me back toward the empty bay. Her head follows it.

'I've registered you in the book,' she shouts. 'You're all good. No-one will clamp you.'

Meredith drives a chunky SUV with cartoon shades suction-capped to the windows. The backseat has a child's booster seat on one side and a clear plastic tub on the other. Both are strapped down with seatbelts.

'Pop the files in the tub,' she says through the passenger window. 'And take out Abadi, Samson and Wright. They're the ones we're going to see.'

I do as instructed and climb into the front seat. Inside, the car looks and smells like it's been detailed that morning.

'I know, right?' She grins. 'Who has a full-time job, kids and a clean car?' She peers left and right and shoots out in front of a trades van trawling for a park on the street. I feel the world whoosh past my ears and grab for the door handle. 'It's not me who does it, although that should be obvious. Greg vacuums it *every week*. Can you believe that?' She accelerates down the street. I close my eyes and keep my head still. Jacaranda trees, the only legacy of the former residential streetscape, make flickering shadow patterns on my eyelids.

'He's insane. It's the same in the house. Beds made every morning. Dishes put away after every meal. If it was me, there'd be crap everywhere. Are you a neat freak too? I hope not. You won't cope this afternoon if you are. Abadi's okay. He's quite a sweetie, actually. Really trying hard to get back on his feet. But Samson,' she pushes out a long, noisy breath, 'she has different ideas about how to keep a house. Some people find it a bit confronting.' I feel her shoot me a look. 'You'll be alright, won't you? You didn't strike me as the judgy type.'

'I'll be fine.' I open my eyes and look down at the files on my lap. 'Who's first?'

'Thought so. I wouldn't have brought you otherwise. Public housing tenants get enough mud slung at them without me bringing more of it into their homes.' She pulls up at the traffic lights and I risk a look through the spotless windscreen.

'Have a look at the Samson file. She's in Maylands in a four-by-two with six grandchildren. The mum's in prison for unpaid fines.'

I open the file. It's a fat one. The papers at the top chronicle an ongoing complaint to the Department of Housing about a broken oven. Correspondence back and forth between Mrs Samson, Meredith and the department argues whether the damage was fair wear and tear or the fault of the tenant. Mrs Samson, the department says, has been using the oven to dry clothes, which is why the element is scorched. Mrs Samson says the oven was twenty years old and not working when she moved in. A page from a Department of Housing maintenance schedule, photocopied multiple times and undated, has a line highlighted in yellow stating that ovens should be replaced every fifteen years. An image of my own oven floats above the page. It is brushed stainless steel, the type that doesn't make greasy fingermarks, and has a red LED timer display. I'd last used it to keep takeaway pizza warm.

'The part itself doesn't cost much,' Meredith is saying, 'but once you include the call-out fee and labour, she'll be looking at two hundred dollars. How do you pay for that on a pension?' She runs an orange light and swings into the left-hand lane. 'Here we are.'

We whip into a side street, the SUV rolling on its suspension, and pull up at the kerb outside a pale brick bungalow. The windows are uncurtained and behind one of them a shadow bounces between the top and bottom frame and back again.

'Melissa, are you jumping on that bed again?' The voice through the screen door is broad, flat and sounds like Weymouth.

'No, Granny.' The shadow disappears.

'You better not be.'

The shadow, this time with hair and eyes, appears at the windowsill. Meredith waves and the shadow vanishes again.

Inside there is no sign of Melissa. Joleen Samson calls us to the kitchen, through a brick arch opposite the front door. I close the screen door behind me. The door closer is intact and sinks to a closed position with a sigh.

'What's for lunch?' Meredith asks.

'Pasta bake.'

'Yum.'

'It'd be nicer if I could grill the cheese on top.'

'The department hasn't fixed the oven yet?'

'Nuh.'

'When did you hear from them last?'

Joleen puts down the spoon she is using to stir a sauce on the stovetop and picks up her mobile phone. She flicks her finger up the screen.

'Monday.' She passes the phone to Meredith. 'They said they'd received my appeal.'

'Right.' Meredith frowns at the screen and writes in her notepad. 'Who's Sean Callaghan? Is he new?'

'Yeah, just started.'

Meredith tipped the screen toward me. *Sean Callaghan, BComm. (Hons), Policy Officer.* He signed off his email with *Best.*

'I'll call him.'

'Thanks love.'

'How's Melissa?'

'Seems fine. No reason why she shouldn't be at school.' Joleen shifts her weight against the dead oven, presses her lips together and folds her arms.

'No more fever?'

'Nah, but the school said she couldn't come back until next week.'

'Bet she's loving that.'

Joleen snorts.

'This is the investigator I called you about. Frances.'

'You're with some government watchdog, aren't you?' She turns back to her sauce.

'The Commissioner for Public Inquiries, yes.'

'Is he going to do something about my oven?' The tone of her voice suggests she suspects not. Meredith saves me.

'I wanted to show Frances the floor in the girls' bedroom, Joleen.'

'Yeah, go ahead.' She waves her arm toward the hallway.

The bedroom is fitted out with two sets of bunk beds, a wardrobe, and a pine chest of drawers. A faded Disney princess rug is on the floor in between the beds. The boards are otherwise bare and there is a ridge of paint at the bottom of the walls where the beading used to be.

'She's a good granny, Joleen,' Meredith says when we are out of earshot. 'Makes sure the kids eat breakfast every morning before school. Makes them do their homework.' We watch a cockroach scuttle across the chest of drawers to get to a plate dusted in toast crumbs. Meredith frowns. 'It's hard to keep the cockroaches out when you've got gaps between the floor and the walls. A lot of kids do a lot worse. At least these guys get a backyard to play in.'

I cross the floor to look through the window at the lawn that sweeps all the way to the back fence. The wardrobe rocks with my footsteps and I shoot out an arm in defence.

'I know, right?' says Meredith. 'Imagine if that came down on one of the kids.'

'The front foot needs chocking with cardboard.'

Meredith laughs, a dark snort that echoes Joleen's. 'Not quite the solution that's needed here.' She points to the corner of the room. 'Check that out. You'll have to dig for it.'

The placement of the wardrobe has created one of those awkward spaces in a room that are useless for anything other than a dumping ground. The corner is piled with clothes, a conglomerate of pastel colours. I dig, pulling aside pale blue pyjama bottoms and socks patterned with faded My Little Ponies. My fingertips dive into something soft and wet. I actually hear a squelch and then breathe in a puff of mould. I pull my hand away and liquid drips onto the clothes.

'Here,' Meredith passes me a wet wipe from her bag. 'I come prepared.'

I clean my fingers and pick through the remaining clothes. An orange, now split open, nests in the folds of a pink fleece jumper. I pass it to Meredith, taking care to keep it intact, and she transfers it to the plate with the crumbs. I move the jumper and the tracksuit pants that lie underneath, finally exposing the floor. Similar to the rest of the room, the beading at the base of the wall is gone, but instead of a two-centimetre gap between the floor and the wall, the floorboards are shattered, long shards drooping downwards and leaving fist-sized holes that reveal the space under the house. I prod the ends, feeling the spongey wood, the cellulose eaten away by the white-bodied colony that lives somewhere within marching distance of the house.

'How long has it been like this?' I ask, rocking back on my haunches and steadying myself with my hands.

'Not long after Joleen moved in so, maybe two years.'

'And the Department knows about it?'

'Yep.'

'And what did they say?'

'It couldn't be white ants because the house has been treated.'

'Right.'

'Yeah. Good logic there, hey?'

'What do they say it is then?'

'The kids must have broken it.'

'How?'

'They weren't clear.'

'But this is obvious white ant damage. You can feel it. Has anyone come out to inspect it?'

Meredith gives another one of her dark snorts.

CHAPTER TWENTY-TWO

Meredith takes me to the Wright tenancy, then we stop at a deli for lunch.

'I usually try to time it so I'm in the area at midday. Best continental rolls in Perth, but you've got to be early, or they're all gone.'

We get lucky and take our rolls to a picnic table between the shopfront and the carpark. Meredith jams one end into her mouth, rips it off and chews. I do the same. I'm hungrier than I thought and get halfway through mine before I come up for air. Meredith scratches the side of her mouth and I wipe mine and suck a glob of pickled eggplant off my finger.

'They're adorable, aren't they, the Wrights?' she says.

I nod, washing down the roll with water from my bottle. William and Barbara – Bill and Ben – Wright live in a blue fibro cottage buried in pots of rose geraniums, fishbone ferns, cyclamen, and pansies. They chatted to us over milky tea in bouncing sentences and hard Gs. *Ten-pound Poms*, they told me, *and proud of it*. They'd raised three children since coming over on the boat and had lived in the blue house since Bill retired after he fell from a roof at work. He tapped his leg with his cane and grinned at the hard knocking sound it made.

'I always said he had hollow legs, and now he's got a real one,' laughed his wife.

'Shame I didn't land on my head,' said Bill. 'Would've done less damage.'

'I see them every six months,' Meredith says, munching on her roll. 'Never any problems, although the department takes advantage.'

She switches to a Scouse accent. 'I don't like to complain, love, but do you think you could get them to look at the hot water? They don't return my calls and we've been having cold showers for the last month.'

Meredith slides the Abadi file between us and scoops up the sliced olives that have fallen onto the bare tabletop. She tosses them into her mouth. 'We'll go see Aaron on the way back to the office. This is his first time in public housing and I'm hoping it won't be for long. He's a nice man, got a cute kid, gets on with his ex. It's just a shame he lost his job. It wasn't his fault. His employer lost a major contract and didn't have the work. I'm hoping he'll pick something up soon.'

'There's plenty of work out there.'

'Yeah,' Meredith grimaces. 'Problem is, one of the big contractors was going to take him on and he didn't pass the pre-employment medical.'

'Drug screen?' I ask, thinking of the pathology request form in Jack's apartment.

'Yeah. Meth. He told me it was a one-off and he's never taken it before.'

'Right.'

Meredith shrugs. 'Maybe he has, maybe he hasn't. I told him it doesn't matter, just to make sure he doesn't do it again.'

We gossip about Weymouth on the way to Aaron Abadi's apartment. Meredith was in the same year at school as Dave's girlfriend. They stayed at Meredith's house the last time they were in the city and, according to Meredith, she's just what Dave needs to keep him in line. Not that it should be a woman's job, she points out as she shunts the SUV through another orange light. And Jack, she says, could do with a partner too. She wonders out loud if he prefers men or women and I say *women* maybe a little too definitely. I see her smirk out of the corner of my eye.

'Maybe we should all get together for a drink next time they're here,' she says. The handbrake screeches, and she opens the car door. 'Come inside and meet our Aaron.'

*

This apartment block is a good forty years older than Harbour Lights. The staircases on each end are open and evaporative air-conditioning units jut from windows. The building casts shadows over the surrounding 1940s bungalows, and the footpath is slippery with damp and smells of figs. It's in a part of the city where single-storey homes are being sacrificed to infill, taking advantage of the nearby train line and hipster shopping strip. From the third floor, I can see the central business district through an orange haze that will blow away in an hour when the wind turns. If this building wasn't government-owned, it would have already been sold and redeveloped with three times the number of apartments.

Meredith knocks on the screen door at number fourteen. It rattles and she opens it to knock again on the solid core front door.

'Coming!' calls a man's voice from inside, and a heartbeat later, the lock clicks and the door swings open. Aaron Abadi beams at Meredith and gives me a generous smile. 'Welcome! You must be Frances. Meredith said you were coming.' He offers tea, shuffles us to a cracked leather couch covered in a checked picnic rug and, after putting the kettle on, sits himself on a yellow plastic stool with fat, rounded legs. His knees prop up well above his hips and he leans his elbows on them, hunched over.

'Meredith said you work for some government watchdog,' he says, repeating Joleen's line from earlier in the day. 'I bet you see some things.'

'Frances is OK,' interjects Meredith, 'I knew her in school.'

'You're from Weymouth? Been up there lately?'

'Just last week,' I reply. 'Went up to see my dad. He was in hospital.'

'Yeah, Meredith said that's why you couldn't come last week. I'm sorry to hear it. Is he OK now?' His question is warm. I like him and find myself smiling and nodding reassuringly. He tucks a dark curl behind his ear, and I silently curse when I catch myself doing the same.

'He is, yeah, thanks.' I return my hand to my lap.

'I worked up there on that new Department of Housing block of flats.'

I suppress a smirk. I'd love to see Duncan hear his baby called a block of flats.

'I didn't know I'd be living in public housing myself in two years,' he adds.

'Things will turn around for you, Aaron,' says Meredith, 'don't you worry. Just keep on the straight and narrow and you'll have a job in no time.'

'Yeah, I messed up there, hey? Won't happen again.'

I believe him. He looks too clean, his skin too fresh, his apartment too cosy, to be a meth-head. Maybe he was telling the truth, maybe it was a one-off.

'What did you say your name was again?' He leans forward and my limbs loosen.

'Frances Geller.'

'I thought so. I've watched your brother play. Fastest man on the wing I've ever seen. The way he shepherded that ball ...' He shakes his head and smiles.

The looseness abandons me, and a familiar weight lands on my chest. 'I stayed in one of those apartments when I was there,' I say. Meredith gives me a look. 'They're pretty flash for government housing.'

Aaron frowns at the abrupt change of topic and glances at Meredith. 'Yeah, they've been finished well. Underneath, though, the structure is the same as everywhere else. Nothing special. In a few years, it won't look much different to this, depending on the punishment it gets.'

Meredith asks Aaron if everything is going well with his tenancy. She asks if the department has visited lately, what the neighbours are like, whether he is receiving his monthly statements, and whether they are accurate. He tells her that he is still waiting on someone to come out and fix the window in the bathroom. It's jammed shut and mould is growing around the frame and in the grout. He's worried that if it gets out of hand, he'll be blamed for it and lose his bond.

'What about the extraction fan, does that help?' Meredith asks.

'Nah, it's broken. I'm waiting for it to be replaced.' He shrugs. 'They don't cost much. Maybe I'll do it myself, fix the window as well while I'm at it.'

'Well, it's an option,' Meredith concedes, 'but make sure you get the department's permission first. Does it need to be wired in?'

'No idea.'

'Don't go doing any electrical work.'

'I won't.' He grins at her in exactly the same way my dad used to do when he was reassuring my mum. I don't believe him for a minute and grin back at him.

'What did you mean by *punishment*?' I ask.

He looks sheepish. 'I don't mean to judge, but some tenants, well, they don't know how to look after a place. It's not their fault, maybe they just never learned how, but doors can get banged pretty hard sometimes, windows broken. One dude, Yamatji guy next door, he was working on car parts in the living room. He had newspaper spread under them, but that will only soak up so much oil, you know?'

'That flat looks empty,' Meredith said, frowning. 'Is he still there?'

'Nah, he was evicted. Not that you'd ever know. He was quiet as. Never heard a peep out of him.'

She writes in her notebook. 'Well, unless there's anything else, Aaron, we'll head back to the office.'

'Nah, I'm good. I'll let you know about the bathroom.'

'Ta. Look after yourself and your boy.'

'Will do.'

He sees us out and Meredith pauses at the window next door. It is covered with a pull-down blind. She mutters something about checking the tenant's file and we walk to the end of the balcony.

'Nice to meet you, Frances,' Aaron calls from the front door as we turn down the open stairwell. I look back, and he's waving. 'Careful on those stairs, they can be slippery.'

CHAPTER TWENTY-THREE

Our meeting with the Assistant Director for Homelessness Strategies is delayed by my trip home and then again by Neil's availability for a pre-meeting briefing, but Belinda and I eventually get to speak with Duncan Wolf this week. His executive assistant tells us it will be at the north metropolitan office, not the corporate head office in the city. Duncan is being strategic. I knew he wouldn't dare schedule a meeting with Neil at a suburban office, but he wants me to know I'm far enough down the food chain to be forced to get in the car and drive out to meet him on his terms. It doesn't make a difference anyway. On the day he is available, we are finishing up in the north and his office is a mere walk down the corridor.

He keeps us waiting. We are still squashed in behind Colin and have packed away the last of the files by the time his EA comes to fetch us. He's not actually in his office when she ushers us inside and she has a panicked look on her face when she says he was here just now and she's sure he won't be far away. When he returns, he's wiping his hands on his trousers. We both remain seated when he offers his hand.

'So good to see you again, Frances. Belinda.' He eases himself into a high-backed leather chair behind his desk and sighs. 'I hear you're finishing up here today.'

'We are, yes,' I confirm. 'Your staff have been very cooperative.'

'But you're running behind schedule. Will the commissioner still meet his tabling deadline?'

'As a matter of fact, he will. We have contingency in the project plan.'

'Of course you do, Frances, of course.' He leans back and places his elbows on the arms of the chair. The action makes his over-large jacket flop open, and I can see that even more flesh has fallen from his chest. I wonder how he's done it. At this rate, he's going to need a new suit. 'How's your dad?'

I ignore him. 'We have some feedback for you today, if you don't mind, Duncan. Some indicative findings from the east metropolitan region.'

Duncan sits forward again. 'You'll provide me with a written copy, I assume?'

'Of course we will.' I take a sheet of paper out of my folder and slide it across the table to him. 'As you know, we've been auditing the defects process and checking whether all identified construction issues have been addressed before practical completion is confirmed by the department's project managers.'

Duncan hums as he runs his eyes down the page. I explain that the project managers have been diligent in holding their building contractors to account. Duncan stops humming and gives us a satisfied smirk.

'Except one.' I point to a spot halfway down the page. 'The project manager in charge of the Dryandra Estate has signed off on the installation of roof insulation, but our inspector says it's missing from one in five residences.' I wait while he takes this in. The humming starts again. He looks out the window.

'That's disappointing,' he says. 'Sloppy. We've had performance problems with this chap before. I'll speak with him and have him rectify it.'

'It might be more than sloppy, I'm afraid. The same insulation company won contracts for other estates in the east metro district. We're going back to check those next week.'

'Same project manager?' Duncan asks.

'Yes.'

He sighs. 'So it's not a one-off. Grounds for dismissal.'

'If we find anything, it will be serious misconduct and possibly even fraud.'

'If I remember correctly' – Duncan actually steeples his fingers and I will Belinda not to snigger – 'he's not a permanent public servant, he's just here on a fixed-term contract. It will be easy to remove him if it is misconduct. In fact, I might terminate his contract anyway. We can't have sloppy work like this. It's a distraction.'

'How the department chooses to manage the issue is up to you; however, we do need a written response so we can acquit it in the report.'

'Of course. I assume you won't need to go back to the east metropolitan office if we terminate?'

'I think we will anyway, Duncan. Just to be sure.' I can't quite keep the satisfaction out of my voice, and I feel Belinda shift in her seat.

Fifteen minutes later we are across the road in a coffee shop eating cheesecake. Belinda has already steepled her fingers twice, cracking herself up and spraying crumbs across the table.

'It doesn't matter how many fixed-term project managers he throws under a bus,' she says, 'it still has to be in the report. The minister will chew him out.'

'Will he though? Simon Tallent doesn't seem like the chewing kind.'

'Maybe not, but when he's facing the wrath of Jaelyn Worner, he might feel the need to push people under a bus himself.'

Belinda is right. Jaelyn will be onto this, whether or not it's an isolated case of sloppy project management. She'll claim it's a deliberate attempt by the government to save money at the expense of public housing tenants' health and safety. She'll drag a single mum with four kids outside their house on the hottest day in summer with a thermometer showing the temperature in her children's bedrooms. One of the children will have a chronic medical condition that flares up in the heat.

'Look out,' says Belinda, nodding at the door. Meredith strides in, red-faced and flustered.

'Oh good, I caught you,' she gasps. 'Duncan's EA said you might be here. Do you have a few minutes?'

'Sure, take a seat.'

'I'll go back up,' Belinda offers.

'No, you're good, stay.' Meredith flaps her hand at her and sits down.

'You know Aaron, who we met on Monday? Remember he had a neighbour who was evicted? Aaron thought it was because he damaged the floor. Car parts and oil and stuff.'

I nod.

'I pulled his file. The tenant's name is Richard Cameron, a Yamatji man from up our way. That was his first tenancy, although he's lived in public housing before when he was a kid. There's nothing on his file about the floor damage, not even anything about housekeeping or maintenance. Nothing. He's been a perfect tenant for two years.'

'Maybe Aaron got it wrong. Maybe he was evicted for something else.'

'He was, I spoke with his tenancy manager. Unruly behaviour, neighbour complaints, drunkenness.'

'Drugs?'

'Not the kid I know.'

Belinda snorts. I know what she's thinking. She had the same look on her face when I told her about Aaron and his one-off positive drug test. Meredith glares at her.

'Ever been drunk, a bit rowdy maybe?' she snaps.

'Yeah, once or twice.'

'Exactly. Doesn't mean you're doing meth in the toilets at work, does it?' Belinda shrinks and Meredith turns back to me. 'Remember Aaron said he never heard boo from him? Kind of makes the unruly behaviour part difficult to believe. And TAG's known Richard for years. We've been visiting his family since he was in high school. He finished year twelve, got an apprenticeship. A real success story. He lost his job when the company went under, but he's not the first person that's happened to, and he hasn't caused any trouble since he moved in.'

'Except for fixing car parts on the floor of his rental,' I point out.

'His mum said that's how he's been making money. And anyway, there's no reported damage. He's not a bad kid.'

'Maybe he just went on a couple of benders and was unlucky to have a snarky neighbour. Even good kids do that.'

'I'm not buying it.' Meredith shakes her head, clenches her jaw. 'Anyway, Richard's mum says he's living in the bush camp down near the refineries on the coast. I'm going to go visit him, get his side of the story. Want to come?'

I feel rather than see the ceiling slide above me. My stomach rises. 'Why isn't he back with his mum?'

'Doesn't get on with the new man. I'm going on the weekend. Apparently, that's the best time to catch him.' She narrows her eyes. I know my forehead is sweating. 'Do you have a problem with that? You won't see any worse than you did the other day.'

'No, I'm good, but what about the complaints? Aren't they on file?'

'No, nothing there. But that's not unusual, there's often a lag. They'll be sitting in someone's inbox waiting to be archived.'

We make a time for Meredith to pick me up from my apartment and she bounces back out of the café. Belinda is quiet in the car on the way back to the office. I figure she's smarting from Meredith's crack. I leave her alone so I can feed my own anxieties. I've been to the bush camp before. Just the once. Around thirty people live there, in tents and humpies screened from the trucks and commuters by coastal scrub. From time to time, it makes the headlines because it's been threatened by fire, or a bad strain of influenza has ripped through the camp. Or someone dies. Mostly people are happy to leave it alone. I'm one of those people.

I pull into the basement carpark and Belinda speaks up.

'You know, we have access to that database. The one with the drug-test results.'

'We do? Who gave us that?'

'The lab. That police inquiry follow-up that Bigfoot allocated to James? He needed access. They didn't like it and he had to sign a confidentiality agreement, but they gave him a login. We could look up Richard, see if he's ever been tested for drugs.'

I pretend to be concentrating on getting the car into the only bay that's vacant on our allocated section of the basement. It's not like Belinda to suggest something that we are expressly prohibited from doing. But she's got a point. The information is there for the taking. The only problem is the access log. Some people who appear in government databases are tagged. Police officers, politicians, criminals. You can't access their information without an alert being triggered. Even I have a tag on my records. You can't look up my driver's licence without a red light flashing on a government desk somewhere. If I inadvertently set off one of those red lights, I'd have some difficult questions to answer.

Belinda steps in before I work out what to say.

'It wouldn't help Meredith though. It's not like she can use the information if she obtains it illegally.'

'No, she can't.'

'Yeah, sorry. Forget I mentioned it.'

CHAPTER TWENTY-FOUR

Duncan is as good as his word. By the time I am summoned to Neil's office the next day, he has sacked the project manager and sent us a hand-wringing letter for our files. It is on Neil's desk when I enter. Neil rests on hand on it and tells me *well done*.

'Thanks, boss,' I answer. Neil winces at the honorific. 'It was all Belinda, though, she's the one who did the hard work.'

'I'll make sure I congratulate her, um, when I do my rounds.' He winces again, as though caught out in a deliberate ploy to ingratiate himself to the staff. I want to tell him that we love him for doing it even though he hates it, but that will only make him more embarrassed. 'Admirable that the department acted quickly,' he says. 'It'll look good for them when the report is tabled. How'd you get on at the east metropolitan office today?'

We'd got on splendidly. We'd even been allocated an enclosed office, offered coffee, and provided with a neat stack of project files for the Agonis and Melaleuca estates. Every hour on the hour, the district manager knocked politely on the door and asked us if we needed anything. He'd even let me use his office to take a call on the landline. *Phone call for you, Ms Geller,* he'd said, rubbing the back of his neck and showing me the way.

We worked through the defects reports in the files, checking each item against the purchase orders, invoices, photographs and project manager sign-offs. I was in heaven. I had a long list of ticks and crosses running down my spreadsheet, but it wasn't until the afternoon that we had our big breakthrough. Belinda took her own phone call, and when she returned, she was bouncing.

'We were right,' she said as she closed the door behind her.

'That was Kim. It's not just the Dryandra Estate, it's Agonis and Melaleuca as well.'

Kim is the building inspector we use on our inquiries when we have to do something more active than scrutinise invoices. He'd been onsite all morning, climbing in roof spaces and checking whether the insulation had been laid.

Belinda leaned over the notes she'd written. 'There's no insulation installed in sections one and two of Agonis, or in sections one and three of Melaleuca.'

'So, maybe forty percent of the units haven't been done?'

'About that, yeah.'

'Bastards.'

'And the project manager's signed off on practical completion?'

'He sure has. And approved payment.' Belinda passed me the practical completion sign-off and the invoice approval. The project manager's signature was scratched across both documents. 'So,' she said, lowering her voice and glancing at the closed door, 'do you think it's sloppy or deliberate?'

'It could be either. Certainly, deliberate on the part of the contractor. He couldn't miss noticing that forty percent of the product is still sitting on the back of his truck.'

'Unless he didn't order it in the first place.'

'Yeah, unless he didn't order it in the first place. If that's the case, it's planned, not sloppy. But either way, it's material enough to report to the fraud squad.'

I tell this to Neil and his head nods up and down, his eyes on the opposite wall. He can see another Alston. Sacking the project manager won't cut it now.

'I suppose you'd better draft a letter to the police commissioner,' he says. 'I'll send it today. And speak with public affairs to arrange a media release.'

'Will do.' I stay seated and he glances at the clock above my head and swallows.

'Is there anything else?'

'Actually, yes.' I've learned from Eric to hold the best for last. I brief him on my phone call for the next fifteen minutes. When I finish, we agree to hold off on the media release. I go back to the pod to tell James I'll be pulling rank over his trip to the South West and visiting Riverside Seniors' Housing myself.

*

We end the week with our first beer in the new pod. James bought a six-pack of Coronas at lunchtime, marvelling at the good fortune of having a bottle shop within walking distance of the office. We clink our bottles together and tilt them at Belinda.

'Your first fraud case,' James says. 'Well done.'

'We don't know if the police will lay charges yet.' She hedges, but her eyes are shining, and she has a satisfied smile on her lips. 'It could turn out to be as Duncan claims, just sloppy.'

'Nah. More likely to be corruption than incompetence.'

'Isn't that supposed to be the other way around?' I ask.

'Not when you've been around the block as many times as I have. Eric would have agreed with me.' We're silent until he adds, 'And anyway, the fraud squad will ping the contractor. That one's a no-brainer.' He stands and drains his bottle. 'And the Opposition, not to mention the media, will have a field day with this whole private-sector landlords thing. Good luck getting that one through the court of public approval now.'

James is right, the Hon. Simon Tallent will have to answer some difficult questions about how his department will manage a private sector housing programme when they can't keep tabs on their existing contractors. I'm guessing any future supermarket encounters might not be as jovial as the last one.

'I'm off.' James' bottle clunks into the bin and he picks up his backpack. 'Enjoy the game tomorrow night. And boss, stick to the speed limit on Monday. It's not the Mid West where there's only one patrol car every five hundred kilometres.'

Belinda shuffles her papers into her mobile pedestal, and I turn back to my screen as a new email flashes to the top. It's Kerry, the village manager at Riverside. She's looking forward to seeing me on Monday morning and reminds me that there is usually a speed camera just after the turn-off from the highway. It seems everyone has my demerit points at heart.

'I'm done too,' says Belinda. 'How about you?'

'No,' I wave her away, 'I need to review this media release. You go. I'll see you at the gate at six tomorrow. Don't forget your scarf.'

'I won't. Don't stay too late.'

I stay for another hour then take the bus home past the park. Uplights have been switched on at the base of the lemon-scented gums and they glow alternating colours of blue and yellow in anticipation of the game this weekend. As the bus trundles west, empty except for me and two other slumped office workers, the rest of the park is a solid, dark mass.

Both of my exhausted travelling companions leave at the stop nearest the fish and chip shop. One walks inside, the other sets off at pace toward the bottle shop four doors down. She wears a pretty skirt with a fitted waist and a pattern of bright orange and red flowers. In the bus, it had flowed over her knees and now as she walks, it swishes with her steps. I look down at my own black pencil skirt, and the white blouse that is tucked into the waistband. I don't do colour at work. I can't think of the last time I chose an item of clothing with a pattern other than a team scarf. I have an unexpected and unwanted mental image of Bigfoot and stretch my feet out in front to examine my shoes. They are black, but at least today they have a heel, and a bow on the toe.

I buy myself a takeaway laksa at the restaurant on the corner of my building and take the two covered and environmentally inappropriate Styrofoam bowls up to my apartment. I haven't cooked all week and a pile of plastic containers is sitting on my draining board. People like me are killing the planet. I pour the noodles, soup, and delicious seafood of questionable origin into one bowl and set myself up at the kitchen table. I sit down, get up again, and fetch a bottle of wine from the fridge. I fill my glass, a *South African pour*, as Eric used to say, referring to pubs that apparently don't have lines etched into their glassware to indicate the standard sizes of drinks.

I contemplate my screen as I drain half the glass. The wine is sweet, a chenin blanc from down south. I put the glass down, stretch my back, and run my hands through my hair. My lips are dry, and I wipe them with my tongue, tasting the sugar from the wine. The soup is still too hot to eat, so I take a spoonful of the coconut liquid from the edge of the bowl and slurp. It runs down my throat, more peppery than I anticipated and I cough, splattering the screen with oily, yellow spots. I use a tissue to smear them across the glass, take a deep breath, and type the URL for the state forensics laboratory into my search engine.

The databases tab is in the main menu. I follow the dropdown box to the one I want and click on the Staff Login button. It brings up a confidentiality agreement box, outlined in double red. *By accessing the State Forensic Laboratory Database, I agree to use the information contained within for the sole purpose of…* Yeah, whatever. I've assessed the risk of getting caught and figure with only ten records to check, I'd have to be pretty unlucky that any of them will have a security tag. I click to confirm that I understand and agree to my obligations and type in James' email address. The password is easy: Belinda, with a *3* instead of a *B* and an exclamation mark instead of an *i*. When the system rejects it, I add her birthyear and I'm in.

I retrieve the savaged A5 sheet of paper with the green serial numbers from under the photography book and lay it out next to the beheaded spreadsheet that I promised I would discuss with

Bigfoot. As I thought, the numbers are the same.

The database is searchable by case number and item number. I decide to try case numbers first. I type in the first number at the top of the green inked list and hit the enter key. *Please enter a valid case number*, the system asks. I re-type it, six numbers, a space, then three letters, and I'm rejected again. I try the second number, then the third, until I've worked my way down the list. The system rejects them all. Eric's numbers are not case numbers.

I refill my glass and try for item numbers. I imagine pressing the enter key and watching the screen load to reveal a bloodstained shirt or maybe the kitchen knife that belonged to the murderous mining camp chef. I've never been to the state forensics lab. Eric went, but only after a long back and forth between Neil and the attorney-general, who claimed that the lab's location was necessarily secret, the address provided on a need-to-know basis. Neil said that parliamentary oversight of executive government was a sufficient need-to-know. The attorney-general said that, as the chief law officer in the state, he believed that was an incorrect reading of Neil's legislative powers. Neil said, fine, let's ask the courts to decide. The attorney-general changed his mind but refused to give Neil the address and insisted on Eric being driven there by one of his staff. Apparently, the staffer didn't get the joke when Eric whipped out a blindfold to wear in the car.

I start at the top again and type the first of the green numbers into the item number box. Instead of a photo of a bloody knife, I get another system request. *Please enter a valid item number.* I try the second, third, and fourth numbers on Eric's list, but I know I'm defeated. The torn page isn't the smoking gun I was hoping for.

CHAPTER TWENTY-FIVE

It's Saturday and Belinda and I are back at the stadium watching the AFL. The home team is up by fourteen points, but we haven't scored a major since the second quarter and the visitors are closing the lead. They score again and the ball goes back to the middle. We have the biggest, heaviest ruckman on the ground, and he goes up and taps the ball to the midfield, who sends it hand over hand into our fifty. Belinda yells *just kick the damn thing* and Venter boots the ball to the goal square. It goes to ground, and everyone piles on. We can't see who has possession. Neither can the umpire. He blows the whistle and prepares to throw it up. The big men fly again, but it's Venter who comes in over the top and takes the mark. The crowd explodes. Scarves are waved. We hold our breath as he tucks his mouthguard into his socks and checks his shoelaces. He lines up. The clock counts down. He kicks, and it goes through. The siren sounds and we go into the fourth quarter back to a fourteen-point lead.

'I need to pee,' says Belinda, and pushes her way through the row. Everyone is standing, stretching their legs, and talking to the people behind them. The woman who has the reserved seats next to me unscrews the lid of her thermos and pours the last of her tea. She always brings a ziplock bag of jelly snakes and offers me one. I choose green and bite off its head.

'We'd be trailing without Venter,' she says. 'That's his fourth goal today.'

'He reads the play better than any of our other forwards.'

'And he's fit. And fresh. The whole package.' She twinkles at me. 'And he's single, too.'

'Hey, you said you'd show me photos of your new grandson this week,' I remind her. She digs in her backpack, and we spend the rest of the break cooing over a chubby baby swaddled in team colours.

Belinda misses the first five minutes of the final quarter and the first of three goals that the visitors kick in succession to take the lead for the first time since the start of the game.

'That's the way to do it, lads,' says the guy with the orange dreadlocks who sits behind us. 'Keep it interesting. Keep us guessing. Don't want us to get complacent now.'

The next three shots at goal are ours and we kick behinds each time.

'I hope the sandwiches are good at the goal-kicking clinic next week,' shouts the orange man. The crowd around us chuckles.

The visitors take the ball back down the other end. They are one point in front and have two minutes to go. They start playing kick-to-kick, running down the clock. One of our centres intercepts a lazy punt and runs the ball through the middle. He's got gas but the other team is closing in. I look for the shepherd on the wing, can almost picture Matt on the centre's right flank, arms out, calling for the ball, but of course he's not there.

I can't breathe. Our guy bounces once, twice, and kicks toward goal just as he gets taken down. There's no-one in the goal square and the ball dribbles through. We are back in the lead.

The ball goes to the centre again. We get clean possession out of the ruck but from there the final three minutes are scrappy and literally pointless. The siren sounds and the crowd rises, victorious.

Belinda and I sing along to the team song and wave our scarves in the air. I press one end of mine into my eyes without Belinda noticing. The team goes into a huddle on the ground and then breaks apart to take mini Sherrins to the kids in the crowd. Venter heads toward our block and Belinda squeals. She grabs my hand and pulls me along our row and down the stairs, bumping people aside. We end up on the fence as he arrives.

'He won't give you a ball, you know,' I tell her. 'They're for the kids.'

'Get something for him to sign,' she gasps. 'Quick.' We both reach into our bags, and I pull something out first. I thrust it into his hand as I realise it is the photo from Eric's mobile pedestal.

'Hey, cool,' he looks up from the photo and into my face. I feel myself blush, am mortified and blush even deeper. 'Where are you from?' His voice is deep and oddly authoritative for a young man.

'Weymouth.'

'Up north? So not from South Africa, then?' He looks disappointed.

'No, sorry.'

'My parents used to take me camping here when we were kids,' he says, tapping his finger on the faded riverbank. 'Have you been?'

I shake my head.

'I hope you get to go someday. It's magic.'

He signs the back of the photo and accepts the store receipt that Belinda pushes at him.

'Nice, are you wearing it today?'

Belinda twirls.

'Good choice, the colour suits you.'

He turns away from us and I watch as he talks to a small boy through the fence. The boy's dad lifts him up so he can hear over the crowd. I do a double take. The dad is Aaron, in a team cap and scarf. Venter holds out his arms and pulls the boy over the fence and onto his hip. Aaron gives the boy his scarf, which Venter gently wraps around his neck, and they pose for the camera. The boy beams and the crowd sighs. When he's back at his dad's feet, he raises his hand for a high five and then runs around himself in the tight space between his dad and the fence. Aaron ruffles his head and then turns to me.

'Hey, Frances.' He raises his hand in the air even though he is only four feet away.

'Hey, Aaron, how's things?'

He pushes his way through the crowd. 'So you're an Eagles supporter, then.'

'It's mandatory for anyone living north of the river.'

'Ah, so that's how they became the biggest club in the country.'

I tap the side of my nose and he laughs. Belinda nudges me.

'Hi, I'm Belinda,' she says, hand outstretched. He takes it and gives her a warm smile. I feel the tiniest clench in my jaw.

'Enjoy the game?'

'Sure did. It's always good when we come out in front.'

'The umpires didn't help though.'

'Do they ever?

'What will they do when there are two West Australian teams in the grand final?'

'Take the day off, I guess.'

Belinda squats in front of Aaron's son, who has directed his interest back to the ground where the team mascot is performing backflips.

'Who's your favourite player?'

He looks at her as though she's lost her mind. 'Venter.' He turns back to the fence shaking his head like the union officials in the carpark. 'Of course.'

She looks back up at us and makes an *o* with her mouth.

'Sass. I like it. What's your name?'

'Declan.'

'My name's Belinda. Pleased to meet you, Declan.' She holds out her hand. He considers it, then looks up at his dad. Aaron nods, and Declan allows his hand to be shaken for the briefest of seconds before returning it to the fence in a solid grip. I watch him run it up and down the rail, getting rid of the girl germs.

Aaron asks me about the inquiry, and I tell him about my exciting life reconciling contractor payments and project sign-offs. I ask him about his job hunting and he tells me he has an interview with a building contractor next week.

'They've got a few projects on the go. Multistorey residential. More housing for poor people.' He gives me a lopsided smile.

I find myself smiling back. 'We need it. The public housing waiting list isn't getting any shorter.'

'Now you're sounding like Meredith.'

'I don't have half Meredith's energy.'

'No-one does. She's like the Energizer bunny. She told me she's found my neighbour, Richard, said he's sleeping rough. I hear you're going to see him tomorrow.'

I nod, just the once and feel my throat close over and my smile fall. I'd been trying to forget my promise to visit the bush camp. He frowns, not understanding. 'Don't worry, you'll be okay with Meredith, she knows her way around. Just don't ask too many questions. The folks down there might be homeless, but they're not public property. They like their privacy.' Declan tugs at his dad's scarf. 'Looks like it's time to go. Good to see you again. Nice to meet you, Belinda.'

'You too, Aaron.'

'Good luck with the interview next week,' I call out to him as they turn back through the thinning crowd. He looks over his shoulder, smiles, and waves. Belinda nudges me again.

'Damn, Fran. You kept him a secret.'

'There's no secret to keep.'

'Really? Look at him. Straight off the front cover of a romance novel. That hair. Those eyelashes. Don't tell me you didn't notice.'

'He's just another cute single dad who spends too much time at the gym. They're a dime a dozen in this city.'

Belinda cackles and I tell her to hurry up, we've got a train to catch, and turn my burning face into the crowd.

*

Belinda gets off the train at the city station and I continue on down the Fremantle line. The win has lifted my spirits – probably not as much as the wine we drank – but as I look out through the dark windows, I keep picking at the problem of the serial numbers. I was certain the forensics database would deliver them. For no reason whatsoever, I'm convinced that the format looks scientific, like the numbers belong with men in white coats and sterile laboratories. I feel like I'm missing something that is just out of reach.

My mind keeps churning as I get off the train and walk through the station to the end of my street. It was a late game and even the corner supermarket with its extended trading hours is closed. The street parking that is usually nose-to-nose with vehicles in the daytime is empty except for a blue Mercedes in the universal parking bay in front of the shops. It doesn't have an ACROD sticker but I'm too tired, I've drunk too much, and I don't have the energy to photograph the numberplate and report it. I swipe myself into the lobby, press the lift button and wait.

Nothing happens.

I grope in my handbag for my phone to check the building management updates. I'm still searching when the lobby doors swish open and one of my neighbours walks in. We are wearing the same scarves.

'Good win tonight, hey?' He nods at a handwritten note tacked to the wall, which of course I did not read. 'The lift's out. You'll need to take the stairs.' He ushers me through the door to the emergency stairwell, tuts at the brick that's been used to chock it open, and with a cheery wave, jogs up the steps. The door closes behind me with a definitive click.

I'm not good with stairwells. I avoid them if I can. The narrow spaces can make it difficult for me to get a vertical fix, even when I don't have three glasses of wine in me. Admittedly, the stairwell in our building is one of the better ones. It's well lit and clean, although it still smells of damp concrete. Big yellow numbers announce the floor at each landing and the metal piping on the balustrade is solid and industrial. I let my hand slide along it as I step up.

I reach the first landing and turn for the next set of stairs when the spins hit. The wall circles to the right, settles back into place, then takes off again. I grip the balustrade and eyeball the corner. It slows, settles, stays in place. I lift one foot and place it on the first step, taking care to set it down heel first, where the weight is most reliable. I bring my left foot next to it and wait, keeping my eyes on my feet. I know that if I look up it will be disastrous. Nothing moves. I try again. At this rate, it will be past midnight before I get to my apartment. I wonder about giving up and spending the night on the landing, but I can feel the cold and grit of the undressed concrete through the soles of my boots and decide I've got no option but to keep going.

I heel-toe my way to the landing and turn for the next set of stairs. Above me, a door opens and closes. My neighbour, I guess, although it seems to have taken him a long time to get there. Maybe he stopped jogging once he turned the corner and was out of sight. I have two floors to go. I ease my foot onto the next step, but this time my boot heel comes down shy of the lip and slips backwards. I grab at the metal balustrade, but my foot twists to the side and my calf, knee, thigh, and hip follow in turn, scraping over the rough concrete as I twist. My fingers knock against a join in the metal pipes, and I let go with a yelp. Then my shoulder blade connects with the concrete and my head whips backwards onto the step above.

CHAPTER TWENTY-SIX

By the time I come to, blood has seeped through my tracksuit pants and onto the floor. I put my hands onto the cold concrete and crawl – actually crawl, thank God no-one saw me, how embarrassing – back up to my floor. I don't bother with undressing. I go straight to bed, in my clothes, with the doona pulled over my head to shut out the unstable world.

I wake up in the morning burrowed tight under my doona and with cold, early morning air on my face. I can see behind my eyelids that today will be another bright one with a cloudless sky. I do a stocktake. We won the game last night and are through to the finals. I've had a win at work. Eric's numbers are not from the forensics database. Aaron has nice eyes. Last night I fell up the stairs and probably have bloodstains on my clothes.

I wake up again an hour later and have to rush because Meredith is picking me up in fifteen minutes. My hip hurts and when I peel off my jeans, they reveal a line of scraped skin and emerging bruises all the way to my ankle bone. I shower, flinching as the water hits my broken skin, and find clean clothes. In the kitchen, I make coffee, eat a banana and take my meds. On the other side of my balcony windows, the tea-coloured lake is unruffled. If I open the doors, I will hear the birds, but I don't have time this morning. I return to my bedroom, both arms outstretched to avoid the door frame, and wedge my tender feet into hiking shoes. By the time Meredith calls from downstairs, I've also bolted down two pieces of vegemite toast and brushed my teeth.

Meredith is idling in the supermarket delivery dock. 'Far out, Frances, this is all right.' She leans forward to gaze through the windscreen at the edifice of my building. 'Public sector accountants must get paid well.'

'Yeah, we do okay.' That's not strictly true. Public service salaries are pretty ordinary. It was Mum's insurance company that funded my digs. Matt bought a car and a lifestyle.

The Sunday paper is neatly folded on the passenger seat, and I pick it up before climbing in. *Shots fired through window* says the headline. The photo above the fold shows a neat fibro cottage with two women standing in the driveway. Their faces have been pixelated, but there is no mistaking they are mother and daughter. Meredith glances at it. 'Pricks.'

'One of yours?'

'No, that's a privately owned house up in the hills, but I heard that the tenants are ex-public housing. One of our success stories apparently. But it seems some wankers don't like it. There was a pointed note in the letterbox. The *n* word was used.' She grinds the car into reverse and shoots us backwards into the street. Brakes screech behind us. We both turn and look through the rear window. I'm expecting shouting, but the driver, wearing sunglasses and a blue baseball cap with a fancy white logo on the crest, just shakes his head and waits for us to get out of his way. The bonnet of his car, a gleaming royal blue that matches his cap, is so close we can't see the grill. Meredith waves and mouths *sorry*, puts the car in drive and pulls away at a more considered pace.

We take the coast road south, crossing the river and skirting the port. The ocean on our right is as unruffled as the lake, all the way to the horizon. The sun picks out the aluminium hulls of fishing dinghies. Dads will be catching whiting and pink snapper, taking it home for a Sunday dinner with hot chips, beers, and cool drink for the kids. In front of us, steam rises from the stacks of the Kwinana industrial strip. Meredith turns east, away from the strip and the calm, blue ocean. I see signs for the Motorplex, a recycling plant, and a Noongar heritage trail. A truck loaded with a bobcat and limestone blocks eases its way out of a side road dredged with fine, white dust. I wrinkle my nose to suppress a sneeze and fail. We pass a sign advertising pick-your-own strawberries and I grip the door handle in readiness; the turn-off is fifty metres on our right.

Meredith flings us across the oncoming lane then abruptly slows to a crawl. We navigate the maze of sand tracks, Meredith leaning out the window and asking for Richard. I sit in the passenger seat, my feet planted, looking at my phone and trying not to see.

'Skinny kid, dark skin, looks about sixteen but he's really twenty-two.'

'Yeah, that's him.'

'Keep going and take a left at the red station wagon.'

'The kid from up north? He's been living down the back. Ask for Lenore and she'll show you.'

The tracks wind left and right, back on themselves, dead end, and finally narrow to walking tracks. Meredith noses the car into a wattle bush after a glance at my shoes. 'Good girl.'

We continue on foot, our heels digging into soft sand and our hands waving away the flies that have appeared with the sun. I can feel my bruised hip stiffening and rub it through my jeans. I hope we don't have too far to go. We left the main road ten minutes ago, but the traffic sounds close, the limestone trucks seeming to roar past only metres away. I can't see them through the bush, only the stacks from the refineries jutting into the blue sky.

We pass a station wagon and I do a double take. The mattress is still on the ground near the rear wheel arch, black with mould. Someone has cleared away the bottles and cans and closed the tailgate. Probably the same person who's moved in. Through the window I can see a grey doona spread over another mattress and two pillows placed side by side. Two plastic tubs are stacked next to the passenger door. I lean closer and see a green Milo tin and next to it a yellow packet of two-minute noodles.

'Can I help you?'

The question comes from under the same bushes that had partly shielded the mattress from the newspaper photographers. I squint into the shadow and make out a man in his sixties sitting on a low camp chair, the type you take to concerts in the park. He has a Coke in one hand and raises it to his mouth as he squints back.

'We're looking for Richard Cameron.' Meredith drops to her haunches and takes off her sunglasses. 'Do you know him?'

The man under the bush closes one eye, opens it again and returns the can to the cupholder in his chair. He twists it in, leans back, recrosses his pale ankles. 'He isn't here. Lenore put him on the bus this morning. Made him go to Centrelink.'

'On a Sunday?'

'So he could be there first thing tomorrow morning.'

'Where's he gunna sleep tonight?'

The man shrugs. 'Probably at the golf course. That's what Lenore would've told him. Away from the drinkers. Away from here.'

'How is he? Is he doing okay?'

'Of course he's not fucking doing okay. He's been hanging out here, hasn't he?' He leans forward, jams his elbows onto his thighs. 'I know who you are. You're the woman from TAG, the one that the journalists interviewed after poor Stacey died. You should know better than to ask stupid questions like that.'

'I'm just looking out for him. See if there's anything I can do.'

'Do your fucking job, that's what you can do. If you'd done that properly in the first place, that young kid wouldn't be here.'

'Shut up, Frank, leave the poor girl alone.' A woman who I guess is Lenore trudges through the sand track behind us. She's wearing thongs and making hard work of it. They're angled on her feet, so her heels sit half on the sand, half on the rubber. White patches of vitiligo pattern her legs. 'They told me someone was looking for Richard.' She plants her feet and breathes hard. Puts her hands on her hips to support her chest. 'He won't be back 'til tomorrow.'

'I'll see if I can catch him at Centrelink,' says Meredith, 'maybe get him into crisis accommodation in Fremantle.'

'Nah, not there. Richard's clean, I don't want him getting mixed up with any of that lot. He's better off sleeping in a tent down here where someone'll look out for him.' She eyeballs me and Meredith in turn and the message is clear. *We'll look after our own, thank you very much.* When her eyes settle on my face, she pauses. Nods. The fire goes out. 'Sorry for your loss, love. He was a real nice kid, your brother.'

CHAPTER TWENTY-SEVEN

On Monday morning, my phone directs me to the next exit off the south-bound freeway and then right again. Riverside Seniors' Housing is in a nice part of town, walking distance to shops and the river, and wide verges with tall street trees. There are people on the footpath, taking their time, holding the hands of toddlers and pulling wheeled shopping baskets. I drive to the end of the street, a cul-de-sac, where a high, pale wall is bordered by a thick row of agapanthus. Their purple heads are nodding in the breeze that has just started blowing. Security panels are mounted to the side of the entrance, and I can see the edges of automatic steel gates tucked behind the walls. My tyres bump as I drive over the channels set into the concrete for their wheels.

Inside the walls, covered parking bays are lined up along either side of the driveway and I swing into the nearest bay marked *Visitors Only – No Resident Parking*. The nose of my car faces a wheelchair-wide path running straight to glass doors. A sign planted in the grass at knee height points me to the office. The doors swing open and a woman with glossy brown hair and a wide smile waves both arms in the air like she's signalling an A380. This will be Kerry, the village manager. She of the speed camera advice.

I climb out of my car into the heat of the sheltered carpark. I left the city early when the easterly still had a cold bite to it, but the temperature was nudging upwards by the time I left the suburbs, and the paddocks began. It should be cooler, down here and away from the concrete and steel heat sink, but that wind crosses the desert and brings the warming land with it. Puffs and columns of bushfire smoke were already rising and drifting westward over the coastal plain. I'd had the car air-conditioning set at twenty-two degrees and stopped at the new service station on the side of the highway for an iced coffee. I scuttle to the cool of the office. I need to pee.

To my Mid West eye, the low, flat paddocks south of the city are always green, even when it's warm like this. They might not be the deep, lush green of late winter crops, but the drying grasses retain a succulence that we don't get at this time of year where I'm from. Up there, the paddocks will be the dull, no-colour of the manila folders that rode down on the passenger seat next to me. The sun and the dry air are sucking the wheat dry. In the next few weeks, the farmers will be out in the paddocks, competing for drivers and road space with the iron-ore trucks.

'How're those fires looking?' Kerry asks after I've visited the ladies room and joined her in her office. She's settled behind her desk, which is a model of organisation. Plastic binders are stacked on a wire frame, and I count sticky labels in seven different colours. 'I heard one got away from them.'

I shake my head as I try to read the labels upside down. It's a skill, a public investigator super-power. 'I don't know. They didn't look like much from the road.' The emergency services app on my phone said there was nothing near the highway, but if the smoke remained overnight, the easterly could push it into the metropolitan area, and it advised people with respiratory issues to stay alert and indoors.

'One of our oldies is worried,' she says. 'The family farm is on the other side of the national park. He keeps ringing them to check on the sheep. Wants to make sure the new people know to leave the gates open.'

I spend the morning in an air-conditioned room looking onto a pebbled courtyard with native plants and a water feature. Yellow-and-black honeyeaters dart from the branches to the fountain and back again. They shake their feathers and drops of water catch the light. Classical music floats down from a ceiling mounted speaker.

Riverside is dedicated to seniors, people who have retired on a pension and with no home of their own. For some, it's the most comfortable place they've ever lived. *I feel like I'm in paradise*, said Evie, on the front page of the *South West Herald* when it ran a puff-piece for the local member of parliament. He was standing next to the Minister for Housing squinting into the sun under the headline. *A New Era in Public Housing.* Duncan stood on the other side, the three of them looming behind the tiny woman in their dark suits. The article said that Evie raised four children with her husband, John, who passed away two years ago. In the photo, she cradled a grey poodle. Even in the black-and-white newsprint I could see he had cataracts.

The files for Riverside are waiting for me in two neat stacks next to a plate of biscuits and a thermos of coffee. Kerry assures me I can have real coffee if I prefer. The residents, she says, run a café on the ground floor and some of them are accomplished baristas. I work through the first stack of files, comparing the defects reports to the project manager's paperwork and making ticks and crosses on my spreadsheet. I'm happy as a clam. The coffee is strong, and the biscuits are homemade, with flecks of macadamia and white chocolate. They're definitely not gluten-free. James will be disappointed when I tell him about the hospitality. I feel bad for usurping him and making the trip myself, but the guilt doesn't last long. I wonder if I'll be given lunch.

At noon, Kerry knocks on the door and asks if I would like to join her and the President of the Residents' Association in the café. Of course I would. She locks the door to my room, takes me to the ladies room to freshen up, and walks me through the gardens to the café. There is a stream of people heading in the same direction.

'Monday is Chinese day,' she says. 'Very popular.'

The smell of oyster sauce, chilli and frying meat draws us inside the café, where red paper lanterns are strung on either side of the entrance. I salivate despite the midmorning biscuits. Kerry takes us to a window table where an elderly man in a light brown suit is sitting with his hands folded together on the white tablecloth. He stands when we arrive and shakes my hand. He is terribly thin, and for a moment I have an image of future-Duncan. It occurs to me that my nemesis' weight loss might not be intentional, and I make a mental note to ask Neil when I'm back in the office.

'Welcome, Frances,' says the thin man, 'I'm Geoff Andrews, President of the Residents' Association. The vice-president was to be joining us today to make a lunchtime foursome, but I'm afraid he had to take his wife to the city for a medical appointment. My wife, Elaine, has joined us instead.'

Elaine beams at me from her chair and pats the seat next to her.

'Nothing too serious, I hope,' I reply as I sit where I'm invited.

'Just the usual six-monthly check-up. It's all part of getting old. You'll have to do it too if you're blessed to get to our age.'

'I'm sure Frances and her generation will live longer than any of us, Geoff.'

'I'm sure she will, my dear, I'm sure she will. Frances, can I get you something to drink? We have wine and beer, or you might prefer a soft drink if you are working.'

It's an instruction rather than a suggestion. 'Just an orange juice please,' I reply.

'Good choice, I'll have the same. And you, Kerry?'

Kerry opts for water and Geoff rises onto his skinny legs again and heads toward the bar, his hands moving across the backs of chairs and his head nodding to the residents on either side.

'Geoff has been president here since we opened,' Kerry tells me. 'I've learned so much from him. He's still a warden of the church across the road.'

Geoff returns, followed by a younger woman carrying a tray of drinks and a man balancing four bowls of meat, vegetables and rice. An extra pot of chilli is placed in the middle of the table.

'Careful, madam,' the waiter tells me. 'It is very hot.' I thank him and he tips his head to the side. 'Enjoy your meal.'

The food is sweet, sour, and the waiter is right, it is very hot. I spread the meat and vegetables and loosen the mound of rice. Steam rises from my plate.

'It smells good, doesn't it?' says Elaine.

'Delicious.' I consider a sliver of steaming meat dangling from my chopsticks.

'We have an amazing chef here. He can do everything: Chinese, Vietnamese, Japanese. We had Singaporean noodles last week. And we only pay ten dollars a meal. Can you believe that?'

I shake my head and breathe steam out of my mouth.

'Not everyone appreciates it, of course. We have the usual contingent who only want to eat mashed potatoes, beans and sausages, but they can always just go to the pub for that, can't they? The local does a very good seniors' meal on Thursdays, if you like that sort of thing.'

'I suppose you have to cater for all tastes.'

'Well, you do, but I don't think that place is here.' She leans in to me. 'Sometimes I think you need to be selective about who comes into a place like this. You know, so we can have a harmonious community.'

I reach for my orange juice and its chunks of ice cubes.

'It's not fair on people if they are never going to fit in,' Elaine continues. 'It's like that shooting in the hills on the weekend. It's not the right way to go about it of course – we must always condemn violence – but people need to live with their own kind.'

Satisfied that she has got her point across, Elaine bends to her plate. I turn to Kerry and ask about village running costs. She rolls her eyes and puts down her chopsticks. Geoff tuts.

'I don't know why they didn't consult with local people before they built,' she says. 'We've got all sorts of issues that we wouldn't have had if someone had just got in their government car and driven down here.'

'The village was built on a swamp,' Geoff explains, 'and they didn't put in enough drainage, so we've got subsidence and cracking in the south-east corner.'

'And the ground floor apartments on the other side get broken into every other week,' adds Elaine.

'That's not a running costs issue, darling.' Geoff pats her leg.

'Well, it is, Geoff, because people can't afford to run air-conditioners, so they leave their windows open at night and thieves just climb in and take what they want.'

'So why don't you get security screens for the apartments on the ground floors?'

'It's not in the budget, darling.' Kerry smiles at me. 'That's what you're all about, isn't it?'

CHAPTER TWENTY-EIGHT

I go back to my desk and fight the effects of too many carbs until it's time to leave. I'm down here for two days and need to check in to my accommodation. Then I'm going to Jana's house for dinner. I leave the files on the table for tomorrow, lock the door, thank Kerry, and head out into lengthening shadows and cooling air.

Steph's sister lives on acreage on the road to the coast. I turn into a gravel driveway signed with a rainbow-painted letterbox and the logo of the Australian organic industry. On one side is a horse paddock and on the other is bush, tall trees and thick undergrowth. Kangaroos are feeding in the paddock. There is no sign of the horses, but at this time of day, they'll be gathered at the gate, waiting for someone to come out of the house with their dinner. The driveway curves right, bringing the house into view, as well as a wide river valley with north-facing slopes covered in vines. On the other side of the valley is a large, white building encircled by deciduous trees planted in even spaces. Everything is backgrounded by tall, solemn forest and the dome of the clear, twilight sky.

'You've come in the back entrance,' says Jana through my open window. She is pushing a wheelbarrow loaded with firewood and her blonde dreadlocks are sewn with purple ribbon. She follows my gaze. 'Pretty view, isn't it? Looks even better from inside with a glass of cab sav by the fire.'

On the other side of a post and rail fence, two horses lift their noses from feed troughs as I follow Jana to her fireplace and her wine bottles. I am uninteresting and they flick their ears and return to their dinner. Jana grills me as we crunch across the gravel.

'You look great. Are you seeing anyone? When did you last see

Steph? Sorry to hear about your dad. How is he now? How's the inquiry? We're all very excited that you've included our little neck of the woods. I can tell you so much. We have such a problem with homelessness down here. Especially with summer coming, and everyone in the city wanting to escape the heat. You should see the tents by the river. It drives the tourist bureau mad. Doesn't set the right example, apparently. Well of course it doesn't, but the solution is to build more public housing, not drive the poor sods out of town.'

She pauses for breath to open the front door, a monstrous slab that wouldn't look out of place behind a moat. I breathe in the smell of roasting meat and work through her questions in order, dodging the one about love interests and filling her in on my dad and the inquiry.

Jana nods as she reaches into a wine fridge that is the same size as the fridge in Joleen Samson's kitchen. 'I heard about the building defects at Riverside. We know what everyone is up to down here – you only need to ask. Kerry and I do yoga together on a Tuesday night. You should come if you're still in town. The instructor is amazing. Studied in India. None of that alt-beats rubbish in the background. Totally quiet, very peaceful. Anyway, Kerry told me about the cracking walls. Duncan's Mansion, we call it. Do you know him? He addressed the council last year. Blah blah bureaucrat talk. Most of us didn't understand a word of it except *No*. Of course, Mike had to go schmooze with him afterwards.'

The wine glass that she passes me is etched with a stylised image of an unlovely horned creature, *Zaglossus hacketti*, the extinct giant echidna of the south-west capes and the emblem of Zaglossus Estate. Clearly Jana's evangelist husband is not a creationist. I take it to the bank of windows that look across the valley and imagine oversized monotremes waddling through the grass, searching for insects. A mob of lazy kangaroos stares back at me before continuing their grazing on Jana's expansive and well-watered lawn.

'Not too shabby, Banana.'

'God, no-one has called me that in years. Cheers.' She joins me, raising her glass. The fingers of her other hand twist through a collection of silver chains at her throat – a pretty metal crucifix decorated with gum leaves, recognisably the work of a famous local jeweller, hangs from one of them. 'The view's rather nice, isn't it?' she adds. 'More trees, less wind.'

It's true. The Mid West landscape of our childhood doesn't lend itself to timber like this. Where we are from, everything that is genetically programmed to grow over two metres develops a pronounced lean away from the south-westerly. Tourists take photos of themselves next to horizontal trees.

'That's the cellar door,' Jana says, waving her glass at the white building. 'Mike's over there right now.' She pauses when we hear the crunch of tyres on gravel and laughs. 'No, he's not.'

The enormous front door swings open and Jana's husband strides through it, arms open and smiling a smile that wouldn't be out of place at a polling booth. I wonder if he's ever considered running for office himself.

He clatters a pair of gold Aviators onto the kitchen bench and nods at my empty glass. 'Fill you up?'

I blink at it, astonished that there is only a mouthful left. I shouldn't on an empty stomach, but I say yes anyway and promise myself it will be the last for the evening. He lifts the opened bottle from the kitchen bench and chuckles.

'I could have guessed Jana would bring this out for you. It's one of her favourites.'

We retire to the couches that are clustered around the fireplace and Mike asks me about the inquiry and what *Doctor* Duncan Wolf thinks about it. Jana rolls her eyes and tells him he should ask the Minister for Housing, seeing as they're related.

'Doctor Wolf and the Minister for Housing have plenty of experience when it comes to parliamentary reviews,' I say.

'Doesn't mean they like them. We don't see the minister down here much. Maybe at the restaurant every now and then, or at church if he's here on the right day. He likes to be wined and dined. But that's the way in, isn't it?'

'What do you mean?' I know exactly what he means. I've had this conversation a dozen times.

'To get government contracts.'

'Well, technically, government contracts go through the online tenders board, not direct to the minister's wife's cousin's husband.'

Mike waves that away. 'Yeah, yeah, just like no politician ever got their relatives plum public service jobs.'

Jana shoots her husband a look. 'Careful. You know Frances doesn't like political gossip.'

'Yeah, fair enough. Anyway, we've all been forced down the tenders board route. And paid for it. Once the bureaucrats get their hands on the deal, you're screwed. I've done a couple of little projects in the city and once they'd added their percentage-for-art and OSH regulations and all the rest of it, it was hardly worth the time it took me away from the winery. And then, to add to the insult, they publish the contract details online. If you want to really make a deal with government worthwhile, you need to go straight to the minister's office.'

He drinks and refills. 'And there's plenty of stuff out there that wouldn't even make it to the tenders board. Like, we've got this land on the corner of the property.' He waves a hand in the direction of some trees. 'It's rubbish land that's no good for vines. The government could use it for a retirement village like Riverside. It'd be perfect, don't you think, to put retirement homes on a wine estate? The oldies would love it. They could even have one of those little shuttle buses to bring them over to the cellar door for lunch. Imagine that. People would be climbing over themselves to get in.'

'I don't think the government builds houses for the sort of retirees you're thinking about, sweetie,' says Jana.

'What do you mean? Poor people don't like wine? That's a bit classist, don't you think?'

Jana gives me an exasperated look. 'People who retire to public housing can't afford the wine that you sell, Mike. And they certainly can't afford to eat lunch every day at your cellar door.'

'Of course it wouldn't be every day. We could have a seniors' discount day every Friday. No, not Friday, we're booked-out on Fridays. Tuesday, maybe, that's our quiet day. Forty dollars for two courses and a glass of house wine. It'd go off.'

Jana gives the same amused bark as her sister. 'Frances, tell Mike how much they charge for lunch at the Riverside café.'

I do, and Mike puckers like his wine's turned to vinegar.

'Ten dollars? We don't do an entrée for under twelve.'

'Maybe you need to rethink your target market.'

'Maybe we dictate the target market.'

Jan raises her eyebrows at me, and I raise my glass to keep my own tongue in my mouth. It's the second time today someone has flagged the idea of a more selective approach to allocating public housing.

I hear tyres on gravel again and see the corners of Jana's mouth twitch upwards.

'I'll go,' says Mike. He opens the door to a pleasant-looking man in a cosy cream Argyle jumper, and chinos. His smile is gentle and takes in everyone in the room.

'This is Toby,' says Jana, twinkling at me, triumphant. 'He's a doctor.'

CHAPTER TWENTY-NINE

Toby turned out to be as pleasant as he looked. He sat next to me on the couch, drank moderately and asked about my work. He remembered the community health inquiry. It made sensible recommendations, he said, that the services in the South West implemented in partnership with general practitioners and the local hospitals.

'I hate to give credit to accountants, but the improvements we made from that report actually saved lives. In most cases, it's as simple as sending the patient's file direct to the GP. It's a shame you didn't include pathology centres in your inquiry, we have a hell of a time convincing patients to have their bloods done before they see their GP.'

The morning after, I wake up to birdsong and the deep green of trees that live with their roots close to water. I press my head into the pillow and do a stocktake. I need to go back to Riverside and work through the second stack of files. I need to get on the road by one to keep my appointment with Neil. I need to ask Kerry for sandwiches for lunch in my office. I could also do with a big glass of water and a couple of ibuprofen. Eric is still missing.

I inspect my stairwell injuries in the shower. The grazes are scabbing over like grazes do, and the bruises have blossomed into an impressive purple avenue. I poke them, exploring the tender flesh. I won't be wearing shorts any time soon.

When I'm showered and dressed, I open the door of my balcony and breathe in the cool, minty smell of the forest on the other side of the river. I keep well back from the railing even though I'm only on the second floor. I shouldn't have had that second glass of wine last night and the forest canopy is tilting to the right and back again. I can't see the river, but I can hear it. It's singing to itself under the trees, and I can picture the bubbling water and the tannin-stained sands on the riverbank. The water will be cold, like the air, and I stay out there for a moment, enjoying the tingle on my cheeks, and steadying myself against the wall.

It is not something that was part of my childhood, this damp, early morning cold. Not unless we went camping by a river in winter or travelled south. One school holidays, we drove Dad's old trayback Nissan around the Capes. We had two whole weeks on the road. Dad got the engineering company next door to his office to make a canopy for the tray and Matt and I slept under it in our single swags. Mum and Dad slept on the ground in their double. They said we couldn't sleep out there with them, and to keep the hatch door closed. When I woke up in the mornings, the thick green canvas over their bodies would be covered in dew and their heads tucked inside.

They placed their swag strategically, where the morning sun wouldn't reach and they could sleep late. I always had books with me and would burrow into my own solitary fug, beanie on my head and propped on my elbows. When I got bored, I would use my finger to draw pictures on the dew-damp windows and breathe in the mysterious smell of tannin-rich water and the musty build-up of fallen leaves.

We were instructed to wake our parents when we needed to pee – under no circumstances were we to go to the toilet block or into the bush by ourselves – and I would watch, fascinated, while Mum wriggled back into her pyjamas inside the swag before she emerged into the morning air. *I'm more comfortable sleeping naked,* she told me when I asked. I tried it myself, but all I felt was less warm. When we returned from the toilet block, Dad would be up, and the first fingers of smoke curling from the fire. The Nissan's tailgate would be down, and bacon and tomatoes lined up on a chopping board.

*

In my hotel room, I make tea and toast and pack my bag. Kerry said she'd be at the village from eight. Riverbank is only a kilometre downstream from my accommodation, but there's no direct road and I have to drive toward town and along the main street before reaching the road that takes me back to the river and the housing estate. At this time of the morning, the only vehicles on the street are trades utes and delivery vans. The utes are clustered around one coffee shop, and I pull in. Men in baggy black tracksuit pants and steel caps adjust their beanies and fold their arms. A chalkboard tells me to smile, the temperature here in God's Own Country will get to the high twenties today.

Eric loved coffee and he loved camping. He told me he used to go with his brother. They'd walk into the national park with all their gear on their backs. Tim was six years older and would carry the tent and most of the food. Eric was in charge of the pour-over strainer that they used to make their coffee in the mornings. He told me his dad would drop them off at the start of the trail and they'd walk up to the foothills, across swaying bridges suspended over broad, shallow rivers and along ridge-top paths. At night, they'd pitch a tent or share a stone *stappers* hut with other people on the trail. When they reached the other end, their dad would be waiting in the car to take them home, where their mum would clean out their backpacks and ask why, once again, they'd only worn one pair of socks for the whole three days.

It was on those hikes with his brother that Eric learned to film nature. His dad bought him a camcorder and Eric took it with him when they walked, slung across his chest. *Most of the first videos were of my feet*, he told me, laughing, until he learned to film at the end of the day instead of on the move. He would lie still in the twilight, and train his lens on rocky outcrops, waiting for the birds that nested in the cracks and holes to fly in and out. He learned to zoom in to capture them regurgitating food for their mate, and to find the bushes and grasses where they foraged.

I imagined myself on a hike with them, carrying my share of the food and filling a water bottle from a fast-flowing stream. We would walk single file on narrow, loose paths and take turns to lead. He would turn to train the camera on me, unaware as I wandered through alpine meadows, and show me the footage around the campfire in the evening. Later, we would drag our double swag outside the hut, telling his brother to stay inside, that we were fine out here alone and not to worry. I would wear a headlamp and read my bird book into the night while Eric slept, watching the stars whirl overhead.

*

When I reach Riverside, Kerry chastises me for buying coffee when the residents could have made me one in the café for free. She has already put a jug of fresh water and a plate of biscuits (almond and dark chocolate) in the room. She promises sandwiches at noon. I work through the files until midday when my sandwiches arrive and continue for another forty-five minutes when it is time to pack up. I've seen everything I need to see, checked off the columns in my spreadsheet, and uploaded photos. Kerry is in her office with Geoff when I emerge with my wheelie case.

'You're off, then?' he asks, standing as I enter the room. 'I hope you got everything you need?'

'I did, thanks.' I nod at Kerry. 'You have a well-organised village manager here.'

'We know,' he says. 'We are blessed to have her. Will you be driving back today or does your boss let you stay in paradise for a few days of rest and recreation?'

'No, I'm heading back, I'm afraid.'

'Well, drive safely. I look forward to hearing about your report.'

I fidget inside my handbag when I'm on the road, multitasking driving with hunting for more ibuprofen. Eventually I give up and pull over. I find the pills in the front pocket, take two with a mouthful of water, and steer back into the traffic.

I pass the next town and a random breath-testing station being set up on the other side of the road. The sun drifts through the windscreen and I can feel the heat on the backs of my hands. I should follow Belinda's lead and keep a tube of sunscreen in the car. The sound system, which is already on low on account of my hangover, mutes and the dashboard display tells me I have an incoming call. I press accept and James comes at me through the car speakers.

'Afternoon boss, this is your friendly reminder that local police are currently targeting speeding.'

I press the volume up button. 'That was last week. Today it's drink driving.'

'Better pull over then, you know you can still be over the limit the day after.'

I let that one go. 'How's progress on those defects reports for the south metro?'

'Slow, I've got to finish the police inquiry follow-up first.'

'When will that be done?'

'Tomorrow, don't stress,' he says. 'Turns out when they pulled the scope, they limited the inquiry to physical evidence only, so I don't have too much to go through.'

I frown at an oncoming car. It is small and green and wandering between the middle line and the verge. It's not me who's over the limit and behind the wheel today. I pull over to the left to give it plenty of space.

'I don't understand,' I say to James. 'I thought that was the point of the inquiry: tracking the movement of evidence.'

'Yeah, it was. In the end. But the original scope included pathology samples. They were the ones that got cut. Good thing too, Eric said there were thousands of them.'

I remember Doctor Toby's comment at dinner last night about the community health services inquiry also excluding pathology. Maybe it's a coincidence, maybe not. The weaving car shoots past me. The driver is on the phone, one hand on the wheel. Not drunk then. He'll go through the RBT station with a zero blood alcohol concentration, but not if he causes a head-on collision first.

'Boss?'

'Yeah, sorry, distracted by an idiot driver.'

'I said I'll have the rest of the defects reports done by the end of the week. Is that still good with you?'

'Yeah, sure, thanks.' I end the call and look in my rear-view mirror at the disappearing green car. Blood alcohol concentrations, like all drug tests, are pathology tests. They go to the state pathology labs for testing, not the state forensics labs, like Belinda thought when she suggested we look up Richard Cameron's records. Different government agencies. Different databases. Different serial numbers.

CHAPTER THIRTY

We are sitting on a balcony looking down over a crowded square. Me, Meredith and Aaron. A pop-up market is in full swing, and people wander from stall to stall carrying spiralised fried potato on skewers and meatballs in paper trays. I can smell beef, cheese and tomato sauce. I nurse my gin and tonic and eyeball the black plastic square that Meredith placed on our table, willing it to buzz and announce that our wedges can be collected from the bar.

She called me at the office that afternoon. 'Aaron has a job!' she'd shouted down the line. 'How awesome is that? I knew you'd be pleased. He said he saw you at the football. I think he likes you, you know. Come out with us tonight and celebrate. We'll be at The Shoe at five thirty.'

She was right, I was pleased, although, if I'm honest, I'd forgotten about Aaron's interview. Despite Belinda's teasing (*Frances has a boyfriend,* was the first thing she said when I returned from the South West) and me grinning like a fool at the stadium, I hadn't spoken with him since the game. But it was easy to meet up with Meredith in the city now that we had moved office. I only had to cross one street to get to the bar that she nominated. I could see the balcony from my workstation.

Now we are gathered around a tiny circular table, and I am wobbling on a stool with uneven legs. It's not my ideal drinking position, but I am next to the balcony railing and can lean on it if I need to.

Aaron brings a bottle of wine, two glasses and a One Fifty Lashes from the bar. 'So, are you a social justice warrior as well?'

'No, she's not,' Meredith interjects. 'She's not allowed. Fierce fence-sitter, this one.'

'Of course she is.' He winks at me. 'Don't worry, I won't tell anyone.'

The black plastic square starts shaking and buzzing, and Meredith rescues it before it walks itself off the wobbly table. When she returns, we both fall on the wedges, and she laughs and says it's a good thing she's ordered a pizza as well. She drops another plastic square on the table and starts on a story about a meeting at the Department of Housing.

'It's a new strategy to reduce the waiting list. Some assistant, assistant director ran the meeting because Duncan was called off on urgent business' – Meredith rolls her eyes – 'and she gave us this thirty-minute PowerPoint presentation on tenant obligations and how the three strikes policy is just delaying the inevitable.'

'The inevitable what?' Aaron asks through a mouthful of hot potato.

'Eviction. She showed us these graphs and claimed that eighty percent of tenants who have one breach of their tenancy agreement eventually accumulate three breaches and have their tenancy terminated.'

'That can't be right,' I say. 'Lots of people only ever have one breach. I see them all the time in the database.'

'It is, according to the Department. Her point was that the three strikes policy isn't needed because it only delays eviction of tenants who are going to get evicted anyway.'

'Big deal. If it doesn't make any difference, just follow due process, and give people their rights. Like she said, the other twenty percent come good.'

'That was our point too, but she was arguing that if the Department evicts them after one breach, the tenancy can be offered to a homeless family on the waiting list sooner.'

I shake my head. The logic doesn't make sense. 'How does that help? The evicted tenants will be straight back on the waiting list. Zero-sum result.'

'Not if they are excluded from the waiting list after eviction.'

I pause, mid-wedge. A glob of aioli plops onto the table. 'You're kidding me. They want to kick someone out after a single breach and then refuse to put them on the waiting list?'

'Not *want to,* they're going to. It comes into effect next week.'

'Far out.' I wipe up the aioli with the side of my finger.

'I know, right?' Meredith refills her glass. She puts it down on the table, where it wobbles before Aaron stills it with a hand on the base. 'It's easy to help people who are easy to help. It can even be marginally profitable if the social housing programme is anything to go by. But the difficult people – the ones who can't stay in a job, never learned to keep house, struggle with addiction or chronic illness – are hard. It takes time and money. But you've got to keep helping – throwing them out onto the street doesn't work.' She points a chip at me. 'Isn't there anything we can do about that? It must be against some sort of law.'

I shrug. 'Not really, no. It's the government's prerogative to set policy as it sees fit. As long as they doesn't breach the fundamental requirements of administrative law, they can be as hideous as they want to be.'

'Fucking arseholes.'

We contemplate our drinks. Aaron breaks the silence by asking me if my brother still plays football. I'm thinking how to reply when a guy in jeans and work boots claps him on the shoulder. I watch as they shake hands and begin a conversation about the game on the weekend.

'You alright?' Meredith leans across the table, her face in mine.

I rub my eyes. I should be fine, but I've been away from my desk all day in meetings with Neil, and ideally my brain could have done with some alone time before social discourse. The last three days had been a slog. I'd made the trip back in good time on Tuesday, watching the residual bushfire smoke drift over the hills, and distracted by the prospect that Eric's green six-number-three-letter combinations were a list of serial numbers for blood test results. It made sense. The numbers had to be related to the part of the inquiry that was pulled. The problem was, I had no access to the database for the state pathology labs and no legitimate reason to request it.

As the temperature climbed and the city traffic grew thicker and slower, my frustration had mounted and my headache returned. I swore and stamped on my brakes as a fat four-wheel drive cut in front of me and swore again as the dark-blue sedan travelling too close behind filled my rear-view mirror. I needed to focus on what I'd just found at Riverside, not an abandoned inquiry into how the police manage forensic evidence. I took the next off-ramp into the CBD streets, shaking off the freeway traffic, and stopped for a bottle of water and more ibuprofen to clear my head. I parked the car, swiped myself through the glass door and into the empty office reception, turned left and walked straight through to Neil's office. I didn't get home until ten that night.

This morning, three days after returning from Riverside, I gave Neil a neat file, cross-referenced to my findings. He's satisfied that everything is in order, and all that's left to do now is for him to hand the report to the Speaker and do his doorstop interview on the Parliament House steps. But I'm still nervous and can't help feeling that I've missed something. My brain keeps running through what I've pieced together, the findings, the documents, and photos that back them up. Our office doesn't need to meet the evidentiary requirements for a criminal conviction – that's the job of the police – but we can't defame someone either, parliamentary privilege or not. It's just not the right thing to do. And it's not like I've found someone stealing pencils this time.

I tell Meredith that keeping the bastards honest is a tough job, but someone has to do it. She laughs and raises her glass.

'I hear you, sister. Oh, I found those complaints by the way, you know, the ones that got Richard Cameron evicted. Anonymous, of course.' She rolls her eyes. 'They were investigated by the same policy officer who's dealing with Joleen Samson. Sean Callaghan. Do you know him?'

I shake my head.

'I've been trying to contact him. He's obviously done the department's course in how to avoid TAG.' She tilts her drink at Aaron. The work-boots guy is back at the bar and Aaron's contemplating his drink, waiting for us to finish. 'Okay, we'll stop talking shop. Tell Frances about your job.'

Aaron's face lights up. He'll be working for a plumbing sub-contractor, *one of the big ones*, he says, on a multistorey public housing project in the inner city, not far from his apartment. He's passed his pre-employment medical and starts on Monday. They're paying well and the subby has a solid pipeline of projects for the next three years, so if he's reliable and does good work, he's set.

I sit up and take notice when he mentions the medical. If my lightbulb moment on the road this week is right, the report will have the same serial numbers as the numbers that have been haunting me since I found the scrap of A5 paper in Bigfoot's folders. I could confirm that Eric's numbers are from pathology reports and might be able to make a case to Neil to access the database. I wonder how rude it would be to ask Aaron for a copy.

'What?' he asks, staring at me.

I decide that I don't know him well enough – yet – to be asking for his medical records. 'Nothing. Sorry.' Meredith rolls her eyes while my brain stumbles, not helped by the two glasses of wine I've drunk. 'What does that mean for your public housing apartment?'

Aaron looks at Meredith, who answers for him.

'He has to submit income statements every three months, and once he's been in work for six months, he needs to give notice and vacate. So, he's got a while yet.'

'What's the rental market like around there?'

'Rubbish. The vacancy rate is at an all-time low, and average rentals on a two-bedroom unit are more than forty percent of what he'll be earning. That is, if you can find anything. The good thing is, if there is anything out there, Aaron will be the one to get it. We give our clients references that show their rental history with the Department. It counts for a lot in the private market. He won't be out on the streets.' Meredith elbows him. 'Just make sure you start looking early, hey.'

'Yes, Mum,' he says, grinning at her and tipping the dregs of the bottle into her glass. 'Want another?'

'I do, but you don't get to buy another round tonight. This one's on me.'

CHAPTER THIRTY-ONE

When the sun comes through my window the next morning, I'm grateful that it's Saturday and I had the foresight to put a glass of water next to my bed. I do a stocktake. The ceiling is horizontal, and I am alone. Eric is still missing, but I might have a lead, and on Monday morning I'll be responsible for all hell breaking loose. I close my eyes. I really hope I've got the last one right.

I sit up, check in with the ceiling again and set about the Saturday routine. I need more meds and bananas and, despite my commitment to a work uniform, I still need to visit the drycleaner every month. There is only so much airing a suit jacket will take before the armpits turn whiffy.

I stuff my jackets into a shopping bag, stuff more shopping bags into my handbag, locate my prescription, and shut my apartment door behind me. My neighbour is waiting at the lift, wearing team colours again, and he lifts a hand in greeting.

'Saturday chores, hey?' He nods at my shopping bags.

'Best to get them over and done with. You?'

'No, I'm in the surgery today.'

'You'll miss the game.'

'I'm recording it.'

We both nod our appreciation of the role of technology in fitting away games into our busy lives and I prepare to scuttle out of the lift.

'Oh, one thing ...'

I stop halfway across the lobby.

'Did you see someone coming down the stairwell after the game the other night? I heard the door close on our floor and thought it was you coming up, but I didn't see anyone.'

I shake my head. 'No, no-one came down.'

'I mustn't have shut it properly. Never mind. Enjoy the game.'

I do a circuit of the shops on the other side of the railway station. Drycleaner, pharmacy, supermarket, and back to the pharmacy. I buy the Saturday paper because I fancy the idea of an old-fashioned sprawl on the couch surrounded by newsprint and coffee. I even buy a doughnut to go with it. As I walk home, I mentally pick through the housing inquiry evidence, looking for holes, for flaws in the logic. It all hangs together, but truth is, I'm terrified. It's one thing to ping people for petty theft and another entirely to accuse someone of criminal misconduct. If this is what Eric wanted, he could have all of it.

It's been two weeks since I got back from Weymouth and there hasn't been much time to think about Eric's near miss with the Mercedes. I've made some half-hearted online searches of the big drug boss who Jason said was driving the car. His name, Graham Griffiths, calls up a string of news articles dating back twenty years. Drugs, firearms, money laundering, alleged police corruption. Sometimes the connection isn't apparent, sometimes he is named. The articles come with photos of bulky men in jeans and short sleeves, wearing bulletproof vests and hip holsters, their faces blurred or cropped out of shot. The most recent article has a montage of boat ramps, desolate white beaches, abandoned shacks tucked behind sand dunes, and rows of plastic bags watched over by AFP officers.

I click on a video of a television news report. The camera pans along a line of thin, tired-looking men in handcuffs and then cuts to the long-faced police commissioner, his expression more disappointed than triumphant. And then there's footage of the big man himself. Although, it turns out, Graham Griffiths is not that big, he's quite short if you compare him to the prison transport vehicle in the background. And lean. He could be a jockey, or a cyclist just returned from the Tour de France. He's handcuffed, being led into the court, and is staring down the lens of the camera. It's a bold stare. He knows what's about to happen in the court room. With the benefit of hindsight, so do I. Judging by the expression on his face, the forthcoming stint inside didn't seem to bother him too much.

I freeze the video as Griffiths blinks, capturing him in an unflattering, eyes half closed, head half turned pose. It has to be him. The architect of my team leader's murder, if not necessarily the one who did the deed. His history, at least according to the world wide web, suggests that he's had plenty of opportunity to engineer a convenient wrongful conviction from time to time, and the motive to keep it under wraps. He'd be well aware of how to manipulate forensic evidence, especially pathology results, given his criminal specialty. And he'd be well connected, I'm guessing – well enough that at least one person who knew about Eric's inquiry would have thought to tip him off. There'd be a whole range of people who could do it. Police officers, lab technicians, ministerial staffers. Our inquiries aren't secret. These days, we even announce our annual programme and post it on our website.

I close my laptop on the alliterative drug trafficker and pick up the paper instead. There isn't much I can do with Jason's revelation. It's not like I can visit the guy in prison and ask him if he killed Eric.

*

By Monday morning, my self-doubt has ticked up another notch or five and I am actually shaking. I do a stocktake – horizon stable, Eric still missing and a person's career about to be destroyed.

When I get to the office, the staff are gathering for a briefing ahead of Neil's doorstop. I squeeze into the boardroom where the

TV screen has been lowered and muted. It shows journalists and camera crew mingling in front of the sandstone box that is our state's Parliament House. The news ribbon says that an announcement from the Commissioner for Public Inquiries is imminent. Bigfoot places herself in front of the screen, clutching a single piece of paper.

When we finally notice that she's there and stop talking, she reads directly from the press release that I helped draft on Friday. The missing insulation wasn't just an oversight, or a one-off. It was widespread fraud, occurring across multiple housing construction projects from the metropolitan area to the South West. Bigfoot tells us that the fraud was identified through the diligent work of our office's Housing Portfolio team. She looks up, frowns, tells us *well done*, and unmutes the television. A voiceover floods the room, but it's not our press release that the newsroom has run with. The police commissioner is ahead of the game.

A senior public servant has been arrested and computers seized by the fraud squad following an investigation by the Commissioner for Public Inquiries, says the news reader. The camera cuts to the head office of the Department of Housing. *Assistant Director for Homelessness Strategies, Dr Duncan Wolf, is led away from government offices by WA Police following a Public Interest Disclosure from an anonymous whistleblower.*

Belinda grins at me. I shake my head to warn her not to say anything and glance around the room. Bigfoot didn't mention that our diligent work had been helped along by a phone call from a disgruntled public servant who was fed up with being told to turn a blind eye.

The investigation found that Wolf may have been complicit in the award and falsification of approvals in relation to the construction of public housing. It is alleged that Wolf ignored recommendations from an independent tender panel and awarded more than five million dollars in roofing insulation contracts to a business associate.

Neil appears on the screen and we all cheer.

'Public Interest Disclosures are a vital part of the public sector integrity framework,' he says, making what I do sound as exciting as Duncan's fingernails. 'We take whistleblowers very seriously.'

The camera pans back to a reporter holding a microphone. *The commissioner found that Wolf directed Department of Housing project managers to approve completed projects, even though the roofing insulation had not been installed. The commissioner has uncovered payments made by the contractor to a bank account controlled by Wolf. It is alleged that the payments were made in exchange for Wolf's involvement in awarding the contract and fraudulently approving contract invoices.*

We can see Neil behind the reporter. His hands are shoved in his pockets, motionless. I can see the smallest upward turn of his mouth, then he glances at the camera, moistens his lips and straightens his back. Belinda sniggers.

The camera cuts again, to a well-dressed elderly couple. I recognise the red lanterns hanging behind them. Of course. Today is Monday, Chinese day in the Riverside café.

'As aged pensioners and with electricity costs the way they are, we rely on good insulation and good household management to heat and cool our home,' says the President of the Residents' Association. 'I close the windows and the blinds in the heat of the day, but our home is still hotter than our neighbours. Our air-conditioning bills are horrendous. Now we know why.'

'Geoff and Elaine Andrews want the government held to account,' says the reporter outside Parliament House.

'Our elected representatives should make sure public servants do the right thing,' declares Geoff. 'And if they don't, they should put their hands in their own pockets and pay our electricity bills themselves.' Elaine nods in agreement beside him.

'Good luck with that,' says James. 'I can't see the Honourable

Simon Tallent sending Western Power a cheque on their behalf.'

'Speak of the devil.'

The Minister for Housing is standing on the top steps of Parliament House, the sky clear behind him. He wears a serious face that says he is disappointed but confident that all can be made well. His white shirt is crisp behind a royal blue tie.

'I know I share the feelings of all West Australians when I say that I am appalled. We expect our public servants to act with the utmost propriety in their custodianship of public resources. It is unthinkable that a senior executive would pocket money meant to house the neediest members of the community.' A small frown appears between the minister's eyes, and he swallows.

'Oh, spare me,' I hear one of my colleagues say. 'Give the man an Oscar.'

'I had no knowledge of any wrongdoing before I was alerted to the misconduct by the Commissioner for Public Inquiries,' the minister states, glancing down at a sheet of paper. I'm guessing this part of his statement was prepared by legal counsel. 'I have ordered an immediate investigation into all outsourcing in my portfolio and will not hesitate to bring criminal charges against any public servant found to be misappropriating public funds.'

'And so, the witch-hunt begins,' says James. 'He'll use this as an excuse to get rid of anyone who doesn't wear the right team's colours, and no-one will stop him.'

James is right. Simon Tallent's public approval ratings are up despite having a senior member of his department charged with fraud. They're not high enough that the premier will be worried about a leadership challenge – although it's obvious that will come at some point – but the government is on a clear upward swing since Tallent abolished the three strikes rule.

A journalist begins to ask a question. 'Is there a culture of—'

But Tallent turns on his heel and marches back into the building.

Someone switches off the television and the screen rolls up to its resting place against the ceiling. James declares a lunchtime break for burgers and beers, and we troop back to the pod to collect our wallets. 'So it wasn't just one dodgy project manager acting alone,' he says, 'it was happening all over the place.'

'And with the guiding hand of Dr Duncan Wolf PSM.' Belinda shakes her head in disgust.

'I wonder if he'll be stripped of that medal?'

Bigfoot stops us before Belinda can answer.

'Frances, can I see you in my office?'

'We were just going out for a celebratory lunch,' protests Belinda. Bigfoot's mouth sets in a line, and Belinda adds, 'Do you want to come with us?'

When Bigfoot's face fails to show any sign of responding, James offers to get mine and bring it back.

'Not the beer,' Catherine says and turns on her heel.

I follow down the corridor to her office, scrolling through a list of potential misdemeanours that I might have committed in the last week. We're not withdrawing to her office for a congratulatory chat, that's clear. No *well done* and clinking of glasses or *have you thought about your next career move.* My director doesn't have a minibar. I suspect that if she ever got the top job and the corner office, she'd put Neil's minibar on the asset disposals list. I remember the RBT station on the highway and wonder if there was also a sneaky traffic camera that I'd missed. The infringement notice would come to the office because I was driving a fleet vehicle. No-one I know has ever committed a traffic offence in a company car. I wonder if the penalty is instant dismissal or some lesser punishment.

Catherine reaches her office and holds open the door to usher me inside. On her desk is a single sheet of paper with rows and rows of tiny numbers and letters. Two rows have been highlighted. I can't read them, but I can read the heading at the top of the page. *State Forensic Laboratory Database – Access Log.*

CHAPTER THIRTY-TWO

I'm awake but I don't dare open my eyes. The ocean is in my head. It rolls its giant weight across the base of my skull, pressing on one side, then the other, and clamping down on my neck. The bed rocks with the movement of the water. It is a gentle swaying, no waves, just a rolling swell, three feet at the most. It would be almost pleasant if I knew I could get out, if I could reach my toes to the sandy bottom and walk them through the salty water to the shore. I imagine this is what seasickness is like, feeling the roll of the ocean with no escape, the land an unswimmable distance away.

If I'm honest, the vertigo could be Meniere's or it could be overwhelming guilt. It turns out that having a legitimate ID and password even if it is your co-worker's and not yours, isn't enough to escape the alerts in the forensics database. The tiny robots that live in the system also identify the computer you use. My computer, obviously, is not a permitted device.

Bigfoot was stern but unexpectedly forgiving. 'Given your excellent track record and no previous missteps, I'm prepared to overlook this. Fortunately, it was a routine report and the State Forensics Laboratory doesn't know it was you or that you were misusing a co-worker's ID. You will, though, need to repeat our online course on information security, and pass it.'

'Yes, Catherine.'

She'd eyeballed me from under her pale eyebrows. 'Don't do anything like this again.'

'I won't.' I'd waited for her to ask me what I'd been doing, what I was looking for. She didn't ask, so I didn't tell.

*

Lying in bed, I tighten my throat and feel my larynx drop as the nausea pushes up from below. My right ear is ringing. It is always ringing. A perpetual summer of cicadas by the beach. I press my tongue to the roof of my mouth and breathe in. I swear I can feel my ear drums flexing, drawing toward each other on the in-breath and rounding outwards when I exhale. I focus on my forehead, on the clear, unburdened space above my eyes. I picture it hollow, a smooth, buoyant void. I need it to be free of the unreliable land and sea, holding its own place, independent and steady.

Vestibular inconstancy notwithstanding, I have to get up. I need to go to work to be on hand to help prepare answers to questions that the media or members of parliament ask about the fraudulent activities of Dr Gordon Wolf PSM, Assistant Director for Homelessness Strategies. The questions will be predictable. *Was the CEO of the Department of Housing aware of Wolf's activities? The Minister for Housing? Why not? Does this indicate a lack of ministerial oversight? A culture of fraud within the public sector?*

The CEO didn't know about the fraud and neither did the minister – or at least we have nothing to suggest that they did. If it wasn't for our whistleblower we might not have found out that the rot had risen as high as Gordon.

'So it was a whistleblower who tipped you off?' James had asked when they got back from lunch. I still hadn't told him. I didn't know how miffed he'd be that Belinda was in on the Public Interest Disclosure and he wasn't. Turns out, he couldn't have cared less.

I nodded in response to his question, working my jaw even though I know it wouldn't do any good. My right ear was already filling with fluid.

'Public servant?'

I shook my head. *Can't say.* Whistleblowers are protected. Since I took the call from Colin in the east metropolitan manager's office,

I'd told only Neil and Belinda. I'd needed her to recheck the records in the metropolitan offices while I was in the South West.

I'd interviewed Colin offsite the day after I returned from Riverside and checked in with him again on Friday. He was doing fine, he said. Happy to have the weight off his chest. Saraj, the sacked project manager, had called him to lodge an unfair dismissal claim. When he told him why, Colin knew he was ethically obliged to make a Public Interest Disclosure.

He struggled with it, he told me, knowing the allegation would bring the department into disrepute and potentially even compromise future public housing projects. *None of us are in this for the money, Frances*, he said. *We believe in what we do.* But it galled him to think that his fellow public servants were lining their own pockets while pretending to be social justice warriors. *In the end, it was a no-brainer.* Colin asked for me, he said, because he'd seen me stand up to Duncan before. The files I reviewed at Riverside confirmed what he'd told me.

By the time I've got my act together, caught my bus, and ridden the lift to the office floor, the workstations are full of diligent investigators quietly totalling numbers and checking boxes. My own little team has departed for their respective Department of Housing offices. Despite the PID report, the housing inquiry still needs to be finished. I have no doubt they will receive total – if somewhat wary – cooperation this morning. Nothing much is going to be expected of me for the next hour or so, so I reach into my bag for the file that has been languishing there since my unsuccessful attempt to log in to the forensics database. So much for pointing the finger at Eric for lax recordkeeping. If Bigfoot knew I'd been carting an inquiry file to and from the office in my handbag every day, I'd be getting a written warning, not just a telling-off in her office.

I open the file to the photocopied outpatient spreadsheet with its sliced-off column headings. I've tucked the torn page with the green numbers in next to it, and now I smooth the page flat, pick up a pen and start doing my thing. I work through the spreadsheet, comparing each serial number against Eric's green-penned list and marking them off until I get a match. *Aggarwal* is the first, then *Alexander, Calder, Chut*. I move down the list, matching numbers to names, until I find the last one – *Stewart*. Helen Stewart, of the misfiled report, who cleaned her oven. Tenancy renewed. I read my new list: *Aggarwal, Alexander, Calder, Chut, McKenna, Meleshe, Paine, Patel, Simpson, Stewart*. Now I have ten real people instead of ten numbers. All I have to do is find out who they are and why their mysterious serial numbers were so important to my missing boss.

Noises from the foyer tell me that my team has returned. I slip the notes I've made into my handbag, login to the cloud in its mysterious location, and make a show of searching for the community health file. Miraculously, all the documents that I scanned in are there, right where I put them. I remember the level five analyst's offer to find the original of the beheaded outpatient spreadsheet, scroll through the list of documents and surprise myself again. It's there, helpfully titled *Outpatient List*. I open it, perhaps just a little too excited that the solution to the serial numbers is as simple as an orderly filing system.

It isn't. The spreadsheet is the same one: same names, same dates, and on the electronic version, the column headings are clear and present and highlighted in bold. But the column I want is missing. I look back and forth between the photocopy and the screen. At some point, someone has deleted the column of six-number-three-letter numbers from the electronic spreadsheet. The hard copy version is all I have. Maybe I'll need to ask Aaron for his medical records after all.

CHAPTER THIRTY-THREE

I'm so popular after the fraud case, I even have an email from alice@eikendalpharmacies.com – Eric's sister – waiting for me when I get home that afternoon. *Dear Frances, I have just seen the news. Congratulations! I remember Eric always thought there was something going on in Housing, and he knew that if anyone could uncover it, it would be you. He would be so very proud. I hope you are well. Alice Rensburg.*

I email her back, thanking her and asking after her greyhounds. *Come up and see for yourself sometime*, she answers immediately. *You are always welcome here. Are you doing anything on the weekend?* I'm not and we make a time.

My browser is still open at the paused news report of Graham Griffiths entering the court. I close it and scroll through the rest of the images. Some are head-and-shoulders corporate shots, bland suit-and-tie affairs with honest-white backgrounds and a professional smile. It is the same smile as Simon Tallent's, with healthy, white teeth and clear skin, but none of the local-member's warmth. Griffiths is also smiling in the photo where he is being led back to the prison transport van after the hearing. There's no warmth there either, only triumph. The jury found him guilty on minor supply charges but were unable to reach a verdict on the trafficking offence. There was insufficient evidence, apparently, to place him at the scene. I'm pretty sure I know why.

There are other photos, loads of them in fact. Climbing in and out of dark Mercedes, twirling his scarf victoriously at the football, handing over a cheque to the chair of a charity that runs men's shelters. Even drug traffickers understand sport and homelessness. Except he's not a drug trafficker. Not according to the court.

According to the court, he's just a petty supplier, caught with a commercial quantity hidden in the frame of his thousand-dollar mountain bike. No different to someone who breaks up their stash and sells it to punters in nightclubs for one-night hits. Punters like Aaron. Punters like Matt.

But I realise the timing's all wrong for Griffiths to want to get rid of Eric. The big drug bust occurred just after Eric disappeared. At that point, Griffiths was expecting to be banking millions of dollars, not defending criminal charges. He had no reason to silence my boss.

I have my own near miss driving to Alice's house that weekend. She lives on a gravel road that turns off the South Western Highway an hour out of the city. It takes me past horse paddocks and up the side of the escarpment into white gum woodlands. Wandoo, as Duncan so helpfully pointed out to Belinda before her diligent auditing put him in prison. In my rear-view mirror I can see the the coastal plain under a haze, and the refineries in the distance. They disappear as I crest a ridge and drop down again, following the narrow road as it curls around the side of a river valley. Alice's house is above me, somewhere behind the trees and granite outcrops, not yet in view. The road takes a sharpish turn right somewhere up ahead and I remember having to swing wide the last time I came here. I'm looking for the turn-off when a trail bike bursts out of a side road on my left, skids in front of the car and guns up the gravel.

I brake hard, my back wheels sliding, and stare at the red dust billowing behind the bike. My left rear wheel has dropped into the soft shoulder and next to it, a trail post for the Bibbulmun Track marks the unseen junction, the yellow triangle pointing along the road. I restart the car, spinning the back wheel as I coax it back onto the road, and when I'm level again, I roll forward into the falling dust, looking for the yellow triangle's mate. Unsurprisingly, it points uphill in the same direction as the bike.

I follow the dust, watching for hidden side roads this time. As I climb, I catch glimpses back down the valley as it winds out of the hills to the coastal plain. Up here, I can see how much the bush has faded in the dry spell. Leaves that are usually plump and glossy at this time of year are dull and dusty, making the bush look worn and defeated before summer even begins. Here and there, patches of dark green give away the location of imported gardens and their secluded houses. Bore-fed oases in the bush. The occasional straight line suggests more horse paddocks and, farther west, a parade of power lines marches south through the national park.

As pretty as it is in winter, I wouldn't live in these hills. It's one thing to go camping in the forest as a kid with your parents, or visit a vast wine estate like Jana's and Mike's, but another entirely to be in the bush all the time. The *sense of enclosure* that people describe about living in the valleys and under the tree canopy only makes me feel trapped. I like to see a faraway horizon. A nice flat one, that I can run toward in case of a fire or if some bush-dwelling carnivore jumps out from behind a shrub and wants to eat me. Trees are lovely, but oppressive in numbers. I take one last turn, pressing my foot to the floor to convince my city-size four-cylinder engine to take the sudden, steep incline, and the CBD towers come into view. I can see the horizon again.

It's not so much a view of the city as of the sky. The cluster of towers that surround our new office is barely more than a white smudge. The low, flat horizon, even in its documented vastness, is also inconsequential. It is the sky that is the hero up here. Today, it is a washed-out blue. Like the bush, it is faded from the early start to the warm weather. It sucks water from leaves, soil and the surface of dams but there is no trace of moisture in it, no deep colour, just bleached dry air above my head. I fill my lungs and lift my back away from the car seat, close my eyes, feel the lightness of it, and breathe the trail bike away.

The gravel road continues south from here, through the national park that stretches east before becoming farmland, and south before hitting the ocean. I turn into Alice's property just before the road disappears over the hill. On the left is a wrought-iron sign spelling out *Eikendal* in curly script, and I pass between banks of agapanthus and twin jacaranda trees. The gravel becomes a red bitumen driveway. It swings into the side of the hill, and I see a lemon tree and the white gable and green front door of Alice's house. I park my car under an eponymous oak planted in front of the entrance and rap on the brass lion's head door knocker. Alice appears, framed by the view of the city behind her.

We drink tea and eat shortbread on the terrace where we celebrated Eric's thirtieth birthday. Eric preferred big horizons too, she tells me after I confess my tree-change hesitancy. She points through the door to a photo on the wall. It shows a river running through reeds, low trees, and bare orange hills below an infinite sky. It is, of course, the same picture on the photo that I found in the bottom of Eric's mobile pedestal.

'He took it on a family canoeing trip,' she says, 'from our campsite on the third day. Those orange hills, they're in the Richtersveld. The river is the border between South Africa and Namibia.' She looks at the framed print, in shadow behind the doors. 'He was so proud when someone offered to buy it.'

'He said he used to go hiking there with his brother.'

'Oh yah, all the time back home. Mostly in the Drakensburg, though, and not so much after we came here. They walked part of the Bibbulmun once. He didn't like it. Not enough mountains and too many trees.' She looks out at the flat plain. 'At least from my house you can see what's coming for you.'

I tell her what Jason told James and Belinda, about the near miss with the Mercedes. She nods, her eyes still scanning the horizon.

'I remember that. The gardener recognised Graham Griffiths on the television when he was arrested. It was brave of him to come forward, I think.'

'He says the police never looked into it.'

'No, that's not right – they did.' She turns her attention back to me, nods her head emphatically. 'They took it very seriously. The commissioner himself briefed us, even sent officers out here to check our security. In fact, I think, without the gardener's information about Eric, Griffiths wouldn't have gone to jail at all.'

'Why is that?'

'The investigating team raided his apartment after Jason came forward. They didn't find anything to do with Eric, but that's when they found the drugs that put Griffiths in jail. We thought we had a breakthrough, but there was nothing.'

'Do you think he was involved in Eric's disappearance?'

Alice sighs and it sounds like defeat. She presses the tip of a finger into the crumbs of shortbread that have scattered onto the table. 'No, I don't think Graham Griffiths is the big deal the papers made him out to be. Anyway, let's not dwell on that. How's your potassium these days?'

I blink and do the so-so thing with my hand. 'How did you know?'

'About the potassium? Eric told me.' She looks at me as though I am completely daft and pats my leg. 'You're important to him, Frances. His protégé. We can't have you having a heart attack just because you don't manage your potassium levels. You should take supplements. Sometimes bananas don't cut it.'

I watch her gather up our plates and cups, her thick, blonde hair curling above her shoulders and her blue blouse tucked in at her waist. She's right, of course, and I'm sure she's not just pushing supplements because she sells them in her pharmacies. The meds I take to keep the spins at bay strip potassium from my bloodstream. That's not a good thing if you want your heart to keep beating nice and regular.

As I leave, we pause next to the framed photo. Alice turns on the lights so we can see it better. Unlike the photo from Eric's mobile pedestal, this larger version captures the detail in the reeds by the riverbank and the ripples in the water. I imagine a sea breeze blowing over it from the west.

'Are there crocodiles in the Orange River?' I ask her, thinking of the wild rivers in the Kimberley.

She laughs. 'No, not like here. There were hippopotamus once, but they're all gone now. We saw baboon when we were there, and someone ahead of us saw a leopard kill. But not the leopard. You'd have to be very lucky to see one.' She is silent for a moment and then holds a finger to the glass. 'Just here. I think. No. Here. Can you see it?'

I move in close to the photo. Her finger is above my head, and I rise onto my toes to see. The rockface is tawny and speckled in afternoon shadow. The veldt grass, growing in clumps in between the rocks, is faded like the winter grass in the bush outside Alice's house. If there is a leopard looking back at the camera, it would have seen Eric better than we can see him.

'Maybe. No.'

She laughs again. 'Neither can I. But we give Eric the benefit of the doubt anyway.'

Alice sends me off with a bag of lemons and I promise to buy some potassium chloride from my local pharmacy. The gravel crunches as I leave the solid surface of her driveway. I stop and wind my window down to listen for the return of the trail bike over the crest of the hill, but the air is silent and still. The easterly has died. I let the car roll down the road, my right foot resting on the brake. At the bottom, back in the river valley, I stop and check again. If anything, the air is even more still than it was on the ridge. It is thicker, too, down here and the trees are taller, reaching overhead. If it is ever possible to hear the sound of the river from the road, I can't hear it today. I guess it has slowed to a trickle with the warm weather and lack of rain. I feel my familiar unease, surrounded by timber and hillsides, and the back of my neck prickles. Now that I'm on the flat road, I pick up the speed and head back to the highway.

I'm feeling sad about Alice's reference to Eric in the present tense when I realise what I've done. I check my phone but down here it gets no signal. The giveaway is the dry riverbed, which I definitely didn't cross on the way in. I continue up the other side of the valley, looking for a place to turn around. Over here, in the shadow of the south-facing slope, the air is cooler, even a little damp. Less likely to spontaneously combust.

I find a driveway and pull in. It is barred by a cocky's gate, the paddock behind it green with winter grass. A horse crops at it, ignoring the car the way only horses can. Overgrown wheel ruts run along the fence line toward some stables, and I can see a second gate, wooden and hung between two red-brick piers, at the opposite end of the paddock. Beyond it, a colonnade of deciduous trees, the green of their leaves at odds with the surrounding bush, and above them a slate roof. I realise I am at the back gate and that the main entrance to this particular hills' hideaway must come off a different road. I back out and point the car the way I came in. The horse looks up, impassive. I'm about to tell him he needs a good brush when I notice the sign propped against the fence, nestled in the winter grass. It is a piece of cut-off flooring timber attached to a rusted chain. At some point the rust has won and someone has moved the fallen sign to one side. I can see the outline of letters above the grass. They have been inscribed with a wood-burning iron. *Wandoo*. The local word for white gum. The owner won't be home because he's in a prison cell. I know, because I put him there.

CHAPTER THIRTY-FOUR

I look at the horse, who is ignoring me again, and pull back into the driveway. It can't hurt, I think. After all, Duncan is locked up ten kilometres away and I know he's single and has never had kids. The property will be empty. Someone, obviously, is looking after the horse, but maybe it's just an agistment and they only come here once a day. It's not like he's wanting for feed with all the grass at his feet. I lock the car and climb the gate.

Underfoot, the soil is a mix of clay and sand, and my feet sink and slip along the wheel ruts. I pass a sheep trough, green with algae, a ball float bobbing at one end. The water is low, and I press down on the float to open the valve, but nothing happens. The pump must either be broken or switched off. Churned-up sand around the trough suggests that the paddock has been home to more than one horse, but the sole occupant today is still pretending disinterest. I cross the paddock and ask him where his pals have gone. He snorts and purses his lips at my outstretched hand but in the absence of food doesn't bother shifting his feet. Instead, I go to him and run my hand over his neck. It is gritty with dust and loose hair. Maybe if there is a brush in the stables and he'll let me, I'll give him a quick once-over. Maybe I can check the pump while I'm there. I give him a scratch, which makes his tail swish, and tell him if I find some oats, I'll give him a treat. I'm halfway to the stables when I hear his heavy tread behind me.

I hadn't picked Duncan for a horsey person. He seems too involved in urban matters, the intricacies of city construction projects, of concrete and site drainage, planning codes, and coordination of subcontractors. I had figured his interest in Indigenous flora and fauna was a considered front, an outward suggestion that he might have a heart for living things. Maybe I was wrong. A wattlebird watches me from the branches of a wedding bush as I approach. He thinks about it, then takes himself off to a banksia tree near the fence line. I wonder how far they range and whether he visits the prison.

The stables themselves are wood with an iron roof. There's room for three horses plus a tack room. Halters hang from nails and a three-tier rack stands in one corner, empty except for a worn saddle, the type you see in riding schools, the girth strap slung over the top. I breathe in the smell of leather, straw and molasses. Three feed bins are lined up against the wall and I prise open the first and sink my hand into the oats inside. I spread my fingers and rake my hand through their gritty, slippery warmth. It reminds me of the stables at Ray's property and I breathe in the homely smell of grain.

A knock against my shoulder makes me overbalance onto the bin. My thighs dig painfully into the metal lip, and I jam the heels of my hands against the wall. I push myself upright and receive a whiskery tickle on my neck and a puff of wet snot across my chin. I have to put my body between the horse and the open bin to stop him from dropping his head into the oats. He's a big horse – bigger than I first thought – and strong. If he got his head down, I wouldn't be able to get it up again. Not until he'd finished and that could be a while. I close my fingers around some oats, grasp the lid and hammer it back into place.

He feels for the oats immediately, nudging my hand open and snuffling them out. When there are no more left, he snorts and tosses his head.

'Jeez Louise,' I tell him, 'go easy.' I put my hand up to stroke his muzzle, but he turns his head away. 'Fine then, be like that.'

The first stall is empty except for a pile of clean straw in the corner. When I open the door of the second stall, the horse follows me inside, sniffs and turns himself around to look at me.

'What?' I ask him. 'Is something supposed to happen?' He shifts his weight. I look over my shoulder and see a grooming brush on the ledge between the second and third stalls. The third stall, I see, has been repurposed for storage. There's no fitting a horse in there, even a small one. It is the usual household overflow of plastic storage tubs, gardening tools, two bicycles with peeling handlebar tape, and discarded furniture, even an old dressing table with a speckled, tri-fold mirror. For a single man, Duncan has accumulated a lot of crap.

'Who the hell are you?'

I recoil so violently I smack my shoulder into the side of the stall. I go to rub it but realise I've already slid my other hand into the grooming brush and scratch myself instead. The woman in front of me looks at the brush, outrage flaming her cheeks.

'What the fuck are you doing with my horse?'

The animal in question bumps her chest with his muzzle then begins to explore her pockets. She pushes him away. 'Get off, Shayne.'

I slip my hand out of the brush and put it back on the ledge. 'Sorry, sorry.' I try to squeeze between her and the horse, but she blocks me.

'I asked you what you're doing here.'

'Nothing. I'm just. I took a wrong turn.' I babble. 'I ride too.'

'And you thought, here's a nice horse that some bastard isn't looking after properly so I'll do it myself.'

'No. No, nothing like that.'

'What then? Looking for some free tack?' She pulls a mobile phone out of her pocket. I already know there's no signal, but what if she takes my photo and sends it to Duncan? I think about my car, parked at the gate. She's probably already got a photo of the licence plate.

'I'm really sorry,' I say. I put my hands up in what I hope looks like I'm surrendering and absolutely not a threat to her horse or her riding gear. 'I shouldn't have come in. I'd be pissed off too if it was my place.'

She stares me down. Waits. I wade in again.

'It's just that it's so pretty here, with the paddock and the stables, and you have such a lovely horse.' The look on her face tells me I'm embarrassing myself and then I remember. 'And his water was low, and it's really hot today and I didn't know how often someone comes by, so I thought I'd check the float.'

She raises her eyebrows but is otherwise unmoved.

'It's not working,' I add.

'Pump's turned off,' she says. 'The fucking useless owner is in prison and the pump housing is locked. I have to come in and fill the trough with a hose.'

'Ouch.'

'Yeah, I know. Arsehole. He won't even give me a key to the back gate. I have to get the feed delivered to the verge and wait for someone to let me in.' Shayne nudges her again and she pockets her phone. 'Yeah, yeah, come on then.'

I follow her out of the stall, and she hands me a plastic lunchbox filled with carrots.

'Here you go, take him outside and feed him while I run the hose out. He can have all of them, just one at a time.' She takes hold of his top lip and tugs on it. Her face softens. 'Chew your food, you greedy bastard, or you'll get wind like last time.' She slaps him on the rump, and he ambles out into the paddock. I follow. He's munching on his first carrot when his owner marches out of the stable door, a coil of hose over her shoulder.

'I'm Tahnee, by the way.'

'Frances.'

'Nice to meet you, Frances.'

I watch her place the hose in the trough and trudge through the sand back to the tap. I wonder how she knows Duncan. They don't look like they're related. She's darker, and has the broad, flat vowels of someone who's grown up in the Mid West. As far as I know, Duncan is five generations Scottish settler, no siblings, just a rumour of a stepmother. Also, he has no interest in horses or physical activity of any kind. Maybe the stables were built before he bought the place. Maybe Tahnee just drove by one day and asked if she could pay to keep her horse here.

Impatient with the pace at which I'm handing over the carrots, Shayne sticks his nose into the lunch box and knocks it to the ground. As I bend to pick it up, I hear shouts and the sound of tyres skidding on gravel. I look up in time to see four mountain bikes take the bend in the road toward the river. The fat wheels remind me of Eric's bike and the way James teased him about riding it in the city.

I feel the prickles in the back of my neck again before I make the connection. I wave the empty lunch box at Tahnee and head back to the stables. Inside, I rest it on the lid of the feed bin and trot past the two empty stalls to the third. The items that had been stacked inside have now been covered with a horse rug, grey, woollen and heavy. I lean over the rail to lift the corner and glimpse a fat, grooved tyre tread.

'Well, that's all done.'

I wheel around. Tahnee is standing in the doorway, the sun behind her, feet planted. She reaches down and turns off the tap, her face fixed on mine. 'You all good?'

'All good.' I make a show of dusting my hands on my thighs and retrieve the lunch box. I brandish it at her again, my excuse to return to the stables, and my heart hammers in my chest as I cross the floor toward the doorway. For a moment I don't know if Tahnee will stand aside. I don't know if she knows either, but then she holds out her hand for the lunch box.

'Thanks for that. He can be a pain when I'm trying to feed him and fill the trough at the same time.'

'No problem. I'll be off then.'

My cheeks are still burning when I reverse the car out of the driveway. I put my hand to them and am so mortified by the heat that I redden all over again. Tahnee has every right to be annoyed with me, first for finding me cosying up to her horse and second for snooping around in her stables. If I was her, I'd have walked me off the property with threats to call the police if I ever came back. Instead, she's texted me her phone number, saying I can come out and ride Shayne any time I like. *Take him through the house gate. Just give me a call – the first couple of times he'll try and put it over you if he thinks he can get away with it.* I can't see it happening myself, at least not until next winter. The thought of being alone on horseback in the dry bush doesn't appeal. And then there's the whole vertigo thing, which I didn't explain. Best just to forget it ever happened, a chance encounter that, against the odds, I managed to exit with my dignity intact.

I cross the dry riverbed, find the right road and head west. The car climbs out of the valley and when I reach the crest of the hill and see the coastal plain again, my phone starts beeping. Five missed messages, all from Meredith. I wait until I'm back at the junction with the highway, pull over, and call her back. She picks up on the second ring.

'Oh God, Frances, Aaron is dead.'

CHAPTER THIRTY-FIVE

I drive straight to Meredith's house. She texts me an address near the port. I park on the street in front of a weatherboard-and-iron cottage with a native garden and the spotless SUV parked under a car port. Meredith answers the door and ushers me past a room where two children in front of a television blink through the doorway with big eyes and open mouths, their legs encircling twin bowls of popcorn. In the kitchen, Meredith tears at a box of tissues and blows her nose. It's all her fault, she says, for finding Aaron the job and insisting that he take it. She knew the developer had a bad reputation. The plumbers had told her.

'He pushes the contractors too hard. They cut corners. I should have known the site was unsafe, but sometimes a job's a job, you know, and it's so important for kids to see their dad go out to work every day.'

Fresh tears start and I pull out more tissues. Meredith ignores them and drags a glass of wine along the bench toward her.

'I should have known better.' She drains the glass and reaches into the fridge for the bottle. 'That poor little kid.'

'Declan? Where is he now? Is he with his mum?'

She nods, pressing her lips together and blinking hard. 'But what's he going to do without his dad?' She looks at me with watery eyes. 'He was just so good, Frances. One of the good ones.'

And then my visit is cut short because the front door screen clatters and heavy footsteps – a working man's tread – thump down the hallway. Voices from the front room call *Daddy!* and Meredith launches herself out of the kitchen. When I catch up, she's encircled, and a small voice at her knees is explaining that *Mummy is sad because her friend died.* Greg nods as I negotiate my way around the huddle. I let myself out.

*

Aaron's funeral is delayed while the coroner investigates. He'd fallen through an opening on the second floor, according to news reports. No-one saw it happen, but an unnamed worker speculated that he'd tripped over building materials that had been hoisted up on Friday. *I knew they were a hazard,* the man was reported as saying. *I wish I'd said something.*

The Minister for Housing said he had questions about why the worker was onsite without authorisation on a Saturday, an observation that Jaelyn Worner echoed except her take was predictably different.

'The current government is putting contractors under pressure to achieve impossible deadlines. Workers are returning to site on weekends, exhausted, and without sufficient breaks. Under these conditions, this sort of tragedy is inevitable.'

A squat, bald man with the union logo distorted across his stomach read out the list of stop-work orders that had been issued against government contractors in the past four months, and held up a frayed safety harness that he claimed a worker had been ordered to use only last week.

On Monday, I sit at my workstation and flick through Aaron's Facebook page. His posts are pictures of Declan, construction work and beach sunsets. His profile picture is old. It occurs to me that it could even be a wedding photo. He's wearing a suit and has been positioned in front of a spray of white bougainvillea. Curious, I open his Albums tab and find one marked *Wedding*. I see row upon row of pictures of a glowing woman in a long white dress standing in front of the same flowers. Her long dark hair and large blue eyes shine against all the white. The sun bounces off her lifted cheeks. In one photo, she is looking off to the side, her hand outstretched. An invitation to someone to join her. Someone she loves. My eyes prickle and I reach for my bag to find a tissue.

I feel a hand on my shoulder and warm breath next to my ear.

'Aw, is that his wife?'

'Ex-wife.'

'She looks so happy.'

'Yeah.' I dab at my eyes and Belinda pats my shoulder.

'I wonder why they separated,' she says, leaning into the screen.

I shrug and blow my nose. She straightens up and adjusts the bag on her shoulder.

'We're off. Are you finishing up?'

'No, I've got work to do and I'm meeting Meredith at six.'

'Better get off Facebook then.' She prods James' chair with her foot. 'Come on, Uncle, I want to get home.'

I take Belinda's advice and log off Facebook. I need to finalise the housing inquiry report. Now that Duncan has been arrested and the whistleblower story is all over the media, Neil wants it tabled in parliament ASAP. And Bigfoot is riding me hard again. She wants the team moving on to the next inquiry. I know what she's thinking. If we can finish another one before the end of the financial year, she'll beat her KPIs and become the next in line for her own boss's job.

I hear footsteps behind me and check over my shoulder again. Bigfoot is standing over the photocopier, in the utility area between the open-plan workstations and the enclosed offices. She won't be pleased if she finds out how I've spent my time today. The housing file is open on my desk, but it's all show. Despite my looming deadline, I've barely looked at it in between scrolling through Facebook and trying to hack in to the state pathology lab. I've completed (and passed) the information security course that Bigfoot made me do, but I'm over my guilt and I still haven't found a way to prove that the green-inked serial numbers are pathology reports. And it's not like I can ask Aaron now. My own blood tests get issued to my GP and she just tells me whether my potassium levels are in the normal range. I suppose I could request a copy, but it's a month until my next appointment.

Bigfoot jabs at the control panel, sighs, jabs again. The machine whirrs and I watch as she braces her back and stretches her hips from side to side. She has the same spider sense as Simon Tallent and turns her head to catch me watching her. Her gaze flicks to the clock on the wall. The office is empty, and all of the lights have timed out except the one over the pod. She picks up her printing, puts a blank sheet over the top and walks toward me. I shut down the login screen before she reaches the pod, but she's narrowed her eyes and I'm fairly sure I've been caught out.

'They've all gone home, have they?'

'Just walked out the door.'

'Hmm. How's progress on the housing report?'

'Yeah, good, thanks.'

She waits.

'I should have the draft to you by the end of the week.'

She shakes her head and presses her tongue to the roof of her mouth the way she does when there's no argument. 'Neil wants to review it over the weekend. I'll need it by Wednesday if I'm going to check it first. Close of business will do.' She scans my workstation. 'You've always got everything in hand, though. Shouldn't be a problem as long as you give it your complete focus.'

I'm about to protest that sorting out her old community housing papers set me back a few days, but the *complete focus* crack is a clear warning that she's onto me and anyway she's already marching back down the corridor, slapping her printing against her leg with each uneven step. Outside my window, the string of lights that lines the balcony of the bar across the road flickers on, and the first

Monday-afternoon office refugees have taken up positions at the tables. I contemplate calling Meredith and cancelling. If I order in a laksa and stay for another couple of hours, I'll make a good dent in the report. But Bigfoot is right, I do have everything under control and two full working days are enough to get a decent draft to her by Wednesday afternoon. I log off and head for the lifts.

CHAPTER THIRTY-SIX

Meredith is sitting at the same table where we celebrated with Aaron ten days ago. She has three wine glasses in front of her, one empty and two fresh. I climb onto the opposite stool, and she slides a glass toward me, leaving a trail of condensation in its wake. The table is steady, and I bend down to look at the floor. Someone has placed a wedge of cardboard under one of the legs.

'Thanks for coming.' She looks up and her eyes are puffy. 'Sorry about yesterday. I wasn't holding it together very well.'

'Don't worry about it. I don't think you're expected to hold it together when this kind of thing happens.' By the time I'd driven home from Meredith's yesterday, it was late afternoon, and I hadn't eaten since the shortbread at Alice's house. Meredith texted me as I arrived home, juggling a leaking box of noodles, a slippery bottle of Riesling and my door key. I'd had to put the noodles on the floor to let myself in and left a yellow stain on the carpet. The text was signed off by Greg. *Thx for coming around. M says sorry she was in a state. She says The Shoe tmrw @ 6? G.*

'I shouldn't have sent Aaron there,' she says, her finger rubbing the condensation of her glass. 'The union guys said the developer is some fly-by-nighter who thinks he's going to get rich quick by dabbling in property. Worker safety is just another cut into his margins. It's cheaper to pay off safety inspectors.'

'Is that right?' My public investigator brain files the information and I picture a potential lead story on the evening news, with a shamefaced government inspector being led into court. Maybe I'm becoming more like Eric after all.

'The guys say he's also mixed up in dodgy land deals. You should look into that. Nail the bastard.'

'Dodgy deals with government?'

She waves a hand in the air, narrowly missing a passing suit. He veers and gives us both a look. 'Some right-of-right faction of the incumbent party. You know the type, pro-development, climate-change sceptics.' She lifts her glass and drains it. 'They all drink together. Go to the same church together. Probably all eugenicists.'

'I don't think that's a thing anymore.' I remember her crack about Duncan being a Nazi.

'Don't you believe it.' She climbs down off her stool and points to my half empty glass. I shake my head and watch her negotiate around tables toward the bar. She trips over a backpack that's leaning against a chair, rights herself, and gives me a thumbs-up. I flag a passing glassie and ask if we can have a jug of water. She looks me in the eye and tells me *absolutely*. It's on the table by the time Meredith returns with two glasses of wine. She laughs and knocks back a glass.

'Fair enough, Frances. Keep me hydrated. I'll be glad you did that at two a.m. tomorrow. Tell me how the inquiry's going. That Public Interest Disclosure must've been a gift.'

I fill her in on the dross of completing the inquiry report, finalising the evidence file, tying up the loose ends. As I speak, I see her eyes glaze over and I hear how boring it sounds. I'll be spending the next two days annotating, cross-referencing, scanning and stapling. At the end of it, I'll have a report bound in the official colours of the commissioner's crest and I'll sit in the Public Gallery while the Speaker lays it on the table of the Legislative Assembly. I remind myself that this report has helped put a corrupt official in jail and stopped the flow of millions of dollars of public money into private hands. I look for the inner glow of self-satisfaction and can't find it.

'Old news.' Meredith is staring at a homeless guy pushing a

supermarket trolley across the square. Her glass is empty. She waves her hand in the air again. 'The fraudulent Dr Wolf is old news, old hat, yesterday's villain, at least until his trial date comes up. Tell me something new.'

I'm not supposed to – it's not an official inquiry, just my own personal campaign – but my glass is empty now too. I tell her about Eric's list of green numbers, how I suspect that they are serial numbers for pathology reports. I explain that Eric must have recognised them from his work on the police inquiry that was going to reveal flaws in the chain of custody for forensic evidence; the inquiry that was pulled halfway through to exclude pathology samples. I tell her that I've matched the numbers to the names of ten real people courtesy of our community health inquiry.

As I speak, I realise that these ten names could be the reason why the police inquiry was pulled. That they might be the key to Eric's disappearance. I become convinced that these ten people have been involved in court cases that someone didn't want Eric to investigate. Something that required them to have a blood test. A wrongful conviction or a miscarriage of justice that allowed someone to go free. I wonder about the time Eric was run off the road by a van and whether it was a freak accident after all.

Meredith's eyes narrow. 'These ten names, where did you find them?'

'In a community health inquiry file.'

'The one where that arsehole reporter took pot shots at my clients?'

'That's the one.'

'Can I take a look?'

I've gone this far, and while I was talking, I drank the third glass of wine that materialised on the table, so I say yeah, sure, why not, and we climb off our stools and cross the road to the office. That in itself is an adventure and as we are waiting at the lights, I look back up at the bar and see the suit glaring down at us.

'Forget him,' says Meredith, tugging me across the road. 'He's tall and cute but he's too uptight for you.' When we get upstairs, she visits the ladies room and returns to the pod with two of James' beers from the staff kitchen.

'Show me.' She grabs Belinda's chair and pulls it up to my workstation. I squeeze in next to her, login to the cloud and bring up the community health file. Meredith scrolls through the document list.

'Why do you have a Department of Housing tenancy report in here?'

'Eric had put it in the hard copy file. He was working on two inquiries at once, so I'm guessing he was just sloppy.'

'Seems a bit of a coincidence to me.'

I shrug. Most people don't believe in coincidences, but I do. I've interrogated enough data to know there is an awful lot of randomness out there in the world. Our brains don't like that. We want to see patterns, linkages, to be able to predict what happens next, to know whether we will be the person to be struck by lightning or the guy standing next to us and what we could do to be the one who survives. It's too unsettling to think that things might happen for no reason at all.

Meredith opens the document. 'Fairly typical tenant.' She frowns, pulls her laptop out of her backpack, and logs into the TAG tenancy database. 'Where are your ten mystery people?'

I show her my notes. She scans the list and nods. 'Thought so. They're all ours. Public housing tenants.' She starts typing on her keyboard. 'Aggarwal: he was in Harbour Lights in Weymouth, but only for a couple of months it seems. Alexander: he had an apartment in the same building as Aaron. Calder: one of ours. Chut: he's ours too. They're all here. And here's your model tenant.'

I lean over her laptop. She's got to *Stewart*. A photo in the top left-hand corner shows a calm face and a fall of brown, curly hair. A red stamp across the screen declares Helen Stewart to be *Inactive*. 'What does that mean?'

'Polite term for evicted. Same as all the others, except Simpson.'

At that moment, the office lights time out. I leave the pod to press the button again and when they blink back on, I hear a clatter from the corridor that leads to the enclosed offices. Clearly someone in there didn't expect the lights to be reset. I think about walking down there to commiserate with whoever is working late but rethink it. I've had three wines and I've got a half-drunk bottle of One Fifty Lashes in my hand. It might not look good, especially if the candle-burner is Bigfoot. Also, she might follow me out of her office and then I'd have to explain why I have a tenancy advocate sitting at my workstation and looking through our files. I return to the pod on the balls of my feet as Meredith drains her bottle.

'You know, we hear all sorts of things at TAG, but they're generally just scuttlebutt.' She looks at me apologetically. 'I love our tenants, I really do, but they're not above slinging mud at the department to take the attention away from themselves. Last year, we heard that tenants were being evicted for what they claimed was no good reason. When we investigated, the department was slow to come back to us. Eventually they produced something – a complaint from a neighbour or photos of property damage – but we had a few tenants swear black and blue that it was fabricated. I remember Helen.' She taps the photo on the screen. 'Lovely woman. Husband in prison, teenage daughter. Moved down from the Mid West to give both of them more opportunities even though it meant leaving country. I probably shouldn't say this, because her name wasn't made public, but it was her house that got shot up the weekend we went to find Richard Cameron.'

I remember the paper folded on the front seat of Meredith's car. Two women, a mother and a daughter, standing outside the front of a cottage, their faces pixelated in the photo.

'Why was she evicted?'

'Her file doesn't say, but I don't remember her making a fuss about it. We keep records of when tenants have issues that might prevent them from paying rent or looking after their property. Hospital admissions, death in the family, that sort of thing. We do it so we can advocate on their behalf when the department comes down on them. Ms Stewart has nothing like that on file.'

I drain my beer while Meredith stares at the screen and taps her teeth. Outside my window, banks of lights flick on and off as cleaners move from floor to floor in the surrounding office towers. A glassie cleans the empty tables on the bar's balcony. The glowering suit has gone, and the square with the pop-up market is empty except for a few late commuters scurrying to the train station. The homeless man with the supermarket trolley has returned to wherever he goes to find shelter each night.

Meredith gasps. 'Oh, of course.' Her fingers scramble across the keyboard and she sits back. I look at the record she's brought up on the screen. Aaron Abadi. A big red *Inactive* stamp shows in the top left-hand corner. She gives me an apologetic look. 'Remember he said he passed his medical? Well, the reason he was in public housing was because he lost his job after failing one. I got a copy from him at the time so I could check if the result was from something else, like painkillers or prescription medication.'

'And was it?'

'No, but that's not the point. Look.' She taps on the screen, where she's brought up a document displaying an incomprehensible list of drug names and blood concentration figures. At the top of the report is the logo of the state pathology labs and a laboratory reference number – six numbers followed by three letters.

Meredith leans back into the chair. 'So, you were right; your mysterious numbers are for pathology reports.'

The numbers glow on the screen. I rub my eyes and peer at the tiny text. *Amphetamine type substances – detected.* Aaron Abadi's one-off hit was captured in a pre-employment medical test and lost him his job. I was on the right track after all.

Meredith grins at me, pleased with herself, but instead of triumphant, I feel sad and deflated. It's one thing to know what the numbers are, but I don't know where the knowledge gets me. So what if Eric had written a list of laboratory reference numbers on a scrap of paper? They were probably part of the police inquiry before the scope was pulled. There was nothing that tied them to his disappearance or even to the drug dealer who'd nearly run him over when he turned into the park that day. And as for his notes being in the community health file, maybe that was just sloppy recordkeeping. I'd had to clean up his files myself before the police searched his workstation.

I stare at Aaron Abadi's name stamped with the ugly red *Inactive* label. 'I don't know what to do with this.'

Meredith belches, reaches for Belinda's *Powered by Plants* water bottle, and drains it. Despite the number of wines she's downed, she still leaves a red imprint on the valve. I make a mental note to clean it and refill the bottle before we leave. 'Did this community health inquiry look at whether patients had blood tests as well as attending their follow-up appointments?'

I remember nice Dr Toby at Jana's dinner table. 'No, just follow-up appointments.'

'So, let's say Eric saw the laboratory reference numbers in the community health inquiry papers and recognised them from the police inquiry. If he knew they weren't supposed to be looking at them, what would he do?'

'Probably nothing. Not officially, anyway. He wasn't the project manager, just helping out the team.'

'Seems a bit strange, though, that your office was looking at something that wasn't in scope. At the very least, that's a breach of privacy. Wouldn't Eric have wondered who was looking at them? Wouldn't he have asked questions?'

No, I think, Eric wouldn't have questioned another project manager's work. That would've involved going to Bigfoot and risking a lecture about staying in your lane. But Meredith has a point. I'd assumed that Eric was the one doing the looking. I look at the date on the photocopied spreadsheet. I'd need to check, but I'm fairly sure it was printed before Eric was brought onto the community health inquiry. So if it wasn't Eric doing some unauthorised investigating, who was it?

'But why are they all public housing tenants?' I ask her. 'That's got nothing to do with the community health inquiry either.'

'Maybe the lab was checking for drugs.'

'No, that doesn't make sense.' I explain how it works with my own blood tests. 'The lab only screens for what the medical practitioner requests. The doctors in the hospitals aren't going to be testing outpatients for methamphetamine, they'll be looking at blood sugar levels, cholesterol, that sort of thing.'

'Who says these tests were requested by medical practitioners?'

I shake my head. I don't get it, she's lost me.

She jabs her pen at the laboratory reference number written down next to Meleshe's name. 'I'm willing to bet this pathology report wasn't requested by a doctor in a hospital. I reckon it's a drug test requested by a future employer. And I'll also bet the result was positive and his eviction was not long after. You know what I think? I think the government was accessing pre-employment drug screening to kick users out of public housing. And your Eric found out.'

We stare at each other for half a second and then my reaction is swift and emphatic and surprises us both. 'No, they can't do that.' I feel my face flush, an angry, indignant red. 'It's illegal.'

The idea of public servants accessing sensitive personal information for political reasons is both ridiculous and nauseating, the thing of conspiracy theories. Something Eric would dream up.

Far-fetched conjecture about a powerful, cruel and tight-fisted state turning its back on the vulnerable. And then I remember the Minister for Housing's comment about the new boy at the Tigers and how he doubted if he would *keep clean* for long enough to use the opportunity. I think of Matt, and the way he was dumped from his job and couldn't afford a rental. The wait for public housing, they told him, was over two years.

The beer in my gut rises up my throat. The ceiling tips to one side. It moves slowly at first, teasing me, before racing to the floor and back up again, spinning around and around until I put my head between my knees and vomit into Belinda's wastepaper bin. From across the room, I hear the ping and hush as the elevator arrives and the doors open and close. When I've finished, Meredith is holding my hair and wiping my face.

'See, you are a social justice warrior after all.'

CHAPTER THIRTY-SEVEN

When it was built thirty years ago, the remand centre was surrounded by bush and swamp. We drove past it once, the four of us. I was still in primary school and about to meet the puppy that I'd been promised for my first double-digit birthday. Matt wanted to call him Bruiser, but I wanted a girl dog, with long, soft ears. I was going to call her Princess. We were travelling slowly along an empty four-lane highway built in anticipation of commuters who wouldn't arrive for another ten years. Dad was looking for the turn-off, a gravel road that would take us past small holdings of boggy paddocks choked with arum lilies and wet-footed paper barks. The sign for the prison was on the opposite side of the highway to the road where my puppy lived, and it drifted into view through the banksia and she-oaks. Blue and white and official, it signalled something that was not part of my world. Was the puppy scared, I asked Mum and Dad, living so close to a jail? No, she wasn't scared, Dad said. The puppy knew she was a good dog, and no-one would come along and lock her up.

It was an ugly thought then, and it is again today, contemplating human beings locked behind walls and wire and observation towers. There is a special kind of fear being in sight of a place designed to hold people against their will. This time, I approach the prison from a new crossroad, four lanes separated by a swale and a traffic barrier. The road has bulldozed its way through the banksia bush and the prison perimeter fence is visible through the remnant trees left on the road reserve, presumably to leave space for another lane when the surrounding land fills with suburbs. They are already encroaching on the prison. Brick-and-tile houses on trucked-in sand that has been packed and packed again to lift houses up and away from the groundwater. The colour real estate lift-outs in the weekend paper show pictures of long-legged water birds and drainage systems that have been turned into water features. Another section of the paper reports on rising damp in new housing estates, and developers and local councils bicker over whom is responsible. I wonder if the lawsuits will be enough to distract people from the incarcerated souls living on their doorstep and whether it will take a breakout for them to sit up and notice.

The entrance to the prison is only one hundred metres from the new intersection between the two highways and is no longer a blue-and-white sign in the bush. Low buildings line the entrance road and there is space for a visitor to pull over in front of a map helpfully placed at driver eye-level. I don't want the office buildings with their garden beds of replacement native plants. I'm going straight to the prison entrance, where I'll be met by uniformed officers who will put my bag in a secure locker and give me a yellow sticker to put on my suit jacket. It will leave a glue mark there that will only come off the next time I send the jacket for dry-cleaning.

Belinda is with me, and she is fidgeting. I watch her eye the six-sided watchtower on our left and then swing her gaze to the one on our right. The glass is milky green.

'Do you think it's bulletproof?' she asks.

'Would you go up there if it wasn't?'

The watchtowers stand at the wide-angled junctions of high concrete walls. They are topped with metal tubes and stained black from rain at the top, and brown from bore water at the bottom. The water-wise plantings of native bushes don't apply to the outside walls of the main prison. Flat, lime-green lawn and a perimeter road are all that skirt the concrete walls, giving a clear line of sight to each corner. I can't picture Duncan, with his love of native birds and flowers, in this place and I almost convince myself that he can't be here if I can't imagine it. I half expect the guard behind the thick glass in the reception to shake his head and say they have no prisoners with that name.

He doesn't, though, because Duncan is here, and I have an appointment to meet him at ten o'clock. He will have been taken to one of the meeting rooms reserved for official visitors like us and will be waiting. Inside the gate, our identities and belongings are confirmed and scanned. We are allocated an escort and admitted through a series of doors. The corridors are wide, the floors grey vinyl and the walls a colour that a real estate agent once told me is called greige. Our escort peers through a window in one of the doors, unlocks it, and sits us down on one side of a table that is fixed to the floor. Duncan is sitting on the other side. He has his own escort and both officers stand behind him. He nods at us as we enter but doesn't rise or attempt to shake hands.

'Frances.' He's wearing a dark green pullover and I'm a little disconcerted at the lack of a collar. I only ever see my male colleagues in business shirts – James excepted of course – and the sight of Duncan's neck is oddly intimate.

'Good morning, Duncan. Thank you for seeing us.' My words come out stilted and formal. Duncan notices and smirks at my discomfort.

'Always a pleasure to assist the commissioner's office.'

'We want to talk to you about termination of public housing tenancies.'

'That's outside of the inquiry scope.'

'But within the commissioner's powers.'

'A new inquiry? When you still had all that file testing to complete in my offices? You are so terribly efficient.'

'We've found a large number of tenancies on file that were terminated with no clear reason.'

'Well, that's sloppy on the tenancy managers' part. Bad

recordkeeping. But I'm sure you'll find, with careful file review, that everything is in order.'

'According to the Tenants Advisory Group, a significant number of those tenants were users of illicit drugs.'

'A significant number of people in public housing are users of illicit drugs. That's not news. We'd like to change that, but I'm afraid the law says we can't. Unfortunately, we're not allowed to move people on if they use drugs.'

'But you did, didn't you,' interjects Belinda, 'You unlawfully accessed their medical records and started evicting anyone with a positive drug test.'

'We don't have authority to do that, Miss Lim. It's not possible.'

'The TAG records suggest that you found a way.'

He laughs. 'I doubt the TAG have recordkeeping standards that would satisfy the commissioner. But even if the records were accurate, it's just coincidence, not causation. I would expect you'd be familiar with the concept.' He draws two overlapping circles on the metal surface of the table, his fingers leaving damp contrails. 'Think about the number of people who take illicit drugs and the number of people in public housing. You're going to get some degree of overlap. It's obvious.'

I watch the lines of moisture evaporate and feel my neck tighten. The same incomplete circles are still between the pages of my landscape photography book, marked out in green pen.

'Who was sending you the lab results?' Belinda asks. 'Who approved it from their end?'

Duncan makes a show of slowly turning his head toward her and taking his time before he answers. When he does, it's me he addresses.

'Misuse of sensitive personal information stored in public sector databases is a very serious issue. The commissioner will need more than overlapping numbers to make those kinds of findings in a public report.'

'You'd be aware, of course, that the state pathology lab recently moved to a fully electronic document management system,' I tell him. 'It logs access and movement of all pathology reports, including drug tests. The records will be with the commissioner this afternoon.'

Duncan just smiles. 'The famous paperless office. It won't be too long before it puts you out of a job, Frances.' That lean again.

'Did you know?'

'Does it matter?' He spreads his arms wide to indicate his current accommodation. 'What difference would it make?'

'You could tell us who else was involved, who gave the instruction to use the information.'

Duncan folds his hands on the table and considers them. They look empty and derived of power without his phone. 'Management directives can be funny things in a complex bureaucracy,' he says into his upturned palms. 'I don't expect this is something you people would understand, with your black-and-white interpretation of the rules.'

Belinda snorts and, to Duncan's credit, he doesn't even flinch, let alone look up at her. 'You will know, of course, that there has been enormous pressure on the minister to clean up public housing and reduce the waiting list. The public expects to see their taxes put to good use. The minister has made it clear to the department that he wants results. Of course, we have programmes for achieving that, as you also know. The social housing initiative, tenant behaviour management. These things only go so far. When you get multiple questions in parliament and are pilloried on the six o'clock news over and over again for the condition of public housing and antisocial tenants, you can't blame junior officers for showing some resourcefulness in tackling the problem.'

'You knew about it then?'

'I didn't say that.' He leans back in his chair and crosses one ankle over his knee. 'You know, Frances, recruitment of junior officers is something your office could usefully investigate. There was a time when one could only enter the public service through a graduate programme. There was none of this coming in at level six or seven. The graduate programme was essential in teaching new public servants about ethical conduct like the treatment of sensitive personal information. It used to ensure that officers knew how to do the right thing. Now we get all sorts, academics, bankers, even former ministerial staffers. You should look into it.'

He folds his arms and I figure that's as much as he's going to give me. I thank him for his time. Belinda makes one last scrawl in her notebook and slaps it shut.

Duncan stands in the half second before I leave my seat and the vertical movement disrupts my balance. I grab for the side of the table, and my papers slide to the floor. He watches me steady myself while Belinda gathers them up. I keep my eyes on the table surface, but I can feel his gaze through the top of my head and know it is calculating.

'So, what's it like,' he asks, evenly, 'having to deal with this thing? What do you call it? Meniere's Disease?'

'Mostly fine.'

'But sometimes not.'

'No, sometimes not.'

'Like being seasick on dry land.'

'Yeah. Like that.'

'I suppose you don't go sailing?'

'No.'

'No ocean cruises with pink cocktails.'

'No ocean cruises, no sail boats, no catamarans.'

'Shame, you're missing out.'

'I'm sure I still live a very full life.'

Our escort catches my eye and I nod. He unlocks the door, but before we can walk through, Duncan clears his throat. 'You know, Frances, what happened to your brother was tragic.'

Belinda breathes out in one long hiss, and I feel prickles run through my body. I turn on my heel and our escort takes a step towards me. Stops just short of grabbing my arm. Duncan smirks.

'But it wasn't the department's fault. Catherine Matthews should know better than putting you in charge of the housing portfolio and letting you carry on with this personal vendetta. Does Neil know? Maybe the minister needs to have a word with him.'

Duncan's at least two metres away and on the other side of the bolted-down table. The guard has positioned himself in front of him without appearing to move. If I had something solid to throw – a cricket ball, a knife – I'd do it. My arm actually shakes with the need to hurl something into his face. Instead, I walk out the door.

The escort takes us back down the wide linoleum corridor. When we are back out in the sunshine on the right side of the gates, I catch myself rubbing my hands and wrists. A solid man in a too-tight suit, exactly the kind you'd expect to meet outside the entrance to a prison, gives me a nod as he walks past.

'Here,' says Belinda. She passes me a tube of antibacterial hand gel before using it herself.

CHAPTER THIRTY-EIGHT

I have a band around my forehead. I've been wading through the state pathology lab's database for the past two hours and my head is thumping. The background screen is a virulent green. I wonder if that's deliberate, designed to discourage loiterers, like the ultraviolet light used in public toilets. I squeeze my eyes, but all it does is put temporary circles in my field of vision.

It doesn't help that Bigfoot is suspiciously nonplussed about yesterday's visit to the prison. I made sure I got Neil's permission and promised it wouldn't stop me getting the draft report to her by close of business today. I even reminded her that she was the one who gave me Eric's papers to sort in the first place. All she managed was a half-hearted chastisement about following instructions.

'Yes, I did,' she said, 'but what did I tell you to do with them?'

'Sort them and give them back to you.'

'And let me know if you found anything.'

'Yes, Catherine.'

'Not run off with your own investigation behind my back.'

'No, not that.'

She braced her back with her hands and I remembered her leaving work to attend a physio appointment. 'You know, Frances, Neil rates you. I rate you. That's the only reason why he agreed to this. But if you uncover anything, there's a process you have to follow, you don't go running off to the commissioner.'

'I come to you first.'

'That's right. I can't have your back if I don't know it's exposed.'

The green screen is starting to pulse. I reach for my water bottle, but it's empty.

'Here,' says Belinda, passing me an unopened bottle. 'You'll go to hell for using single use plastic but at least you won't die of dehydration.'

I crack the seal and drain the bottle in two long draughts.

'How's it going?' she asks.

'Meh. Nothing's leaping out at me.' I push back from the desk and focus on the horizon, where the hills make a hazy line to the west. It will be hot out there today, hotter than the weekend. I hope Shayne's water trough has been topped up.

'What've you got so far?'

I'm working through a list of public housing tenants, looking up their names in the pathology database, recording the date and result of any drug tests, and going back into the Department of Housing database to check their tenancy status. I don't have the access logs yet, so I can't check who was here before me. That's next-level approval, and subject to what I can find in the database itself. It is picky, repetitive work. Exactly the kind I like. But today my right ear is full of fluid and the ceiling keeps tipping. I'd really like to lie down on the floor, but I worked hard to convince Neil to give me access to the database and I've got a deadline to produce results. I check the number of records on the spreadsheet I'm creating.

'Sixty so far, not counting the ten that Eric found,' I reply.

'How many have been drug tested?'

'Twelve.'

'And how many of those have been evicted?'

'Three.'

'That's not many. Are the reasons recorded?'

'Yeah. Disruptive behaviour and failure to maintain the property.' The tenancy files might or might not have documentation to back that up, but even if they do, my numbers aren't telling a story of a wicked public housing landlord evicting the poverty-stricken for minor drug use.'

'How much of an issue is it really, though?' Belinda asks. 'I mean, the law allows tenants to be evicted if they use a property for illegal activities. Doesn't that cover drug use?'

'Smoking a joint on your couch while you're watching the footy is a bit different to running a meth lab in the spare room.'

'It's still illegal though. I think a lot of people would think we're splitting hairs.'

'I bet the same people would change their tune if they were evicted for being high after a night out in Northbridge. How's that any business of your landlord? As long as you pay the rent and keep the place clean who cares if you like to get high on a Saturday night?'

Belinda raises her hands and I realise I've been making my point a little too forcefully 'Okay, okay. I'm just saying. I wouldn't like a drug addict renting my property.'

We both turn back to the screen. I can feel the heat coming off my face and I'm annoyed that I raised my voice. Duncan was right, I can't make this personal. What Belinda and I think isn't important. What matters is that the department acts in accordance with the legislation, obeys the rules, and doesn't get ahead of itself.

Belinda points at the screen where I've recorded the number of drug tests and her voice is conciliatory. 'Those are high, though. Would you have thought that twenty per cent of the general population had been drug tested in the last year?'

'No. Maybe. I don't know.' I think about it. 'Twelve out of sixty. That's one in five. No, of course not.'

She returns to her own workstation and starts typing into her search engine. 'According to the state pathology lab, they ran ninety thousand drug tests last year. I'm guessing that includes the idiots who swallow bleach, so maybe it's not all illicit drugs. There are two and a half million people in the state, so that means at the most three, maybe four, percent of people in the general population are drug tested each year. That's a lot less than twenty per cent.'

'So, if the department has been using drug tests to kick out tenants, they're not just harvesting existing results, they're targeting tenants for drug testing.'

'Yep, looks like it.' She swings back to me, legs dangling. 'That could be an interesting finding: *Government coerces public housing tenants to have illegal drug tests.* But then again' – I watch her weigh it up – 'I'm still not sure if anyone will care. Won't most people say that people who get public housing shouldn't be spending their money on drugs anyway?'

'That's not really the point though, is it? If the government wants to drug test tenants, they need to pass laws to make it legal.'

'Maybe they will, they've got a majority.'

Belinda is right. Again. If we table a report that says the government was forcing tenants to be drug tested, the Minister for Housing will just say that's in line with public opinion, if not technically within the black-and-white letter of the law. Nothing to see here. And if Meredith and her fellow advocates at the Tenants Advisory Group make a noise about it, he'll stand on his elected mandate. *Hard-working taxpayers won't tolerate drug users benefiting from the public purse, blah, blah, blah.* I suspect he'd be right. We will, as Belinda said, look like we are splitting hairs. Or worse, be accused of taking a partisan position.

I have no doubt that Eric knew about it. There was a reason he wrote down those ten numbers and I'm convinced they have something to do with his disappearance. All of them except Simpson and Helen Stewart returned positive drug tests, and all have been evicted except Simpson. If the department had been evicting tenants for drug use, logic would say that Helen Stewart, whose test was negative, would still be in public housing and not in a private rental where her new neighbours think she doesn't belong. Maybe I'm on the wrong track. Maybe I should be looking at wrongful convictions after all.

I fall back against my chair and stare at the ceiling. The panels are curved. Long wavy lines that are supposed to absorb noise. I wonder how much more they cost than the usual flat panels, whether they were purchased after following a competitive tender process, and what percentage noise reduction we got for the money. Everyone wears headphones in the office these days anyway so I can't really see the point. Looking at them makes me feel queasy again so I close my eyes and breathe out.

'Come on, it's not that bad.' James is back.

'Yes, it is.' Belinda replies for me. 'She's tired, annoyed and probably dehydrated.'

'Sleep and water will fix two thirds of that.'

'And the charity box chocolates will do the rest.'

'I'll go get some.'

'Have a look at my photos first.'

I close my eyes and listen to Belinda tell James about our visit to the prison. She'd finally relaxed once we were back in the car and insisted on doing a circuit of the carpark while she took photos on her phone. They're now sitting in my phone as well. She was so pleased with herself for surviving the ordeal, she sent them to everyone she knew. I hear her chastising James because he didn't reply to her text.

'How would you get public housing tenants to get drug tested?' I ask him when she finally leaves for reception. 'It's not like you can just get them to rock up to a lab voluntarily.'

'Get the police to do it, I guess.'

'Yeah, but how? Stake out their properties? Wait for them to come home looking under the weather and tap them on the doorstep?'

'Don't ask me, ask a cop. We know plenty of them.'

'Do we though? Someone we could ask this sort of thing?'

'What about the guy that tipped off Eric? You know, the guy who told him about the cook and his knife and how it went missing in police custody.'

'His brother-in-law, Rassie.'

'Yeah, him. Eric said he worked in internal affairs.'

'That could work.' Belinda returns and passes me a handful of tiny chocolates. 'We met him at Eric's thirtieth, remember? Dutch accent. Alice's husband.'

I text Alice to ask her if Rassie would mind giving us some off-the-record advice on drug testing in exchange for a beer. I shut down the computer and follow Belinda and James to reception. In the lift, Belinda argues with James about what to have for dinner. They leave me at the ground floor, agreeing that they will eat the steaks James defrosted that morning, but undecided about whether to barbeque or stir-fry. I watch them cross the road to the train station. James takes Belinda's hand as they step off the curb and she lets him, smiling up at his face. My phone pings. It's Alice.

I'm sure Rassie would love a beer, but he's a plumber, so unless your criminal has flushed the drugs down a toilet, he might not be much help!

CHAPTER THIRTY-NINE

I ride the bus home, past the darkening park. I look down at my phone from time to time to see if there's anything I've missed. Each time I tap the screen, it lights up the same message. Rassie's a plumber. He doesn't work for internal affairs. Alice doesn't send a second text. No jokes about how easy it is to confuse plumbing and internal police investigations. No questions about why I asked. No offer to put me in touch with another relative who works in internal affairs.

The bus passes the corner of the park and into the suburbs. As we trundle through the intersection, the lights change to orange and a dark-blue sedan shoots past us in the right-hand lane. The bus driver is forced to brake, and the only other passenger – the woman with the swishy skirt (she is wearing a red pantsuit today) looks at me and rolls her eyes. Cosy houses line the street. They are the same vintage as the house that the TAG now occupies, only here the suburb has remained residential, gentrified and quietly lush. It is a white-picket-fence and tuckpointed suburb. A place for university-educated parents to send their children to bed at the same time every night and oversee their teeth-brushing in the morning. A place where every child wears a school uniform and gets a packed lunch. What will those children make of life on the other side of the city, I wonder, when (if) they discover that the children there go to school after sleeping in a room with five other kids and a hole in the floor. The kids who live here would be hard pressed to understand a year-long battle to get your oven fixed or what it's like to have your clothes dried inside of one.

The bus lurches as the driver slams his brakes again. I hear him swear. My backpack tumbles off the seat. My red-suited companion staggers as she is thrown down the aisle. She grabs a handrail, swings sideways, and I see her ankle roll. I flinch, anticipating the pain, but she rights herself, and looks back at me with a grin, shaking one leg in the air. I'm confused until she points to her foot. We're both wearing Docs. I give her a thumbs-up and she bounces down the steps to the street, giving the driver a wave and a thank you.

In front of the bus, parked in front of the Buses Only sign, is the car that cut in front of us at the lights. The driver, a tall, fit-looking man in a baseball cap and a hurry, puts his hand up to the bus driver with an apologetic wave. He meets my eye, narrowly misses shirtfronting the lady in red, then turns on his heel and ducks into the fish and chip shop. The bus driver shakes his head, reverses, and pulls back out onto the road.

When I get home, I eat sliced banana on a toasted bagel for dinner. I think about adding a handful of spinach, but the packet has developed the swampy odour of decaying leaves, so I toss the packet in the bin and drizzle honey over my banana instead. It's not a substitute for whatever minerals I'm supposed to get from spinach, but it does taste better. I chase it with the dregs of a bottle of wine and open my laptop to FaceTime Belinda.

She answers, waves, swallows. I've caught her mid-chew. I can see the television news in the background behind her head. I tell her about Alice's text. Rassie's a plumber, not a cop. Did we get that wrong?

'No, Eric definitely said it was his brother-in-law who told him about the chef. Did he only have the one?'

'Eric only has one sister. How else can you have a brother-in-law?'

'Brother's wife's brother?' she offers.

'No, Alice and Eric only have one brother, the guy in Cape Town, and he's not married. Never was as far as I know.'

Belinda turns away from the camera. 'James? Did Eric definitely say he got the tip-off about the chef's knife from his brother-in-law or was it some other relative?' The camera wobbles around the room and instead of the tiled floor of Belinda's bedsit, I see long, dark floorboards and an arrangement of leather couches. I grip the kitchen bench to steady myself.

'No idea. That was almost two years ago now.' I hear the rhythmic thud of a knife on wood and the camera swings upwards to reveal James at a long island bench, chopping carrots. In the foreground, a hand reaches out to steal a carrot and gets waved away by the knife. Belinda's face comes into view.

'Aren't you having second thoughts about the drugs angle anyway?' she says. 'I thought the data wasn't giving you anything.'

'Maybe, maybe not. What's for dinner?'

'Some sort of beef and vegetable stir-fry involving garlic. Oh, hang on.'

The camera drops to the floor again. The volume on the television ratchets up.

'Turn on the news, Frances. Channel Seven.'

I find the remote. The Channel Seven news desk is telling us that the government, in a late-night sitting of parliament, has passed legislation to clean up public housing. The camera cuts to Parliament House, where the Minister for Housing is back on his favourite step. Once again, the sky is clear behind him, and he smiles an easy smile that says he has the backing of the premier and the entire Cabinet. It looks like he is wearing the same shirt and tie he wore when he slayed Duncan.

'Public housing tenants now have real reasons to walk away from poor life choices,' he says to the interviewer. 'Our government is providing them with incentives to kick illicit drugs. From next month, all public housing tenants and people on the waiting list will have to undergo mandatory drug screening. People who test positive must undertake counselling and submit two negative test results within three months.' He turns to the camera and looks straight down the lens. 'When you come clean, you will secure your place in public housing.'

The camera switches to a familiar, scowling face. Like the minister, Meredith is standing on the Parliament House steps, but the shadow of the building falls across her. She balances the ubiquitous stack of files on her narrow hips.

'Having a roof over your head is the number one factor in kids doing well at school, parents getting jobs, and everyone in the community living long and healthy lives. This government wants to pull the rug out from under the feet of people who are struggling, literally, the one thing that stands between their kids and a life on the streets. It is cruel and heartless, and the minister and the premier should be ashamed of themselves.' The camera cuts back to a distanced view of the minister and his clutch of reporters and cameramen. He is standing in the sun, head and shoulders above them.

'The government's *Come Clean* campaign launches on television and online tonight,' says the voice over. The news report banner cuts in and a car advertisement starts.

'It looks like you were right.' James' head fills my laptop screen. 'They were probably trialling it before going public. That's what you're seeing in those records.'

'I can't say I disagree with him,' Belinda's voice comes from somewhere behind James. 'People can't expect the public to give them a house while they're spending money on drugs. And anyway, the private sector already does it. Workers in the mining industry have to take mandatory drug tests before being allowed on site.'

I say nothing. I think there's a difference between keeping workplaces safe and denying people a home, but the old habit of not commenting on government policy is ingrained. Even with my workmates, even in private.

'I guess that's it, then,' says James. 'No point reporting on what they've just made law. What are you thinking, boss?'

I don't know what I'm thinking. Meredith is right, *Come Clean* is bad policy, but Belinda and James are right too. If no-one was going to care about drug users being evicted from public housing, they're going to care even less now. I can't help but think the announcement's too much of a coincidence coming two days after we visited Duncan in prison. I wonder who he called. Would it have been direct to the minister's office, or did he tip off a visitor and have them make the call for him?

I listen to the sounds of domesticity filtering through my laptop speaker. Pots clanging, kitchen drawers opening and closing; the same sounds as at Jack's. I turn off the television and press my finger into the toast crumbs on my plate. 'I'll wave the white flag tomorrow morning.'

Belinda and James chorus goodnight and James' kitchen blinks off my screen. I send a meeting request to Neil's EA for tomorrow. I hope she doesn't invite Bigfoot. I feel like enough of a quitter without having my director gloat over my backdown. She'll be nice in front of Neil – *at least you can be satisfied that you covered all bases*, that sort of thing – but she'll have *told you so* written all over her face. Or maybe she won't. Bigfoot didn't seem to be all that worried about my impromptu prison visit. Maybe she has other things on her mind. Maybe she's not just sensible shoes and a work uniform and has a family – possibly even an aging parent like me – to worry about. She wasn't interested in the reason for my unauthorised forensic database snooping either. Maybe I just don't feature as high in her list of priorities as I think I do.

As I take my plate and glass back to the kitchen, my laptop beeps. Neil's EA has accepted the meeting request. I'm to be in Neil's office at eight am. I take the last of my wine to the balcony to watch the final colours of the sunset. Below my feet, a shiny, dark-blue sedan is parked in the universal parking bay, and I look down just in time to see a baseball cap with a fancy white logo disappear into the driver's-side door.

CHAPTER FORTY

Neil lets me drop the forensics investigation without losing face. *You never know if you don't ask the question,* he says. Bigfoot, if anything, looks like her attention is anywhere but in Neil's office. She stares out of the window and doesn't even blink when Neil compliments me on my enthusiastic pursuit of human rights, *even if it hasn't come to anything this time.* She only comes to when he asks about progress on the housing inquiry report.

'Right,' she exclaims, clapping her hands together and startling both of us. 'Now there'll be nothing in the way of meeting our deadline.' She hands me her corrections on my draft, telling me to dot the I's and cross the T's and get it back to her by close of business. Neil nods his encouragement, and we walk back to her office. She disappears inside and closes the door without a word.

I take Bigfoot's notes back to the pod and get to work. Two hours later, and as much as I love detail and tying up loose ends, I'm dragging my feet. I know the report is important. It will be used by the public prosecutor when Duncan goes to trial and has to be watertight. I've inserted my footnotes and annotations diligently, aware that each finding will be pored over. I've done this before, I can do it again. But my care factor has gone. Duncan has done a lot worse than just line his pockets with public money, I'm sure of it. He's used people to make himself look good. As Meredith said, he's taken away one of their basic human needs – a roof over their heads – just so he can reduce the waiting list and meet his KPIs. I don't care that the government has now made it legal, I don't care if the general public agrees with them; I want Duncan to pay for his callous indifference to people who don't get to live in hillside mansions. I stab at the keyboard. At least I can take comfort that this report will keep him out of the realms of power. He's facing seven years in prison if he's convicted of the roof-insulation fraud. He must be in his late fifties now. A conviction will mean the end of his public service career.

Belinda has sorted purchase orders, invoices and Kim's inspection reports by district and housing estate. I check each bundle, tally the discrepancies between what was bought and what was delivered, and place the papers in the evidence file. Later, I will scan everything to PDF and put them in the electronic archive.

Only one contractor was involved in the fraud. Batt Brothers Supply and Installation – a partnership between twin brothers, Bevan and Brian Batt. I shudder. It's almost as bad as Graham Griffiths. There should be a Commissioner for Names to protect innocent infants from their parents. I look up Bevan and Brian Batt online to see if there's anything alarming in their history that I should know about before I put their names in a public report. I find lots of advertisements for Batt Brothers. Pictures of a round, smiling cartoon man wearing blue overalls. With his chubby tummy and short legs, I can't see him ever crawling into a roof space, but I guess that's not the point. He looks friendly, honest and unthreatening, and given that it's the mum part of their mum-and-dad customer base who arranges things like roof insulation, it's probably hitting the mark. Although not anymore.

Alongside the advertisements are links to news reports about the *public housing scandal* and photos of two very un-smiley men climbing into a Range Rover. Then I find a photo of the brothers at the football. They are standing in a corporate box, twirling their scarves over their heads. Next to one twin, is our very own Dr Duncan Wolf, team cap pulled low over his head and a wide grin splitting his face. On his other side, in the visiting team's colours and with a beer in hand, is Graham Griffiths.

CHAPTER FORTY-ONE

It's twilight by the time I email the draft report to Neil and Bigfoot, and shutdown my laptop. I would have finished earlier except I went for a walk around the city blocks while I stewed over Graham Griffiths and his connection to the Batt brothers and my incarcerated nemesis. It can't be a coincidence that someone doing time for supply of methamphetamine is on flag-waving terms with Duncan and his partners-in-fraud. Not when Duncan is also waging a war against drug addicts in public housing. But I can't make the two pieces fit. If Graham is a supplier and he's buddies with Duncan, which I am sure he is, you'd think he'd be leaning on him to keep his buyers where he can find them. But Duncan is turfing Graham's customers out of their homes.

I catch the bus, order takeaway online from my phone, and stew some more as I ride past the park. The missing piece is there some-where but keeps slipping just beyond my grasp. My annoyance finds other things to latch onto. A previous passenger has spilled coffee and it has created a sticky river flowing under my seat. Someone has scratched the word *fuck* into the glass, in tiny letters just above the window ledge. Somehow, the size of the script and the obvious care taken to avoid being caught is more irritating than the super-sized scrawl of the usual graffiti tags. Another commuter boards and, although every other seat is free, he sits facing me and sticks a chewing gum in his mouth. I feel my own jaw tighten as he masticates.

When we reach my building and its avenue of pines, the same blue sedan – a Mercedes, no less – is parked in the universal parking bay out the front. I resist the urge to kick its tyres, but there are people in the street, so I leave it. If it's still there after I've collected

my noodles, maybe I can trip on some loose paving ⟨
of sticky honey soy sauce from my takeaway on the t⟨

There's an unusual number of people about. The a⟨
members stride up and down, sculling from Cam⟨
from the gym's full-height windows spill onto the footpath. A row
of treadmills and stationary bikes are lined up facing the street, all
occupied by people sweating out their day. The Merc driver better
not be on one of those, I think, or it will be more than the bonnet of
his car that gets the honey soy treatment. The corner supermarket
is lit up as well, and a small crowd spills onto the footpath, which
has been decorated with a red carpet and wine barrels sprouting
black flags. Black-clad waiters carry silver trays of tiny plastic
tasting cups. The cashier at the Thai takeaway recognises me and
passes my order through the servery.

'Promotion?' I ask him.

'Inaugural street party, apparently,' he replies with a grin.
'Sponsored by a winery. I heard the local member of parliament is
giving a speech. We weren't invited but it's good for business. We've
already had customers ordering takeaway after too many of those
plastic cups.'

I take another look at the black flags. They unfurl in the westerly
to reveal a rippling and familiar image of *Zaglossus hacketti*, the
stylised emblem of Zaglossus Estate, owned by Jana's husband. It
seems he's taken his own advice to wine and dine the minister.

'I might have a few of them myself.'

'Enjoy.' The kitchen passes him another order and he checks the
name on the ticket before calling it out into the street.

I wave my thanks and wander toward the supermarket, scanning
the crowd for Mike. They are a mix of sweaty shoppers in tracksuit
pants and crumpled office workers clutching cups of wine with
relief. I've almost reached a young woman balancing a tray, when
the traffic lights change and the unmistakable figure of the Hon.
Simon Tallent jogs through the intersection. He's looking straight

. me and speaking on the phone. When he sees that I've clocked him, he breaks into a wide smile, pockets the mobile and raises his hand in greeting. It's the same self-assurance, the same belief that he speaks for the majority, that he carried when he looked down the camera from the steps of Parliament House. But even from here I can see that the smile doesn't reach his eyes, that it is the smile of the Cabinet minister, not the local member. He beckons me over, but I point to my takeaway, and shrug my apologies. He nods, full of ministerial understanding, then returns his attention to his phone, tapping furiously in good imitation of his incarcerated underling. I turn around. I have my own wine at home.

On my floor, the fire door is chocked open, even though the lift is working again. It creates a soft whistle that I can only just hear underneath my tinnitus. I contemplate closing the door, shuffling aside the brick paver wedged into the gap, but figure someone has left it open for a reason and pad down the otherwise silent corridor. I've got my door key out this time, so I don't need to juggle my bag and the sweating plastic box. The yellow stain on the carpet outside my door is still there. I'm surprised building management haven't emailed me a *please explain* and decide it would be prudent to put stain remover on it before I eat and forget again. I drop the takeaway on the kitchen bench and search the cupboards under the sink for the pink-and-white spray bottle. I'm head down and bum up when I hear my front door click.

I try to leap to a less vulnerable position but fail and bang my head against the U-bend, so I sit on the kitchen floor instead, aiming the stain-remover bottle with one hand and rubbing my skull with the other.

'Hello?'

No-one replies and I contemplate whether that is a good or a bad thing. I can't remember if I let the front door swing shut behind me or left it open. Maybe I left it open and the draught from the fire door has made it swing shut. I strain, but now I can't hear the whistle of the draught at all. It occurs to me this would make sense if my front door is shut. The problem is, I don't know if there is someone on this side of it with me, or whether the click was the sound of them making their escape.

I get to my feet, holding the spray bottle in front of me with my fingers curled around the plastic trigger, and step through the kitchen toward the front door. As I pass the hallway that leads to my bedroom, I pause. Through the open door, the doona hanging over the foot of my bed is smooth and undisturbed. The striped shirt I'd put on this morning and discarded in favour of the white one I'm wearing now is still draped over the chair because I was too lazy to hang it up again. If someone is in there, I can't hear them.

I turn my head to look back over the living room. I'm holding my breath and exhale through my mouth as silently as I can, suspecting I am being overly dramatic. I still have my trigger finger on the spray bottle. The coffee table is a mess, I notice. Newspapers, a wine glass, a dirty plate, my landscape book and my computer. If someone had been in here, they weren't inclined to do any cleaning or steal my laptop. The tension drains out of me in a rush. I let my gun-arm fall, deflated, and check the front door. It's locked.

I put the spray bottle on the kitchen bench, retrieve my dirty dishes from the coffee table and put them in the sink. I open a rosé and fork noodles onto a clean plate. If the intruder – if there ever was one – is still here, they can accost me over dinner. My overfilled glass sloshes as I dump it on the table, and I remember the yellow stain on the carpet. I take the spray bottle to the front door, get down on my hands and knees, and make a white fluffy circle of foam over the mark. I'm sitting back on my heels, pre-occupied with watching the bubbles burst and pop when I sense a shadow behind me. I try to swing around but the sudden movement and the proximity of a tall figure makes the corridor lurch and, before they can speak, I'm on the floor, my eyes squeezed shut and my fingers digging into the deep carpet pile.

CHAPTER FORTY-TWO

'Whoa, sorry! Sorry. Are you OK?'

I press my tongue against the roof of my mouth and tighten my throat against the rising nausea. I can smell chemicals and realise I've landed in the stain remover. My hair is damp. I breathe, but it only intensifies the sharp smell, and I screw up my nose.

'Talk to me, tell me what's happening.'

I can't place the voice and I risk opening my eyes. The skirting board flies past me in a blur but in front of it I recognise the face. It's my neighbour, with two frown lines between two brown eyes hovering above the carpet. His hands are also braced on the floor, and I reach out and pat one in what I hope is a gesture of reassurance. He takes it as a signal for help and grips it, slipping his other hand under my armpit and lifting me to a sitting position against the wall. My vestibular system screams. I squeeze my eyes closed and wait for my brain to adjust to my new position. Damp is seeping through my skirt to my butt, and I wonder what the stain remover will do to the fabric. I hear a groaning noise. It's me, protesting at the vertical shift. I cradle my face in my hands and push down the bile. If I vomit now, it will make more than just a small yellow circle next to my door.

'It's vertigo, right? Just stay where you are for now. Sip this.'

I feel cold glass slide into the palm of my hand. Gripping it is beyond me. A warm hand wraps around mine and and together we raise the glass to my lips. I sip. Breathe. Sip. Breathe. I can't hear anything over the ringing in my ears. I feel something hard knocking against my back and realise it's me, rocking backwards and forwards against the wall.

It could be five minutes or twenty but eventually the hammering in my chest softens and the world behind my eyelids settles into place. I risk taking another look. I'm propped facing down the corridor and can see all the way to the fire door, which is closed. My neighbour is sitting cross-legged in front of me, tapping on his phone. The glass is on the carpet next to him. He looks up, smiles.

'You're back.'

I nod.

'How do you feel?'

'It's almost over.'

'We'll wait another minute and I'll help you inside. I have a patient with Meniere's. Do you have rescue meds?'

'I'll be fine.'

'Okay, but just say the word and I'll get them for you.'

I reach for the glass, drink more water, keep my eyes open, and nod when I'm ready to stand. He lets me do it in my own time and together we shuffle back into my apartment and onto the couch. I stare at the blank television screen while he moves around my kitchen. He returns with my bowl of noodles and a folded-up towel.

'I can't stay, I have an appointment in half an hour.' He places the television remote on the arm of the couch. 'Can I call anyone? What about your friend? The one who just left.'

I blink at him, consider making a quip about not having any friends who know where I live, but my tongue is rooted to the floor of my mouth.

'You must've just missed him,' he says. He puts a card on the table. 'Here are my contact details. Call me if you need anything. Anytime.'

I listen for the click of my front door lock. I really want to get up and check it but even bending forward makes the room start spinning again. I console myself that my neighbourly neighbour could be wrong. The person he saw leaving could have been knocking on any of the six doors on our floor; it didn't have to be mine. And the noise I heard could have been anything, including my tinnitus.

I use the remote to switch on the news. It's two minutes into the broadcast and I've missed the top stories. I lift my food, noodle by noodle, to my mouth. Early season fires on the east coast are threatening homes, the television says. Helicopter footage pans across sheets of flame-igniting gum trees. The shire president of a coastal town stands with his back to an orange horizon and says they will know within the next twelve hours whether residents will be told to evacuate. In the meantime, people should remain indoors with their windows closed and be ready to leave. The emergency services number and the name of the local news radio station scroll underneath.

The screen shifts to a crowd gathering beneath a spreading tree at the entrance to the cemetery located only a kilometre from my apartment. A long, dark vehicle floats past them and they drift into its wake. At the front walks a woman with dark hair tied back in a low ponytail. I recognise her from her late husband's Facebook page. She holds the hand of a boy wearing a black suit and white sneakers. His eyes are wide and fixed on the rear window of the hearse. Behind him walks a phalanx of union men, Eureka Stockade flags pinned to their jackets. Their eyes are hidden behind their black sunglasses, but their tightly held mouths give no doubt about their mood. In front of them, to one side of Aaron's widow, walks a man in a black suit, black shirt, black tie, gold-rimmed Aviators. As they approach the chapel and the hearse turns to the side entrance, he places his hand on the woman's back and guides her to the front door. A row of foreheads frown and one union man bends into another, who shakes his head. The usurper removes his glasses, and a sidebar gives viewers his name. *Mike Vargus, CEO of Lignum Partners and Zaglossus Estate.* I blink, and then blink again. So much for *a couple of little projects in the city.* I'm guessing Mike didn't invite the funeral party to his promotion event downstairs with the minister.

CHAPTER FORTY-THREE

The next day I take the bus to the university and walk into the park. I should have gone grocery shopping – I'm still out of bananas – but today I need trees, not fruit. I miss the view from our old office. The bus trip past the park each day doesn't compensate for being able to gaze across a green canopy when my eyes need to unfocus and give my brain a break. In our new corner pod, we can look into the distance, but the colour scheme is grey and brown instead of green and blue, and it's not a nice brown either. Not the brown of rich, crumbly soil or chocolate cake, but the dirty, washed-out brown-orange-grey of city heat, car exhaust and smoke. I need to bathe in the bush.

It hadn't taken long to find out what the internet had on Jana's husband. He took to the lectern after escorting Aaron's widow to her seat and used the opportunity to preach a few quotable life messages.

'Nothing will change Aaron's destiny, but what you do now will change yours,' he told the grieving gathering. 'God wants you to prosper, to live your best life. Name it and claim it.'

The Twitterati had sneered. *Trickle-down economics with hymns, and God blessed him with wealth because he had the foresight to be baptised into the same religion as the Minister for Housing.*

The building unions, famous for their conservative Catholic roots, were also quick to take him down. 'Michael Vargus thinks the capitalist system is divinely ordered to reward good Christians. If he put more money into his building sites than into his church, people like Aaron Abadi would go home safe to their families at night.'

Meredith, I saw, had stayed out of the spat. I couldn't even spot her in the funeral footage.

I'm more interested in the connection between Mike and the Minister for Housing's former Assistant Director for Homelessness Strategies than I am in Mike's personal theology As objectionable as it is, I couldn't care less whether Mike thinks his personal wealth is divinely ordained, although I wonder what Jana's position is on that.

I walk the same route that Belinda, James and I walked on the Saturday after Eric disappeared, wondering if I need to look at the records for the construction site where Aaron died. Duncan – or at least Duncan's office – would have awarded the contract to Mike Vargus. After Mike's rant about the tenders board, I'm thinking Duncan might have been than awarding roofing insulation contracts to his mate.

The sun has more of a sting to it than it did on our walk twelve months ago and I follow the bush side of the road in the shade. Saturday morning traffic noises drift up the escarpment, but the park is otherwise silent. Whatever creatures live under the bushes and in holes in the ground, they are quiet, sleeping safely, hidden away for the day. The river drifts into view as I walk and even the river craft move silently. I take my time, mindful of my episode on the carpet last night. I pass an empty carpark, the place in the road where James found the sunglasses, and the sand track with the discarded pile of clothing. The glasses, I realise, are still in my jacket pocket, one of those internal ones that I never use except when I go hiking. I pat myself down, feel their bony wings against my ribs, and try them on. They are heavy on my face, but have a blue-green tint, the type that softens and cools the world around you. I leave them there even though I know they will make red indents on the side of my nose.

Voices rushing up behind me shout *car!*, then shoot past before I've even jumped aside. A peloton of maybe ten, twelve, riders, tightly bunched. I catch words like *shareholders* and *targets*. It is reporting season for the corporate world and the cyclists will be swapping their bikes and lycra for Teslas and suits on Monday morning. Maybe even before then. They vanish around the next corner as one, leaving me with the silent bush and the background hum of traffic. Eric didn't ride in a peloton. He was contemptuous of the group riders in their sponsored vests. He rode alone in his home-brand t-shirt and cycling shorts, setting his own pace. I knew he rode with a camera strapped to his back and would stop to capture the bush, recording its changes in seasons. Occasionally – very occasionally – a child might foreground a wattle bush in flower or be an artistic blur on a tree-top walk, but he wasn't interested in photographing people. He would have chafed, I imagine, at the crowds that day and the missed opportunities to stop in a quiet place and wait for non-human creatures to emerge in the twilight.

The sounds of the cultivated sections of the park float around the corner. Car engines firing, people laughing, children shouting, doors slamming shut. I reach the carpark and climb the lookout, my feet ringing on the open metal treads, and count three lazy columns of smoke in the hills. Up here, above the canopy, the sea breeze whispers against my cheek. I turn my head to face it and catch the glint of car roofs along the road I've just walked. I realise the car that the cyclists were shouting to avoid never passed me and, looking at the full car bays underneath my feet, congratulate the driver for wisely choosing a parking spot farther away from the crowds.

Below me, family groups amble up the long, sloping lawn that divides the park from east to west. I hang onto the rail, willing my vestibular system to behave, and watch children clatter up the steps. When they reach the top, they stop abruptly and blink at me, a stranger and unaccompanied. They look for their parents and sidle around to the opposite side of the platform, as far from me as possible, staring past their feet at the world below.

Vehicles nose into the carpark, pause, and reverse out again. Only one bay is free, its blue-stencilled wheelchair clear from this angle. I watch drivers and passengers eyeing it, wondering whether to risk a short stay while they unload grandma and their eskies. It can be a long walk from the next available carpark. A four-wheel drive enters, reverses back onto the road, then brakes abruptly as the driver sees reversing lights flash on one of the parked vehicles. Another would-be picnicker on the road behind him blasts his horn in annoyance. The four-wheel drive is not willing to give up the opportunity though, and stays where he is, blocking the road, while the exiting car edges out of its bay. I can see his fingers tapping on the steering wheel, a North Face logo, and a backpack on the passenger seat. A solitary hiker, impatient to get on one of the trails through the park before it gets too hot. The exiting car straightens up and squeezes through the gap in the driveway, hiking man pulls in, and the driver who was forced to wait accelerates away, one finger jammed hard against his windscreen, his face contorted from the insult of having to wait.

I head back down the stairs. I've drunk all my water and can feel my heart flip-flopping in my chest. It does that when my potassium is low. I remember Alice's exhortation to buy potassium chloride tablets. I haven't done that yet, of course. I get a bottle of orange juice at the café, drain it, and look for a fruit bowl on the counter, hoping for one-dollar bananas, but all they have is apples. I fill the orange juice container with water and drain it again. A family vacates a deeply shaded patch of lawn, so I claim it and ease myself onto the grass. I pull back my toes to stretch out my calves. As I bend forward, heat flashes at the base of my skull and the world sways sideways. Bile rises in my throat. I slide my hand backwards along the grass, lowering my head to the ground as slowly as I can manage, my eyes fixed on the hills beyond the river. The columns of smoke have begun to disperse, spreading as they hit some mysterious layer of air. I close my eyes and wait for it to pass.

I wake up when the shade shifts, and the sun hits my bare shins. I pull my legs underneath me and lift myself onto my elbows. Picnic rugs, eskies and their disgorged contents are clumped across the grass, and the air is warm and moist from the enveloping vegetation. The sky over the hills is a dirty colour, dulled by smoke and heat. I drink the last of my water, refill the bottle from the fountain near the café and set off under the avenue of lemon-scented gums, heel-toeing to lengthen my calves after my nap.

Our old office comes into view through the column of trees. My calves are really tight now and I'm breathing harder than I should. A bicycle – a single one this time, and riding on the footpath instead of the road – shoots past me. I don't hear it approach and I miss my footing as I jump to one side. The rider raises his hand in apology but doesn't turn around to see if I'm okay. He continues toward the roundabout and turns right to coast down the hill and into the city. I brace my hands on my hips to lift my chest and breathe deep. As my shoulders drop, I close my eyes and will my heart to steady. My old bus stop is a few metres down from the roundabout. If I can make it there, I'll catch the bus home.

I open my eyes again and focus on the city towers. My head feels tight like I'm wearing a swimming cap and the sounds of the park have dulled as though I'm underwater. The towers shimmer, or maybe it's just my eyes. A figure moves in front of them. For a moment I can't tell if it is something near the horizon or in the park, and then it comes closer, consolidating. I can see a North Face logo at eye level, crossing the road toward me. He moves with an appearance of urgency, his arms held out in front. I can see his blond hair and his mouth working, and I concentrate on the shapes it makes until I hear steps and feel something hard catch me behind my back.

'Frances? Frances!'

My name doesn't come from the hiker, who seems to dissolve. I squeeze my eyes hard and open them again, but he's gone. I turn toward the voice, which is now asking me if I'm okay, and see our old gardener, Jason, his protective earmuffs clasped around his neck. It's his arm around my back and I register that it's taking a good part of my weight. I try to right myself.

'I don't think that's a good idea, mate,' he says, putting his other hand under my arm. He's supporting me like I'm his grandmother. 'I've got you. Let's walk you back to the office, hey?'

I don't walk so much as shuffle in a repeat of my disgrace the night before. We cross the road, Jason briefly letting go of my arm to put up a hand to traffic, and circle around the blower vac he's left on the footpath.

'It can wait', he says. I hear the glass doors of the building lobby slide open and feel the air-conditioning on my face. I'm lowered onto a cool leather seat, eased onto my back and my feet lifted onto the cushion. Jason unlaces my shoes, and I wriggle my toes in the cool air.

'What was that all about?'

'It's nothing, I'm just a bit dehydrated.'

'How? It's not even thirty degrees outside. I thought you were from Weymouth. You should be used to weather hotter than this.'

I turn my head and see a bowl of fruit on the coffee table in front of me. It has bananas.

'Can I have one of those?'

'You can have all of them if you like. They won't last until Monday, and they'll only get binned when the cleaners come.'

He passes me one and I eat it half peeled, like a cartoon monkey.

'You don't look great, if you don't mind me saying. Maybe you should go to the hospital.'

'No, I'm fine, really.' I think of the bottle of rescue meds in my bathroom cabinet. 'I've got medication, I just need to go home and take it. The twenty-seven bus goes straight past my building.'

Jason checks his watch. 'Are you sure? There's one due in twenty minutes. I'll walk you across the road when you're ready.'

I drain my water bottle again and Jason passes me a can of

lemonade. 'You look like you need the sugar.' I drain that too and wonder how long it will be before my bladder protests against the surfeit of liquid I've drunk. Or maybe I've already sweated it out. My body seems to think it is going somewhere and needs to be replenished.

Jason settles himself onto the armchair opposite me, removes his earmuffs and unlaces his boots. He has tan lines and grass clippings above the cuffs. Underneath, his skin is as pale as an office worker.

'Who was the guy?' he asks.

'What guy?'

'The guy with the backpack. He sounded like he knew you.'

I try to remember, but all I can get is a fuzzy image of a North Face logo. 'He was in the carpark earlier. Some random hiker.'

'Some random creep more like it. He was a solid bloke, but he took off pretty quickly when I turned up. It was lucky I was outside doing the footpath. I saw you on the road. You weren't exactly walking in a straight line. You looked like you needed a hand.'

'Thanks. I think I did.' I wriggle my toes in the cool air, remembering the last time Jason spotted someone on Fraser Avenue. 'James told me what you said about the day Eric went missing,' I say, 'about the near miss.'

'That was Eric's fault, to be honest. The Mercedes was travelling pretty close behind the other bike and Eric slipped in between them. The driver had to brake hard.'

'James said he was the drug trafficker, the one they sent to prison.'

'The driver of the Merc? No that wasn't him.'

'But wasn't that what you told the police? That Graham Griffiths nearly took him out. That's why they raided Griffiths' house. It's how they got him on supply charges.'

'No, no, no. That's not how it was. Griffiths was there, he just wasn't in the car. He was the guy on the bike, riding next to Eric into the park. They were talking. He was wearing sunglasses just like yours.'

CHAPTER FORTY-FOUR

The paddocks have browned off even more since I was here last weekend. Winter grass that was heading a week ago looks brittle and horses stand in the shade instead of basking in the spring sun. Belinda tugs her sleeve over her wrist as I turn the car off the highway and light streams through her window. We crest the ridge and the bush shimmers in front of us. Through the trees, we glimpse a column of smoke to the south, rising straight upwards.

'That's a long way off, isn't it?'

'At least fifty kilometres,' I reassure her. 'And when the sea breeze comes in, it will push it in the other direction.' We drop down into the valley and the trees close over. The air is instantly warmer, thicker.

'Does the sea breeze even make it this far?'

I risk a glance away from the road. She has a sheen of sweat on her temple. 'Of course it does, just a few hours later than on the coast.'

'When it's too late anyway.' She shudders as the tyres crunch over the dry gravel. 'Why would anyone want to live out here?'

'It's pretty in winter.'

I don't know why I'm defending the tree-change lifestyle. It's not my thing personally and development up against the national park doesn't seem right for a whole bunch of reasons. There's the combustibility of the bush for a start, which is the stuff of nightmares, but also the impact on groundwater from clearing and bores. There are no aquifers up here, just water bodies sitting in rock fractures. And not everyone is connected to scheme water. Alice, I remember, has installed a forty thousand litre tank behind her house.

'Tell me again why we are driving into a bushfire trap on a Sunday.'

'Jason saw Graham Griffiths riding into Kings Park with Eric on the day Eric disappeared. Graham knows Duncan and Duncan's dodgy business associates. Eric's bike has never been found, but I saw a bike that looked like Eric's in Duncan's stables.'

'So, you think Graham murdered Eric somewhere in Kings Park and got Duncan to stash the bike on his property.'

'Something like that.'

'With all of those people around.'

'Look in the glovebox.'

Belinda opens the glovebox and takes out the sunglasses.

'Do you remember those? They're the ones James found on the road the day after Eric disappeared. Near where we found those clothes. They couldn't have been dropped by someone at the concert. It's too far away.'

'Even so, they could've been dropped by anyone. And Eric didn't wear that brand. He didn't wear any brand. He bought his sunglasses at the service station.'

'They're not Eric's, they belong to Graham Griffiths. Jason said he was wearing glasses exactly like these on the day he saw him with Eric.'

'You can't be serious? We've driven all the way out here because of a pair of scratched Wayfarers? There'd have to be dozens of lost sunglasses in the park. Odds are, half of them are Raybans. I hope you don't apply this type of logic to our inquiries.'

'It was Eric's bike in Duncan's stables, though. I'm sure of it.'

'OK then.' Belinda tugs at her sleeve against the sun and pouts at the trees. 'But if we die in a bushfire, it's your fault.'

I slow down as we drive along the valley floor, looking for the hidden road and listening for surprise trail bikes. Belinda sees the yellow triangle before I do, and I have to reverse before making the sharp turn. Of course, because I pick this moment to back up, a four-wheel drive appears in my rear-view mirror, and I need to stand on the brake as he wrenches his steering wheel to avoid rear-ending me. He stares steadfastly ahead as he passes, no winding down the window to check if we are alright, like you'd get in Weymouth. I remind myself that despite the green canopy, technically we are still in the city.

The intersection is more of a convergence than a T-junction; it's no wonder I took the wrong road on my way out of the valley that day. It takes us under paperbarks and over the dry river crossing. Down here, there is still a hint of green and the smell of boggy mulch, but I wouldn't bank on the fire-retardant properties of the remnant moisture. Belinda shuffles in her seat.

I swing the car around to park with its nose into the gate and stamp on the brake for a second time. Belinda lurches forward.

'Oof, steady on.'

'Sorry. Unexpected obstacle.' We both lean forward to peer over the bonnet. Tahnee has received a delivery of feed and two hessian sacks have been dumped in front of the gate. A padlock hangs off the chain, and I remember Tahnee's complaint about not getting a key. Shayne is standing with his head hanging over the gate, his lips straining for the bonanza that is just out of reach. When he sees me, he snorts hello but when I walk over to him, he won't let me scratch his muzzle. I climb over the gate, and he tosses his head and makes a show of cantering away. He stops after a few metres and looks back over his haunches to see what I'm doing.

What I'm doing is being batted away by Belinda as I offer to help her over the gate.

'Go away, farm girl, I'm not completely useless.'

We trudge through the sand toward the stables. The water in the trough is low again, so I guess Tahnee is still coming out here every day to top it up. Nothing much has changed inside. The solitary saddle is still there. I run my hand over the firm leather, and it comes away coated in dust. The tack hangs from the walls and in the middle stall, the brush is where I left it.

Belinda sniffs. 'Smells like horse.'

'Well, yeah, I suppose it would.'

She cracks the lid on one of the feed bins and, like me, dives her hand into the oats. 'It's warm,' she says, surprised.

'Moisture content might be a bit high.'

She cocks her head.

'Microbes breed where there's water' – Belinda pulls her hand out – 'and that creates heat. It's pretty dangerous in silos. If the temperature gets too high, the grain can spontaneously combust.'

'You love all this country stuff, don't you, Fran?' She pushes the lid back into place. 'Why do you live in the city?'

The horse rug that Tahnee had thrown over the rear stall is still in place, and I reach over the wall and flick it off. Dust and horsehair fly upwards and I turn my face away, squeezing my eyes and mouth closed. That doesn't stop it from getting up my nose and setting off a round of sneezing. Belinda laughs at me from the door, well removed from the dust cloud.

'That'd be why. Can't be a farmer if you're allergic to dust.'

I want to tell her that dust will make anyone sneeze when it's forced up their nasal passages, but my eyes and nose are streaming, and I can't find a tissue in my pockets. I lift up my t-shirt and wipe my face on that instead.

'You're gross, Frances.'

'Make yourself useful and pass me the hose.' I retreat outside, wash my face down, and dry it on my grubby t-shirt. Inside the stables, Belinda is a silhouette, moving toward the back wall.

'Where did you see the bikes?'

'Leaning against the barrier between the second and third stalls.'

'Are you sure?'

'Yep.'

'I can't see them.'

I follow her in, lean over the wall. They're gone. They're not anywhere else in the stall either. The same plastic tubs are stacked in the corner, the same antique dressing table against the back wall. The tools are still there too, only the bikes are missing.

I consider jumping the wooden gate to the house and searching the garden, but I can't bear the thought of getting caught again. It was bad enough having to talk my way out of being in the stables – if Tahnee found me snooping around the house, she'd definitely report it to Duncan. Instead, I roll the hose out to the trough. The water in the bottom is tepid and Shayne positions himself ready for the good stuff to flow. I trudge back through the sand to turn it on, grab the grooming brush and give him a once-over while he drinks. A muddy puddle forms at his feet.

'Won't Tahnee wonder who filled the trough?'

'I'll text her. She was pretty relaxed about me coming over to ride her horse, so I can't see that she'll have a problem with me topping up his water.'

'What sort of work does she do?'

'Don't know. I don't even know her last name.'

I hear voices and the dry clatter of tyres on gravel. Sunlight flashes off bicycle frames between the trees. Then I hear a crunch and a slide, and the voices become shouts. Then a bang, and the crack and tinkle of plastic and glass. Laughter. I glance at Belinda and start walking toward the car. Four men on mountain bikes are gathered around my rear bumper. They couldn't be more different from the pelotons you see in the city. For a start, they're twenty to thirty years younger and don't have a shred of anything stretchy on their bodies. Their only nod to PPE is the work boots they all wear. No helmets. They see me and start waving their arms. The shouting starts again.

'Move your fucking car off the road before you kill someone.'

'Stupid city bitch.'

'Nah, she's special, mate, she owns a horse.'

'Daddy owns a horse.'

'Not for much longer from what I heard.'

They laugh.

I stay on the paddock side of the gate and finger the phone in my pocket. Orange fragments of my taillight are scattered on the gravel, where my rear wheel is sticking out into the road. I figure making excuses won't be helpful.

'Sorry guys, my bad. We'll be out of here when we've filled up the trough.'

They look over my shoulder and one laughs, a low snigger.

'Aw, look, horse girl has a little Chinese friend.'

'Cute.'

'Malaysian, actually.'

'Whatever. Chinese, Japanese, dirty knees, what are these?' The tallest, who had taken up front position at the gate, plucks his shirt out from his chest with both hands and struts back to his mates.

Belinda turns on her heel. 'I'll turn off the hose.'

'Nah, cutie, don't get offended. Come back. What's your name?' The dude with the pretend boobs places his hands and one foot on the gate to lever himself over. I squeeze my fingers around the thick, wooden block of Shayne's grooming brush.

A dented Land Rover, the type that looks like it belongs in the desert cresting sand dunes, rolls over the dry river crossing and pulls up, blocking the road. Boob-boy pauses. Alice Rensburg leans her elbow on the driver's side windowsill in all of her blonde-haired, blue-eyed Dutch perfection and there is a stillness while the mountain bikers take her in.

She breaks the spell. 'Everything alright here, Frances?'

'None of your fucking business,' replies Boob-boy on my behalf. 'But you could make me your fucking business. If you want.' His mates cackle.

Alice opens her door and climbs down to a chorus of whistles and nudging. She leans back into the car and when she turns around, she is wearing a Go-Pro and carrying a rifle. She looks comfortable with both.

'Frances, Belinda, get in your car.'

We do as we are told.

'You boys can go back home to your mums.'

Alice watches, feet apart and rifle cradled in both hands, while they get back on their bikes. She indicates for us to drive on in front of her. When we've crossed the dry riverbed, she pulls alongside in the Land Rover and tells us to follow her up to the house.

CHAPTER FORTY-FIVE

Alice sits us outside on the terrace overlooking the coastal plain and the distant city. She puts two sweating glasses of water on the table and retreats into the house. Overhead, the wisteria that shaded Eric's thirtieth birthday party is a tumble of bare branches and clusters of soft, purple blooms. Belinda stares at the city and ignores her water. She's pale. I tell her to drink, and she gives me a defeated look but picks up her glass anyway. She runs the side of her finger down the condensation and licks it.

'We've got some charmers in this country, don't we?'

'There are charming men like that everywhere,' answers Alice. She is carrying a tray with a pot of tea, cups, and a plate of biscuits. 'Women, too.' Belinda sighs and Alice passes her the biscuits. 'Not everyone in the hills is like that. Those four are known troublemakers. We'd already heard they were on the prowl today.'

'How did you know we were in the valley?'

Alice nods at a pair of field glasses on the table. 'Rassie said he'd seen you turn off toward the river. I saw your car, and then the bikes coming down the hill.'

'You were watching us?' Belinda looks at me as though this just adds to the overall wrongness of life in the bush. 'Isn't that a bit creepy?'

'Good thing I was though, hey?' Alice's eyes twinkle and she leans back in her chair, crosses one boot over the other knee. She couldn't look more assured if she pulled a cowboy hat down over her brow and rested one hand around the barrel of the rifle she has presumably stowed away somewhere.

'Will you report them?'

'Only on the community watch Facebook group. The police won't be interested.' She turns her attention to me. 'How've you been Frances? You look tired.'

'I'm fine. A couple of wobbles lately, but nothing major.'

'Are you taking your potassium?'

I give her a thumbs-up as I bite into a biscuit. I haven't, but now's not the time to be arguing about how I manage my health.

'Sounds like you need a proper break then. If you really want to get out in the countryside, you should go stay with my brother Tim in Cape Town. He'll take you hiking on the mountain. You'll love it. You'll come back a whole new person.'

Down in the valley, a lazy curl of smoke rises above the green ribbon of trees that track the river. Belinda points to it. 'Is that at the paddock?'

As Alice and I turn to look, the smoke intensifies. Tongues of flame flicker between the trees. Alice swears and bolts to the front door, dragging her phone out of her back pocket.

'Get in the *bakkie*, girls.' She barks instructions to emergency services, and we fly back down the hill, Belinda and I fumbling to fasten our seatbelts while the Land Rover lurches. We grab our seats as Alice unexpectedly turns right instead of left at the bottom of the hill. The road circles around to the front of Duncan's property. She pulls into the brick-paved driveway, leaps out of the vehicle and sprints under the line of trees toward the paddock and the stables. I can see Shayne pacing backwards and forwards across the wooden gate. He's tossing his head, his eyes ringed with white, and he brays when he sees Alice. Behind him, the cocky's gate at the other end of the paddock, where I had parked my car less than half an hour before, is backgrounded in flame. The bags of feed are on fire and the flames are reaching for the lower branches of the roadside trees.

Alice opens the gate and jogs Shayne to the front of the house, her fingers threaded through his mane. I unbuckle my seatbelt and run past her to the stables. The hose is where Belinda and I left it, coiled around the hook on the wall. I lift it off and at that moment Alice threads her arm underneath next to mine and together we run it down the paddock. We reach the end of its length when the water gushes out. I look back and Belinda is standing next to the tap.

The hose only reaches just past the trough, but the pressure is good. The water floods the ground in front of the gate and the base of the trees on either side. It is not enough to douse the feedbags or reach the branches, which are now smouldering, fingers of pale smoke reaching above our heads. Alice runs back to the stables, and I hear thuds and clangs before she returns with Belinda and arm loads of horse blankets. They both run ahead to the fire and begin beating at the flames that are spreading in the grass along the fence line.

I see a flash of red at the top of the hill and seconds later hear sirens followed by the low, insistent blast of a truck horn. Lights flash between the trees, pause as the fire truck takes the turn toward the river and then bathes us in red. The sirens stop and men in yellow onesies with silver reflective tape jump down from the cab and begin unrolling the hoses. A red four-wheel drive pulls up behind the truck and two men in blue uniforms climb out. At the front of the truck, someone barks instructions, someone else moves Alice and Belinda to one side, and water explodes from the hose. Like magic the flames are gone and all I'm looking at are smoking bags of feed and scorched trees. I glance down at my hose and its gallant stream of water and suddenly feel inadequate and small.

A man in a yellow overall takes it from me. 'You did a great job there, ma'am. Let's go turn it off, hey?'

He walks the three of us back to Alice's car, a man in blue trailing behind. At the front of the house, Shayne is cropping the green lawn. It must be getting watered while the owner is in prison.

The firefighters gravitate toward Alice for information. I don't seem to be needed so I wander across to Shayne. The house, I notice now, is as well kept as the garden. It's shaped like a box, an elegant one, with tall, symmetrical windows, twin chimneys, and a central front door topped by a triangular pediment. I'm curious to know what the inside of a corrupt public servant's house looks like and wonder if it would be too rude to peer through the windows. I check over my shoulder. Only Shayne is watching me. Alice and Belinda are talking to the firefighters who, I'm guessing, will send the police to Alice's house to look at the recording on her GoPro.

I ease myself between two rosebushes and cup my hands on the window glass. I expect the room inside to be dark and brooding, but it is full of light, thanks to the height of the windows, which stretch up to the twenty-foot ceilings. The furniture is modern. A pale couch is arranged in front of a fireplace, which has actual wood on the grate, ready to be lit. A spray of native flowers sits on an angular side table and on the floor next to it is propped an unframed painting of black cockatoos flying across a brilliantly blue sky. They look raucous and irreverent, and the style is familiar. I wrinkle my nose at the thought of taxpayer money buying original art to adorn a hills mansion when it could have been used to buy an oven for a family in the suburbs.

I step out of the garden bed. There's nothing to be gained by peering into Duncan's windows other than feeding my own contempt. Shayne has moved further along the lawn and Alice, Belinda and the fireman have disappeared. I follow a path around to the side of the house. Here, slightly recessed from the façade of the main house and hidden from the driveway, is the cutest garden shed I've ever seen. It is the main house in miniature, with a gabled roof, symmetrical windows and a central door topped by a tiny plaster pediment. I try the door, but it's locked, so I look through a window. Unlike the main house, the inside is dark, and I only see shapes at first. A tilt-up door at the back. A ride-on lawnmower. A long workbench with a vice. Shelves underneath holding an array of power tools. Dad would give an arm for a shed like this. My eyes finally adjust, and I see the two bikes that have been left leaning against the wall on the other side of the ride-on mower. I switch windows to get a better view. I am certain they are the same bikes I saw in the stables. I check over my shoulder again, pull out my phone and take a photo. As I cross the lawn, Shayne looks up and snorts a greeting. I follow his gaze to see Tahnee marching around the corner of the house, her face a mixture of relief and fury.

CHAPTER FORTY-SIX

Tahnee speaks to me only after she's interrogated her horse.

'Are you OK?' she asks him, pressing her face into his neck. 'Were you scared? Were you pleased to see Alice?'

I prick up my ears at this last question, my mind making rapid and unreasonable connections until I remind myself about small communities and everyone knowing everyone else. Shayne ignores Tahnee's questions and snuffles at her pockets despite the smorgasbord under his feet. He is rewarded with an apple that Tahnee feeds him in two halves, sliced open with a knife that alarmingly she pulls from her back pocket.

'Sounds like you've met the local boys. Delightful, aren't they? I heard they were especially welcoming to your friend. Arseholes. They've given me and Mum the same lip.' I can see Belinda walking back down the driveway with Alice. Both are coated in dust and ash, which has run in dark brown smears down their arms where they had been splashed with water. Alice wipes a forearm across her forehead, branding herself with mud. I bet we all stink of smoke.

'You found him then?' Alice nods at the horse.

'Lazy sod couldn't be bothered going any further.'

'Why would he, looks like he's found everything he needs right here.'

'He won't be staying for much longer. I've got to go. Deliveries to make.' Tahnee unwinds a lead rope from her shoulder and clips it loosely around Shayne's neck. 'Come on, you old bastard, let's put you back in your paddock.'

Alice drives Belinda and me back up the hill to her house, makes us drink more water, and hands us both a bag of lemons from the basket near the front door. I forget to tie the top of mine before I put it in the car and the fruit tumbles loose on the drive home. One hooks under the brake, and I squash it when I stop at an intersection. The citrus hit cuts across the smell of smoke that we'd brought into the car. Belinda breathes it in.

Tell me again how Alice knew we were at Duncan's place?' she asks.

'Rassie told her he saw us.'

'Yeah, but when?'

'On the road. He must have been the guy that I nearly reversed into when I missed the turn-off.'

She twists in her seat to face me. 'But she didn't actually say that, did she?'

'Well, no, but ...'

'Because that guy didn't look like Rassie. Rassie has dark hair, remember? Smiley eyes. We met him at Eric's thirtieth. The guy in the four-wheel drive was blond. And Rassie would have said hello or waved at least.'

'Maybe Rassie saw us somewhere else, like at the turn-off to the highway.'

'Maybe, but did you notice where the four-wheel drive went? It went straight, not up the hill to Alice's place. That's the way we took to Duncan's to rescue the horse. You know where else that road goes? Nowhere, Frances, that road goes nowhere. The guy in the four-wheel drive went to Duncan's house. He was there while we were in the stables.'

Belinda is right. The road that Alice took to Duncan's house crossed the riverbed upstream and ended in a stub road in front of the house. 'What are you saying? Do you think he was the one who set fire to the feedbags?'

'No, it was those jerks on the bikes who did that. It's just, doesn't it give you the creeps to think he was there while we were snooping around?'

I think about that. If the four-wheel-drive guy went to Duncan's house, it was probably for a legitimate reason. Even prisoners need someone to check that the irrigation is working while they're not at home. But if he'd seen us, whoever he was, he'd definitely tell Duncan. And Duncan would make a complaint to my boss, probably through the housing minister for greatest impact.

'If he was there, though, he must have left before the guys on the bikes showed up. I mean, he would have heard them yelling and come out, right?'

'Not if he didn't want anyone to know he was there.'

I consider my own snooping around the garden shed and curl my toes. 'But why would he want to hide? He would have checked that the house was secure, maybe turned the irrigation on and off, and left again. Ten minutes, max. He would have been back on the highway before those dickheads turned up.'

'Heading toward the prison.'

'So, what if he was? He hadn't seen us, and he'd missed all the action. All he'd have to report was that the hedges need pruning.' I laugh at the prospect of Duncan's theoretical heavy giving him a garden report, but it comes out dry and my breath smells of smoke.

CHAPTER FORTY-SEVEN

I wake up early the next morning, press my head into the pillow, and do a stocktake. My hair still stinks, and my face feels greasy. My tongue is furry with dehydration. I need to drink some water and pee. The ceiling is motionless. Eric is still missing. But I have found his bike, I am sure of it.

I rub my eyes, but it doesn't make my face feel any better. My eyeballs squeak, another sign that I'm dehydrated. I need to top up my fluids and take my medication if I don't want to be on the floor in the next hour. I get dressed, hoping the shower I took last night will be enough to save my co-workers from the smell of smoke that clung to me all the way home even over the smell of the squashed lemon. I eat a piece of toast and run to catch the bus.

I feel the charge in the office as soon as the lift doors open. Julie gives me a tight smile and flicks her eyes back to her screen. There's a buzz coming from the open-plan work area. It drops when I walk in. In the sudden silence, James and Belinda look up from the corner. Neither of them wave. My stomach clenches.

'What's up?' I ask, dropping my bag on my desk. Ridiculously, I keep my voice low to match the volume of the room even though, obviously, everyone already knows what's going on.

'Someone told Neil what happened yesterday,' Belinda stage whispers. 'I told you that guy at Duncan's house saw us.'

There's a post-it note on my screen with a message handwritten in Neil's EA's rounded script. *Neil wants to see you and Belinda at 8:30am.* I look at my watch. It's eight twenty-seven. Belinda is already on her feet, shrugging herself into her suit jacket.

Neil's EA presses her lips together and looks at the clock above her workstation when we reach the other end of the floor.

'Go straight in, ladies.'

I reach for the door handle, and she clears her throat.

'Maybe knock first, Frances.'

The door is ajar, and it swings when I tap on it with my knuckles, making the knock sound tentative and guilty. From behind it comes a deep sigh. Neil will be dreading this. Possibly more than I am. His *come in* is weary and he motions for us to take the two seats that have been positioned side by side in front of his desk. A single page with a large signature block and a blue-and-gold crest hangs from his hand. The *S* and the *T* of the signature are huge compared to the typed font.

'I'm going to assume you know what this is about,' he begins. 'The whole office seems to know already; God only knows how.' At this, he narrows his eyes at the partly open door and Belinda leaps out of her chair to close it. 'Dr Duncan Wolf made a complaint to the Minister for Housing last night and the minister couriered this to me this morning.' He taps the letter with the back of his free hand.

I open my mouth to speak but he waves me away.

'I'll be dealing with this strictly in accordance with our complaints procedure, Frances. You will be provided with a copy of the complaint' – he indicates two sealed envelopes on his desk – 'and given seven days to respond in writing. Your director, Catherine Matthews, will consider the complaint and your response, and make a recommendation. You will be aware, of course, that should the complaint be upheld, it may constitute serious misconduct and carry the risk of possible dismissal.' He passes me the first envelope. 'I am not going to stand you down, but I suggest you take leave for the rest of today and tomorrow to recover from the, ah, incident with the fire. I hope it goes without saying that you are not to contact Dr Wolf for any reason whatsoever.'

I look down at the envelope in my lap. It will, I know, contain a copy of the letter Neil is holding, a copy of our complaints policy, and the yellow trifold brochure for our Employee Assistance Programme.

'Belinda, the complaint against you is less serious – Duncan is aware that you report to Frances and be believes you were likely acting on instruction – but you do need to respond to it.' He passes her the second envelope. 'I suggest that you, too, take personal leave today and tomorrow.'

'Thank you, Neil,' she mutters. We both stand and he looks at us sorrowfully, hands secured in his pockets. Belinda leads the way out of his office, and we hear the door click softly as we pass the EA's empty workstation.

*

I watch the trees scroll past the bus window. The bus is empty at this time of the day, returning to the suburbs after disgorging itself of city commuters, and doesn't stop at all as we pass the park. I don't see any joggers either, just mums unloading toddlers and prams in the carpark near the adventure playground. I wonder if I will be a mum with a pram and a toddler one day. What will it be like, spending my time driving children around and drinking coffee outdoors on a Monday morning? Will I miss the daily commute to the city, the march in the shadows of the office towers, the shiny lift lobbies and the suits and panelled receptions? Will I have to give up my apartment and move to an outer suburb so I can have four bedrooms and a lawn?

Eric's sister Alice never worked in the corporate world. She has spent her working life in suburban pharmacies, behind the counter in shopping centres and high streets. She wouldn't have a reason to visit the city more than once or twice a year. Her clients wear work boots and sneakers. They push prams, lean on walking frames, ride gophers. Alice, I realise, didn't ask us what we were doing at Duncan's house yesterday. She didn't mention Duncan by name, or comment that he was in prison, even though she knew who and where he was, and that I'd played a part in putting him there.

The bus crosses the intersection and enters the suburbs and my phone rings. It's Belinda. From the background noise, she is on the train. We left the office together, a hundred eyes boring into our backs. James made a joke of it as we packed our bags, but I knew he was uncomfortable, left in the pod on his own.

'I remembered where I've seen that guy before,' Belinda says above the sound of the train speakers announcing the next stop. 'The one in the four-wheel drive. Duncan's mate.'

'Is he Duncan's mate though? It might not have been him. We don't even know if he knows Duncan.'

'Of course he does. Take a look at your text messages.'

I open the message and the photo that she's sent me. I've seen it before, but I don't get the connection. I'm the only passenger on the bus so I put her on speaker. 'And?'

'Enlarge it and take a look at the left, no, right, of the main gate.'

I look at the photo again. It's a wide shot of the prison, taken from the passenger seat of my car. I can see the windowsill, angled at the bottom of the frame. I can also see a man outside the gate. It looks like he's on the phone. I slide my fingers across the screen, pulling the shot apart. The man is blond, built, and familiar. He's the guy who nodded at me as we left the prison on the day that we visited Duncan. He's also the guy in the four-wheel drive who I almost rear-ended in the valley yesterday.

'I guess that answers it then. The mystery man in the four-wheel drive was checking Duncan's house for him.'

'That's how Duncan knew we were there.'

'That's how Duncan knew we were nearby,' I correct her. 'This guy didn't actually see us on the property. For all he knows, we were going to see Alice and took a wrong turn. And then we went with Alice to rescue her neighbour's horse. Total coincidence that it was Duncan's place.'

'Neil didn't sound like he was going to buy that kind of story this morning.'

I remember Neil's sorrowful look. 'No.'

'You're not a very good liar, Fran. You've got the wrong face for it.'

'Yeah, well, I'll just tell the truth and Bigfoot can make of it what she will. If it's not misconduct, she'll find something else that ruins my chances of promotion. She'll have me under her thumb forever.'

I'm back home by early afternoon and have been in the door for ten minutes, tops, when someone knocks on my door. I'm only halfway changed out of my suit, barefoot and in stained tracksuit pants and my best white button-down shirt when I drag myself to the door. I'm so tired and cranky that I don't stop to wonder how my visitor has made it up to my floor without being buzzed in first.

CHAPTER FORTY-EIGHT

He is blond and built, the same as in the photo. He nods when I open the door the same way he nodded at me outside the prison. You'd think we'd known each other for years, business colleagues, politely acknowledging each other at the start of a meeting booked weeks earlier.

'You're Duncan's mate,' I tell him. 'How's his irrigation?' He looks confused. 'Dr Duncan Wolf, the corrupt public servant whose house you're looking after.'

His nostrils flare. The muscles on the side of his neck twang. 'That prick? I'm no mate of his. Wouldn't touch him with a ten-foot pole.' He looks at me curiously, like he's expecting me to say something else, then flicks his gaze over my shoulder into the apartment. 'You on your own?' I suspect this is the point where I'm supposed to say that my black-belt boyfriend is here with me but, as Belinda says, I'm a rubbish liar. Instead, I just confirm that yes, I am here on my own, and wait for him to grab my elbow and hustle me downstairs into a white van.

'Mr Griffiths wants to see you.'

'Who?'

'Graham Griffiths. My boss.' He looks me up and down and I confirm that I'll need to get changed.

'I've never met with a convicted drug trafficker,' I tell him, as though he might give me pointers on my wardrobe.

'No need. He'll only see this bit. And it wasn't trafficking.' He indicates the collar of my shirt upwards with a sweep of his hand, lifts the backpack off his shoulder and lets himself in. At my kitchen table, he extracts a laptop and a mobile phone, establishes the connection, and opens Zoom. He sits me in front of the screen and checks that the light is right. It's not. He fiddles with the brightness, checks again, then relocates my floor lamp. After shuffling it from side to side in front of me, he gives me the thumbs-up and opens the meeting room. Griffiths is already there. He could be sitting in a corporate office on the Terrace. Except he's not.

'Frances Geller, pleased to meet you at last.' His accent is rural, like my dad's, and his face and neck have the deep red tan of a man who has done a lifetime of outside work. I can only see as far as the desktop, but he looks like he's retained his lean, pre-prison frame. He wears a white collared shirt and a navy blazer. It is not the same outfit he wore when he arrived at the court. He sees me noticing. 'My business associate kindly brings me suitable clothes to wear to meetings. Thank you for letting him in. It was important to me to meet with you.'

'I'm not sure I had a choice.'

'Of course you did, but I do understand your reluctance. I admit I did ask him to, ah, make his case, if you were not agreeable. He tried to speak with you in Kings Park on the weekend, but I understand you were unwell.' He looks at his hands, which are anchored to the table, fingers spread. 'My condolences on your brother, by the way. I know what it's like to lose family. My mum died young, like yours. Dad remarried a Yamatji woman from up your way. Lives in the city now. She gave me a little sister before he died, but it's not easy.' He waits, but I have nothing to say, no reciprocal words to offer back to him. I'm still at a loss to understand why I'm sitting at my kitchen table under carefully balanced lighting and talking to an imprisoned drug dealer on Zoom.

'I hear no-one was hurt in the incident in the hills yesterday,' he continues, seemingly unfazed by my silence. 'That's good. Obviously, we were concerned about my niece and her horse, but it seems they're both fine and the fences are intact, so we don't need to find alternative agistment.'

'Tahnee is your niece?' I hear my voice squeak.

'Yes, but I wouldn't expect you'd have known that.'

'Is that why this guy was up there yesterday? To look after the horse?' I glance at my intruder standing by the window. He looks at me briefly, gives an oddly awkward smile, then turns back to the street.

'One of the reasons, yes.'

'I can't do anything about the report, you know. It's already with the commissioner.'

'What report?' He looks as confused as his messenger did when I mentioned Duncan in the doorway.

'The housing inquiry. I know your connection to Duncan Wolf. I know you know the Batt brothers.'

'The insulation scandal? The one that's put Dr Wolf inside?' He laughs. 'I don't care about that. I haven't seen Bevan and Brian in years. Although I have to admit, it was pretty clumsy. Not the most elegant of arrangements. No, I've had Vince looking out for you. That's what he was doing yesterday. I can't have what happened to your co-worker happen to you as well.'

'Pardon?' My brain tumbles and I glance at the window. 'Vince' flinches.

'It was my fault Eric was even looking at the forensics evidence issue. I didn't even plan it. We just happened to be riding the same route and stopped at the same lookout in Kings Park. He's a nice young man, by the way, respectful, open, incredibly fit. A lot like Vince. I struggled to keep up with him even though he slowed down for me. He talked about his work and seemed genuine enough, so I told him about my brother-in-law.'

I make the connection. Eric's mystery informant was Graham Griffiths, convicted drug trafficker and, apparently, keen cyclist. That in itself is enough, but Vince is *Vince*? I glare at Ray's son across the room, willing him to turn away from the window. It's at least ten years since I saw him last, but I can see it now, the resemblance to his dad in the set of his shoulders, the muscled, rugby-player's thighs.

Griffiths misconstrues the look on my face. 'You know the case then?'

I do my best to focus on the screen and not leap across the room to shunt my one-time, older-brother's friend in the chest. 'He did time for murder but was pardoned after another inmate confessed.'

'Terrible miscarriage of justice. Unforgiveable. Ian – my brother-in-law – spent seven years in prison. He was just a chef, a cook on a mine site. A father and a husband providing for his family. A good man. It nearly broke him. I've done all I can to help him since those bastards let him go. A home in the hills, a job at one of the local restaurants, a place to agist the horse.'

'So, you do know Duncan.'

'Of course I know Duncan. Everyone knows Duncan.'

I can't see how anyone outside the state public service bubble would have a reason to know Duncan except his mum and his GP, but I let it go. Duncan doesn't appear to be the reason I'm here.

'What happened to Eric?'

'Well, that's where it got complicated,' says Griffiths, spreading his arms along the table. 'I didn't realise that the commissioner publishes notices of his inquiries. Apparently, they're not conducted in secret' – he shakes his head as though he can't fathom why a government inquiry should be conducted in the open, with full transparency – 'so, everyone knew what Eric was doing and as you can imagine, some of the people in my, ah, professional circles weren't enthusiastic about it. Someone had already taken steps to discourage him.'

'Like running him off the road?'

'Despicable. Not the right way to go about things at all.' On the screen, Griffiths' mouth turns down in an expression of disgust that I'm not buying. I'm sure he's had plenty of reasons to persuade people to his way of thinking in the past.

'I arranged to be in Kings Park when Eric was there. That wasn't hard, he's a man of predictable routines. I tried to warn him, encouraged him to let it go, but he was on a mission. You have to admire that.'

'So, you got the inquiry pulled instead.'

'No, no. That wasn't me. Someone else did that. Probably the same person who tried to scare him off with the white-van trick. I know what you're after, Frances, but I'm afraid I don't know who that was or what case they thought Eric was going to bust open. I can't help you there.'

'You must have some idea.'

Behind me, Vince adjusts his stance. Griffiths sits forward and links his fingers together on the table. 'No, I really don't.'

'But they were worried enough to get rid of Eric as well as pull the inquiry, because he was going to make it public.'

Griffiths looks down and considers his hands. They are small but look ropey and strong, like a jockey. When he looks up, his gaze shifts past the camera, and his face has lost its geniality.

'You've thought it through. I should have expected that. Duncan said you were bright. Yes, Eric was going to go public, but they got to him first. And to me.'

I can't believe he's making it all about him. I feel the heat rise up my chest and a mist spray from my lips. 'The police raided your house because a gardener saw you with Eric on the day he disappeared, not because of some conspiracy.'

'But the gardener didn't plant the drugs in my bicycle frame, did he?'

'Are you seriously telling me they weren't yours?' I can hear the contempt in my voice and remind myself that this man's minder is standing in my living room. I'm sure he'll put his allegiances with his boss before the sister of his one-time friend.

'Do you think I'd be stupid enough to keep drugs at my own house?' He looks offended and, at the window, Vince coughs.

'I really have no idea.'

'No, you don't, Frances.' His voice hardens and I get a glimpse of the drug trafficker. 'That's why I want you to drop this rehash of Eric's police inquiry.'

'Because you don't want blood on your hands again. Or the police back in your apartment.'

'Exactly.'

I weigh up my options and figure, why not, I might as well put it all on the table. See what Griffiths says.

'I know what Eric found.'

Behind his open collar, Griffiths' throat flushes, deepening the colour of the sun damage. At the window, Vince shifts his feet again.

'It wasn't about shoddy forensic evidence and wrongful convictions in the courts. It's bigger than that. Eric discovered that Duncan was accessing the state's pathology database – ordinary citizen's private health records – to identify drug users in public housing and kick them out into the streets. That's how he was reducing the public housing waiting list and getting all his pats on the back from the minister.'

Griffiths nods, presses his lips together, and looks out the window. 'I see.' The flush in his throat fades. 'That's not a very nice thing to do, although public opinion might be on his side. So, you think someone in government pulled the inquiry – someone connected to Duncan – and that they also got rid of your boss and put me in prison. Seems like extreme lengths to me, just to achieve some Key Performance Indicators.'

No-one put Griffiths in prison except himself, but I ignore it. 'They did it to make the minister look good. To keep him and the party in government. To make him deputy premier. If I let this go, they'll get away with throwing people out onto the streets just to advance their own careers. People die when that happens.'

'As you well know.' Griffiths leans forward. Swallows. 'You can't change the past, Frances, even if your inquiry does prove that the government acted unlawfully.' He sighs and his face softens. He's no longer the drug trafficker. He looks like any middle-aged, working-class man. He could be my dad. 'I am sorry about Matt – really, I am, he was a nice young man – but no-one will care if government has been evicting drug addicts from public housing. Public opinion isn't on your side. You've got nothing to gain by pursuing this.' Griffiths taps the table and Vince leaves his post. 'Promise me you'll let it go.'

I shrug, knowing I look like a petulant child. He's right. Belinda's right, James is right. Meredith and me, we might think we have the moral upper hand, but we're on our own. On the screen, Griffiths is looking somewhere else. He's finished with me. I'm dismissed. Vince shuts down the meeting and slides the laptop into his backpack. He returns the floor lamp, reconnects it, switches it on and off again.

'I suppose you agree with him.' I hate the whiney tone in my voice but Vince, it seems, is adept at handling the querulous.

'Public policy's not really my thing.'

'But keeping an eye on wayward public servants is?'

He shrugs. 'When it's part of my job.'

'How does your boss know my brother?'

'He didn't.'

'He just said he was a nice young man.'

Vince shrugs. 'He might've met him once or twice.'

'Were you and Matt still in touch when he died?'

Vince stands very still and turns his head toward the window again. For a moment, I think he's not going to answer me, and I feel a rush of panic, a sudden urgency to demand every last bit of information from this boogie-boarder turned minder before he leaves with his laptop and memories of my brother's last months. I see him make up his mind with a small shake of his head.

'Yes and no. I'd call him from time to time. Sometimes he'd answer, sometimes he wouldn't. I took food and stuff to the bush camp a few times, I even saw you there once. You didn't see me.'

'Did he get the meth from you?'

'No.' His answer is swift and firm. 'I don't touch the stuff. I don't get involved in any of that.'

'Of course you don't.' I don't believe him and now I just want him to go. I stand up, hoping to look decisive. 'I guess I won't be seeing you around.'

'That's up to Graham.' He shoulders his backpack and opens the front door. I'm about to lock it after him when he pauses. 'I know I could've done more for Matt. Graham probably would've found him somewhere to live if I'd asked.'

'Why didn't you then?'

'I didn't want Matt to be, you know, exposed to all of this.'

'You mean the drugs? How come it's alright for you to be exposed, but not your friend?'

He looks at the carpet. Rubs his toe into the curry stain that has survived my aborted cleaning attempt. 'Yeah, but I'm not into any of that. Matt was already, um, susceptible.'

I can see Vince is choosing his words carefully, trying not to offend, trying to keep his own emotions in check. But his confession only adds to the list of if-onlys that preceded my brother's death. If only he hadn't been sleeping under that bridge. If only he'd been able to get into public housing. If only he hadn't been kicked out of his private rental. If only he'd bought his own place like I did. If only he hadn't lost his job. If only he hadn't started using in the first place. If only Mum hadn't died.

'Being homeless kind of made him more susceptible, don't you think?'

He answers with a small nod. He's not expecting forgiveness. 'I know. Look, if there's anything I can do …'

I shake my head. I've had enough help from career criminals for one day. 'I don't think so. Maybe think about changing employers. Someone who trades in legal goods and pays taxes.' He grimaces and for half a second I'm remorseful. 'Oh, and maybe try to avoid running red lights and parking in universal parking bays. It kind of makes you stand out.'

He blinks. 'Yeah. Right. Good tip.'

I lock the door, take up his abandoned post at the window and watch him leave the building. He crosses the footpath and stands in the vacant universal parking bay, rubbing his foot over the blue stencil. He pulls a mobile phone out of his pocket and talks into it, glancing up and down the street. He nods when the call ends, looks up at my window, then walks down the street in long strides, deceptively fast, and stops outside the Thai restaurant. I look at my watch. It's time for me to eat too.

Half an hour later, I've cooked dinner. It's a curly pasta with bacon and broccoli. It has parmesan and pepper too, and I'm impressed by the smell rising from my stovetop. I take a bowl to the couch and balance it on my lap. I'm in time for the early news, so I switch on the television instead of opening my laptop. The lead story is about bushfires again. Over one hundred homes have been destroyed and footage from a helicopter shows another being engulfed. I imagine Duncan's house meeting the same fate, the fire from the feedbags spreading across the paddock, mounting the stables, and crossing the tree canopy into the main building. The flames would feed on the pale couch and the wood in the grate would burn without coaxing. The painted cockatoos would melt into rivulets, and the tall, elegant windows shatter outwards.

I'm so engrossed in the mental image of my nemesis's house being annihilated that it takes me a moment to recognise the burnt-out grass on the television screen. It surrounds Duncan's gate. In the background, Shayne has his head down and his butt to the camera. I hammer the volume button on the remote. *Police are questioning public servant, Dr Duncan Wolf, after finding bags of methamphetamine at the scene of the arson attack at his property on the weekend. The drugs have an estimated street value of one million dollars and were found in bags of stock feed.* The screen cuts to the main gate of the prison, where a dark-haired reporter looks directly into the camera and tells us that there will be more to come on this channel as the story unfolds.

I stalk back to the kitchen with my empty bowl, fuming. Graham Griffiths doesn't give a toss about my welfare and wouldn't have cared about Eric's either. And Vince wasn't looking out for me that day either; he was there to pick up the delivery for his boss.

I drop the bowl onto the kitchen bench hard enough to chip the base and I'm ferreting around on the floor to retrieve the shard of porcelain when I step on it with my bare foot.

It's always the little things. The big things – your mother's stroke, your brother's meth addiction elbowing out his football career – are safer bottled up. A three-millimetre chip off a green bowl, though; that can tip the scales. I sit on the floor, dripping blood from my heel, and sob, Griffiths' little lecture on public opinion replaying in my head. Of course, he thinks people don't care about drug addicts. He clearly doesn't himself, or at least not about the misery of addiction. Graham Griffiths only cares enough about drug addicts to feed their habits and to arrange a Zoom meeting from prison so he can redirect my attention away from his own distribution channels.

CHAPTER FORTY-NINE

'They were delivering meth in bags of horse feed?' James hoots. 'I've never heard that one before. What would happen if one of the bags broke open?'

'The horse would run really fast?' Belinda has her back to him, typing as she talks. In front of her, through the windows, clouds are scudding across the sky toward the hills.

'There's an idea. You could give it to racehorses.'

'I think someone has thought of that already.'

'Really? Do people actually do that? I was just joking.'

'What do you think the racing industry doping scandals are all about? Horses kicking back smoking a joint and listening to reggae?'

'Obviously not, no, but meth? You'd have to be some kind of sick bastard to think about giving that shit to a horse.'

'You just did.'

'But I'd never actually do it.'

While Belinda and James debate the ethics of doping horses, I've resumed my search for the smoking gun. Belinda and I are back in the office after our one-and-a-half days in home purgatory and I haven't been allocated another inquiry yet, so I log in to the pathology database. Technically, my access has been rescinded but as they say, the wheels of bureaucracy move slowly. I am certain that somewhere in these records, there is proof that Duncan and his allies have systematically accessed the private medical records of public housing tenants. That they have then evicted anyone with a positive test for illicit drugs. They've done it to reduce the waiting list, to make themselves look good. To get the minister re-elected.

And somehow, for some reason, Graham Griffiths doesn't want me looking at it, just like he didn't want Eric looking at it two years ago. I don't care if public opinion isn't on my side. Public opinion is not my concern. I'm here to call out public servants who break the law, and the law says you can't use someone's private information for anything other than the reason it was given.

'J A M 3 5. It's not long enough and it wants a character.' Belinda exhales behind me. 'Do emojis count?'

'Probably not. Change the J to an exclamation mark and add your name to the end.' I check the date. 'Has your password expired already?'

'No, I'm done with all that tenancy stuff. Bigfoot wants me to look at the government tenders board and make sure that the sale of these public housing sites to the private sector comply with procurement policy. It's going to be boring as batshit.'

Personally, I think it sounds like a great project and I'd offer to do it for her if I wasn't knee-deep in pathology reports. 'Which sites?'

'Harbour Lights in Weymouth, the apartment building where Aaron Abadi lived, and' – she checks her notes – 'the one in Northbridge that's almost finished. Banksia Apartments. I'll say one thing for Duncan, he's committed to native plants. Oh crap.'

'What?'

'Banksia Apartments. That's the development where Aaron died.' She grimaces. 'Sorry, Frances.'

'Show me?'

Belinda logs in and brings up the tender records for Banksia Apartments. The block of land was part of a decommissioned primary school, no longer needed in the inner city as post-war family homes gave way to office blocks and apartments. I want to see how much Mike Vargus paid for it – whether the bureaucrats had screwed him over as he claimed. Belinda clicks on the contract details, and we blink. Mike hasn't used the Zaglossus name to contract for the work. He's used the trading name Lignum, after the settlement inland from Weymouth, on Yamatji country. And he's not a sole trader, it's a four-way partnership: Michael Vargus, Graham Griffiths, and Ian and Helen Stewart.

Belinda turns to me, her fingers suspended over the keyboard. 'That's not what I was expecting. Ian Stewart, isn't he …?'

'The mining camp chef who killed his mate with a kitchen knife. And I'm guessing Helen is his wife.' Which makes Ian Stewart the brother-in-law whose murder conviction Graham Griffiths wanted Eric to avenge.

My desk phone rings. It's the security desk downstairs.

'Your visitor is here to see you.'

'My visitor?'

'She said she has an appointment with you.'

'What's her name?'

'She wouldn't say, except that she had an appointment. I can't send her upstairs without ID.'

I glance at Belinda and back at the screen. 'Fine. I'll be down in a minute.'

Downstairs, the security guard tips his head toward the furthest and worst-lit corner of the lobby. Reclining on a couch is a thin woman wearing jeans, sneakers and a cheesecloth tunic. She has a fall of long, brown curls and a defiant look. As I cross the lobby, her face softens in the same way Tahnee's did when she spoke to Shayne. She motions for me to sit, angling her body away from the door.

'He knew you'd come.' Helen Stewart's voice is the accent of the Mid West, Yamatji country, of nasal resonance and the softened T. 'He knew you couldn't resist it, not after the story broke last night.' She pauses to look me in the eye. 'Even if you wouldn't do what he told you.'

'How's Tahnee?'

'Keeping out of trouble.'

'Was she involved?' I think about her need to leave Shayne after the fire and make her deliveries.

'No, Tahnee doesn't get involved in any of that shit. And Graham doesn't ask her either.'

'Was Vince supposed to collect them, the bags of feed?'

'I don't know. That's Graham's business, not mine.'

'But you're here on Graham's business today?'

Her face hardens. 'He's not some drama queen, Frances. He warned you off for a reason.'

'To keep me away from his drugs network.'

'It's not about the drugs.'

'It sure looks like it to me. I suppose Duncan's taking his cut too, letting him use his place.'

'Duncan? That scumbag?' Her face puckers and she all but spits on the floor. 'He doesn't get a cent out of Graham. Not when Graham found out what he was doing. Graham doesn't do business with people like that.'

While I get a tiny prick of satisfaction from realising that Duncan probably doesn't know his hills property is part of Griffith's distribution channel, I think Helen's comment is a bit rich when Griffiths is making money out of other people's self-destruction. 'Except he does, doesn't he? He got Duncan to award him and Mike Vargus government housing contracts and make sure they only get tenants who are clean. Heaven forbid Graham might end up being landlord to one of his own grubby, drug-addicted clients.'

Helen Stewart's jaw clenches, and I think for a minute she's going to walk out on me, but like Vince did the night before, she composes herself, makes her decision. 'You've got it wrong.'

'So why are you here? As far as Graham knows I've given up on the police inquiry.'

'You're still searching around in that database, though.'

'How do you know that?' I look at my watch. It would be two and a half hours, tops, since I logged on.

She looks at me like I'm daft. 'They've got alerts in the system.'

'And I suppose those alerts get back to Graham.'

'They do, but they also get back to people who will be a lot less happy than Graham about you looking at those records.'

'Look, I get it. Private information is private and has to be kept secure. People have a right to know that no-one is going to be trawling through their records for laughs. But that's the whole point. That's exactly what the government has been doing. Trawling through medical records to find reasons to evict people. It's illegal, and it's unfair. When people become homeless, all sorts of awful things happen.'

To my horror, I feel my eyes swell and a band of heat across my forehead. Behind Helen Stewart's curls I see a familiar shape step across the foyer and stop at the security desk. I shuffle sideways on the bench seat, but Bigfoot sees the movement and looks up. At the same time, Helen turns around to see what has caught my eye. Bigfoot pauses to take her in, then scowls and looks at her watch. I nod, hoping to communicate my absolute confidence that I am down here on legitimate office business.

Helen puts one skinny brown hand on my arm. 'I know it's personal for you, but believe me, Frances, this isn't about drugs. It's personal for me too.' She pulls a folded tissue out of her bra and touches it under my eyes. I feel like a child being comforted by my mother and feel my cheeks redden with the shame of it. When she's done, Helen lets one hand rest against the other, feather-light on my arm. Together we look down at them and the contrast between her skin and mine. I see my dad's disappointment at my three percenters quip, and I realise what she's come here to say.

CHAPTER FIFTY

The office empties. It has drained toward the liftwell in a steady trickle for the past two hours. I stretch my back and reach for my cold mug. James and Belinda left an hour ago with instructions for me not to stay late. Belinda returned ten minutes later with a bunch of bananas from the stall downstairs. I break one off and take it and my mug to the staff room. We have an actual staff room in this office, not just a pocket-sized space carved out behind the liftwell. It has tables and a selection of hard and soft chairs. The food prep bench can fit six people and we don't have to navigate around each other, avoiding body contact to a chorus of *sorry* and *excuse me.*

At this time of day, the chairs have been lifted onto the tables and the cleaner is vacuuming underneath. He kills the motor when I enter and steps aside. I tell him not to worry, remembering my mother throwing up her hands whenever Matt or I began foraging for snacks the minute she'd finished cleaning the kitchen. Matt was worse than me. On weekends, he'd stumble out of his room around noon and graze continuously until dinner time. There might be a lull for an hour or so, but sooner or later the fridge door would crack open, Mum would sigh, and Dad would pat her leg as they sat on the couch watching a movie. In a way, I'm glad she died before Matt. Even though he drove her mad by blowing her shopping budget each week, I saw the way her chin lifted, and her mouth twitched upward as she complained. She seemed to be in constant wonder that this tall, gangly human had come out of her body. It would have broken her to outlive him.

Dad drove to Perth that day, in the old Nissan. I told him not to drive, to catch the plane down instead, but he refused. If he left straight away, he said, he'd be in the city by the time the afternoon flight left Weymouth, and he'd need the car while he has here. I reminded him that I also have a vehicle, but he just grunted something about me needing to get to work, as if I had a car bay at the office back then or would even consider going to work when my brother had just been found wedged between concrete pillars under a freeway overpass, his body in his sleeping bag.

I put my banana skin in the bin of the cleaner's trolley and take my tea back to the pod. It's getting dark and I punch the after-hours light switch. A cold front is coming through and the clear Djilba sky has been replaced with grey, scudding clouds. I've started a new spreadsheet. Names down the left-hand column, and across the top, tenancy start dates, end dates, and length of stay. It's a smaller sample size this time, so small that I don't even need to choose among the population of tenants who have moved in and out; I can use them all. The surnames are as familiar to me as the view of the sea from my bedroom window. They appear in my school year books and in street signs from my childhood. Boyle, Cameron, Davies, Lim, Pedersen, Samson, Worner, Zublinski. I log them all, watching the numbers unfurl. Some have held their tenancies for years, some for months. I wonder where they went when they left, if they got rentals in the private market, or if they're now couch surfing, smoking cones in their granny's garden shed or making do beneath an overpass.

I save the spreadsheet, open my web browser and hold my breath as I type my login details. They are still valid. It seems that health department system administrators have more pressing priorities than cancelling the access rights of government watchdogs. I start typing in the names and logging test results. I don't care if they trigger some electronic tripwire.

There are lots of people with positive results; a solid forty percent of tenants have tested positive for some form of illicit substance in the past two years. Every single person who tested positive was evicted within three months of receiving their results, unwitting participants in Duncan's trial of the *Come Clean* policy. The rest of the short-stayers, the ones with no positive test results – the Zublinskis and the Camerons and the Lims – are either the three percenters or not from around there. David was right about why the locals call it the White Palace.

The after-hours light times out. In the window, the pod's reflection dims, and I see sheets of rain pushing across the northern suburbs. There are people out there, in the wet and the wind. They are curled against roller doors at the back of shops and in warehouse loading bays. Some have sheets of cardboard, some have rolls of plastic, some are in sleeping bags. Some are barricaded by shopping trolleys and backpacks and the bodies of other rough sleepers. Some are alone and vulnerable to passers-by who take out their rage at coming into contact with poverty by stomping on a head and causing an internal bleed that, left untreated for twelve, maybe fourteen, hours, causes a stroke and a lonely death under a freeway.

I catch a flicker of movement in the glass and my heart tumbles in my chest. I swing around in my chair. Bigfoot is standing at the entrance to the pod. Her hand is clenched in a fist, poised to knock on the workstation divider.

'Sitting in the dark, Frances? Why don't you put the timer on?'

The light from my screen gives her face a pale, unnatural pallor against the darkened office. Lit from below, it's not flattering, and makes her look even more gaunt than she is. It occurs to me that she would have walked past the after-hours timer on her way to my work station. She braces her back with one hand. Long days at a desk can't be good for her hip. I'd get up to turn the timer on again myself, but I don't want to leave her alone with my computer screen. Bigfoot is, I realise, the only common denominator between the community health and forensic inquiries, the two inquiries where Helen Stewart appears. The inquiries that both fell short of discovering what is shown on my computer screen.

'I'm done, anyway.' I swing my chair to the computer, putting my back to her and immediately feel uncomfortable. In the glass, I see her half-reflected shape step forward and I feel her bend over me to look at the screen.

'What are you working on at this hour? I thought you'd take the opportunity to have a few early nights.'

'While you're investigating my misdemeanours?'

She sighs. 'Well, if you put it like that, yes. But it's all done now. Neil has my report and recommendations.'

'It didn't take you long.'

'It was pretty cut and dried, really.'

I look at her face in the window. She's doing the same, but I can't read her expression. I swallow, hate myself for my tells, and shut down the screen.

'You're right, I should go home.'

'I'll walk with you to the bus stop.'

CHAPTER FIFTY-ONE

The universal parking bay at the front of my building is vacant when my bus pulls in. Vince must have taken my advice. That, or he's busy elsewhere, keeping tabs on some other public servant whom Griffiths has in his sights. I look around for the blue Merc but, if he's here, he's parked it out of sight. Or maybe he's in the four-wheel drive today, making sure he can drive straight to Duncan's house to collect Griffith's merchandise without having to change cars. I scuttle across the footpath while fat drops of rain fall from the Norfolk Island pines and shelter under the building awning. I need to get supplies from the supermarket. I really should stop making these daily dashes in and out and commit to a weekly shop. It would save me time and probably money. Plus, I'd be more likely to stock up on real meat and vegetables instead of noodles and toast.

I jog to the next shelter, thankful that I've worn my Docs today. There's a lull in the rain, so I dash to the supermarket entry, only just avoiding being run over by a delivery van backing into the loading bay. Inside, the air-conditioning directs its flow toward the doors and a blanket of warm air falls over my face. I'm the only person here apart from a staffer with an oversized mop.

I pick up a basket and head for the fruit and vegetable section near the windows. I don't have my shopping bags with me, but the sky won't fall in if I buy one or two. I choose mushrooms and broccoli, carrots and bok choy, and another hand of bananas. I've come good since my last adventure in the park by supplementing my diet with lunchtime bacon and avocado toasties. Bananas aren't the only food high in potassium, but they'll always be part of my daily routine.

My phone pings and I'm trying to open my messages when I realise that I'm not the only shopper here after all.

'Hello again, Frances.'

Simon Tallent holds two oranges, cupping them in front of his chest. He bobs one up and down, wrinkles his chin, and puts it back on the mound behind him. 'Imported, but what can you do?'

'Eat an apple instead?'

He makes a show of looking into my basket. 'Or bananas. I see Neil made the front page again this week. You did some good work there, exposing Duncan's backhanders.' He shakes his head. 'You never know, do you? Although, I guess it was bound to happen sooner or later.'

'Bound to happen? How do you figure that?'

He rubs his fingers together in the universal symbol. 'Duncan had money trouble. I know, I know, with the house and everything, it looks like he was set for life, but how do you think he bought a place like that and filled it with art on a public servant's salary?'

I shake my head and don't answer. I figure he's going to tell me anyway.

'He plays the stockmarket. Constantly. Haven't you seen him on his phone? He's never off it, always checking in.'

'It's hardly a crime, though. Lots of people do it.'

'But for Duncan, it's an obsession. I had to make him put it away during an Estimates Committee hearing once. He did well on iron-ore stocks as few years ago – you know he's good mates with some of the directors in the Department of Mines – but rumour has it he got burned in that mineral-sands fiasco a few years ago. Borrowed from some business associate' – he laughs – 'probably the Batt Brothers, to cover the losses, then threw that away as well. Don't bet what you can't afford to lose, Frances. It's the golden rule of investing.'

I mumble something non-committal and shuffle around a bin of discounted potato chips, sliding my phone into my pocket. Duncan's stockmarket obsession is interesting in its own way – after all, we'd all thought he was on dating apps – but I really don't care now.

'What are you working on? I hear you're revisiting some old ground, digging through the database at the state pathology lab.'

'It's nothing official yet.'

'Be careful not to get ahead of yourself. You know Neil is obliged to make future inquiries public before he starts accessing government records. You wouldn't want to make him overstep the powers of his office.'

'It's not new, just closing out the housing inquiry.'

'Ah yes, the drugs angle. Duncan told me you accused him of illegally accessing private health information.'

'But that's exactly what he did do, didn't he?'

'The drugs issue is not a story, Frances. You know that; Neil knows that. I've had the department working on the *Come Clean* policy for twelve months. Cabinet is one hundred percent behind it. And they already do it in the United States. I know your friends in the TAG are full of moral outrage, but they're too close to their clients, their judgement is clouded. That Shia LaBeouf-type that your friend Meredith used to hang out with. He was handsome in a swarthy kind of way, if you like that sort of thing, but he was never going to lose the habit. It was only a matter of time before he had an accident at work. It's probably for the best. Now his ex can get on with her life, meet someone more like her, have a couple of proper Aussie kids.'

'That's a bit harsh, don't you think? Shrugging off a life because he took a one-off hit.'

'What you've got to understand, Frances, is that's a way of life for these people. Drugs are an integral part of their society. It's why their own countries don't thrive. There's no point supporting them if they're never going to make it. It's just throwing good money after bad.'

'Is that also your justification for kicking immigrants and Indigenous people out of public housing?'

The minister's phone buzzes. He looks at the screen, frowns, and glances out into the street. A blue Mercedes cruises past in the rain. The light is wrong, and I can't see the driver's face, but he nods in our direction. The minister nods back.

'The administration is responsible for implementing government policy, Frances. You know that. I just set the rules, I don't sign the eviction notices.'

'But you make the decisions to sell off public housing to the private sector. You're the one who tells the buyers that they'll only have to deal with clean, white people.'

He smirks as he considers the two bags of chips in his hands and tosses the curry flavour back into the discount bin. 'I'm just a plain old salt-and-vinegar man myself.' He gives me a calculating look. 'I don't suppose you'll be losing any sleep over Wolf though. He used to brief me on the commissioner's inquiries. He wasn't your biggest fan. He could never work out how someone so obviously unwell could produce such consistent work.'

'I suppose that's who you'll target next, then? Once you've removed the drug users and the refugees and the brown people? People with disabilities will be next to go. Tell me, Minister, is that because a disability means a person can't be trusted to keep their rental clean? Or is it because they're not favoured by God?'

Simon Tallent just laughs. 'God helps people who help themselves. Look around you and tell me which people are putting in the effort. It isn't hard to work it out.'

'You can't be serious.'

'I am deadly serious, Frances, and I'd strongly advise you to drop your unauthorised snooping in government health records. Look what happened to your co-worker.'

'Eric knew?'

'Of course he knew, he just told the wrong people that he knew. What did he think was going to happen when he told Graham Griffiths what he'd found? Did he really think Griffiths would want to stop us from cleaning up public housing? It suits him just fine to have sober tenants in his new apartment building. The rest of them, the ones who can't clean up their act, we keep them on the streets right where he wants them, craving another hit to help them forget their miserable lives.'

I look at a point behind the minister's shoulder. It's a display of discount chocolate. Mint chocolate chip. I like mint and chocolate. My instinct is to ignore the minister's dog-whistling. Graham Griffiths benefits, whether or not people who are down on their luck are kicked out of public housing. He's going to find them and take their money wherever they are. He's a criminal. That's what they do. But like all good redirection, the minister's story has a ring of truth.

'And where does Mike Vargus fit in?' I think about Mike's comments by the fire that evening, about needing to be selective and creating a harmonious community.

'Mike Vargus is a supernumerary, a bit player. I helped him out, he's married to my cousin, after all – but he's just a winemaker playing at property development in the city. He might make a few dollars, but he doesn't understand what drives the margins. Not like Griffiths does. We know you've been in contact with Griffiths, by the way.'

I blink and shift my focal point back to Simon Tallent's face. The chocolate stack wobbles in the background, and I reach for the potato-chip bin to steady myself. The minister frowns and I can see that this is what he despises. Weakness, in any form, is anathema to him. When he speaks, his voice is full of distaste.

'Do you really think it's possible to make calls from a state prison without being recorded?'

'Griffiths told me to back off. Just like you.'

'Of course he did, so he wouldn't have to remove you from the picture like he did Eric.'

Behind him, the blue Mercedes circles around again and this time it slides into a vacant parking bay outside the supermarket windows. The driver's door opens, and a tall, fit-looking man climbs out and dashes across the road. He has his face down to avoid the rain and a blue baseball cap with a white logo pulled low over his eyes. As he steps onto the footpath, he almost shirtfronts a woman in a red coat. My mind jolts back to the fish and chip shop on the day the minister announced *Come Clean*. He's the same person who cut in front of my bus; the same person who's been parking his fancy blue car in the universal parking bay outside my apartment; the driver of the car that Meredith almost hit on the day we went to the bush camp; the suit at the bar. It wasn't Vince at all. The Hon. Simon Tallent MLC has been having me followed.

CHAPTER FIFTY-TWO

I take a step back and into the avocados. One dislodges and falls with a fleshy smack onto the floor. I bend down to pick it up and check my phone, which I'm still clutching after being interrupted by the Minister for Housing. When I right myself and return the bruised fruit to the top of its pyramid, Simon Tallent is tapping at his own phone. Behind his shoulder, the chocolate stack tilts to the right. Don't even think about it, I say in my head, and it wobbles back and forth, undecided. I shift the weight of the groceries on my arm.

'I should finish my shopping. And it looks like you're needed.' I can see the driver of the Mercedes outside the supermarket. He's holding up his phone at the minister through the window.

Tallent looks up, smirks, looks down again and punches the screen with his thumb.

'Sean? No, he's good. He can wait.'

I do a double take at the tall man outside, but all I see is his back retreating down the street. 'That's Sean Callaghan? The new Department of Housing graduate managing Joleen Samson's appeal? I pictured him as shorter.'

Tallent laughs. 'He's related to me, not Jana. Our side of the family are all over six foot.'

'How hard was it to get him a job in the department?'

Tallent narrows his eyes. 'Steph told you.'

'She did.' I called her after Duncan's crack about ministerial staffers and asked her to tell me the gossip she wanted to share that day we had coffee before the football. She'd just laughed and said it wasn't that big a deal. Just another politician parachuting his nephew into a cushy government job.

Tallent dismisses me with an excuse used by the corrupt everywhere. 'Everyone does it. I needed a dedicated resource to put together *Come Clean*. There were no takers inside the bureaucracy, so I put Sean in the seat.'

'Where he has served you well, I'm sure.'

'Like I said, you only need to look around you. It's not hard to see who's willing to work and who's not.

'And he was willing, so he got the job. I bet you're not paying your nephew a graduate's salary.'

'Of course not. Market forces, Frances. He was the only person to put their hand up, so he could command the salary he wanted. That's only fair.'

'When did he tell you about Duncan?'

The minister laughs, actually laughs out loud, throwing his head back and causing shoppers to turn and look. I can't tell if he's truly delighted with my cleverness or whether the mirth is covering something darker.

'No, you've got that one wrong. It wasn't Sean who tipped me off about Dr Wolf, it was Mike Vargus. He bid for the Riverside contract, you know, but the department decided not to go with a developer and manage the project in-house. It's pretty obvious why, thanks to your good work. If Mike was in charge, Duncan and the Batt brothers wouldn't have been able to skim those insulation contracts. Sean just confirmed it for me once he had access to the department's records.'

'So why didn't you just report Duncan to the police? You could have taken the glory of rooting out corruption in your own department.'

'It looks less staged. We weren't a hundred percent sure everyone would be on board with *Come Clean* and a story like that helps build public confidence, especially when there's a respected government watchdog involved.'

'Wasn't that a risk, though? What if we didn't find it? What if the whistleblower didn't come forward?'

And that's where I stop myself, because Simon Tallent is smiling broadly and this time it's a real smile, self-satisfied and making his eyes gleam.

'The whistleblower was genuine; you don't need to worry about that. But his source – his name was Saraj, if my memory serves me correctly – was reluctant to come forward. It seems in a previous life he'd seen what a government can do to people who speak up. He's left the public service now and I believe his redundancy payout was enough to set him up on a lifestyle property in the South West, not far from Riverside as it turns out. Nice life for someone who came here on a boat.'

'You used him. Like you used us.'

'So what, Frances? Parliamentary inquiries get used for political purposes all the time, by both sides of politics I might add. You're kidding yourself if you think you and Neil are immune to all of that.'

'We have evidence of what you're doing, you know. We'll table it in parliament.'

'I don't think you'll be in a position to do that in the near future. Even parliamentary commissioners have to wear budget cutbacks from time to time.' He turns back to the oranges. 'Good to see you again.'

Once again, I'm dismissed. I watch him lift fruit, sniff it, and place the oranges he deems suitable in his basket and drop the rejects back on the tray. I want to scream at him, punch him in the face, or at least say something witty and cutting. Something that will make him question the very worthiness of his soul. But people like the Hon. Simon Tallent MLC, Minister for Housing and soon-to-be deputy premier, don't question their worth. They've had affirmations of their personal value whispered in their ears and shouted on campaign trails all their lives.

I slink away with my healthy groceries. The guy with the mop does double duty, taking my money at the register and helps me load my vegetables into reusable plastic bags. I step through the automatic sliding doors into the wind and the rain.

Sean Callaghan's car is still on the street, but he is nowhere in sight. Lights and music drift on the wind from across the railway line and I figure he's probably gone to the pub to wait while his boss finishes talking with the uncooperative public investigator. I unlock my phone and keep it in my free hand anyway.

I turn in the other direction, toward my own building. I'm going to unpack my groceries, cook some vegetables, eat a banana, take my meds, and maybe drink a ginger beer instead of opening a bottle of wine. Maybe I'll have a bath. I could light the scented candle I was given at the office Christmas party last year, read a book, and avoid the news. Maybe after that, I'll put on fresh pyjamas and log onto Seek, see if anyone in Weymouth needs an accountant. If the minister's parting comment is anything to go by, I'll be needing a new job soon.

I don't bother running through the rain. My bags are heavy, and dry clothes are hanging in my wardrobe only one hundred metres away. The delivery van is still parked in the loading bay, forcing me to step around it. The back door is open and, like Sean Callaghan, I have my head down so I don't see the face of the person who jumps onto the footpath, grabs me and my groceries, pushes me inside and slams the door closed.

CHAPTER FIFTY-THREE

The river widens and slows, islands of reeds appear, and we navigate braided channels to find our way through. On either side of the water, the bare hills recede, leaving shallow, rocky screes behind the pampas grass. The weaver bird nests strung from the blades have become unremarkable now. I barely watch the males as they dart in and out, thrusting their beaks to add new strips of green to their walls.

We've been on the river for three days, a convoy of canoes paddling toward the ocean. Some days we've been thrust forward where the river has narrowed and been forced through impassive granite boulders. I've gripped the ropes on the sides of the canoe as we bounced and lurched, spray in my face and a scream in my throat, and thankful for my commitment to regular medication. Other days we've battled the afternoon sea breeze, unexpectedly fierce this far inland, and arrived at the campsite arm-sore and weary. And there have been days when we've just drifted, letting the current move us downstream. I've leaned against my pack, sapped by the heat, and stared at the green thicket that lines the banks. I've seen vervet monkeys looking back at me with their black faces, hundreds of the ubiquitous weaver birds, and even a fish eagle. Sometimes I've closed my eyes, my lids heating up under the sun, and startled myself awake to the same repeating green and orange panorama.

In the evenings, we've made camp under a sky that turns from Southern Hemisphere blue to pink, to purple, to sequins that rival even the skies over Weymouth. I've seen a shooting star that was so big, so bright, so enduring that I was convinced it was military, a contribution to some conflict farther north. As tents have been erected and sausages turned in frying pans, I've watched baboon families on sun-warmed rock faces across the water. Rock dassies have frowned at me in turn. Other paddlers with energy left after a day on the water have strolled back upstream to leap off cliffs and float back to camp. I've listened to their screams and splashes, content to bathe only in the cooling air.

I drove up here from Cape Town in a hire car that I left in Springbok before catching a bus to the border. The safari company met me there and took me to the camp in the back of their troop carrier. There, I slept in a mud and thatch hut, ate barbequed game and burned citronella candles next to my bed while I waited for the canoes to arrive.

*

I got to South Africa on a superyacht. It was built in Perth, sold to a buyer in Dubai and delivered via Weymouth. The van took me straight to the docks. Unlike he did with Eric, Vince didn't let me stop for iced coffee on the way.

'This should have been done weeks ago,' he told me as he drove north in the dark, 'straight after the shooting. Two days after you first logged into that damn database.' He glanced in the rear-view mirror. Clocked my blank face. 'Didn't Helen tell you it was her house? The papers made it out to be a bunch of redneck locals but the note in the letterbox was for Graham. It was a warning from Tallent to back off. He thought Graham had given you the tip-off, like he did with Eric.'

Vince opened the rear doors only when he had Ray and Jack in sight. Ray patted my back and passed me a document folder, the type that middle-aged couples are always opening at airports when they're looking for their passports.

'You have everything you need in here. If you must get in touch, do it through Vince. Someone at the other end will show you how.' He laid a hand on Vince's shoulder, a paternal gesture that his son leaned into before catching my eye and, to his credit, turning a deep shade of red.

'You're Graham Griffiths' tax accountant.'

Ray shakes his head. 'Was, not anymore.'

'So, you knew about the drugs.'

'That's client privilege, Frances, you should know about that.' He saw my sideways glance at the boat. 'Don't worry, it's only you and Jack, no merchandise.'

'Does Dad know?'

'Not about the drugs, but he knows that we're arranging for you to take a sabbatical. Medical leave, I believe they've called it at your office. And it's probably best that you don't contact him. Not for a while, anyway. Don't worry, we'll take care of the old boy. And he'll be well looked after in the retirement village.' He put his other hand on my shoulder, paternal but there was pressure behind it, guiding me toward Jack. 'And we'll have a quiet word to the others too. This time everyone who needs to know will know.

They shunted me onto the boat with a backpack filled with clothes from my own wardrobe. 'If you don't have sea legs already, you'll have them by the time we get there,' Jack told me. I tucked myself below deck, swallowed a sleeping pill and closed my eyes for thirteen hours. By the time I surfaced, the water was a deep, dark blue and the wind blowing from the west.

*

The canoes clear the reed islands and I see something I haven't seen for days, the glint of corrugated-iron rooftops rising up the hill on the Namibian side. They are farther downstream, says my guide from the back of the canoe. We won't go there; we'll be stopping before the next bend. He points his paddle at a sandbank and dips it into the water to steer us to the right. He has been my navigator for the past three days, pointing out channels and turning our boat from the rear to get us through rapids. It was unnerving at first, sitting at the front of the boat facing into the rocks and the waves, anticipating disaster until the bow swayed sideways. I didn't need to worry, he'd said. It was my job to paddle, his to be the rudder. Eventually I learned to let go, to trust his judgement and anticipate the turn and not the collision.

We pull onto the sandbank and suddenly I am leaving the canoes for the last time. We pull them out of the water and fresh guides in green safari shirts jog down to the water's edge, motioning for us to leave our packs. They will bring them up. Our job is to wash our hands and eat lunch. At the top of the riverbank, we are greeted by waitstaff and picnic tables laid out with cold meats, fruits and fresh bread. We eat, drink wine, and the rest of the group friend each other on Facebook. I tell them I don't do social media and they smile and say *good for you.* They dive online, desperate to catch up on news and check travel bookings. Some are continuing northwards, winding their way through the continent, and not intending to go home for another six months; others are returning home to jobs and university studies. Everyone but me opts for the first bus back. They have hire vehicles to collect, a border to cross, another bus to meet. I tell them I've booked an extra night at the camp so I can visit the gem mines and will catch a lift with one of the guides tomorrow. I wave them goodbye and head back to the river.

I check the mud map that Tim Steyn gave me on the docks in Cape Town and find the path that leads toward the town. I only have to walk a few paces before the pampas grass closes over my head and the camp has disappeared. After half an hour, the track bends to the left and down to the bank. A canoe similar to the one I have travelled in is pulled up on the sand. I sit and drink my water, pop a pill out of its blister pack and run a finger over the embossed oak tree logo on the side of my new medication bag. It was in the backpack that Vince prepared for me and is stocked with twelve months' worth of betahistine, diuretics and rescue meds. All I need now is bananas, and I can get plenty of those here.

*

Bigfoot has everything she needs for Neil's report to parliament, but if she can't get it over the line, she has a back-up plan. We walked the long way to the bus stop that night, sheltering from the rain under shop awnings. It wasn't a coincidence, Bigfoot being the common denominator in the two inquiries that involved Helen Stewart. She'd seen anomalies in residential addresses in the community health inquiry. The inquiry team had trouble tracking down patients who live in public housing. They'd be there one day and gone the next.

She let it go until Eric's police inquiry was approved and she noticed the same names appearing in his working papers. Cameron, Meleshe, Stewart: they were all there, and they all had blood tests done in the months before they were evicted. She had added the missing column to the spreadsheet and was trying to link them all together when she was hit by the car.

'No, I don't know who the driver was. It crossed my mind, especially after the police inquiry was pulled and then Eric disappeared. But it could also just be a coincidence.'

'I don't know if I believe in coincidences anymore.'

'No, coincidences are real. I admit I panicked for a moment and deleted the spreadsheet column with the pathology report numbers. That was a mistake. But don't you go getting all conspiracy theory on me. Anyway, when Neil decided to relocate the office, I put the papers into Eric's old folders, hoping you'd find a pattern that I couldn't see.'

I remembered the night I vomited in Belinda's wastepaper bin.

'Were you in the office that night?'

Her lip twitched upwards in the closest approximation I'd ever seen her give to a smile. 'I was leaving when I heard the commotion. You obviously didn't notice that someone had cleaned up by the next morning, did you?'

I hadn't and muttered my thanks, keeping my eyes on the footpath.

'I'd just about given it up for a lost cause, especially when the government announced *Come Clean* and you had to abandon the investigation, when I saw you talking with Helen Stewart in the building foyer. I recognised her from the photo in her tenancy file, and it all fell into place.'

But Bigfoot didn't know the Graham Griffiths connection; I filled her in as we walked. About how Helen was his half-sister and how he discovered, through Eric, that she'd been evicted from her public housing tenancy for no apparent reason. And removed from the waiting list. With thirty thousand people in front of her, she'd never live in publicly funded housing again. Graham found her and Tahnee squatting in an abandoned kombi in the Kwinana bush camp, too ashamed to tell family. He put them both up in a house in the hills. It was what gave Eric the idea to check the tenancy histories of other evictees. The three percenters and people not from around here.

'Is that why Griffiths invested in Banksia Apartments? To have somewhere that wasn't caught up in the purge?'

'That's what Vince told me. It makes a good story, but I don't know how much of it I believe.'

'And the Minister for Housing had someone plant the drugs in his apartment when he didn't toe the line.'

'Who knows?'

Personally, I think the drugs were Griffiths'. I'm not inclined to give the benefit of the doubt to someone who trades in misery, even if he's probably just saved my life. Vince also told me that when he went to pack a bag for me, he found a gas leak in my apartment. *Just a small one. Not enough to blow up your kitchen when you cooked dinner, but probably enough to turn you blue by morning.* He'd called Alice and she told him to make sure I got plenty of oxygen. *Keep all the windows down in the van on the drive north.*

'But it's not about coming clean from drugs,' I told Bigfoot, 'it's about race and religion. Christianising public housing, forcing everyone else onto the streets and into the bush camps. *God wants Christians to prosper.* Isn't that what the Minister for Housing's church says? He might not sign the termination notices, but he makes sure the Department of Housing knows who is godly and deserving and who isn't.'

We reached the end of another city block, avoiding puddles and hugging the shopfronts, before Bigfoot replied. She narrowed her eyes, staring down the sandstone block of Parliament House at the other end of the Terrace. I knew from experience not to interrupt.

'No,' she said eventually. 'It's not about race or religion. It's about money. It's always about money. This government wants to outsource public housing, but the private sector is interested only as far as it can make a profit. And that's easier to do if you've got tenants who stay put, pay their rent on time and maintain their properties.' She draws a Venn diagram in the air with her hands. 'It shouldn't come as any surprise that it's quicker and cheaper for people in power to decide for themselves which classes of people make good tenants, instead of giving every person a fair go.'

'Which is why they got rid of the three strikes rule.'

'Exactly.'

'That sucks.'

'Yes, Frances, it does.'

*

Dust rises at the foot of the hills on the South African side of the river. The sea breeze is in and carries away any sound that might have travelled across the water. I'm glad I'll be crossing with the wind. My arms are still sore from the battle two days ago and I doubt I'd get far against it on my own. I watch the dust cloud grow as a vehicle crosses the river plain. It heads toward the bank and the windscreen catches the sun.

I strap my bag into the centre of the canoe and climb into the rear seat. It's more difficult on my own, without a guide to hold the craft while I find my balance. I plant my feet, strap the paddle to my wrist, and push off, wobbling like a kid on a bicycle. Bigfoot – I make a mental note to think of her as Catherine from now on – has the recording of my supermarket conversation with the honourable minister. She will have passed it to Jaelyn Worner, and Jaelyn will be waiting for the right time to pass it to the press. I'm guessing the right time will be one month out from the next state election.

The wind catches me, and I float away from the bank. I risk a glance back over my shoulder. Tim was right: this section of the river is invisible to anyone at the camp. On the other side, the four-wheel drive has pulled up to the water. The driver is standing on the foot plate. He's seen me and is signalling with one arm. I can see the camera slung across his chest, the curve of his cyclist's legs, and his blond hair. I point the bow back across the river and dip my oar into the water.

ACKNOWLEDGEMENTS

Thank you for reading *Vertigo*. This is a special book for me, not only because it draws on my thirty years of living with Meniere's Disease, but because it represents a memorable time in my career. Like Frances, I was a public sector investigator and like Frances I delved into the depths of government department files and databases. Like Frances, I loved it. I would like to thank – with much warmth and affection – all of my colleagues at government integrity offices and the thousands of public servants who keep the wheels of the state turning. I would also like to thank the IRL public servants who gave me permission to use their names in this book. Special thanks to Frances, who is the inspiration for the main character and to Jack, for letting me use your name and recreate your enviable lifestyle.

As this book was being typeset, I learned of the passing of Dr Gordon Robertson PSM. Gordon served as the deputy auditor general in Western Australia for ten years. He was my cousin and, as we discovered after the fact, my boss. Gordon was awarded an Australian Centenary Medal for his service to the public of Western Australia and an Australian Public Service Medal for outstanding service to public sector auditing and strategic auditing policy. He was the polar opposite of Frances' nemesis. I think she would have adored him as much as I did.

Thank you to the team at Fremantle Press. Fremantle Press's core purpose is to identify talented new and emerging Western Australian writers and artists, and to publish and distribute our work to the widest possible audience. They have been with me at every turn of my fledging writing career and for that I am truly grateful.

Thank you to the booksellers, distributers, writers, writing centres, conference organisers, reviewers, bloggers, and all of the writing industry in Western Australia and Australia for your continued kindness and encouragement.

Thank you to every reader who has contacted me to tell me how much they enjoyed my books. You have no idea how much this means to me.

Thank you to Marlish Glorie's writing group and my beta readers who claim to eagerly await each new manuscript, declare it a masterpiece, and set me straight on the things I get wrong.

A very special thank you to the Katharine Susannah Prichard Writing Centre for their Flash Fellowship which gave me a week of writing time in the Perth Hills.

And finally, thank you to my family and especially my husband, Ross, who still goes to work every day and comes home to a wife tapping away at her keyboard. Let's go back to the Orange River.

*I acknowledge that this book was written on
Wadjak Noongar boodjar and that the town of Weymouth is created
out of my memories growing up on Yamatji country.
I pay my respects to the elders, past and present, of all Indigenous
people in Australia and affirm my support for their ongoing
connection to country and culture.*

MORE BY KAREN HERBERT

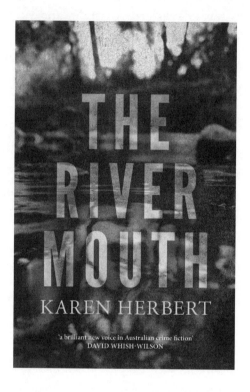

Fifteen-year-old Darren Davies is found facedown in the Weymouth River with a gunshot wound to his chest. The killer is never found. Ten years later, his mother receives a visit from the local police. Sandra's best friend has been found dead on a remote Pilbara road. And Barbara's DNA matches the DNA found under Darren's fingernails. When the investigation into her son's murder is reopened, Sandra begins to question what she knew about her best friend. As she digs, she discovers that there are many secrets in her small town, and that her murdered son had secrets too.

'You're not going to want to put this literary and lyrical crime novel down until you're finished.' AU Review

FROM FREMANTLEPRESS.COM.AU

FROM FREMANTLE PRESS

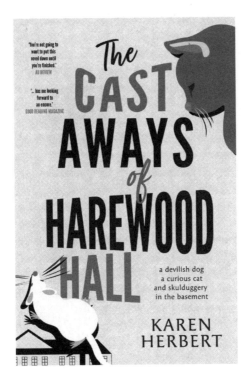

Josh is a sweet, well-meaning university student with a big heart. After he impulsively steals two research mice from a campus laboratory, he hides them in the basement of the retirement village where he works. The mice are happy and so is Josh, until he discovers that the lab mice could cause a deadly disease.

Enter a cat called Harley, a dog called Bobby, the arrival of some mysterious packing boxes, and a strange spike in the village's water bill. As the clock ticks, and disaster looms, can the efforts of the Harewood Hall residents save the day?

'a charming, comforting read celebrating community and kindness.' The West Australian

AND ALL GOOD BOOKSTORES

ALSO AVAILABLE

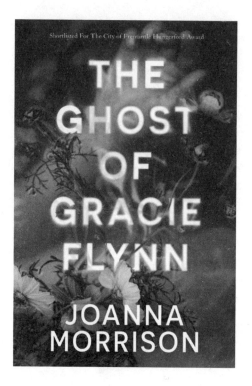

Gracie Flynn may be dead, but she's not gone.

Three university friends are divided by a tragic death. Eighteen years later, chance reunites them. Robyn is still haunted by memories of her best friend Gracie, and Cohen's heart has never healed. Only Sam seems to have moved on and found success and happiness. But death rocks their lives again when Sam's body is found in mysterious circumstances. And the ghost of Gracie Flynn has a story to tell about the night that changed their lives forever.

'a real page-turner … this story of love and betrayal was one of my favourite books this year' Better Reading

FROM FREMANTLEPRESS.COM.AU